INTERNATIONAL BIBLIOGRAPHY OF THEATRE: 1982

Sponsored by The American Society for Theatre Research, and

The International Association of Libraries and Museums
of the Performing Arts

In cooperation with The International Federation for Theatre Research

INTERNATIONAL BIBLIOGRAPHY OF THEATRE: 1982

Edited by Benito Ortolani

Published by the Theatre Research Data Center, Brooklyn College, City University of New York, NY 11210

Distributed by the Publishing Center for Cultural Resources, 625 Broadway, New York, NY 10012

© Theatre Research Data Center, 1985; ISSN 0882-9446; ISBN 0-89062-207-8

This publication was made possible in part by grants from the National Endowment for the Humanities, the Rockefeller Foundation, Dean Witter Reynolds, Inc., the American Society for Theatre Research, and by in-kind support and services provided by Brooklyn College of the City University of New York.

INTERNATIONAL BIBLIOGRAPHY OF THEATRE: 1982

TABLE OF CONTENTS

PREFACE

This first step toward the accumulation of a wide-ranging databank of international theatre research references and the publication of annual bibliographies from that databank was initiated several years ago by a resolution of the officers and members of the American Society for Theatre Research to centralize, computerize and publish such resources for scholars, administrators, artists and students of theatre. More recently Brooklyn College established its Theatre Research Data Center with staff, space and equipment to help get the project underway. Grants from the National Endowment for the Humanities, the Rockefeller Foundation, the American Society for Theatre Research and other private sources then made it possible for the databank to be constructed and for this pilot bibliography to be published. More than sixty theatre scholars, librarians and theatre production people (see **Contributors**) volunteered to cover theatre periodicals and books published in 1982. Other theatre figures from ASTR, USITT, ATA, CORD, ITI(US), SIBMAS, FIRT and fourteen national centers in North America, Europe and Asia advised on the project taxonomy, the content of the databank and the form and content of the data collection sheets and bibliography. The future will include maturation of the databank and bibliographies, installation of the online access system and development of the international network.

We express our gratitude to the many institutions and individuals who made this volume possible. In a special way we thank:

The members and the leaders of ASTR, especially President Joseph Donohue and past President Bernard Beckerman, the Executive Committees and the Committee on Research, especially past Chair Helen Krich Chinoy;

President Robert Hess and the Theatre Department of Brooklyn College, City University of New York;

President Harald Zielske and Dr. Otto Schindler for the International Bibliography Commission of SIBMAS;

President William Green and the University Commission of FIRT;

Dr. Heinrich Huesmann, Deutsches Theatermuseum, Munich;

Professor Heinz Kindermann, Margret Dietrich and Professor Wolfgang Greisenegger, Institut für Theaterwissenschaft, University of Vienna;

Professor Alessandro d'Amico and Dr. Teresa Viziano, Museo Civico dell'Attore e dello Spettacolo, Genoa;

Professor Rosanne Potter and Mr. Steven Kunz, Iowa State University;

Mr. Charles Boeheim and Ms. Betsey Jackson, Spires Consortium, Stanford University;

Mr. Benjamin S. Klein and Ms. Pat Reber of the CUNY/University Computer Center;

Ms. Betty Smith and Ms. Shirley Fenton, University of Waterloo; and

Professor Barry Brook and Ms. Dorothy Curzon of RILM, Graduate Center of the City University of New York.

In addition to the financial support of the National Endowment for the Humanities, we are particularly thankful for the help of its officers, especially Dr. Harold Cannon and Ms. Pat Shadle. Finally we thank our field consultants and hard working field bibliographers, whose generous contributions have made this work a reality. Their names follow.

CONTRIBUTORS

TAXONOMY TASK FORCE

Oscar G. Brockett, University of Texas, Austin
James Ellis, Mount Holyoke College
Gil Lazier, Florida State University
Alan Woods, Ohio State University

SPECIAL ADVISORS

John Ball, University of Toronto
Hedwig Belitska-Scholtz, National Széchényi Library, Budapest
Bernard Beckerman, Columbia University
Elizabeth Burdick, International Theatre Institute, New York
Joseph Donohue, University of Massachusetts, Amherst
Christopher Edwards, The Rose Bruford College of Speech and Drama, London
Henrich Huesmann, Deutsches Theatermuseum, Munich
Siniša Janić, Museum of Theatre Art of Serbia, Belgrade
Liudmila Levina, State Central Theatre Library, Moscow
Kai-Yu Liu, Chinese Theatre Association, Beijing
Irene Peypoch, Negociat de Cultura, Barcelona
Margaret Loftus Ranald, Queens College, City University of New York
Rolf Rohmer, Theaterhochschule, Leipzig
Otto G. Schindler, University of Vienna
Thomas Siedhoff, University of Bayreuth
Barbro Stribolt, Drottningholms Teatermuseum, Stockholm
Dorothy Swerdlove, Theatre Collection, New York Public Library
Alessandro Tinterri, Museo Civico dell'Attore e dello Spettacolo, Genoa
Teresa Viziano, Museo Civico dell'Attore e dello Spettacolo, Genoa
Zbigniew Wilski, Polska Academia Nauk, Warsaw
Wei-Jie Yu,. Shanghai Academy of Drama
Natalia Zhilina, State Central Theatre Library, Moscow
Harald Zielske, Free University, West Berlin

PROJECT FIELD REVIEWERS

Arnold Aronson, New York, NY
James R. Brandon, University of Hawaii
Oscar G. Brockett, University of Texas, Austin
Liz Fugate, University of Washington, Seattle
William A. Gibson, University of Idaho
Patricia A. Greiner, Casper, WY
Constance F. Gremore, Metropolitan State University
Frank S. Hook, Lehigh University
Frederick J. Hunter, University of Texas, Austin
Heather McCallum, Metropolitan Central Library, Toronto
Barbara Mittman, University of Illinois, Chicago
Richard Plant, Queens University, Kingston
Louis Rachow, Hampden/Booth Theatre Collection & Library, New York
Nancy Ruyter, University of California, Irvine
Allegra Fuller Snyder, University of California, Los Angeles
George Winchester Stone, New York University

CONTRIBUTERS – Cont'd

FIELD BIBLIOGRAPHERS

Arnold Aronson	New York, NY
Jerry Bangham	Alcorn State University
Thomas L. Berger	St. Lawrence University
Ned Bowman	Scenographic Imports, Norwalk, CT
John W. Brokaw	University of Texas, Austin
Monica Burdex	California State University, Northridge
Marvin Carlson	Graduate Center, City University of New York
Barbara Clayton	University of Wisconsin, Madison
Ginnine Cocuzza	New York, NY
Johnnye L. Cope	North Texas State University, Denton
Barry Daniels	Kent State University
Peter A. Davis	University of Oregon
Richard Devin	University of Washington, Seattle
Weldon B. Durham	University of Missouri
Carl F. Ferré	North Texas State University, Denton
Kathy Foley	University of California, Santa Cruz
Liz Fugate	University of Washington, Seattle
Paul J. Gaffney	University of Texas, Austin
Steven H. Gale	Missouri Southern State College
Patricia A. Greiner	Casper, WY
Constance F. Gremore	Metropolitan State College
James V. Hatch	Hatch-Billops Collection, New York
Ramon Hathorn	University of Guelph
Temple Hauptfleisch	Center for South African Theatre Research, Pretoria
Frank S. Hook	Lehigh University
Frederick J. Hunter	University of Texas, Austin
Vera Jiji	Brooklyn College, City University of New York
Eugene Jones	The Aracoma Story (Theatre), Logan, WV
Gerald Kahan	University of Georgia
Ann Marie Koller	Palo Alto, CA
Barbara Mittman	University of Illinois, Chicago
William Nelson	Carnegie-Mellon University
Robert J. Owczarek	Boston University
Irene Peypoch	Negociat de Cultura, Barcelona
Jerrold Phillips	Northeastern University
Richard Plant	Queens University, Kingston
Margaret Loftus Ranald	Queens College, City University of New York
John W. Robinson	University of Nebraska, Lincoln
Bari Rolfe	Oakland, CA
Loren K. Ruff	Western Kentucky University
Nancy Ruyter	University of California, Irvine
Patricia Sandback	San Diego State University
Otto G. Schindler	University of Vienna
Guntram Schneider	University of Vienna
Eleanor Silvis-Milton	University of Pittsburgh
Caren Steinlight	State University of New York, Plattsburgh
Alessandro Tinterri	Museo Civico dell'Attore e dello Spettacolo, Genoa

FIELD BIBLIOGRAPHERS

Susan Tuck	Sherborne, MA
Ronald W. Vince	McMaster University
Carla Waal	University of Missouri
Richard Wall	Queens College, City University of New York
Daniel Watermeier	University of Toledo
Margaret B. Wilkerson	University of California, Berkeley
Simon Williams	University of California, Santa Barbara
Leigh Woods	Indiana University, Bloomington

BIBLIOGRAPHY PROJECT STAFF

Editor: Benito Ortolani   **Associate Editor:** Margaret Loftus Ranald

THEATRE RESEARCH DATA CENTER

Director: Irving M. Brown   **Systems Analyst:** Rosabel A. Wang

Staff: Jill Dolan, Catherine Hilton, Donna Mehle, Charlotte Rea, Belén Negrón, Jeff Reynolds, Richard Ruskell, Martha Buckwalter, Aviv Orani

INTRODUCTION TO THE BIBLIOGRAPHY

The heart of this bibliography is the listing of items in the **Classed Entries** section. It contains the most complete information on each entry. There are several means of access to these entries.

The **Taxonomy** serves as the primary table of contents. It is a systematic organization of the field of theatre, and its structure dictates the placement of items in the Classed Entries according to their content. Thus users may determine through the Taxonomy the location in the Classed Entries section of items of interest to them and browse through those and related adjacent fields.

Access of a more specific sort may be gained through the **Subject Index**, in which a wide range of topics is arranged alphabetically. Under each subject heading is set forth the number of each classed entry to which that heading pertains and the time period, geography and essence of the classed entry from which the subject entry was generated. There are headings in the Subject Index for historical periods and centuries, and each classed entry is listed under one or more of these.

Two other indexes provide additional access to the classed entries. The **Document Author Index** lists the authors of the classed entry documents; the names of authors discussed in the indexed documents may be found in the Subject Index. The **Document Geography Index** lists the numbers of the classed entries items according to the geographical area to which the content of the referenced documents pertains.

NOTES ON THE TAXONOMY

The taxonomical categories are intended as practical aids for the location of entries, not as a theoretical statement about the controversial problem of theatre systematics and terminology.

COLUMN 1

Sec. B (Basic Theatrical Documents) includes production documents themselves, not items about them. Playtexts as a rule are not included.

Sec. C (Theatre in General) is used only when Sections D-N do not apply. "Theatre" is understood as "live presentations by performers for audiences". It includes mimetic and non-mimetic forms.

Sec. F (Drama) includes items related to playtexts and their performance, where the spoken word is traditionally considered the dominant element.

COLUMN 2

Subsets of **Sec. C (Theatre in General):**

Comprehensive is applied to entries encompassing all or most aspects of theatre or dealing with the phenomenon of theatre, especially in a theoretical manner.

Multiple application is used in all other cases in which a particular aspect could apply to several theatrical forms in Column 1, e.g., stage lighting.

COLUMN 5

The categories in this column describe the document's treatment of its subject. Treatment does not form a group of items in the classed entry section: it is included in each entry.

Studies of criticism/critics treats as its primary object criticism in itself, its nature, methodology, and development, as well as the persons who practice it.

Critical studies presents an evaluation resulting from the application of criteria.

Studies of theories/theorists considers theory itself, one or more specific theories, or those who discuss or propose theories.

Studies of history/historians treats as its primary object theatre history itself, its methods and problems and the persons who write history.

Historical studies refers to brief treatments of one or a few events.

Histories-general covers the whole spectrum of theatre—or most of it—over a period of time and typically appear in one or several volumes.

Histories-specific covers a particular genre, institution, or component of theatre.

Histories-sources refers to source documents that are not primarily critical or historiographical in nature.

Histories-reconstruction denotes entries that attempt to reconstruct some aspect of the theatre.

Histories-oral applies to sound or video recordings of interviews.

Studies of research/researchers discusses research methods and problems and the persons who are involved in research.

Biographical studies are articles on part of the subject's life.

Biographies denotes a book-length treatment of an entire life.

Linguistic studies deals with issues pertaining to the meaning or value of the language itself, not to textual accuracy.

Textual studies examines the texts themselves for origins, accuracy, and the like, not evaluation.

Technical studies examines theatre from the point of view of the applied sciences or discuss particular theatrical techniques.

Textbooks/manuals/guides teaches or describes procedures.

NOTES ON THE SECTIONS OF THE BIBLIOGRAPHY

CLASSED ENTRIES. Each citation includes the standard bibliographical information: author(s), title, publisher, pages, and notes, preface, appendixes, etc., when appropriate. Journal titles are usually in the form of an acronym, for which see the **List of Periodicals**. Pertinent additional information is provided in square brackets.

When the title is not in English, a translation in parentheses follows the original title. Established English translations of play titles or names of institutions are used when they exist. Geographical names are given in standard English form as defined by **Webster's New Geographical Dictionary** (1984). Names of institutions, companies, buildings, etc., unless an English version is in common use, are as a rule left untranslated.

An indication of the time and place to which a document pertains is included wherever appropriate and possible. The geographical information refers usually to a country, sometimes to a larger region such as the Middle East or English-speaking countries. England, Scotland, Wales, and Great Britain are used depending on the scope of the document. The geographical information is relative to the time of the content: Russia is used before 1917; East and West Germany after 1945; Roman Empire until its official demise, Italy thereafter. When appropriate, a precise date related to the content of the item is given. Otherwise the century or centuries are indicated, sometimes with a well-known historical period. When the document covers more than two centuries the term "Multi-period" is used.

Unless the content of a document is sufficiently clear from the title, the classed entry provides a brief abstract. Titles of plays not in English are given in English translation in the abstract, except for most operas and titles that are widely known in their original language. If the original title does not appear in the document title, it is provided in the abstract, in parentheses following the English title. English form is used for transliterated personal names. In the subject index, each English spelling refers the user to the international spelling, under which all relevant entries are listed.

Affiliation with a group or movement and influence by or on individuals or groups is indicated only when the document itself suggests such information. When a document belongs to more than one Column 1 category of the taxonomy, the entry may be cross-referenced to the other applicable Column 1 category. Playtexts and reviews of performances or publications as a rule are not included; exceptions are made in the case of playtexts with substantial commentary, newly discovered important plays from the past and translations from less accessible languages. Reviews having the scope of review articles are also included.

SUBJECT INDEX. Play titles not in English are in the original language with a translation in parentheses. A subject heading containing only the English translation refers the user to the original-language heading. English spellings of transliterated personal names are cross-referenced to the international spelling, under which all appropriate items are listed. Named chronological periods should be cross-checked with appropriate centuries.

DOCUMENT AUTHOR INDEX. Only the names of the authors of the classed entries are included. Authors discussed in the entries may be listed in the subject index.

DOCUMENT GEOGRAPHY INDEX. Document geography refers to the area covered by the document, not to its place of publication.

A TAXONOMY OF THEATRE

Column I	Column II	Column III	Column IV	Column V
			Subset each as follows:	Studies of criticism/critics
				Studies of history/historians
				Studies of research/researchers
				Studies of theories/theorists
A) Reference Materials	Bibliographies	Choreography/choreographers	Characters/roles	Bibliographical studies
	Catalogues	Librettos/librettists	Plot/subject/theme	Biographical studies
	Collected materials	Plays/playwrights	Structure/language	Critical studies
	Descriptions of resources	Scores/composers	Genres	Historical studies
	Dictionaries	Scripts/scriptwriters	Adaptations	Linguistic studies
	Encyclopedias		Editions	Technical studies
	Guides		Translations	Textual studies
	Indexes			Biographies
	Lists		Composition	Histories-general
	Yearbooks		Health/safety/logistics	Histories-oral
B) Basic Theatrical Documents	Miscellaneous texts	Audience	Psychology/behavior	Histories-reconstruction
	Playtexts		Reactions/comments	Histories-sources
C) Theatre in General	Comprehensive		Relationship to performer	Histories-specific
	Multiple application			Reviews of performances
D) Dance	General	Design/technology	Camerawork/camera operators	Reviews of publications
	Ballet		Costuming/costumers	Textbooks/manuals/guides
	Ethnic dance		Health and safety	
	Modern dance		Lighting/lighting designers	
	Popular dance		Machines/equipment	
E) Dance-drama	General		Make-up	
	Kabuki		Masks/wigs	
	Nō		Properties	
F) Drama	General		Scenery/scene designers	
	Comedy		Sound	
	Experimental forms		Technicians/crews	
	Tragedy	Financial operations	Earned income	
G) Media	General		Fundraising/gifts and grants	
	Audio forms		Government funding/subsidies	
	Film		Planning and accounting	
	Video forms			
H) Mime	General	Institutions	Producing/performing	
	Pantomime		Research	
			Service	
			Social	
I) Mixed Performances	Court Masque	Legal Aspects	Special	
	Performance Art		Training	
			Liabilities	
			Licensing and regulations	
			Performance rights	

Performance management
- House management
- Performance coordination
- Stage management
- Technical direction

Performance/performers
- Acting/actors
- Dance/dancers
- Music/musicians
- Singing/singers

Performance spaces
- Amphitheatres
- Audience areas
- Construction/renovation
- Found spaces
- Halls
- Musicians/chorus areas
- Planning/design
- Religious structures
- Stage
- Support area
- Theatres

Personnel
- Dramaturgs
- Health and safety
- Labor relations
- Middle management/agents
- Top management/producers

Public relations
- Advertising and development
- Audience relations
- Community relations
- Press relations

Relation to other fields
- Anthropology
- Economics
- Education
- Other arts
- Philosophy
- Politics
- Psychology
- Religion
- Sociology

Staging
- Choreography/choreographer
- Conducting/conductors
- Directing/directors

Training
- Nonformal training
- Teachers
- Teaching methods
- Training aids

J) Music-drama
- General
- Musical theatre
- Opera
- Operetta

K) Popular Entertainment
- General
- Cabaret
- Carnival
- Circus acts
- Commedia dell'arte
- Pageants
- Parades

L) Puppetry
- General
- Shadow puppets

M) Ritual and ceremony
- General
- Civic
- Religious

N) Individuals
- Beckett
- Brecht
- Calderón
- Cechov
- Corneille
- Goethe
- Ibsen
- Ionesco
- Molière
- O'Neill
- Pirandello
- Racine
- Shakespeare
- Wagner

CLASSED ENTRIES

REFERENCE MATERIALS

Bibliographies

1   Bonafede, Cecilie Wiborg. "Ibsen-bibliografi 1979-1980."
(Ibsen Bibliography, 1979-1980.) *IÅ*. 1981-82: 119-136.
1979-1980.

2   Carpenter, Charles A. "Modern Drama Studies: An Annual
Bibliography." *MD*. 1982 June; 25(2): 222-310.
Twentieth cent. Related to Drama.

3   Cocuzza, Ginnine, ed.; Cohen-Stratyner, Barbara Naomi,
ed. *Performing Arts Resources*. Vol. 7. New York: Theatre
Library Association; 1982. x, 80 pp. Pref.
Multi-period. ■Bibliography of pertinent materials for those in the
performing arts.

4   Cohn, Alan. "More Tennessee Williams in the Seventies."
TWNew. 1982 Spring-Fall; 3(2): 46-50. [Supplement to the
bibliography *Tennessee Williams in the Seventies*, published
TWNew, Vol. 2, No. 1.]
Twentieth cent. ■Bibliography of essays about and interviews with
Tennessee Williams.

5   Haase, Yorck Alexander, comp. "Bibliographie deutschsprachiger Theaterliteratur 1981." (Bibliography of Theatre
Literature in German, 1981.) *TH*. 1982; 13: 135-142.
Multi-period. ■Listing of books in German on theatre and drama
published in 1981.

6   Jacobs, Henry E. *Cymbeline*. New York: Garland; 1982.
xvii, 591 pp. (Garland Shakespeare Bibliographies Series
3.) Pref. Index.
1609-1982. ■Annotated bibliography of *Cymbeline* criticism. Related to
Individuals: Shakespeare.

7   Magister, Karl-Heinz. "Shakespeare-Bibliographie für 1980
mit Nachträgen aus früheren Jahren." (Shakespeare Bibliography for 1980 with Addenda from Earlier Years.) *SJW*.
1982; 118: 209-282. Notes. [Concluded on January 31,
1981.]
Multi-period. ■Entries from multi-national publications. Related to
Individuals: Shakespeare.

8   Moudouès, Rose-Marie. "Bibliographie." (Bibliography.)
RHT. 1982; 34(4): 305-577.
Multi-period. ■Annual bibliography of articles and books on theatre.
Related to Theatre in General.

9   Klein, Dennis A. *Peter and Anthony Shaffer: A Reference
Guide*. Boston: G.K. Hall; 1982. xi, 110 pp. Pref. Index.
England. Twentieth cent. ■Chronology and annotated bibliography.

10   Wearing, J. P. "Nineteenth-Century Theatre Research: A
Bibliography for 1981." *NCTR*. 1982 Winter; 10(2): 93-
109. Index.
English-speaking countries. 1787-1914. Related to Theatre in General.

11   Hadamowsky, Franz. *Bücherkunde deutschsprachiger
Theaterliteratur*. (Bibliography of Theatre Literature in
German.) Vienna, Cologne, Graz: Böhlau; 1982. 407 pp.
(Maske und Kothurn, Beiheft 6.) Pref. Index. [Part 2, 1945-
1979: Part 1 not yet published.]
Germany. Austria. Switzerland. 1945-1979. ■Listing of approximately
10,000 books in German, published between 1945 and 1979. Part 1
covers general reference materials and books on special fields, Part 2,
theatre history, Part 3, lives and works of individual dramatists and
theatre people. Index does not include plays.

12   Haring-Smith, Tori. *A.A. Milne: A Critical Bibliography*.
New York: Garland; 1982. xxxii, 344 pp. (Garland Reference Library of the Humanities 305.) Index.
Great Britain. Twentieth cent. ■Published writings by and about Milne,
recent adaptations of Milne's juvenile books.

13   Attisani, Antonio; Buffa, Cristiano. *Leggere lo spettacolo —
Catalogo dei libri e delle riviste di teatro e danza usciti in
Italia nel 1981*. (Reading the Performance: Catalogue of
Books and Magazines of Theatre and Dance Printed in Italy
in 1981.) Florence: La casa Usher; 1982. 227 pp. (Quaderni
4.) Index.
Italy. Multi-period. Related to Dance.

14   Colecchia, Francesca, ed. *García Lorca: An Annotated
Primary Bibliography*. New York: Garland; 1982. xxiv, 281
pp. (Garland Reference Library of the Humanities Series
259.) Pref. Index.
Spain. 1900-1936.

15   "Research Update." *ChTR*. 1982 Fall; 31(4): 11. Biblio.
USA. 1982. ■Bibliography of current research in creative drama and
children's theatre.

16   Coven, Brenda. *American Women Dramatists of the Twentieth Century: A Bibliography*. Metuchen, NJ: Scarecrow P;
1982. v, 237 pp. Index.
USA. Twentieth cent. Related to Drama.

17   Elliot, Paula. *Performing Arts Information, 1975-1980: A
Bibliography of Reference Works*. Manhattan, KS: Kansas
State Univ. Libraries; 1982. vii, 41 pp. (Bibliography Series
15.) Index.
USA. England. 1975-1980. ■Annotated bibliography of English-
language bibliographies, dictionaries, encyclopedias, indexes, calendars,
directories, guides to opportunities, collective biography, new journals,
filmographies and discographies.

18   Johnson, Claudia D.; Johnson, Vernon E. *Nineteenth-
Century Theatrical Memoirs*. Westport, CT: Greenwood;
1982. xvii, 269 pp. Index.
USA. England. Nineteenth cent. ■Bibliographical listing of memoirs
and autobiographies including brief biographical sketches of artists.

19   Kaiser, Ernest. "Blacks and the Mass Media: A Bibliography." *Fds*. 1982; 22(3): 193-209.
USA. 1971-1982.

20   King, Kimball. *Ten Modern American Playwrights: An
Annotated Bibliography*. New York: Garland; 1982. xv, 251
pp. (Garland Reference Library of the Humanities 234.)
Index.
USA. Twentieth cent. ■Concerns Edward Albee, Amiri Baraka, Ed
Bullins, Jack Gelber, Arthur Kopit, David Mamet, David Rabe, Sam
Shepard, Neil Simon and Lanford Wilson.

21   Landrum, Larry N. *American Popular Culture: A Guide to
Information Sources*. Detroit, MI: Gale Research P; 1982.
xvii, 435 pp. (American Studies Information Guide Series
12.) Pref. Index.
USA. Multi-period. ■Annotated bibliography. Related to Popular
Entertainment.

22   Seligman, Kevin L. "Bibliography of Flat Pattern Sources."
TD&T. 1982 Fall; 18(3): 23-28. [Part One, A-J.]
USA. Twentieth cent.

23   Seligman, Kevin L. "Bibliography of Flat Pattern Sources."
TD&T. 1982 Winter; 18(4): 20-25. [Part Two, K-W.]
USA. Twentieth cent.

24   Work, William. "The ERIC Connection." *ChTR*. 1982
Summer; 31(3): 13-17.
USA. 1979-1981. ■Annotated bibliography on relationships among
language arts skills reported in ERIC (Education Resources Information Center).

25   Work, William. "The ERIC Connection." *ChTR*. 1982;
31(1): 22-23.
USA. Twentieth cent. ■Annotated bibliography of creative drama and
theatre research available from ERIC (Educational Resources Information Center).

REFERENCE MATERIALS – cont'd

Catalogues

26   *Il magnifico apparato – Pubbliche funzioni, feste e giuochi bolognesi nel Settecento.* (The Magnificent Pomp: Public Ceremonies, Entertainments, and Games in 18th Century Bologna.) Culture and Civil Life in the Eighteenth Century in Emilia Romagna. Bologna: Clueb; 1982. 163 pp. Pref. Illus.
Italy. Eighteenth cent. ■Catalogue of exhibition at Palazzo Pepoli Campogrande, June-September 1982.

27   Bondoni, Simonetta M. *Teatri storici in Emilia Romagna.* (Historical Theatres in Emilia Romagna.) Bologna: Grafis; 1982. 248 pp. (Istituto per i Beni Culturali della Regione Emilia Romagna.) Notes. Illus.
Italy. 1600-1982. ■Exhibition catalogue with essays on theatrical heritage.

28   Bowlt, J.E. *Russian Stage Design: Scenic Innovation (1900-1930).* Jackson, MS: Mississippi Museum of Art; 1982. viii, 344 pp. Pref. Index. Biblio. Illus.: Photo. B&W. Color.
Russia. 1900-1930. ■Exhibition of scenic innovations from the Lobanov-Rostovsky collection. Related to Theatre in General: Design/technology.

29   Smith, Ronn, ed. "Directory 1982/83." *ThCr.* 1982 June/July; 16(6): 7-238. Index.
USA. 1982. ■Alphabetical listing of manufacturers of theatrical supplies and equipment.

Collected materials

30   Anderson, J.J. *Newcastle upon Tyne.* Toronto: Univ. of Toronto P; 1982. xvii, 216 pp. (Records of Early English Drama Series.) Pref. Index. Biblio. Illus.: Plan.
England. 500-1559. ■Compilation of records pertaining to medieval productions.

31   Engle, Ron, ed. "Theatre History Obscurities." *THSt.* 1982; 2: 129-135. Illus.: Photo. B&W.
Europe. North America. Nineteenth cent. Twentieth cent. ■Reproductions of pictorial materials not previously published or not readily available, including material related to Jenny Lind, Fritz Leiber's *Hamlet*, Rose McClendon, *Ben Hur*.

32   Guibert, Noëlle; Razgonnikoff, Jacqueline. "A quoi on joue?" (Playing at What?)*CF.* 1982 Mar.; 107: 3-14.
France. 1650-1982. ■Citations from various historical periods regarding acting and compendium of terms related to acting.

33   Wagner, Cosima; Mack, Dietrich, ed. *La mia vita a Bayreuth – Lettere e appunti 1883-1930.* (My Life in Bayreuth: Letters and Notes 1883-1930.) Milan: Rusconi; 1982. 905 pp. Notes. Illus.
Germany. 1883-1930. ■References to Bayreuth Festival. Related to Individuals: Wagner.

34   Anon. "Payne Memorabilia Donated to University of Texas Library." *ThNe.* 1982 Apr.; 14(4): 12.
USA. 1946-1982. ■Brief note of materials donated: i.e., medals, citations, recognition of achievements of B. Iden Payne, who initiated repertory movement in England, served as general director of Shakespeare Memorial Theatre at Stratford-upon-Avon, directed John and Ethel Barrymore and Helen Hayes. Related to Drama: Directing/directors.

35   Wilmeth, Don B. "The Shubert Archive." *ThNe.* 1982 Mar.; 14(3): 4.
USA. 1902-1982. ■Holdings of Shubert Archive, one of the largest theatre collections, will soon be available. Mentions biannual newsletter, *The Passing Show*.

Descriptions of resources

36   Anon. "Newsletter." *NCTR.* 1982 Summer; 10(1): 37-38.
Nineteenth cent. ■Recent publications, works-in-progress, forthcoming conferences, queries of interest to students of nineteenth century theatre.

37   Obermaier, Walter. "Nestroy-Neuerwerbungen der Wiener Stadt- und Landesbibliothek." (Nestroy: Recent Acquisitions at the City Library of Vienna.) *Ns.* 1982; 4(2): 50-53. Illus.
Austria. 1982. ■Notes on manuscripts by Johann Nestroy recently acquired by the manuscript collection of the City Library of Vienna. Related to Drama.

38   Bandy-White, Linda. "Miscellaneous Letters." *PS.* 1982 Summer; 6(2): 11. Illus. Loc.: The Shubert Archive, 149 W. 45th St., N.Y.C. 10036.
USA. 1920-1923. ■Describes contents of 28 boxes of letters between Shuberts and employees or prospective employees, with specific references to Helen Möller and Georgie Price.

39   Levy, Suzanne. "Correspondence: 1900-1906." *PS.* 1982 Winter; 6(1): 2-4. Illus.
USA. ■Description of 42 volumes of letters and clippings on Shubert artistic and financial operations.

40   Malnig, Julie; Nelson, Steve. "Archive Update." *PS.* 1982 Summer; 6(2): 12. Illus. Loc.: The Shubert Archive, 149 W. 45th Street, NY, NY 10036.
USA. 1909-1929. ■Shubert materials on theatres, real estate, unsolicited manuscripts, correspondence and the 1914 film, *The Life of Our Saviour*. Related to Media: Film.

41   Marder, Louis. "The Bard on Broadway: Historic Collection Exhibited in New York City." *ShN.* 1982 Winter; 32(5-6): 34.
USA. 1982. ■Theatre memorabilia displayed at the Museum of the City of New York.

Dictionaries

42   Gale Research Co. *International Authors and Writers Who's Who, with International Who's Who in Poetry.* Ninth edition. Detroit, MI: Gale Research P; 1982. 752 pp.
Twentieth cent. ■12,500 biographies of authors, writers, poets, with appendices of pseudonyms and literary agents.

43   Cohen-Stratyner, Barbara Naomi. *Biographical Dictionary of Dance.* New York: Schirmer Books; 1982. vi, 970 pp. Pref. Biblio.
Europe. North America. South America. 1550-1982. Related to Dance.

Guides

44   Bergeron, David M., ed.; Lindenbaum, Linda, ed. *Research Opportunities in Renaissance Drama.* Vol. 25. Lawrence, Kansas: UP of Kansas; 1982. vii, 150 pp. Pref.
England. 1500-1700. ■Survey of areas in Renaissance drama which suggest profitable research opportunities.

45   Parker, Valeria. "The Starving Artist: Self-Inflicted Myth." *CAM.* 1982 Nov.; 4(11): 41.
USA. 1982. ■Guide to resources for performers such as art advocacy, funding and support organizations.

46   Schlischefsky, Alexander; Sydow, Annegret. *Arbeitsfeld Theater.* (Theatre as a Sphere of Work.) Wilhelmshaven: Heinrichshofen; 1982. Unpaginated. (Theaterpädagogische Bibliothek 1.) Gloss. Index. Biblio. [New edition.]
West Germany. Twentieth cent. ■Employment, schools and organizations for theatrical employees.

Indexes

47   Hauger, George. "English Musical Theatre 1830-1900." *TN.* 1982; 36(2): 55-64.
England. 1830-1900. ■Corrections and additions to Allardyce Nicoll's *History of English Drama and Twentieth Century Drama*.

48   Hauger, George. "English Musical Theatre 1830-1900." *TN.* 1982; 36(3): 122-125.

REFERENCE MATERIALS — cont'd

England. 1830-1900. ■Index to the list of authors in *Theatre Notes*, volume 36, number 2. Related to Music-Drama: Musical theatre.

49   Alvarez, Max Joseph. *Index to Motion Pictures Reviewed by Variety, 1907-1980.* Metuchen, NJ: Scarecrow; 1982. viii, 510 pp. Pref. Index.
USA. 1907-1980. ■Motion picture index compiled from reviews in *Variety.* Related to Media.

Lists

50   Billington, Michael. *The Guinness Book of Theatre Facts and Feats.* Distributed by Sterling Publishing. Enfield, Middlesex, England: Guinness Superlatives Ltd; 1982. 240 pp. Index.
Multi-period.

51   Ollén, Gunnar. "Strindbergsförestállningar 1981." (Strindberg Productions, 1981.) *MfS.* 1982 Apr.; 66: 1-13 .
1981. ■Reports on productions in Sweden, Holland, Belgium, USA, East and West Germany, Finland, Denmark, Italy, Venezuela, England and Austria.

52   Schindler, Otto G., ed.; Schneider, Guntram, ed. *Theater in Österreich: Verzeichnis der Inszenierungen, 1980/81.* (Theatre in Austria: List of Productions, 1980-81.) Vienna: Verband der wissenschaftlichen Gesellschaften Österreichs; 1982. 187 pp. (Jahrbuch der Wiener Gesellschaft für Theaterforschung.) Pref. Index. [Annual publication.]
Austria. 1980-1981. ■New productions and guest performances at Austrian theatres and companies, including festivals and some non-professional groups: index of names, play titles, companies and places.

53   O'Neill, Patrick B. "A Checklist of Canadian Dramatic Materials to 1967. Part I: A to K." *CDr.* 1982; 8(2): 173-303.
Canada. Twentieth cent.

54   McGee, C.E.; Meagher, John C. "Preliminary Checklist of Tudor and Stuart Entertainment: 1485-1558." *RORD.* 1982; 25: 31-114. Pref. Biblio.
England. 1485-1558.

55   Guibert, Noëlle; Razgonnikoff, Jacqueline. "Les Comédiens Français de A à Z." (Actors of the Comédie Française from A to Z.) *CF.* 1982 Oct.; 112: 27-32. [Cross ref to v. 113 1982 Nov., v. 114 1982 Dec.]
France. 1680-1982. ■Dictionary of actors and actresses from Auge to Beaubour.

56   Guibert, Noëlle; Razgonnikoff, Jacqueline. "Les Comédiens Français de A à Z, 3." (Actors of the Comédie Française from A to Z, 3.) *CF.* 1982 Dec.; 114: 20-28. [Cross ref to v. 112 1982 Oct., v. 113 1982 Nov.]
France. 1680-1982. ■Dictionary of actors and actresses from Chaumette to Delvair.

57   Volz, Ruprecht. "Strindbergpremieren in Deutschland 1981." (Strindberg Premieres in Germany, 1981.) *MfS.* 1982 Apr.; 66 : 14-16.
Germany. 1981. ■Reports on German productions of Strindberg plays.

58   "Premiär." (Premiere.) *Entre.* 1982; 9(5): 38-39.
Sweden. 1982. ■Openings September-November, 1982.

59   "Premiär." (Premiere.) *Entre.* 1982; 9(6): 30-31.
Sweden. 1982-1983. ■Openings November 1982-February 1983.

60   "Premiär." (Premiere.) *Entre.* 1982; 9(1): 38-39.
Sweden. 1982. ■Openings January-March, 1982.

61   "Premiär." (Premiere.) *Entre.* 1982; 9(3): 30-31.
Sweden. 1982. ■Openings April-July, 1982.

62   Engle, Ron, ed. "Mid-America Theatre Conference Theatre History Symposium 1982." *THSt.* 1982; 2: 139-140.
USA. 1982. ■List of papers presented at symposium on 'Makers of the Modern Theatre,' held in Kansas City, MO, March 19-21.

63   Helbing, Terry. "Active Lesbian/Gay Theatre Companies." *GTAN.* 1982 Aug.; 4(1): 12.
USA. Europe. Australia. 1982. ■Alphabetical listing with addresses. Related to Drama.

64   Hill, Philip G. "Doctoral Projects in Progress in Theatre Arts, 1982." *TJ.* 1982 May; 34(2): 241-246.
USA. 1982. ■Dissertations in progress.

65   Loney, Glenn. *Twentieth-Century Theatre.* New York: Facts on File; 1982. v.1: xvi, 256 pp./v.2: 264 pp. Pref. Index. Illus.: Photo. B&W.
USA. England. 1900-1982. ■Premieres, revivals, theatres, productions, births, deaths and artists' debuts. Related to Theatre in General.

66   Anon. "Dokumentation." (Documentation.) *TH.* 1982; 13: 119-134. [Column.]
West Germany. Austria. Switzerland. 1981-1982. ■Main theatres, productions in 1981-82 and plays for 1982-83.

Yearbooks

67   *Österreichischer Bundestheaterverband. Bericht. 1980/81.* (Austrian Federal Theatres: Report, 1980-81.) Vienna: Österreichischer Bundestheaterverband; 1982. 454 pp. Pref. Illus.: Maps. [Annual report.]
Austria. 1980-1981. ■Includes Burgtheater, Staatsoper and Volksoper. Texts of agreements, listing of radio and television broadcasts, guest performances abroad and in provinces, listing of new productions and casts, statistics on plays, authors and composers, spectators, prices, etc.

68   Rubin, Don, ed.; Walsh, Paul, ed.; Wilson, Marg, ed. *Canada on Stage: Canadian Theatre Review Yearbook, 1981-1982.* Toronto: CTR Publications; 1982. 398 pp. Notes. Index. Illus.: Photo. Print. B&W.
Canada. 1981-1982. ■Professional theatre activity: listing of winter theatre, festival theatre, summer theatre and theatre for the young by province. Includes the productions, casts and dates performed at each theatre, with list of awards. Related to Theatre in General.

———

Other entries with significant content related to Reference Materials: 133, 172, 955.

BASIC THEATRICAL DOCUMENTS

Miscellaneous texts

69   Gordon, Mel. *Lazzi: Comic Routines of the Commedia dell'Arte.* New York: Theatre Library Association; 1982. 80 pp. Pref. Biblio. Illus.: Dwg. B&W.
Italy. 1550-1680. ■207 lazzi in outline, scenarios and character glossary. Related to Popular Entertainment: *Commedia dell'arte.*

70   Bryer, Jackson. *The Theatre We Worked For: Letters of Eugene O'Neill to Kenneth Macgowan.* New Haven, CT: Yale UP; 1982. xiii, 274 pp. Pref. Notes. Illus.: Photo. Dwg. B&W.
USA. 1920-1959. Biographies. ■Edited letters from Eugene O'Neill to Kenneth Macgowan, discussing Provincetown Players, O'Neill's plays and personal life. Related to Individuals: O'Neill.

71   Feit, Ken. "Stories Told by Children." *Tk.* 1982 July-Aug.; 2(5): 38-39. Illus.
USA. 1971-1972. ■Stories collected by itinerant storyteller Ken Feit from school children during a workshop.

Playtexts

72   Gray, John. "Rock 'n Roll." *CTR.* 1982 Summer; 35: 67-131. Pref. Illus.

BASIC THEATRICAL DOCUMENTS — cont'd

Canada. 1981. ■Nostalgic musical romp by author of *Billy Bishop Goes to War*, followed by interview with the author. Related to Music-Drama: Musical theatre.

73   Baker, Donald C., ed.; Murphy, John L., ed.; Hall, Louis B., Jr., ed. *The Late Medieval Religious Plays of Bodleian MSS Digby 133 and E Museo 160*. London: Oxford UP; 1982. cix, 284 pp. (Early English Text Society 283.) Pref. Notes. Index.
England. Medieval period.

74   Bowers, Fredson, ed. *The Dramatic Works in the Beaumont and Fletcher Canon*. Vol. 5. New York: Cambridge UP; 1982. vii, 670 pp. Pref.
England. 1600-1625. ■Continuation of Bowers' scholarly editions of the Beaumont and Fletcher canon.

75   Jones, Henry Arthur; Jackson, Russell, ed. *Plays by Henry Arthur Jones*. New York: Cambridge UP; 1982. x, 228 pp. (British and American Playwrights: 1750-1920.) Pref. Notes. Biblio. Illus.
England. 1882-1897. ■Introduction, biographical record and texts of *The Silver King, The Case of Rebellious Susan* and *The Liars*.

76   Racine, Jean; Knight, R.C., transl. *Jean Racine: Four Greek Plays*. New York: Cambridge UP; 1982. xvi, 223 pp. Pref. Notes. Biblio.
France. Seventeenth cent. French classicism. ■Translations with introductions of Jean Racine's *Phèdre, Andromaque, Iphigénie* and *Athalie*.

77   Turrini, Peter; Roger, David, transl. "*Josef and Maria*." *Gambit*. 1982; 10(39-40): 57-77. Illus.
Austria. 1982. ■Text, with brief commentary of *Josef and Maria (Josef und Maria)*. Simultaneous premieres at Orpheum, Graz, and the Österreichische Gewerkbund, Vienna. Illustration from a 1982 production.

78   Müller, Heiner; Hood, Stuart, transl. "*The Mission*." *Gambit*. 1982; 10(39-40): 111-129.
East Germany. 1981. ■Text and brief critical commentary on *The Mission, or Memory of a Revolution (Der Auftrag oder Erinnerung einer Revolution)*. Premiere Kleine Bühne of the East Berlin Volksbühne, January 1981, directed by the author.

79   Corneille, Thomas; Mandel, Oscar, transl. *Ariadne: A Tragedy in Five Acts*. Gainesville, FL: UP of Florida; 1982. xii, 82 pp. Pref. Biblio. Illus.: Print. B&W.
France. 1672. ■Text with critical and historical analysis of *Ariadne (Ariane)*.

80   Matagorō II, Nakamura, adap.; Brandon, James R., adap. & transl; Berberich, Junko, transl; Feldman, Michael, transl. "*Chūshingura: The Forty-Seven Samurai* (A Kabuki Version of the Play)." 147-221 in Brandon, James R., ed. *Chūshingura: Studies in Kabuki and the Puppet Theater*. Honolulu, HI: Univ. of Hawaii P; 1982. xii, 231 pp. Pref. Notes.
Japan. Tokugawa period. Eighteenth cent. ■Translation and adaptation of text, with introduction. Related to Dance-Drama: *Kabuki*.

81   Fassbinder, Rainer Werner; Gooch, Steve, transl. "*Cock-Artist*." *Gambit*. 1982; 10(39-40): 15-36. Illus.
West Germany. 1968-1979. ■Text and brief critical commentary of *Cock-Artist (Katzelmacher)*, with photographs of 1971 German production. Premiere at Anti-theater, Munich, 1968, filmed 1968.

82   Gahl, Christoph; Vivis, Anthony, transl. "*Intensive Care or An Endless Vegetable-like Existence*." *Gambit*. 1982; 10 (39-40): 131-156. [Translation of *Intensivstation*. First broadcast Sept. 22, 1980, Hessischer Rundfunk.]
West Germany. 1980. ■Text of *Intensive Care* with brief critical commentary, translated from Christoph Gahl's *Intensivstation*.

83   Hacks, Peter; Hilton, Julian, transl.; Bönisch, Hanne, transl. "*Market Day at Plundersweilern*." *Gambit*. 1982; 10 (39-40): 79-110. Illus.

West Germany. 1975. ■Text and brief critical comment on *Market Day at Plundersweilern (Das Jahrmarktsfest zu Plundersweilern)*, after Goethe. Premiere Berlin, November, 1975. Illustration from an otherwise unidentified production of Peter Hacks's *Seneca's Death (Senecas Tod)*. Infl. by Johann Wolfgang von Goethe.

84   Krötz, Franz Xaver; Gooch, Steve, transl. "*Homework*." *Gambit*. 1982; 10(39-40): 157-180. Illus.: Photo.
West Germany. 1971-1979. ■Text of *Homework (Heimarbeit)*, with brief critical commentary. Premiere April 3, 1971. Photographs from unidentified German production of Krötz's *Neither Fish nor Fowl (Nicht Fisch Nicht Fleisch)*.

85   Müller, Harald; Gooch, Steve, transl. "*Flotsam*." *Gambit*. 1982; 10(39-40): 181-205.
West Germany. 1974. ■Text of *Flotsam (Strandgut)* with brief critical commentary. Premiere at Schiller Theater, West Berlin, 1974.

86   Roth, Friederike; Schmid, Estella, transl. "*Piano-Play*." *Gambit*. 1982; 10(39-40): 37-56.
West Germany. 1970-1981. ■Text, with brief commentary of *Piano-Play (Klavierspiele)*. Premiere at Malersaal des deutschen Schauspielhauses, Hamburg, 1981.

———

Other entries with significant content related to Basic Theatrical Documents: 317, 322.

THEATRE IN GENERAL

Comprehensive

87   Wilson, Edwin; Goldfarb, Alvin. *Living Theater: An Introduction to Theater History*. New York: McGraw-Hill; 1982. xiv, 482 pp. Pref. Index. Biblio. Illus.: Photo. B&W.
Multi-period. Textbooks/manuals/guides. ■Survey of world theatre history from beginnings to present.

88   Conolly, L.W., ed. *Theatrical Touring and Founding in North America*. Westport, CT: Greenwood; 1982. xiv, 245 pp. Pref. Index. Biblio.
Canada. USA. 1700-1980. Historical studies. ■Collected essays on varied subjects in theatre history.

89   Cook, Michael. "World Theatre Day." *CTR*. 1982 Summer; 35: 132-134. Pref. Illus.
Canada. 1982. Histories-sources. ■World Theatre Day message written by playwright Michael Cook.

90   John, Hans-Rainer. "Das Zentrale Thema bewältigen." (Mastering the Central Theme.) *TZ*. 1982 Feb.; 37: 6-7. Illus. [Monthly column.]
East Germany. Twentieth cent. Critical studies. ■Theatre's social value.

91   Guibert, Noëlle; Razgonnikoff, Jacqueline. "Comme au théâtre." (As in the Theatre.) *CF*. 1982 May; 109: 13-14.
France. 1982. Linguistic studies. ■Theatre terminology in everyday language.

92   Ödeen, Mats. "Teater och berättande." (Theatre and Narrative.) *Entre*. 1982; 9(5): 14-18. Illus.
Greece. France. Multi-period. Historical studies. ■Origin of theatre in religious ritual, origin of drama in oral epic tradition. Drama of ancient Greece and medieval France illustrates Ödeen's theory of perennial conflict between literary and oral culture, and differentiation of theatre and drama.

93   *Il teatro in Italia e in Puglia. Prospettive e realtà*. (Theatre in Italy and in Apulia: Prospects and Reality.) Consorzio del Teatro Pubblico Pugliese. Bari: Laterza; 1982. 151 pp.
Italy. 1960-1981. Histories-sources. ■Proceedings of meeting on situation of theatre, May 8-9, 1981.

94   Sauter, Wilmar. "Teatern inte Litterär!" (Non Literary Theatre.) *Entre*. 1982; 9(6): 23-24. Illus.

THEATRE IN GENERAL – cont'd

Sweden. Twentieth cent. Studies of theories/theorists. ■Supports concept of theatre as theatrical.

95   Patterson, Douglas L. "A Call for Regional Histories." *Tk.* 1982 July-Aug.; 2(5): 50-55. Notes.
USA. 1930-1982. Histories-sources. ■Paper delivered at Midwest Area Theatre Conference in March 1979, calling for serious consideration of theatre history in America outside New York City and launching two-year regional project to compile materials for seven midwestern states.

96   Perosa, Sergio. *Storia del teatro americano.* (History of American Theatre.) Milan: Bompiani; 1982. 204 pp. (Studi Bompiani.) Pref. Index. Biblio.
USA. 1700-1969. Histories-general.

97   Wilson, Garff B. *Three Hundred Years of American Drama and Theatre.* Englewood Cliffs, NJ: Prentice-Hall; 1982. xii, 350 pp. Pref. Index. Biblio. Illus. [2nd Edition.]
USA. 1665-1982. Histories-general.

98   Blum, Lambert; Iversen, Fritz. "Der wahre Wert des Theaters: Indizien zu einem Desillusionierungsprozess." (The Real Value of Theatre: Signs of a Process of Disillusionment.) *Tzs.* 1982; 1: 17-23.
West Germany. 1982. Historical studies. ■Critical comment on background of 'theatre crisis'.

99   Girshausen, Theo. "Erkundungen im Konjunktive: Über Geschichte und Perspectiven der Theaterwissenschaft." (Explorations in the Subjunctive: On History and Prospects of Theatre Research.) *Tzs.*; 1: 101-113.
West Germany. 1800-1982. Studies of research/researchers. ■Development of 'Theaterwissenschaft' (Theatre research) as an academic discipline emphasizing the concept of theatre as autonomous art form. Suggests coordination of semiotic, sociological, empirical, perception-oriented and historical approaches to contemporary theatre.

Relation to other fields: Education

100   Sharpham, John; Sudano, Gary R. "Back to Basics: Justifying the Arts in General Education." *ThNe.* 1982 Jan.; 14(1): 15-16.
USA. 1980-1982. Critical studies. ■Arts instruction shown to be basic part of curriculum.

101   Wicke, Henry A., Jr. "A Rationale for the Arts in Education." *ThNe.* 1982 Feb.; 14(2): 17-18.
USA. 1982. Critical studies. ■Five reasons why the arts are important to all levels of education.

Relation to other fields: Philosophy

102   Hearn, Thomas K., Jr. "A Philosophy for the Arts." *ThNe.* 1982 Feb.; 14(2): 19-21. Biblio.
USA. 1980. Critical studies. ■Basic issues regarding role of arts in society, including effects of technology, secularism, electronic media, dualism and elitism. Presented at the ACUCAA (Association of College, University and Community Arts Administrators) 24th Annual Conference, December 21, 1980, New York City.

Relation to other fields: Politics

103   Romero, Laurent. "Die aktuelle Theaterpraxis oder Die Nostalgie nach grossen Formen der Tradition." (The Present Theatre Practice or The Nostalgia for Great Forms of Tradition.) *MuK.* 1982; 28(1): 51-66.
France. 1960-1981. Histories-sources. ■Interview with critic Bernard Dort, about political values of theatre, theatre concepts of Romain Rolland, Jean Vilar, Roger Planchon and Ariane Mnouchkine, and functions of theatre criticism.

104   Adler, Heidrun. *Politisches Theater in Lateinamerika: Von der Mythologie über die Mission zur kollektiven Identität.* (Political Theatre in Latin America: From Mythological Mission to Collective Identity.) Berlin: Reimer; 1982. 171 pp. (Beiträge zur Kulturanthropologie.) Notes.

South America. 1500-1982. Histories-general. ■Pre-Columbian theatre, dances, ritual performances, missionary drama and contemporary revolutionary and alternate theatre groups.

105   Killens, John Oliver. "The Responsibility of the Writer to the Community." *Crisis.* 1982 Mar.; 89(3): 30-32.
USA. Twentieth cent. Histories-sources. ■Novelist urges Black artists to wage cultural revolution and to use their words for political and social change.

Relation to other fields: Sociology

106   Tiger, Lionel. "The Larger Scheme." *AmTh.* 1982 Nov.; 4(8): 10-13. Notes. Illus.: Photo. B&W.
Europe. USA. Multi-period. Critical studies. ■Examines physical and social evolution of people in relationship to art.

107   Puppa, Paolo. "Kultur – Zivilisation – Peuple nel teatro francese del Novecento." (Culture, Civilization and the People in French Theatre of the 20th Century.) *QT.* 1982 Feb.; 4(15): 189-199. Notes. Biblio.
France. Twentieth cent. Historical studies. ■Cultural politics during Popular Front, with focus on Romain Rolland.

108   Wise, Debra. "Transformation & Communitas." *Tk.* 1982 Jan.-Feb.; 2(2): 20.
USA. 1981-1982. Critical studies. ■How theatre can provide alternative images of community and social relationships.

Staging

109   Kröplin, Wolfgang. "Synthetisches Theater. Alexander Tairows Theaterprogramm und der Einfluss der Oktoberrevolution." (Synthetic Theatre: Alexander Tairov's Idea of Theatre and the Influence of the October Revolution.) *TZ.* 1982 Nov.; 37(11): 51-52.
USSR. 1914-1950. Studies of theories/theorists. ■Tairov's changing idea of theatre and differentiation from the civic literary theatre.

Multiple application

110   Malpede, Karen. "Women in Theatre: Compassion and Hope." *Tk.* 1982 Mar.-Apr.; 2(3): 4-6. Notes. Illus. [Excerpts from full-length book.]
Multi-period. Histories-specific. ■Excerpts from introduction to book of same title concerning historical involvement of women in the making of theatre from ancient ritual to present.

111   Gleiss, Jochen; Kranz, Dieter; Linzer, Martin; Markwart, Enno; Waschinsky, Peter. "Theater der Nationen Sofia '82." (Theatre of Nations, Sofia '82.) *Tz.* 1982 Sep.; 37(9): 57-64.
Bulgaria. 1982. Reviews of performances. ■Reports on Theatre of Nations festival.

112   Kozlinski, Wotjek. "Artists and Critics: Incompatible Yet Inseparable." *CTR.* 1982 Winter; 33: 100-102. Illus.
Canada. 1982. Studies of criticism/critics. ■Criticism conference held at Queen's University, Kingston, ON.

113   Ryga, George. "The Artist in Resistance." *CTR.* 1982 Winter; 33: 86-91. Pref. Illus.
Canada. 1982. Histories-sources. ■Text of an address at Populist Theatre Festival.

114   Wagner, Anton. *From Art to Theory: Canada's Critical Tools.* CTR. 1982 Spring; 34: 59-76. Notes. Illus.
Canada. Twentieth cent. Studies of criticism/critics. ■Bibliography and research in criticism.

115   Charles, Amy N. "Sir Henry Herbert: The Master of the Revels as a Man of Letters." *MP.* 1982 Aug.; 80(1): 1-12.
England. 1594-1670. Biographical studies. ■Survey of Sir Henry Herbert's literary works.

116   Shapiro, Michael. "The Children of Paul's and Their Playhouse." *TN.* 1982; 36(1): 3-13.

CLASSED ENTRIES

THEATRE IN GENERAL — cont'd

England. 1575-1600. Historical studies. ■Rebuttal of W.R. Cair's article 'La Compagnie des Enfants de St. Paul'.

117 Cascetta, Annamaria; Antolini, Fabio; Cuminetti, Benvenuto; Bernardi, Claudio. *I discorsi del teatro — Percorsi e problemi della scena che cambia.* (Theatre Talks: Methods and Problems of the Changing Stage.) Milano: Vita e pensiero; 1982. 229 pp. (Comunicazioni sociali 3.) Pref. Notes.
Europe. Twentieth cent. Critical studies. ■Western dramaturgy model crisis: separate analysis of its constituent elements (text, actor, direction, stage space).

118 Gervais, Jean. "Entrevue: l'itinéraire de Jacques Lasalle." (Interview: Jacques Lasalle's Itinerary.) *PrTh.* 1982 Winter-Spring; 14-15: 77-94.
France. 1981. Studies of theories/theorists. ■Author, actor, director Lasalle on directing, styles of acting and actors, his theatre of suspicion, doubt and everyday occurrence and his rejection of traditional theatricality and stage extravagance. Mention of Jean Vilar, Gérard Philippe, Roger Planchon, Stanislavski, Brecht and Grotowski.

119 Romero, Laurent. "Remembrance of Things Past: French Theater Praxis Today." *MD.* 1982 Sep.; 25(3): 387-398.
France. 1950-1980. ■Interview with critic Bernard Dort on important trends, political aspects and director's role.

120 Fischer-Lichte, Erika. "Theatergeschichte oder Theatersemiotik — eine echte Alternative? Versuch einer semiotischen Rekonstruktion der Theatergeste auf dem deutschen Theater im 18 Jahrhundert." (Theatre History or Theatre Semiotics – A Real Alternative? Toward a Semiotic Reconstruction of the Gesture in German Theatre of the 18th Century.) *MuK.* 1982; 28(3-4): 163-194. Notes.
Germany. Baroque period. Eighteenth cent. Studies of theories/theorists. ■Formulation of specific gestural codes for each period proposed as main task of semiotic approach to theatre history. Application to theatrical gesture of German baroque period reflecting Enlightenment views of human nature.

121 Otto, Werner. "Theatergeschichte(n) 8: Verrohung in der Theaterkritik. Die Auseinandersetzungen um Aufgabe, Grenzen und Stil in der Theaterberichterstattung. 1902." (Theatre History 8: Brutalization in Theatre Criticism. The Discussion on Task, Limits and Style in Reporting about Theatre, 1902.) *TZ.* 1982 Aug.; 37(8): 47-49. Illus.
Germany. 1902. Studies of criticism/critics.

122 Davis, Nicholas. "Allusions to Medieval Drama in Britain. A Finding List/1." *MET.* 1982; 4(2): 75-76. Pref.
Great Britain. 1180-1621. Histories-reconstruction. ■Gives account of three hitherto unreported allusions.

123 Mariotti, Arnaldo. *La penna trovarobe — Indagine su una critica teatrale al di sopra di ogni sospetto.* (The Propman Pen: A Research on Exemplary Performance Criticism.) Florence: Libreria Editrice Fiorentina; 1982. 82 pp.
Italy. Twentieth cent. Studies of criticism/critics. ■Collection of opinions of 20th century authors, actors, directors, spectators and critics on profession of theatre criticism.

124 Marko, Susanne. "Teatern som liv och livet som teater." (Theatre As Life and Life As Theatre.) *Entre.* 1982; 9(1): 9-15. Illus.
Italy. Poland. Denmark. 1970-1981. Histories-sources. ■Theatre Festival in Santarchangelo, begun in 1970, had performances by 50 groups in 1981. Pedagogy and research by Eugenio Barba's International Theatre School of Anthropology (ISTA). Infl. by Jerzy Grotowski.

125 Yamaguchi, Masao; Walker, E.A., transl. "Theatricality in Japan." *MD.* 1982 Mar.; 25(1): 140-142. Notes.
Japan. Twentieth cent. Histories-sources. ■Theatricality expressed in space, time and character.

126 Ödeen, Mats. "Teater som 'live show'." (Theatre as 'Live Show'.) *Entre.* 1982; 9(1): 16-21. Illus.

Sweden. 1970-1981. Critical studies. ■Pornographic shows for male audience represent aesthetics of dominance. Grp/movt: Living Theatre.

127 Anon. "Artistic Priorities: A Fireside Chat." *AmTh.* 1982 Apr.; 4(1): 11. Notes. Illus.: Photo. B&W. 1.
USA. 1982. Histories-sources. ■Gordon Davidson, Alan Schneider and Peter Zeisler comment on artistic issues.

128 Anon. "Gorelik, Stavis, Corrigan: New ATA Fellows." *ThNe.* 1982 Nov.; 14(8): 3,4. Illus. B&W. 3.
USA. 1982. Biographical studies. ■Accomplishments of newest American Theatre Association Fellows.

129 Carmines, Al. "How It All Began: The Flowering of Off-Off Broadway." *AmTh.* 1982 Oct.; 4(7): 6-7. Notes. Illus.: Photo. B&W. 1.
USA. 1950-1970. Historical studies. ■Review of off-off Broadway movement as exemplified by the Judson Dance Theatre.

130 Carter, Heather L. "What Is It — Research or Research?" *ChTR.* 1982 Spring; 31(2): 26-31. Biblio. Illus.: Diagram.
USA. Twentieth cent. Studies of research/researchers. ■Most valuable theatre research has a firm base in theory and considers readers' needs.

131 Dasgupta, Gautam; Fierstein, Harvey; Fornes, Maria Irene. "Portraits in Words." *PerAJ.* 1982; 6(2): 27-28.
USA. 1960-1980. Histories-sources. ■Joseph Papp, Maria Irene Fornes, John Vaccaro, Harvey Fierstein, Jean-Claude Van Itallie, Kevin O'Connor, Liz Swados, Ron Link and Gautam Dasgupta relate their experiences with Ellen Stewart.

132 Haskins, James. *Black Theater in America.* New York: Thomas Y. Crowell; 1982. vi, 184 pp. Illus.: Photo. B&W.
USA. 1700-1982. Histories-sources. ■Survey of Black artists' contributions to theatre.

133 Hatch, James V. "Sitting at the Banquet, Talkin' with Ourselves (An Open Letter to Theatre Scholars and Historians on the Status of Black Theatre Research and Publication)." *BALF.* 1982 Winter; 16(4): 168-170. Biblio.
USA. 1970-1982. Histories-sources. ■Appeal for Black theatre scholars to join mainstream journals and funding, with bibliography. Related to Reference Materials: Bibliographies.

134 Helbing, Terry. "Gay Theatre City by City." *GTAN.* 1982 Aug.; 4(1): 6-11.
USA. 1981-1982. Histories-sources. ■Reports of gay theatre activities during the 1981-82 season from Austin, Baltimore, Boston, Chicago, Dallas, Los Angeles, Minneapolis, New York, Phoenix, San Francisco, Washington and West Palm Beach.

135 Odom, Leigh George. "*The Black Crook* at Niblo's Garden." *TDR.* 1982 Spring; 26(1): 21-40.
USA. 1866. Histories-reconstruction. ■Performance history of the September 16, 1866, production of *The Black Crook* at Niblo's Garden, New York.

136 Smart-Grosvenor, Vertamae. "Showstoppers: A Few Riffs and Strokes for Some Star Folk with Style." *Ebony.* 1982 Oct.; 13 (6): 75-77.
USA. Twentieth cent. Histories-sources. ■Brief vignettes/commentary on several Black stars, including Ntozake Shange, Cecily Tyson, Diana Ross, James Baldwin, Lena Horne, Rosalind Cash, Billy Dee Williams.

137 Thibeau, Alice. "Asian American Theatre, Genre beyond Stereotype." *CAM.* 1982 May; 4(5): 35. [Column: Bay Area Arts Forum.]
USA. Twentieth cent. Histories-sources. ■Artistic and administrative development of Asian American theatre.

138 Kartusch, Susanna. "Soviel unbenutzte Phantasie: Schauspieler im Kinder- und Jugendtheater." (So Much Unused Fantasy: Actors in Children's and Young People's Theatre.) *Tzs.* 1982; 2: 32-39. Illus.
West Germany. 1980-1982. Histories-sources. ■Acting in children's theatre.

THEATRE IN GENERAL — cont'd

139 Riewoldt, Otto. "Die Regisseure sind die grossen Verhinderer." (The Directors Are the Ones Who Hinder.) *TH*. 1982 Sep.; 9: 7-9.
West Germany. East Germany. Twentieth cent. Histories-sources.
■Interview with former East German author, Thomas Brasch, on theatre politics and aspects of repertory.

Audience

140 Meyer, Gerhard. "Lebensbedingungen — Bedürfnisstruktur — Theaterbesuch. Zu den Wechselwirkungen und Schlussfolgerungen." (Conditions of Life — Structure of Needs — Theatre-going: Interaction and Conclusions.) *TZ*. 1982 Jan.; 37: 24-25.
Germany. Eighteenth cent. Nineteenth cent. Studies of theories/theorists. ■Relationship of audience to theatre based on Goethe's description of audience.

Audience: Composition

141 Gurr, Andrew. "The Many-Headed Audience." *ET*. 1982 Nov.; 1(1): 52-62. Notes.
England. 1594-1610. Historical studies. ■Examines test cases of bawdry in *Othello* and *The Winter's Tale* to infer audience composition from text and sense of text from audience composition. Related to Individuals: Shakespeare.

142 Guibert, Noëlle; Razgonnikoff, Jacqueline. "Des *Chevaliers du lustre* aux *Enfants du paradis*." (From *Knights of the Chandelier* to *The Children of Paradise*.) *CF*. 1982 May; 109: 3-12.
France. 1600-1950. Historical studies. ■Audience composition, hired clappers (*claques*), seating and terminology at Comédie Française.

143 Ring, Lars. "Publiken på Drottningholm." (The Audience at Drottningholm.) *Entre*. 1982; 9(1): 34.
Sweden. Twentieth cent. Histories-sources. ■Research methodology, including cultural profiles, analysis of audience at Drottningholm summer performances.

144 Milloy, Marilyn. "Vivian Robinson Giving Black Theater a Boost." *Ebony*. 1982 Sep.; 13(5): 15.
USA. Twentieth cent. Histories-sources. ■Brief tribute to Robinson and her organization, Audelco (Audience Development Committee), which works to develop Black audiences for theatre.

145 Thorpe, John. "Playing the City/Finding the Audience." *CAM*. 1982 Apr.; 4(4): 39. [Column: Bay Area Arts Forum.]
USA. Twentieth cent. Histories-sources. ■Experiences of Black actresses performing in San Francisco, problems of attracting Black audiences to Black theatre. Comments on theatre locations, community self-esteem and attitude towards theatre.

146 Weinstock, Gloria. "Oliver Pitcher and the Changing Role of the Black Playwright." *CAM*. 1982 May; 4(5): 11.
USA. Twentieth cent. Histories-sources. ■Reflections on pressures of commercialism, double audiences, stage images of Blacks and non-musical Black theatre, trends in Black theatre and female playwrights, and efforts to attract a paying Black audience.

Audience: Psychology/behavior

147 Wardetzsky, Kristin. "Junge Leute vor der Bühne: Zum Rezeptionsverhalten Jugendlicher, 2." (Young People Before the Stage: On the Reactions of Adolescent Audiences, 2.) *TZ*. 1982 July; 37(7): 37-40. [Second of a series of articles.]
East Germany. Twentieth cent. Technical studies. ■Changing young people's behavior by addressing their problems on stage.

148 Wardetzsky, Kristin. "Junge Leute vor der Bühne (1)." (Young People in the Theatre, 1.) *TZ*. 1982 June; 37(6): 48-50. [First of a series of articles.]
East Germany. 1982. Technical studies. ■On the behavior of young people in the theatre.

149 Tindemans, Carlos. "Bedeutungszuweisung im Theater: Entwürfe zur methodischen Analysierbarkeit des Bewusstseinsprozesses des Theaterzuschauers." (Message Transmission in Theatre: Outline for Methodical Analysis of Audience Consciousness.) *MuK*. 1982; 28(3-4): 290-325. Biblio.
Europe. Twentieth cent. Histories-sources. ■Interviews with spectators of *The People Shows No. 64* and a performance of *Reindeer Werk*, using concepts of 'ethogenics' (R. Harré) and 'frame analysis' (E. Goffman) to analyze the processes of perception.

Design/technology

150 Arnott, Brian. "A Point of View." *CTR*. 1982 Winter; 33: 9-13. Illus.
Canada. 1982. Critical studies. ■Designer discusses potentials of technology.

151 Benson, Susan. "Artists not Craftspeople." *CTR*. 1982 Winter; 33: 30-39. Pref. Illus.
Canada. 1982. Histories-sources. ■Susan Benson, head of design at Stratford Festival, on design problems.

152 Doherty, Tom. "Recognizing the Designer." *CTR*. 1982 Winter; 33: 40-43.
Canada. 1982. Histories-sources. ■Profile of Associated Designers of Canada.

153 Scales, Robert R. "The World Backstage." *CTR*. 1982 Winter; 33: 14-19.
Canada. 1982. Technical studies. ■Interrelationship of technical theatre, new technology and personnel.

154 Schick, Rick. "Realizing a Concept or The 15 Percent Solution." *CTR*. 1982 Winter; 33: 20-25. Illus.
Canada. 1982. Technical studies. ■Effective use of technology for set, lighting and sound design within budget constraints.

155 "75 Jahre *Bühnentechnische Rundschau*." (75 Years of *Bühnentechnische Rundschau*.) *BtR*. 1982 Oct.; 5: 18-19.
Germany. 1907-1982. Histories-sources. ■Celebration of 75th anniversary of the journal *Bühnentechnische Rundschau*.

156 Ottolenghi, Valeria. "L'animazione teatrale." (Theatrical Animation.) *QT*. 1982 Feb.; 4(15): 5-79. Notes. Biblio.
Italy. Twentieth cent. Studies of theories/theorists. ■Problems of theatrical animation. Related to Media: Film.

157 Verdone, Mario. "Lo spettacolo futurista." (Futurist Performance.) *TeatrC*. 1982 May-Sept; 1(1): 1-18.
Italy. 1909-1929. Historical studies. ■Futurist performance and its contribution to renewal of European scenography and technology.

158 Corbett, Tom. "Adhesive Formulation." *ThCr*. 1982 Aug.-Sep.; 16(7): 33, 62-68.
USA. 1982. Technical studies. ■Adhesive bases and their uses.

159 Weisfeld, Zelma H. "Designers and Denver Combine for USITT Conference." *ThNe*. 1982 Summer; 14(6): 15.
USA. 1982. Histories-sources. ■Report on USITT (United States Institute for Theatre Technology) conference including scenography (lighting design, costumes and scenery), health and safety commission, costume commission, local sessions and final meeting.

160 Freitag, Paul. "Microprozessoren steuern und regeln die Bühnenmaschinerie." (Microprocessors for Controlling Theatre Equipment.) *BtR*. 1982 Oct.; 5: 17-18. Illus. Schematic.
West Germany. Twentieth cent. Technical studies. ■Scene shifting by microprocessor.

161 Zotzmann, Adolf. "Zu den Ausführungen eines Schnürmeisters." (A Head Fly-Man Answers Criticisms.) *BtR*. 1982 Aug.; 4: 22-23.
West Germany. 1982. Technical studies. ■Response to criticisms of new technical facilities.

THEATRE IN GENERAL — cont'd

Design/technology: Costuming/costumers

162   Seligman, Kevin L. "Costume Pattern Drafts." *TD&T*. 1982 Spring; 18(1): 14-15. [Reprint of 1920 article by W.E. Leggatt and T.W. Hodgkinson.]
Twentieth cent. Technical studies. ▪Drafting patterns and instructions for gentlemen's frockcoat.

163   Böhm, Gotthard. "Kostüme: Lohengrin aus der Kiste." (Costumes: Lohengrin from the Chest.) *Bühne*. 1982 Dec. : 40. Illus.
Austria. 1982. Histories-sources. ▪Notice on an exhibition of historical costumes at the Austrian Theatre Museum.

164   Clark, Fiona. *Hats*. Distributed by Drama Book Publishers. London: B.T. Batsford; 1982. 96 pp. (The Costume Accessories Series.) Illus.: Dwg.
Europe. Multi-period. Histories-specific. ▪Descriptive history of headgear, primarily in Western civilization.

165   Cumming, Valerie. *Gloves*. Distributed by Drama Book Publishers. London: B.T. Batsford; 1982. 96 pp. Index. Biblio. Illus.: Dwg. Color.
Europe. Multi-period. Histories-specific. ▪Survey of handwear, primarily in Western civilization.

166   Williams-Mitchell, Christobel. *Dressed for the Job: The Story of Occupational Costume*. New York: Sterling Pub. Co.; 1982. 143 pp. Pref. Index. Illus.: Dwg. Print. Color.
Europe. Multi-period. Historical studies. ▪Clothing worn by farmers and laborers.

167   Schoeman, Liesbet. "Benodigde basiese kennis vir kostuumontwerpe vir 'n hoërskoolproduksie, deel 3." (Essential Basic Knowledge for Designing Costumes for a High School Production, Part 3.) *TF*. 1982; 3(1): 65-72. Biblio. Illus.
South Africa, Republic of. 1982. Textbooks/manuals/guides.

168   Bruun-Rasmussen, Ole; Petersen, Grete. *Makeup, Costumes and Masks for the Stage*. New York: Sterling; 1982. 96 pp. Index. Illus.: Photo. Dwg. B&W.
USA. Twentieth cent. Technical studies.

169   Cesnakas, Mary M.; Jaros, Anne. "A Revolutionary Approach to Corsets." *ThCr*. 1982 Mar.; 16(3): 27, 50-51. Illus.
USA. Twentieth cent. Textbooks/manuals/guides. ▪Making period corsets from high impact polystyrene vacuum form plastic.

170   Davis, Richard A. "Found Object Costuming." *ThCr*. 1982 Jan.; 16(1): 30, 64-66.
USA. Twentieth cent. Textbooks/manuals/guides.

171   Norcross, Beverly. "Tabards of Junk." *ThCr*. 1982 Jan.; 16(1): 30, 64. Illus.
USA. Twentieth cent. Textbooks/manuals/guides. ▪Construction of tabards from cake pans and other items.

172   Riley, Robert. "F.I.T. Design Lab." *Pb*. 1982 Nov.; 1(1): 90. Illus.
USA. Twentieth cent. Multi-period. Histories-sources. ▪Gifts of theatrical costumes to research collection of F.I.T. (Fashion Institute of Technology). Related to Reference Materials: Description of resources.

173   Smith, Ronn; Wallach, Susan Levi. "On Pins and Needles." *ThCr*. 1982 Nov.-Dec.; 16(9): 24-27, 61-67. Illus.
USA. 1982. Technical studies. ▪Description of work in the costume shops of John Reid, Jimmy Meyer, Mary Macy, Schnoz & Schnoz and Sherred, Berger & Lovett.

174   Stribling, Lauretta. "Old Shoes from New." *ThCr*. 1982 Jan.; 16(1): 31, 68-69. Illus.
USA. Twentieth cent. Textbooks/manuals/guides. ▪Transforming modern shoes to period.

175   Wallach, Susan Levi. "All Dolled Up and No Place to Go." *ThCr*. 1982 Nov.-Dec.; 16(9): 23, 67-71. Illus.

USA. Twentieth cent. Histories-sources. ▪Designers talk about costumes and lighting for *A Doll's Life*.

176   Wallach, Susan Levi. "In Matters Quite Costumical: The Design Work of Patricia McGourty." *ThCr*. 1982 Mar.; 16(3): 13-17, 40-44. Illus.
USA. 1982. Histories-sources. ▪Survey of costume designs.

Design/technology: Health and safety

177   Kaelin, Valerie C. "Political Analysis of Stress in Costume-Related Fields." *TD&T*. 1982 Fall; 18(3): 11-14.
USA. Twentieth cent. Technical studies. ▪Ways of reducing tension in costume shops.

Design/technology: Lighting/lighting designers

178   Dolgoy, Sholem. "Lighting: Untapped Potential." *CTR*. 1982 Winter; 33: 26-29.
Canada. 1982. Technical studies. ▪National Ballet's designer discusses lighting design.

179   Filion, H.P.; Nutt, T.C. "Montreal Studio 51: A New Lighting Installation." *Tabs*. 1982 Nov.; 39(2): 28-29.
Canada. 1980. Technical studies.

180   Guibert, Noëlle; Razgonnikoff, Jacqueline. "L'éclairage." (Lighting.) *CF*. 1982 Jan.; 105: 3-28.
France. Multi-period. Historical studies. ▪Evolution of lighting materials and techniques.

181   Bradley, John. "A Season with a New Galaxy." *Tabs*. 1982 Nov.; 39(2): 24-25.
Great Britain. 1981-1982. Technical studies. ▪Brief description of Galaxy lighting control system at Royal Shakespeare Theatre.

182   Harral, Amanda. "Lighting Workshop." *Tabs*. 1982 Nov.; 39(2): 5.
Great Britain. 1982. Technical studies. ▪Description of business that combines lighting equipment retailing with architectural and equipment consulting.

183   Walne, Graham. "Going to Church." *Tabs*. 1982 Nov.; 29(2): 21.
Great Britain. Twentieth cent. Technical studies. ▪Brief description of lighting installation in church.

184   Masini, Ferruccio. "Sulle luci." (About Lighting.) *QT*. 1982 Feb.; 4(15): 185-188.
Italy. Twentieth cent. Histories-sources. ▪Lighting in *La gabbia di Pandora (Pandora's Cage)*.

185   Ballard, Rae Ellen. "Dance Lighting in Alternative Spaces: Edward Effron in Profile." *ThCr*. 1982 Mar.; 16(3): 19, 45-47. Illus.
USA. 1982. Histories-sources. Related to Dance.

186   Bodenhausen, Karl Heinz. "The Control of Electrical Light Sources." *TD&T*. 1982 Summer; 18(2): 18-23.
USA. Twentieth cent. Technical studies. ▪Intensity control of lamps.

187   Laine, Barry. "Illuminating Lady." *BaNe*. 1982 July; 4(1): 26-28. Illus.
USA. 1958-1982. Histories-sources. ▪Interview with Jennifer Tipton, lighting designer. Related to Dance.

188   Loney, Glenn. "Painting with Lights." *ThCr*. 1982 May; 16(5): 15-17, 32-40. Illus.
USA. Europe. 1982. Biographical studies. ▪Survey of Beni Montresor's lighting designs and lighting for film. Related to Media: Film.

189   Reinecke, R.E. "A Microcomputer-Controlled Chaser." *ThCr*. 1982 May; 16(5): 56-59. Illus.
USA. 1982. Technical studies. ▪Wiring and programming computers for chase effect.

190   Rubin, Joel E. "Stage Lighting and the State of the Art." *TD&T*. 1982 Fall; 18(3): 5-10.

THEATRE IN GENERAL — cont'd

USA. 1982. Technical studies. ■New lighting technology and its effects on present lighting designers.

191   Whaley, Frank Jr. "Property Master's Notebook: Let There Be Light." *ThCr.* 1982 Aug.-Sep.; 16(7): 37-39, 68-73. Illus.
USA. Multi-period. Historical studies. ■Overview of light sources, from ancient Egypt to the advent of incandescent lamps.

192   Frauendienst, Wolfgang; Bergfeld, Wolfgang; Tome, Konrad. "Die Lichtregieanlage Sitralux B 40 im Nationaltheater München." (The Sitralux B 40 Lighting Control System at the Munich National Theatre.) *BtR.* 1982 Feb.(1): 10-12. Illus.
West Germany. 1981. Technical studies. ■Head of Nationaltheater München discusses creation of Sitralux system and significant advances in lighting control and design.

Design/technology: Machines/equipment

193   Tolnay, Paul. "Nekrolog." (Obituary.) *BtR.* 1982 Apr.; 2: 23-24.
Hungary. Twentieth cent. Histories-sources. ■Demise of Asphalaia water-hydraulic system at Magyar Operaház (Budapest State Opera).

194   Johnson, William S., Jr.; Wolff, Fred M., ed. "An Effective Heat Source for Shop-Built Vacuum Forming Machines." *TD&T.* 1982 Spring; 18(1): 10-12.
USA. 1982. Technical studies. ■Specifications for heat unit with schematic diagrams for building complete vacuum forming machine.

195   Pike, Leon. "High and Low Tech Pneumatics: The Tube Lift." *ThCr.* 1982 Mar.; 16(3): 22, 47-49. Illus.
USA. 1982. Technical studies. ■Use of compressed air to move raked platform.

196   Scales, Robert R. "Pneumatics: Single Movement Effects." *ThCr.* 1982 Mar.; 16(3): 52-56. Illus.
USA. 1982. Technical studies. ■Use of carbon dioxide tank and fire extinguisher for remote control of stage devices.

197   Slabaugh, Richard. "A Wood Graining Tool." *ThCr.* 1982 Aug.-Sep.; 16(7): 32, 58-62.
USA. Twentieth cent. Technical studies. ■Description of a tool made of cardboard tubing and Ethafoam rope.

Design/technology: Make-up

198   Baygan, Lee. *Makeup for Theatre, Film and Television: A Step by Step Photographic Guide.* New York, NY: Drama Book Publishers; 1982. xix, 182 pp. Biblio. Pref. Illus.: Photo.
Multi-period. Textbooks/manuals/guides.

199   Black, George. "Character Make-up for Small Theatres." *TD&T.* 1982 Fall; 18(3): 18-19.
Twentieth cent. Textbooks/manuals/guides. ■Basic techniques for greasepaint or creme.

200   Le Roux, Abri. "Die grimeerontwerp van *Report to the Academy.*" (The Make-up Design for *Report to the Academy.*) *TF.* 1982 May; 3(1): 18-25. Illus.
South Africa, Republic of. 1979. Technical studies. ■Description of make-up design for ape-like character in production of *Report to the Academy.*

Design/technology: Masks/wigs

201   Miller, Mary Jane. "Three Self-Reflexive Masks." *ThR.* 1981-82 Winter; 7(1): 26-37. Notes. Illus.
Multi-period. Historical studies. ■Nature and function of masks illustrated through examples of a Tsimshian double stone mask, a Hopewell culture skull mask and an electronic mask by Joseph Svoboda for Carl Orff's opera *Prometheus.*

202   Havel, Kathy. "Using Ethafoam for Commedia Masks." *ThCr.* 1982 Jan.; 16(1): 28, 61. Illus.

USA. Twentieth cent. Textbooks/manuals/guides. ■Steps in making Ethafoam masks.

203   Oertling, John T. "Reassessing Papier-mâché Masks." *ThCr.* ; 16(1): 28, 62-63. Illus.
USA. Twentieth cent. Textbooks/manuals/guides. ■Construction methods for papier-mâché masks.

Design/technology: Properties

204   Reed, Patrick. "Actor-Proofing Furniture." *ThCr.* 1982 May; 16(5): 66-67. Illus.
USA. Twentieth cent. Textbooks/manuals/guides. ■Use of steel tubing and plywood to build Victorian period sofa.

205   Smith, Ronn. "Merchandising on Broadway." *ThCr.* 1982 Oct.; 16(8): 30, 58-60.
USA. Twentieth cent. Technical studies. ■Ways general managers obtain props by soliciting donations from manufacturers.

Design/technology: Scenery/scene designers

206   Bains, Yashdip Singh. "Painted Scenery and Decorations in Canadian Theatres 1765-1825." *THC.* 1982 Fall; 3(2): 109-125. Notes.
Canada. 1765-1825. Historical studies. ■Examination of staging practices.

207   Ritterhouse, Jonathan. "Herbert Whittaker: A Theatre Life." *THC.* 1982 Spring; 3(1): 51-78. Notes. Illus.
Canada. 1911-1982. Biographical studies. ■Career chronology of designer, director and critic.

208   Berry, Ralph. "Metamorphoses of the Stage." *SQ.* 1982 Spring; 33(1): 5-16. Notes.
England. 1590-1610. Historical studies. ■Metamorphosis of Elizabethan stage into ship, promontory, island or other places as demanded by script.

209   Börsch-Supan, Helmut. "Karl Friedrich Schinkel und das Theater." (Karl Friedrich Schinkel and the Theatre.) *KSGT.* 1982; 32: 3-26. Notes. Illus.
Germany. 1815-1829. Biographical studies. ■Architect and painter also known as theatre architect and stage designer. Relationship between work for theatre and other works of art.

210   Rydzyk, Hans-Jürgen. "Die Bühne wird zum Bild: Zu Karl Friedrich Schinkels Entwürfen zur *Zauberflöte.*" (The Stage Becomes a Picture: On Karl Friedrich Schinkel's Designs for *The Magic Flute.*) *KSGT.* 1982; 32: 27-57. Illus.
Germany. 1815-1816. Historical studies. ■Production at Königliches Hofoper (Royal Opera House, Berlin).

211   Schlemmer, Oskar; Bistolfi, Marina, ed. *Scritti sul teatro.* (Writings on the Theatre.) Milan: Feltrinelli; 1982. 245 pp. Pref. Notes. Index. Biblio. Illus.
Germany. 1888-1943. Studies of theories/theorists. ■Anthology of theatrical writings by designer Oskar Schlemmer.

212   Cambellotti, Duilio; Quesada, Mario, ed. *Teatro Storia Arte.* (Theatre, History, Art.) Palermo: Edizioni Novecento; 1982. 304 pp. (Narciso 4.) Notes. Illus.
Italy. 1933-1954. Biographies. ■Collection of designer Duilio Cambellotti's writings on theatre, activities as a critic and an autobiography.

213   Leacroft, Richard. "Serlio's Theatre and Perspective Scenes." *TN.* 1982; 36(3): 120-122. Illus.: Photo. B&W. 3.
Italy. 1545. Histories-reconstruction. ■Reconstructs Serlio's drawings of his tragic, comic and satiric scenes, and finds discrepancies.

214   Sprovieri, Giuseppe; Bonanni, Francesca. "Testimone di Antonio Valente." (Testimony of Antonio Valente.) *TeatrC.* 1982 May-Sep.; 1(1): 39-57. Biblio.
Italy. Twentieth cent. Biographical studies. ■Memoir of scene designer and architect.

THEATRE IN GENERAL — cont'd

215 Verdone, Mario. "Antonio Valente: scenografo e scenotecnico." (Antonio Valente: Scene Designer and Technician.) *QT*. 1982 Aug.; 5(17): 179-190.
Italy. 1919-1955. Biographical studies. ■Artistic production and relationships with directors and other designers.

216 Mellgren, Thomas. "Gunilla Palmstierna-Weiss." *Entre*. 1982; 9(3): 10-17. Illus.
Sweden. Germany. Twentieth cent. Histories-sources. ■Interview with set, costume and lighting designer Palmstierna-Weiss. Infl. by Peter Brook; Antonin Artaud.

217 "Computer Calculation of Lumber Required for Flat Construction." *TD&T*. 1982 Winter; 18(4): 18-19.
USA. Twentieth cent. Textbooks/manuals/guides. ■TRS-80 Model 1 Level II program for computing lumber needs for flats.

218 USITT Graphic Standards Board. "Recommendations for Graphic Language in Scenic Design and Technical Productions." *TD&T*. 1982 Spring; 18(1): 8-9.
USA. 1982. Technical studies. ■Conventions for standardization of symbols to improve communications.

219 Aronson, Arnold. "Eugene Lee." *TD&T*. 1982 Summer; 18(2): 4-11.
USA. Twentieth cent. Biographical studies. ■Commentary on designer Lee's work with complete production listing.

220 Aronson, Arnold. "Contemporary American Designers: John Lee Beatty." *TD&T*. 1982 Winter; 18(4): 4-12.
USA. Twentieth cent. Biographical studies. ■Survey of Beatty's sets with biographical material and production chronology.

221 Blackstone, Warren. "Directly Speaking: Facility Fever." *ThNe*. 1982 Feb.; 14(2): 2, 22.
USA. Twentieth cent. Histories-sources. ■Set design and execution should support, not overwhelm, actors.

222 Davis, Rick. "Three American Designers: An Interview with Jane Greenwood, Ming Cho Lee and Michael Yeargan." *ThM*. 1981-82 Winter; 13(1): 76-82. Illus.
USA. 1970-1980. Histories-sources. ■Trends toward realism, and designers' working conditions in commercial theatre and in regional theatre.

223 Funke, Phyllis Ellen. "Altering the Theatre to Fit the Show." *Pb*. 1982 Dec.; 1(1): 44. Illus.
USA. 1924-1982. Historical studies. ■Alteration of theatre interiors to accommodate production design, with emphasis on Broadway theatres and shows.

224 Held, R. L. *Endless Innovations: Frederick Kiesler's Theory and Scenic Design*. Ann Arbor, MI: UMI Research P; 1982. xvii, 258 pp. (Studies in the Fine Arts: The Avant-Garde Series 23.) Pref. Notes. Index. Biblio. Illus.
USA. Twentieth cent. Biographical studies. ■Career of scenic designer and architect, with analyses of scenic work and discussion of his theory of correalism.

225 Hoffman, Karen. "Textural Fiber Hangings." *ThCr*. 1982 Aug.-Sep.; 16(7): 34, 54-58. Illus.
USA. 1982. Technical studies. ■Creating an organic environment.

226 Jackson, Russell. "Alfred Thompson, 1831-1895: A Forgotten Talent." *TN*. 1982; 36(2): 72. Illus.: Photo. B&W.
USA. England. 1831-1895. Biographical studies. ■Career of Alfred Thompson as set designer and costumer at Gaiety Theatre, and as writer for *Mask*.

227 Lieberman, Susan. "Talking Shop/Made to Order." *ThCr*. 1982 Oct.; 16(8): 22, 61-65. Illus.
USA. Twentieth cent. Histories-sources. ■Survey of special effects.

228 MacKay, Patricia. "Scaling *K2* at the Arena." *ThCr*. 1982 Oct.; 16(8): 17, 51.
USA. 1982. Histories-sources. ■Set construction for Arena Stage production of *K2* in Washington, DC.

229 MacKay, Patricia. "A Profile of Oliver Smith." *ThCr*. 1982 Apr.; 16(4): 11-19, 56-70. Illus.
USA. Twentieth cent. Biographical studies. ■Survey of theatre designs with selected chronology.

230 Marsh, John. "Whale Oil and Greasepaint: On Tour with Benjamin Russell and E.C. Williams." *THSt*. 1982; 2: 36-60. Notes. Illus.
USA. 1849-1866. Historical studies. ■Account of two notable panoramas of whaling. Related to Popular Entertainment.

231 Moss, Sylvia. "Robert Fletcher by Design." *ThCr*. 1982 Aug.-Sep.; 16(7): 29-31, 46-50. Illus.
USA. Twentieth cent. Histories-sources. ■Survey of Fletcher's designs for theatre, opera, dance and film. Related to Media: Film.

232 Shank, Theodore. "*Stuck* on a California Freeway." *TD&T*. 1982 Summer; 18(2): 14-16. Illus.
USA. 1982. Histories-sources. ■Production of Adele Shank's *Stuck, a Freeway Comedy*.

233 Shyer, Laurence. "Mass and Detail: A Profile of Tony Straiges." *ThCr*. 1982 Feb.; 16(2): 15, 35-41.
USA. Twentieth cent. Biographical studies. ■Design theories and general biography.

234 Shyer, Laurence. "In Collaboration: Michael Yeargan and Andrei Serban." *ThCr*. 1982 May; 16(5): 23-27, 60-64. Illus.
USA. 1982. Histories-sources. ■Relationship between Yeargan and Serban in designing productions.

235 Smith, Raynette Halverson. "A PVC Gazebo." *ThCr*. 1982 Aug.-Sep.; 16(7): 35, 50-54. Illus.
USA. 1982. Technical studies. ■Use of polyvinyl chloride to build a gazebo.

236 Tawil, Andrea. "Designing Slides for Theatre and Concert Projection." *ThCr*. 1982 Mar.; 16(3): 23, 28-34. Illus.
USA. 1982. Textbooks/manuals/guides. ■Painting slides for projections.

237 Wallach, Susan Levi. "Crawford, Steinbock & Associates." *ThCr*. 1982 Aug.-Sep.; 16(7): 24-27, 96-97. Illus.
USA. Twentieth cent. Histories-sources. ■Interview with Bill Crawford on working techniques in his scene shop.

238 Wallach, Susan Levi. "The Theatre Machine Scenic Shop." *ThCr*. 1982 Aug.-Sep.; 16(7): 24-26, 46. Illus.
USA. 1982. Histories-sources. ■Interview with designer Patricia Moeser.

239 Wallach, Susan Levi. "Bruce Porter-Bruce Rayvid Stage Scenery." *ThCr*. 1982 Aug.-Sep.; 16(7): 20-23, 44-46. Illus.
USA. 1982. Technical studies. ■Interview describing scene shop and working habits.

240 Wallach, Susan Levi. "Broadway Technical Services." *ThCr*. 1982 Aug.-Sep.; 16(7): 20-23, 43-44. Illus.
USA. 1982. Histories-sources. ■Interview with Bob Kaiser on building offbeat scenery.

241 Himstedt, Hellmut. "Blickpunkt Malersaal." (Focal Point: Paint Shop.) *BtR*. 1982 Feb.; 1: 17.
West Germany. 1981. Histories-sources. ■Notes on exhibition of scene painters and sculptors.

Design/technology: Sound

242 Collison, David. *Stage Sound*. Distributed by Drama Book Publishers. London: Cassell; 1982. 187 pp. Index.
1982. Textbooks/manuals/guides. ■Technical handbook for producing appropriate sound effects.

243 Shearing, Jack; Monderloh, Otto; Harris, Gary; Fitzgerald, Richard; Richmond, Charles; Collison, David; Scales, Robert R. "Special Report: Theatre Sound." *ThCr*. 1982 Feb.; 16(2): 22-24, 47-56. Illus.

THEATRE IN GENERAL — cont'd

Twentieth cent. Technical studies. ▪Sound designers' theories.

244 Fasold, Wolfgang; Tennhardt, Hans-Peter; Winkler, Helgo. "Die Raumakustik im Neuen Gewandhaus Leipzig." (Acoustics in the Neues Gewandhaus, Leipzig.) *BK*. 1982; 1: 14-19. Illus.: Photo. Plan. Diagram. 9.
East Germany. 1982. Technical studies. ▪Acoustics of new concert hall, with emphasis on wall surface treatment to reduce standing waves.

245 Collison, David. "I Will Tell You Where to Put Your Loudspeakers." *ThCr*. 1982 Oct.; 16(8): 32-35, 38-42.
USA. Twentieth cent. Textbooks/manuals/guides. ▪Questions and answers on proper placement of theatre loudspeakers.

246 Lambert, Timothy. "Getting Storm and Sea on Tape." *ThCr*. 1982 Mar.; 16(3): 58-59. Illus.
USA. 1982. Textbooks/manuals/guides. ▪Technique for rendering 25 minute build-up of storm at sea.

247 Lucier, Mary. "Chuck London: Shaping Sound at the Circle Rep." *ThCr*. 1982 May; 16(5): 28-29, 54-55. Illus.
USA. 1982. Technical studies. ▪Technique of sound reinforcement.

248 Lucier, Mary. "What's Wrong with Theatre Sound?" *ThCr*. 1982 Feb.; 16(2): 21, 42-47.
USA. 1982. Technical studies. ▪Sound reinforcement and enhancement in theatres of various sizes.

249 Thomas, Richard K. "Approaching Sound Design for Period Plays." *ThCr*. 1982 Jan.; 16(1): 9, 70-77.
USA. Twentieth cent. Technical studies. ▪Adapting period music to tastes of modern audiences.

Design/technology: Technicians/crews

250 "Fachausbildung in der DDR." (Specialist Training in East Germany.) *BtR*. 1982 Aug.: 23-24. [Reprinted from *Podium* 1/82.]
East Germany. Twentieth cent. Histories-sources. ▪Description of training theatre technicians.

251 Perkins, Kathy Anne. "Black Backstage Workers, 1900-1969." *BALF*. 1982 Winter; 16(14): 160-163. Notes. Illus.
USA. 1900-1969. Historical studies. ▪Struggles of Black stage hands to unionize and fight racism in predominantly white unions.

252 Randon, Carl. "Technische Einrichtungen eines neuen Theaters." (Technical Installations in a New Theatre.) *BtR*. 1982 Apr.: 22-23.
West Germany. 1982. Histories-sources. ▪Theatre consultants impose technical tasks with serious consequences.

Financial operations

253 Anon. "A Response from Trustees and Directors: Questions and Answer Section." *AmTh*. 1982 Apr.; 4(1): 7-10.
USA. 1982. Histories-sources. ▪NEA (National Endowment for the Arts) chairman Frank Hodsoll answers questions about corporate contributions to the arts.

254 Downey, Roger. "Trouble in Paradise." *AmTh*. 1982 Dec.; 4(9): 1. Notes. Illus.: Photo. B&W.
West Germany. Twentieth cent. Histories-sources. ▪Economic problems in theatres.

Financial operations: Fundraising/gifts and grants

255 Goldberg, Moses. "American Children's Theatre in the 80's." *ChTR*. 1982 Fall; 31(4): 13-16.
USA. 1980-1982. Histories-sources. ▪Three techniques to obtain funding for children's theatre.

256 Massa, Robert. "Bits." *VV*. 1982 Dec. 21; 27(51): 119. Illus.: Photo.
USA. 1982. Histories-sources. ▪NEA (National Endowment for the Arts) funding policies and brief review of several productions.

257 Visser, David. "Foundations and Shifting Sands." *AmTh*. 1982 May; 4(2): 4-5. Notes.
USA. Twentieth cent. Histories-sources. ▪Ford Foundation & Commonwealth Fund re-evaluate their philanthropic programs.

Financial operations: Government funding/subsidies

258 Anon. "Pratiques: votre dossier n'a pas été retenu pour fins de subventions." (Proceedings: Your Dossier Has Been Closed and Your Subsidy Cancelled.) *PrTh*. 1982 Winter-Spring; 14-15: 37-55. Illus.: Photo. B&W.
Canada. 1970-1982. Histories-sources. ▪Declarations by directors of five companies on fiscal condition of their companies and funding policies of Ministry of Cultural Affairs: (1) Jean-Denis Leduc, Le Théâtre de la Manufacture, (2) Denis Bélanger, Les Pichous, (3) Denis Pronovost, Le Théâtre de Carton, (4) Marthe Mercure, L'Atelier-Studio Kaléidoscope, (5) Jean-Guy Sabourin, Le Théâtre de la Grande-Réplique.

259 Moore, Mavor. "Guardian of the Arts: The Canada Council Celebrates Its 25th Birthday." *OC*. 1982 Spring; 23(1): 13, 48 . Illus.
Canada. Twentieth cent. Histories-sources. ▪Praise for achievements of the Canada Council and warnings about troubled economy.

260 Wehle, Philippa; Ten Cate, Ritsaert; DeFelice, Atanasio. "American Theatre Abroad — The European View." *PerAJ*. 1982; 6 (3): 23-45. Illus.: Photo.
France. Netherlands. Italy. USA. Twentieth cent. Histories-sources. ▪Europeans examine subsidies of American groups.

261 Sander, Anki. "Självfinansiering eller lågpris?" (Self-Financing or Low Prices?)*Entre*. 1982; 9(5): 3-7. Illus.
Sweden. Twentieth cent. Histories-sources. ▪Government support cannot keep up with rising costs. New policies needed to encourage increased box-office income.

262 Baker, Stuart E. "Public Funding and the Theatre — Hard Times Can Make Us Strong." *ThNe*. 1982 Dec.; 14(9): 2.
USA. 1980-1982. Technical studies. ▪Strategies for theatres under severe reduction in government funding.

263 Coigney, Martha W. "Yankee, Stay Home?" *PerAJ*. 1982; 6(3): 111-114.
USA. Twentieth cent. Histories-sources. ▪Calls for U.S. government to subsidize travel of theatre troupes abroad.

264 Hodsoll, Frank. "'Where Do We Go From Here?'." *ThNe*. 1982 Apr.; 14(4): 15-16. [From an address delivered to National Symposium of Theatre Trustees, January 30, 1982 in Pasadena, CA.]
USA. 1982. Histories-sources. ▪Aims and objectives of NEA (National Endowment for the Arts) as seen by chairman Frank Hodsoll.

265 Martenson, Edward A. "The NEA Theatre Program: An Initial Review." *AmTh*. 1982 Oct.; 4(7): 14-16. Notes. Illus.: Photo. B&W.
USA. 1982. Histories-sources. ▪Reviews guidelines for NEA (National Endowment for the Arts) theatre programs and funding.

266 Massa, Robert. "TKTS to Heaven." *VV*. 1982 Aug. 31; 27(35): 79, 81. Illus.: Dwg.
USA. 1982. Histories-sources. ▪Describes TKTS, a half-price ticket outlet financed by The Theatre Development Fund.

267 Michael, R. Keith. "NEA Study Outlines Growth, Problems of Theatre Today." *ThNe*. 1982 Nov.; 14(8): 14.
USA. 1981. Technical studies. ▪Account of statistical NEA (National Endowment for the Arts) report: 'The Condition and Needs of the Live Professional Theatre in America'.

268 Sloan, Lenwood. "A.B. Spellman: NEA's New Vanguard Expansion Arts." *CAM*. 1982 Oct.; 4(10): 33. [Column: Bay Area Arts Forum.]
USA. 1980-1982. Histories-sources. ▪Project Director of NEA (National Endowment for the Arts) Expansion Arts Program reflects on effects of Reaganomics.

THEATRE IN GENERAL — cont'd

269   Zeigler, Joseph Wesley. "Second Thoughts on the Institutional Theatre." *TA.* 1982; 37: 29-38.
USA. 1965-1982. Historical studies. ■Role of NEA (National Endowment for the Arts) in theatre funding and probable impact of recent budget cuts.

270   Blum, Lambert; Iversen, Fritz. "Das Schauspielhaus für Karstadt..." (The Theatre for Karstadt...)*Tzs.* 1982; 1: 47-57.
West Germany. Twentieth cent. Histories-sources. ■Interview with Jürgen Flimm, manager of Kölner Städtisches Schauspiel, on Stadttheater (municipal theatre) system vs. free groups.

271   Blum, Lambert. "Projektsubventionierung." (Project Subsidy.) *Tzs.* 1982; 1: 68-77.
West Germany. Netherlands. 1979-1982. Histories-sources. ■Discussion of subsidy systems for 'free groups.' Schlicksupp Teatertrupp's production of *Flametti*, supported by the Toneelraad of Rotterdam with project subsidy. Related to Theatre in General.

272   Bohn, Rainer. "Dann muss ich eben das Licht ausmachen." (Then I Will Have to Turn Out the Lights.) *Tzs.* 1982; 1: 24-33.
West Germany. 1982. Histories-sources. ■Interview with Wilhelm A. Kewenig, West Berlin Senator for Science and Cultural Affairs, about rise in ticket prices for state theatres.

273   Gruber, Birgit; Bohn, Rainer. "(Wie) soll man das Stadtheater verteidigen?" ((How) Should We Plead For Municipal Theatre?)*Tzs.* 1982; 1: 7-16. Notes. Illus.
West Germany. 1982. Histories-sources. ■Discussion of shortage of public expenditures on theatre, and relation to cultural and social policy.

274   Gruber, Birgit; Bohn, Rainer. "Freie Gruppe — freie Unternehmer?" (Free Group — Free Enterprise?)*Tzs.* 1982; 1: 58-67. Illus.
West Germany. 1972-1982. Histories-sources. ■Interview with Ilse Scheer on economic situation of *Theatermanufaktur*, subsidy and independence. Related to Dance.

275   Rudolph, Hagen. "Sparen an der falschen Stelle." (Economizing in the Wrong Place.) *BtR.* 1982 Aug.; 4: 19.
West Germany. 1982. Histories-sources. ■Effect of unemployment and recession on culture and need for re-evaluating federal and municipal budgets.

Financial operations: Planning and accounting

276   Milhous, Judith. "United Company Finances, 1682-1692." *ThR.* 1981-82 Winter; 7(1): 37-53. Notes.
Great Britain. 1682-1692. Histories-reconstruction. ■Attempt to reconstruct in detail finances of company under Thomas Betterton's management: discusses questionable financial management of Davenant brothers in later seasons.

277   Baugniet, Lanny. "Building a Subscription Audience." *GTAN.* 1982 Aug.; 4(1): 5-6.
USA. Twentieth cent. Technical studies. ■Planning a subscription drive and promoting audience development.

278   Visser, David; Feldman, Laurence. "The Public Partnership." *AmTh.* 1982 Jan.; 3(10): 10. Notes.
USA. 1981-1982. Histories-sources. ■Meaning of trusteeship, and relationship between theatre budgets and contributions from boards of trustees.

Institutions

279   Langford, Roger. "Vancouver's Arts Club: Getting Bigger." *CTR.* 1982 Winter; 33: 96-99. Illus.
Canada. 1964-1982. Histories-sources. ■Development into a three-theatre complex.

280   Mercer, Ruby. "The Gamble That Paid Off." *OC.* 1982 Summer; 23(2): 12-14. Illus.

Canada. 1982. Histories-sources. ■Interview with Mario Bernardi on his resignation from Canadian National Arts Centre.

281   Crane, Gladys M. "Women's Program Update." *ThNe.* 1982 Mar.; 14(3): 9.
USA. 1980. Histories-sources. ■Brief report on involvement of minority women, mention of Black Theatre Program and process of selecting women for membership.

Institutions: Producing/performing

282   Langerman, Deborah. "Technique as Message." *Tk.* 1982 May-June; 2(4): 27-29. Notes.
Twentieth cent. Critical studies. ■Political theatre groups' desire to reach a broad, non-elitist audience.

283   Kutschera, Edda. "Theater der Jugend: Im Angstdreieck." (Young People's Theatre: In a Triangle of Dread.) *Bühne.* 1982 Dec.: 14-15. Illus.
Austria. 1982. Histories-sources. ■Current state of Theater der Jugend and its repertory.

284   Englund, Claes. "Låt oss få se Szajnas teater i Sverige!" (Let Us See Szajna's Theatre in Sweden.) *Entre.* 1982 ; 9(4): 24. Illus.
Bulgaria. 1982. Histories-sources. ■Report on Theatre of Nations festival sponsored by ITI (International Theatre Institute).

285   Brennan, Brian. "Theatre 3: A Critical Obituary." *CTR.* 1982 Winter; 33(102-105). Illus.
Canada. Twentieth cent. Histories-sources. ■Recent demise of leading alternative theatre.

286   Runnells, Rory. "Winnipeg: Two Years and Counting." *CTR.* 1982 Fall; 36: 113-115. Illus.
Canada. 1980-1982. Histories-sources. ■Brief update on activities of Manitoba Theatre Center.

287   Simpson, Herbert. "Summering in Stratford: Hotbed of Theater Arts." *Dm.* 1982 May; 56(5): 46-48, 50.
Canada. 1981-1982. Histories-sources. ■Contribution of movement specialists to Shakespeare Festival productions: choreographer Judith Marcuse, fight director Patrick Crean, weaponry buff Braun McAsh and movement coach Jeffrey Guyton. Importance of dance training for actors.

288   John, Hans-Rainer. "Sozialistisches Theater in der Karibik." (Socialist Theatre in the Caribbean.) *TZ.* 1982 May; 37(5): 51-57. Illus.
Cuba. 1982. Historical studies. ■Description and evaluation of the Festival de Teatro de La Habana and an interview with Raquel Revuelta, director of the Teatro Estudio Habana.

289   Parmalee, Cricket. "The New Theater of Cuba." *Tk.* 1982 Mar.-Apr.; 2(3): 21-22. Illus.
Cuba. 1981. Histories-sources. ■History of Teatro Nuevo, the New Theatre Movement in Cuba, as presented at a festival featuring Grupo Teatro Escambray, Cubano de Acero, and others.

290   Ross, Ciro Bianchi. "The Cubans Bring Teatro Nuevo to the USA." *Tk.* 1982 May-June; 2(4): 6-9. Illus.
Cuba. USA. 1982. Histories-sources. ■Introduction to the Grupo Teatro Escambray, a professional regional theatre, including synopsis of four Cuban folktales.

291   Lewin, Jan. "Festival of Fools." *Entre.* 1982; 9(4): 10-16. Illus.
Denmark. 1982. Histories-sources. ■Third Festival of Fools presented work of 50 international experimental groups.

292   Gair, Reavley. *The Children of Paul's: The Story of a Theatre Company, 1553-1608.* Cambridge UP; 1982. x, 213 pp. Pref. Notes. Index. Biblio. Illus.
England. 1553-1608. Historical studies. ■Interaction between major boys' company and domestic political forces.

293   Lead, Brian. "The Forgotten Theatres of Furness." *TN.* 1982; 36(1): 27-33.

THEATRE IN GENERAL — cont'd

England. 1796-1811. Historical studies. ■Overview of the theatres and theatrical productions of the Furness Peninsula.

294 Oaks, Harold R. "Political Trends in Western European Children's Theatre." *ChTR.* 1982 Winter; 31(1): 3-7. Notes.
England. Netherlands. Denmark. Finland. Twentieth cent. Histories-sources.

295 Pry, Kevin. "Theatrical Competition and the Rise of the Afterpiece Tradition." *TN.* 1982; 36(1): 21-27. Chart. 2.
England. 1700-1724. Historical studies. ■Argues that competition between Lincoln's Inn Fields and Drury Lane was major influence in increase of afterpieces.

296 Ranger, Paul. "A Matter of Choice: A Comparison of Locations and Repertoire in Some English Provincial Theatres." *NCTR.* 1982 Winter; 10(2): 61-84. Notes.
England. 1787-1817. Historical studies. ■Henry Thornton's theatre management. Distinctive audiences in each town required different managerial approaches and repertoires. Includes sample repertoires.

297 Thomsen, Christian W. "Die 'New York Street Theater Caravan': Poesie des Widerstands und der Revolution im politischen Volkstheater." (The 'New York Street Theatre Caravan': Poetry of Resistance and Revolution in the Political Popular Theatre.) *MuK.* 1982; 28(2): 143-153.
Europe. USA. 1969-1981. Historical studies. ■Political and social work, techniques of production, tours in Europe, biographical notes on leader, Marketa Kimbrell. Infl. by Jerzy Grotowski; Lee Strasberg; Tadeusz Kantor.

298 Beauman, Sally. *The Royal Shakespeare Company: A History of Ten Decades.* New York: Oxford UP; 1982. xii, 388 pp. Pref. Index. Illus.: Photo. B&W. 49.
Great Britain. 1875-1975. Histories-specific.

299 Nilsson, Reidar; Rezmerski, John. "Tukak' Teatret." *Tk.* 1982 July-Aug.; 2(5): 6-10. Illus.
Greenland. 1975-1982. Historical studies. ■Social and symbolic bases of Tukak' Teatret, an Inuit theatre company inspired by storytelling traditions.

300 Ashley, Wayne; Holloman, Regina. "From Ritual to Theatre in Kerala." *TDR.* 1982 Summer; 26(2): 59-72.
India. 1981. Histories-sources. ■History of the 1981 performance by the Natana Kala Kshetram theatre company of *Sree Muchilot Bhagavathi,* part of a new theatrical form including ancient ritual, epic and Puranic material.

301 *Il Teatro Municipale 'R. Valli'.* (Romolo Valli Municipal Theatre.) Reggio Emilia: Edizioni del Teatro Municipale; 1982. 58 pp. Illus.
Italy. 1852-1982. Historical studies. ■Theatre's activities.

302 Squarzina, Luigi, ed. *Il Teatro Argentina e il suo Museo.* (The Teatro Argentina and Its Museum.) Rome: Officina Edizioni; 1982. 101 pp. Illus.
Italy. 1700-1982. Historical studies.

303 Volpi, Gianna. *Spoleto Story.* Milan: Rusconi; 1982. 257 pp. Pref. Illus.
Italy. 1958-1981. Histories-sources. ■Chronology of performances of Festival dei Due Mondi in Spoleto with monographs on collaborators and short critical notes on the most important performances.

304 Englund, Claes. "Kommunal teater i ekonomisk press." (City Theatre under Economic Pressure.) *Entre.* 1982; 9(1): 18.
Norway. Twentieth cent. Histories-sources. ■Oslo Nye Teater, funded by city, with emphasis on comedy and children's theatre.

305 Janzon, Leif. "Eg é fra Bergen!" (I Am from Bergen.) *Entre.* 1982; 9(2): 49. Illus.
Norway. 1876-1981. Histories-sources. ■Repertory of oldest theatre, Den Nationale Scene, in Bergen.

306 Mellgren, Thomas. "Vi har ett bastant motstand mot de stora gesterna, den rena teatern." (We Are Strongly Opposed to Big Gesture, Mere Theatre.) *Entre.* 1982; 9(2): 40-41. Illus.
Norway. 1980-1981. Histories-sources. ■Svein Erik Brodal, artistic director of Det Norske Teatret, oversees varied repertory including new scripts, American musicals and international avant-garde works.

307 Lewis, Allan. "The Rumanian National Theatre and Radu Beligan." *NSEEDT.* 1982 June; 2(2): 7-8.
Rumania. 1980-1982. Histories-sources. ■Discussion of theatre and its artistic director/administrator.

308 White, Kathy. "The Dundee Rep." *Tabs.* 1982 May; 39(1): 4.
Scotland. Twentieth cent. Historical studies. ■Report on exhibition representing a quarter-century of production by Dundee Repertory Theatre, displayed in collection of photographs by Alex Coupar.

309 Capmany, Aurelio. *El Café del Liceo.* (The Liceo Cafe.) Barcelona: Alba; 1982. 195 pp. Pref. [Revised edition of *El Café del Liceo: 1837-1839, The Theater and Its Carnival Dances.*]
Spain. 1837-1839. Historical studies. ■The Gran Teatre del Liceo and its carnival dances.

310 Lundin, Immi. "Rapport från barnteaterns aktuella landskap." (Report from the Present Landscape of Children's Theatre.) *Entre.* 1982; 9(3): 3-9. Illus.
Sweden. Norway. Denmark. 1982. Histories-sources. ■Children's theatre intent on bridging generation gap.

311 Norén, Kjerstin. "Gatuteaterns språk." (The Language of Street Theatre.) *Entre.* 1982; 9(5): 8-13. Illus.
Sweden. Denmark. 1970-1982. Histories-sources. ■Jordcirkus and Solvognen ensembles present productions and happenings as political protest and artistic experimentation. Infl. by Living Theatre; Bread and Puppet Theatre.

312 Sander, Anki. "Teater som lukrativt språklaboratorium." (The Theatre As a Lucrative Language Laboratory.) *Entre.* 1982; 9(1): 28-32. Illus.
Sweden. 1974-1981. Histories-sources. ■English repertory companies performing in Sweden, including the English Theatre Ensemble, led by Tommy Iwering, and the English Theatre Company, led by Richard Jacques and Christer Berg.

313 Allen, Judith. "Atlanta's 80-81 Season." *OvA.* 1982 Nov.; 10: 7-8.
USA. 1930-1982. Histories-sources. ■Synopsis of modern Black theatre companies, with some background on beginnings.

314 Anon. "Newsreel." *M.* 1982, Fourth Quarter; 14(4): 23. [Theatre notes.]
USA. 1982. Histories-sources. ■Notes on historic theatres.

315 Anon. "Around the Circuit." *M.* 1982 Fourth Quarter; 14(4): 24. Illus. [Theatre notes.]
USA. 1982. Histories-sources. ■Assorted news items about various historic theatres.

316 Anon. "A Photo History of La Mama." *PerAJ.* 1982; 6(2): 18-26. Illus.: Photo. Poster.
USA. 1960-1980. Histories-sources.

317 Berkowitz, Gerald M. *New Broadway: Theatre Across America, 1950-1980.* Totowa, NJ: Rowman and Littlefield; 1982. x, 198 pp. Pref. Index. Biblio.
USA. 1950-1980. Historical studies. ■Critical survey of selected regional theatres. Related to Basic Theatrical Documents.

318 Berson, Misha. "The People's Theatre Festival." *Tk.* 1982 May-June; 2(4): 34-36. Illus.
USA. 1978-1982. Histories-sources. ■Intentions and organizational problems.

319 Bliss, Shepherd. "Bread and Puppet Theatre: Resurrection Circus." *Tk.* 1982 Nov.-Dec.; 3(1): 22-27. Illus.

THEATRE IN GENERAL — cont'd

USA. 1962-1982. Historical studies. ■Description of annual event. Related to Popular Entertainment.

320 Buttitta, Tony; Witham, Barry B. *Uncle Sam Presents: A Memoir of the Federal Theatre, 1935-1939.* Philadelphia: Univ. of Pennsylvania P; 1982. xv, 249 pp. Pref. Notes. Index. Biblio. Illus.: Photo. Dwg. B&W. 19.
USA. 1935-1939. Histories-specific.

321 Davis, Jed H.; Corey, Orlin. "The Four Stories of CTF." *ChTR.* 1982 Winter; 31(1): 12-15.
USA. 1957-1982. Histories-sources. ■Aims, structure and development of Children's Theatre Foundation.

322 Davis, Jed H.; Evans, Mary Jane. *Theatre, Children and Youth.* New Orleans: Anchorage; 1982. 362 pp. Index. Biblio. B&W. Color.
USA. 1960-1982. Critical studies. ■Practices in children's theatre with guidelines for producing plays. Related to Basic Theatrical Documents: Miscellaneous texts.

323 Dewberry, Jonathan. "The African Grove Theatre and Company." *BALF.* 1982 Winter; 16(4): 128-131. Notes.
USA. 1820-1826. Historical studies. ■Relocation and final closing of the African Grove Company's theatre.

324 Fark, William E. "The New Old Globe: A Year of Celebration." *PArts.* 1982 Jan.; 16(1): 20-25. Illus.: Photo.
USA. Twentieth cent. Histories-sources. ■Opening of rebuilt Old Globe Theatre in San Diego with first professional resident acting company.

325 Feingold, Michael. "The Phoenix Theatre 1953-1982." *VV.* 1982 Dec. 21; 27(51): 117, 130. Illus. Photo.
USA. 1953-1982. Historical studies.

326 Fischer, Corey. "Some Notes on Workshops." *Tk.* 1982 July-Aug.; 2(5): 19-21.
USA. 1960-1982. Histories-sources. ■Personal experiences of one of the founders of A Traveling Jewish Theatre.

327 Klett, Renate. "Die berühmteste Theaterfrau der Welt feiert ein Jubiläum: 20 Jahre Ellen Stewart und ihr La Mama Theater." (The Most Famous Theatre Woman of the World Celebrates a Jubilee: 20 Years with Ellen Stewart and Her La Mama Theatre.) *TH.* 1982; 13: 94-99. Illus.
USA. 1962-1982. Historical studies.

328 Leverett, James. "The Wooster Group's 'Mean Theatre' Sparks a Hot Debate." *AmTh.* 1982 Jul.-Aug.; 4(4-5): 16-20. Notes. Illus.: Photo. B&W. 7.
USA. 1982. Critical studies. ■Prompted by New York State Council on the Arts' withdrawal of funding, Wooster Group's *Route 1 & 9* dramatizes the group's history and philosophy.

329 Loney, Glenn. "La Mama Celebrates 20 Years." *PerAJ.* 1982; 6(2): 6-17.
USA. 1960-1980. Histories-sources. ■Ellen Stewart discusses her personal history, experiences with grant agencies and notable playwrights and producers.

330 Lynch, Twink. "Community Theatre Leaders: There's a Need for Professional Training." *ThNe.* 1982 Nov.; 14(8): 2, 15.
USA. 1917-1982. Histories-sources. ■Training for leaders of community theatre: responsibility, personnel, methods and impact on community.

331 Malone, Diane. "The Small Professional Theatre Movement." *ThNe.* 1982 Jan.; 14(1): 14.
USA. 1980-1982. ■Contributions of small professional theatre movement to artists, audiences and society.

332 Malpede, Karen. "A World Without War: Playmaking with New Cycle Theater." *Tk.* 1982 Nov.-Dec.; 3(1): 6-10. Illus.
USA. Twentieth cent. Histories-sources. ■Report from playwright and co-founder.

333 Munk, Erika. "Against Scapegoats." *VV.* 1982 Feb. 23; 27(8): 84.

USA. 1982. Studies of criticism/critics. ■Warfare between critics and non-commercial theatres.

334 O'Quinn, James. "Southern Exposure." *AmTh.* 1982 Dec.; 4(9): 1-2. Notes. Illus.: Photo. B&W. 2.
USA. 1982. Histories-sources. ■Report on ROOTS (Regional Organization of Theatres-South) Conference Festivals: performances by Free Southern Theatre, South of the Mountain, Southern Theatre Conspiracy's Seven Stages and Birmingham Creative Dance Co.

335 Regan, F. Scott. "Things I Hope I Never Hear Again." *ChTR.* 1982 Summer; 31(3): 22.
USA. Twentieth cent. Histories-sources. ■Negative attitudes and misconceptions about children's theatre.

336 Richards, Sandra. "Black Repertory Group's Youth Outreach Program: Co-operation Is the Key Word in the Youth Performing Arts Company." *CAM.* 1982 Aug.; 4(8): 23. [Column: Bay Area Arts Forum.]
USA. Twentieth cent. Histories-sources. ■Philosophy of program aiming at development of Black youth through participation in the performing arts.

337 Robinson, Edward A. "The Pekin: The Genesis of American Black Theater." *BALF.* 1982 Winter; 16(4): 136-138. Notes.
USA. 1905-1911. Histories-sources. ■Brief history of the first professional Black theatre company in Chicago.

338 Roth, Martha. "Learning to Live with Our Differences." *Tk.* 1982 May-June; 2(4): 14-16. Illus.
USA. 1981. Histories-sources. ■Feminist theatre group, At the Foot of the Mountain, held a series of discussion evenings with women from different racial, ethnic and class backgrounds.

339 Sarlós, Robert K. *Jig Cook and the Provincetown Players: Theatre in Ferment.* Amherst, MA: Univ. of Massachusetts P; 1982. xii, 265 pp. Pref. Notes. Index. Biblio.
USA. 1912-1929. Histories-specific.

340 Shewey, Don. "One More Time." *VV.* 1982 Mar 9; 27(10): 88. Illus. Photo.
USA. 1982. ■Describes Second Stage, theatre that gives revised contemporary plays second productions.

341 Smith, Louise. "Otrabanda: Ten Years on the Mississippi." *Tk.* 1982 Nov.-Dec.; 3(1): 11-15. Illus.
USA. 1970-1982. Historical studies. ■Otrabanda Company's touring productions by raft to communities along the Mississippi River.

342 Wallach, Susan Levi. "Robert Brustein and Robert Orchard." *ThCr.* 1982 Oct.; 16(8): 13-15, 43-45, 48-51. Illus.
USA. 1982. Histories-sources. ■Interview concerning the American Repertory Theatre of Cambridge, MA.

343 Yarbo-Bejarano, Yvonne. "The Image of Chicana in Teatro." *Tk.* 1982 May-June; 2(4): 19-21. Illus.
USA. 1970-1982. Critical studies. ■Examines portrayals of Chicanas in plays written for and performed by Teatro de la Esperanza.

344 Stuttgarter Ensemble. "Wir verlassen die Weihestätten: Die Pläne des 'Stuttgarter Ensembles'." (We Abandon the Sacred Conventions: The Plans of the Stuttgarter Ensemble.) *Tzs.* 1982; 1: 44-46.
West Germany. 1982. Histories-sources. ■Statement of Stuttgarter Ensemble under Hansgünther Heyme on its withdrawal from subsidized theatre system and foundation of Stuttgarter Fabrik.

345 Badisches Staatstheater Karlsruhe; Generallandesarchiv Karlsruhe. *Karlsruher Theatergeschichte: Vom Hoftheater zum Staatstheater.* (History of the Theatre in Karlsruhe: From Court Theatre to State Theatre.) Karlsruhe: Braun; 1982. 168 pp. Biblio. Illus.
West Germany. 1600-1982. Histories-specific. ■From court theatre to the Badisches Staatstheater.

346 Fischer, Gerhard. "Ulrike Meinhof's *Revolt* and Other Plays." *ThM.* 1981-82 Winter; 13(1): 83-88. Notes. Illus.

THEATRE IN GENERAL — cont'd·

[Second International Children's and Youth Festival, Grips Theater, West Berlin, June 6-15, 1981.]
West Germany. 1981. Reviews of performances. ∎Youth theatre groups in Berlin.

347 Hofmann, Jürgen. "Kultur im Widerspruch (2): Frankfurter Fermente oder Zurück zur neuen Bürgerlichkeit." (Culture in Contradiction, 2: Frankfurt Ferments or Back to the New Bourgeoisie.) *Tzs.* 1982; 2: 103-129.
West Germany. 1981. Critical studies. ∎Remarks on reopening of Alte Oper (Old Opera) and appointment of East German director Adolf Dresen as general manager of Schauspiel Frankfurt. Discusses Frankfurt's cultural policy and alternative theatre, seen as re-establishment of 'bourgeois' ideology in West Germany.

348 Joerder, Gerhard. "Du musst nur die Laufrichtung ändern." (You've Just Got to Change the Direction You Run.) *TH.* 1982 July; 7: 41-45. Illus.
West Germany. 1980-1982. Histories-sources. ∎Changes in repertory and subscription organization at Stadttheater Konstanz under new manager, Hans J. Amman.

349 Lange, Mechthild. "Für die schweigende Mehrheit?" (For the Silent Majority?)*TH.* 1982 Apr.; 4: 52-55. Illus.
West Germany. 1982. Histories-sources. ∎Describes commercial situation and repertory of four private theatres: Hamburger Kammerspiele, Altonaer Theater, Theater im Zimmer and Ernst-Deutsch-Theater.

350 Rischbieter, Henning. "Zwei Gesichter Thalias in Hamburg." (The Two Faces of Thalia in Hamburg.) *TH.* 1982 Apr.; 4: 39-51. Illus.
West Germany. 1982. Histories-sources. ∎Conditions and repertory at Deutsches Schauspielhaus and Thalia Theater, including portraits of eight actresses.

351 McCaslin, Nellie. "The Yugoslav Festival of the Child." *ChTR.* 1982 Fall; 31(4): 9-11.
Yugoslavia. 1958-1982. Historical studies. ∎Sterijino Pozorje (Yugoslav Festival Theatre) and 1982 festival work of Drago Putnikovic.

Institutions: Research

352 Pauli, Manfred. "Schauspielkunst — Zentrum der Theaterarbeit: Versuch eines Reports vom IX. Weltkongress der FIRT, September 1981." (Dramatic Art — The Thrust of Theatre Work: Report on the 9th World Congress of FIRT, Leipzig, September 1981.) *TZ.* 1982; 37(1): 37-40, 72.
East Germany. 1981. Histories-sources. ∎FIRT (International Federation for Theatre Research) report includes selection from main lecture by Joachim Fieback about dramatic art on stage plus description of FIRT and its aims.

353 Buck, Richard M. "TLA: Preserving Theatre's Heritage in Print." *ThNe.* 1982 Summer; 14(6): 13.
USA. 1937-1982. Histories-sources. ∎Activities of the Theatre Library Association (TLA) including conferences, awards (George Freedley Memorial Award and the Theatre Library Association Award) and publications (*Broadside, Performing Arts Resources*).

Institutions: Service

354 Kilbourn, William; Roberts, Jean; Gardner, David; Peacock, David; Des Landes, Claude; Learning, Walter. "The Canada Council and the Theatre: The Past Twenty-five Years and Tomorrow." *THC.* 1982 Fall; 3(2): 164-192. Illus.
Canada. 1957-1982. Histories-sources. ∎Transcript of panel discussion on achievements of Canada Council.

355 Marder, Louis. "London's Theatre Museum Threatened, Fought For, and Saved." *ShN.* 1982 Winter; 32(5-6): 27-28.
England. 1971-1985. Histories-sources. ∎Description of campaign to open museum, and description of its space, facilities and collections.

356 Monroe, John G. "Charles Gilpin and the Drama League Controversy." *BALF.* 1982 Winter; 16(4): 139-141. Notes.
USA. 1921. Historical studies. ∎Drama League's attempted rescission of an award to Charles Gilpin.

357 Wilkerson, Margaret B. "Pre-Convention on Black Theatre." *ThNe.* 1982 Apr.; 14(4): 7. [First of three articles in *The Black Theatre Bulletin* included as part of *Theatre News.*]
USA. Nineteenth cent. Twentieth cent. Histories-sources. ∎Goals and objectives of Black Theatre Program particularly regarding a first preconvention to be held prior to American Theatre Association Convention in New York City: includes brief history of theatre for Black Americans.

Institutions: Social

358 Kidd, Ross. "Popular Theatre and Popular Struggle in Kenya: The Story of the Kamiriithu Community Educational and Cultural Centre." *Tk.* 1982 Sep.-Oct.; 2(6): 46-54, 56-61. Notes. Biblio.
Kenya. 1976-1982. Historical studies. ∎Rural labor community's cultural center and theatre: Kenya's first popular native language theatre.

Institutions: Special

359 Hecht, Stuart J. "Social and Artistic Integration: The Emergence of Hull-House Theatre." *TJ.* 1982 May; 34(2): 172-182 . Notes. Illus.
USA. 1890-1928. Historical studies. ∎Dramatic productions at settlement house as a means of encouraging individual expression. Movement from production of plays with realistic social themes to artistic achievement and promotion of playwrights.

360 Mayo, Anna. "Stomping at the Savoy." *VV.* 1982 June 1; 27(22): 90. Illus.: Photo.
USA. 1982. Histories-sources. ∎Description of 27th Annual Obie Awards ceremony.

361 Thomas, Jeffrey. "Indian Time Theatre." *Tk.* 1982 Nov.-Dec.; 3(1): 53. Illus.
USA. 1982. Histories-sources. ∎Plan for promoting Native American consciousness through theatre presentations on reservations.

Institutions: Training

362 Mwansa, Dickson; Kidd, Ross. "Third World/Canada Popular Theatre Exchange." *Tk.* 1982 Mar.-Apr.; 2(3): 23-25. Notes. Illus.
Canada. 1981. Histories-sources. ∎Activities at workshop to improve performance techniques for community involvement.

363 John, Hans-Rainer. "Erkennen and Bekennen." (Discerning and Confessing.) *TZ.* 1982; 37(2): 29-30. Illus. [Second of a series.]
East Germany. 1981. Histories-sources. ∎Interview with Hans-Peter Minetti on training at the Hochschule für Schauspielkunst Ernst Busch.

364 Kamlongera, Christopher F. "Theatre for Development: The Case of Malawi." *ThR.* 1982 Autumn; 7(3): 207-222. Notes. Illus.
Malawi. Twentieth cent. Histories-sources. ∎Educational uses of 'Theatre for Development' exemplified through traveling group of performers from University of Malawi playing in many villages.

365 Kentridge, Matthew. "The Tandem Theatre of King Edward School — A Polite View." *TF.* 1982 May; 3(1): 11-17.
South Africa, Republic of. 1982. Historical studies. ∎History, uses and performances of a school drama club theatre.

366 Altenbaugh, Richard J. "Proletarian Drama: An Educational Tool of the American Labor College Movement." *TJ.* 1982 May; 34(2): 197-210. Notes. Illus.
USA. 1925-1936. Historical studies. ∎Summary of drama programs in three labor colleges.

THEATRE IN GENERAL — cont'd

367 Merin, Jennifer. "The American League." *CTR*. 1982 Summer; 35: 57-60.
USA. 1971-1982. Histories-sources. ■The League of Professional Theatre Training Programs' experiment in setting and maintaining training standards.

368 Neely, Kent; Vogel, Frederic. "A Professional Evaluation of Academic Theatre Management Training." *TD&T*. 1982 Spring; 18(1): 4-7.
USA. 1982. Critical studies.

369 Tarleton, Bennett. "Utah's Comprehensive Arts Education Plan Moves Ahead." *ThNe*. 1982 Feb.; 14(2): 1, 3.
USA. 1982. Histories-sources. ■Includes components of program, specific objectives and accomplishments and people responsible for administering plan.

Legal aspects

370 Jungmar, Susanne. "Slutstrid i rätten om Manifestet." (The Final Struggle in the Case of the Manifesto.) *Entre*. 1982; 9(6): 26-27.
Sweden. 1981-1982. Histories-sources. ■Court case grew out of controversy over repertory and management of Göteborg Stadsteater (Gothenburg City Theatre).

Legal aspects: Liabilities

371 Davidson, Randall W.A. "Liability and the Technician in the Entertainment Business." *TD&T*. 1982 Fall; 18(3): 15-17.
USA. Twentieth cent. Histories-sources. ■Technicians' responsibility and wisdom of carrying liability insurance.

Legal aspects: Licensing and regulations

372 Feingold, Michael. "Killer Quiz Stays Crits." *VV*. 1982 Aug. 24; 27(34): 105.
USA. 1982. Histories-sources. ■Third annual humorous Dramatic Licensing Quiz.

Performance management

373 Paavolainen, Pentti. "Une saison individuelle à Lappeenranta en 1980-81 — un défi à plus d'un théâtre/Lappeenranta's Original Theatre Season 1980-81 — A Challenge for Many Theatres." *NFT*. 1982; 34: 10-12.
Finland. 1980-1981. ■Lappeenranta City Theatre repertory and policies.

Performance management: Stage management

374 Dilker, Barbara. "Stage Management Overview." *ThCr*. 1982 Apr.; 16(4): 50-56.
USA. 1982. Critical studies. ■Attempts to define stage manager's duties.

Performance spaces: Amphitheatres

375 Anon. "Antikes Amphitheater in Plovdiv wieder Spielstätte." (Historic Amphitheatre in Plovdiv is a Working Theatre Again.) *BK*. 1982; 1: 4. Illus. 1.
Bulgaria. 114-1982. Histories-sources.

Performance spaces: Construction/renovation

376 Axtell, William. "Air Casters for Multi-Use Space." *ThCr*. 1982 Mar.; 16(3): 22, 49-50. Illus.
Canada. Twentieth cent. Technical studies. ■Transforming Center in the Square from concert hall to intimate auditorium.

377 Harris, Richard. "The Mill at Sonning." *Tabs*. 1982 Nov.; 39(2): 11. Illus.
Great Britain. Twentieth cent. Technical studies. ■Brief description of renovated watermill theatre, including equipment listing.

378 Hegglin, W. A.; Ammann, H.; Zotzmann, A. "Das neue Theater-Casino in Zug." (The New Theatre-Casino in Zug.) *BtR*. 1982 Oct.; 5: 20-24. B&W. ar. pl.
Switzerland. 1980-1982. Histories-reconstruction. ■Renovation and reconstruction of important architectural building.

379 Anon. "Pasadena Playhouse Begins Million-Dollar Renovation." *ThNe*. 1982 Dec.; 14(9): 11. Illus.: Photo. B&W.
USA. 1917-1982. Histories-sources. ■Announcement of renovation, including brief history.

380 Dandridge, Susan. "San Diego on the Thames." *Tabs*. 1982 May; 39(1): 4-5.
USA. Twentieth cent. Histories-sources. ■Report on Shakespeare Festival and Old Globe Theatre, with emphasis on destruction by fire in 1978 and the 100-day reconstruction.

381 Howard, John T. "The Boston Metropolitan Theatre Center." *TD&T*. 1982 Summer; 18(2): 12-13.
USA. 1982. Technical studies. ■Transformation of film-vaudeville house into modern theatre roadhouse. Related to Popular Entertainment.

382 Harris, Richard, ed. "The Watermill Theatre." *Tabs*. 1982 May; 39(1): 8.
Wales. Twentieth cent. Histories-sources. ■Description of new theatre built from an old watermill.

383 Krengel-Strudthoff, Inge. "Das neue Stadttheater Esslingen." (Esslingen's New Municipal Theatre.) *BtR*. 1982 Dec.; 6: 18-20. B&W. Plan. Fr.Elev.
West Germany. 1977-1982. Histories-sources. ■Planning and construction of a provincial theatre.

Performance spaces: Halls

384 Goldie, Terence W. "Newfoundland Theatre: The Proper Thing." *CTR*. 1982 Spring; 34: 180-184. Illus.
Canada. 1970-1982. Histories-sources. ■Longshoreman's Protective Union Hall has housed various kinds of theatre.

385 Orrell, John. "The Theatre at Christ Church, Oxford, in 1605." *ShS*. 1982; 35: 129-140, plate II. Notes. B&W. Fr.Elev. Loc.: British Library.
England. 1605. Historical studies. ■Probably earliest design of hall arranged for visit of James I, marking Inigo Jones' introduction of perspective scenery into English drama. Infl. by Sebastiano Serlio.

386 Benini, Enrica. "Il teatro di Vasari per le nozze di Francesco de' Medici con Giovanna d'Austria (1565)." (The Theatre by Vasari for the Wedding of Francesco de' Medici with Giovanna d'Austria, 1565.) *QT*. 1982 Feb.; 4(15): 136-150. Notes. [An example of purchaser-artist relationship in Florentine milieu.]
Italy. 1565. Histories-reconstruction. ■Theatre built by Giorgio Vasari in Palazzo Vecchio for performance of *La Cofanaria (The Casketmaker)* by Francesco d'Ambra at wedding of Francesco de' Medici with Giovanna d'Austria. Infl. by Giulio Camillo Delminio.

Performance spaces: Planning/design

387 Hamann, Ernst-Otto. "Vor 100 Jahren: Der Brand des Wiener Ringtheaters." (100 Years Ago: The Fire in the Ringtheater in Vienna.) *TZ*. 1982; 37(1): 47-48.
Austria. 1881-1981. Historical studies. ■Fire's effect on subsequent theatre construction.

388 Blanco, Milagros Ayala. "Ein Theater für Havannas Pioniere." (A Theatre for Havana's Young Pioneers.) *BK*. 1982; 1: 3. Illus.
Cuba. 1978-1982. Histories-sources. ■Ernesto (Che) Guevara Theatre in Lenin Park, with 718 seats before a 50 ft. wide (max.) proscenium opening and 79-ft. deep stage house.

389 Bredenbeck, Günter. "Zu Fragen der Lüftungs- und Klimatechnik in Theatren." (Questions about Ventilation and

THEATRE IN GENERAL — cont'd

Air Conditioning in Theatres.) *BK*. 1982; 1: 29-30. Illus.: Diagram. 2.
East Germany. 1982. Technical studies. ■Special problems of air conditioning a theatre.

390 Harris, Richard, ed. "The Barbican Centre and Strand." *Tabs*. 1982 May; 39(1): 3.
England. Twentieth cent. Histories-sources. ■Description of specifications for lighting system, sound and communication, stage equipment and seating for the Barbican Theatre, Concert Hall and Cinema.

391 Marder, Louis. "London Globe Plans Groundbreaking in 1983." *ShN*. 1982 Winter; 32(5-6): 27-28.
England. 1972-1983. Histories-reconstruction. ■Replica of '1599 Globe,' and overview of international fundraising efforts.

392 Marder, Louis. "C.W. Hodges Reveals Latest 3rd Globe Replica Plans." *ShN*. 1982 Winter; 32(5-6): 30.
USA. England. Twentieth cent. Histories-reconstruction. ■Summary of plans for Wayne State University.

393 Anon. "Nekotorye problemi proektirovnya i stroitel'stva kyl'turnoprosvetitel'nikh uchrezhdenii." (Some Problems of Designing and Building Performance Spaces for Cultural Institutions.) *STT*. 1982(4): 2-3.
USSR. Twentieth cent. Histories-sources. ■Measures to improve functioning of cultural institutions: recommendations by Council for Cultural and Educational Activity of the Ministry of Culture.

394 Kranz-Michaelis, Charlotte. "Werner Ruhnaus Podienklavier." (Werner Ruhnau's 'Podium-Piano' Stage.) *BtR*. 1982 June; 3: 10-15. Illus. Photo. B&W. Architec.
West Germany. 1957-1982. Technical studies. ■Evolution and application of 'podium-piano' stage.

395 Wever, Klaus; Biste, Rudolfe. "Die Spielkonzeption der Schaubühne 'Inszenierten Raumes' und ihre technische Umsetzung im Mendelsohn-Bau Berlin." (The Acting Concept of the 'Enacted Space' and its Technical Realization in the Mendelsohn-Bau, Berlin.) *BtR*. 1982 Apr.; 2: 10-19. Illus. B&W. Architec.
West Germany. 1971-1982. Technical studies. ■Two designer/architects discuss planning of space, including technical and artistic decisions.

Performance spaces: Stage

396 Johnston, Alexandra F. "York Pageant House: New Evidence." *REEDN*. 1982; 2: 24-25. Notes.
England. 1388. Histories-reconstruction. ■A record of pageant wagons stored in Palace of Archbishop of York.

Performance spaces: Theatres

397 O'Neill, Patrick B. "Saskatchewan's Last Opera House: Hanley 1912-1982." *THC*. 1982 Fall; 3(2): 137-147. Notes. Illus.
Canada. 1912-1982. Historical studies. ■Traces history of Hanley Opera House. Related to Music-Drama: Opera.

398 Schwarzer, Erwin. "Theater in der Volksrepublik China." (Theatre in the People's Republic of China.) *BtR*. 1982 Feb.; 1 : 19-20.
China. 1981. Histories-sources. ■Account of a tour by a retired theatre architect.

399 Adams, John Cranford. "How Large Was the Globe Playhouse?" *SQ*. 1982 Spring; 33(1): 93-94. Notes.
England. 1576-1647. Histories-reconstruction. ■John Orell's description of Globe Theatre shown incorrect.

400 Dunbar-Naismith, James. "Return to Tradition: Some Interesting Developments in Post-War British Theatre Design." *EHN*. 1982 June; 9(2): 80-91. Illus.
England. 1945-1980. Historical studies. ■Developments in theatre architecture: return to traditional forms.

401 Hume, Robert D. "The Nature of the Dorset Garden Theatre." *TN*. 1982; 36(3): 99-109.
England. 1673. Historical studies. ■Substantial differences in function of Dorset Garden and Drury Lane: managers, physical stage, productions.

402 Ingram, William. "Henry Laneman." *TN*. 1982; 36(3): 118-120.
England. 1582. Histories-sources. ■Evidence that Henry Laneman was owner of Curtain Theatre.

403 Langhans, Edward A. "Conjectural Reconstructions of the Vere Street and Lincoln's Inn Fields Theatre." *ET*. 1982 Nov.; 1(1): 14-28. Notes. Illus.
England. 1661-1674. Histories-reconstruction. ■References to theatre interiors by contemporary playgoers and playwrights.

404 Marder, Louis. "London Globe Project Organizes for Action." *ShN*. 1982 Fall; 32(4): 19.
England. 1982. Histories-sources. ■Description and statement of principles.

405 Heliot, Armelle. "Nouvelle aventure pour le théâtre de l'Athénée." (New Adventure for the Athénée Theatre.) *CF*. 1982 Feb.; 106: 21.
France. 1982. Histories-sources. ■Reopening of the Athénée Theatre under state auspices.

406 Tosi, Guy. "The Italian Theatre — A Pattern for Europe." *EHN*. 1982 June; 9(2): 40-67. Illus.
Italy. 1400-1799. Historical studies. ■General outline of theatre architecture and stage design.

407 "New Life for the Southern Theatre?" *M*. 1982 First Quarter; 14(1): 16. Illus.
USA. 1890-1982. Histories-reconstructions. ■Efforts to restore Ohio theatre, description and history.

408 Anon. "West Coast/Newsreel." *M*. 1982 Second Quarter; 14(2): 15.
USA. 1982. Histories-sources. ■News items relating to historic Mid-Western theatre buildings.

409 Aronson, Arnold; Davy, Kate. "Theatre Architecture." *TD&T*. 1982 Winter; 18(4): 12-17.
USA. 1969-1982. Technical studies. ■Architectural survey of university theatre buildings.

410 Baumann, Wallace. "Knoxville Theatres 1872-1944." *M*. 1982 Fourth Quarter; 14(4): 15-17. Illus.
USA. 1872-1944. Historical studies. ■A history of legitimate and film houses. Related to Media.

411 Glazer, Irvin R. "Newsreel." *M*. 1982 First Quarter; 14(1): 18.
USA. Twentieth cent. Histories-sources. ■Notes on theatres that have been saved or torn down.

412 Hale, A.B. "Tampa." *M*. 1982 Fourth Quarter; 14(4): 9-12. Illus.
USA. 1926-1982. Historical studies. ■The Tampa Theatre, originally a cinema designed by John E. Eberson, now a national historic site used for a wide variety of performances. Related to Media: Film.

413 Lindy, Sharon. "Midwest." *M*. 1982; 14(1): 19.
USA. Twentieth cent. Nineteenth cent. Histories-sources. ■Architectural notes on historic theatres.

414 Longfield, Robert. "Researching Theatres...and Theatre History." *M*. 1982 First Quarter; 14(1): 12.
USA. 1900-1940. Studies of research/researchers. ■Techniques of researching historic theatres and theatre history.

415 Diederichsen, Diedrich. "Fiction of Function: Problems of Theatre Building." *EHN*. 1982 June; 9(2): 69-79. Illus.
West Germany. 1945-1980. Historical studies. ■Forms of theatre architecture developed after World War II.

THEATRE IN GENERAL — cont'd

Performance/performers

416 Nygren, Christina. "Teaterhösten i Peking." (Fall Theatre Season In Beijing.) *Entre.* 1982; 9(6): 25-26. Illus.
China. 1982. Histories-sources. ■Survey of productions by Chinese and foreign troupes, with discussion about problem of adapting traditional forms to contemporary life.

417 Haughton, David. *Lindsay Kemp.* Fotografie di Guido Marari. Milan: Domus; 1982. 144 pp. Pref. Illus.: Photo.
England. 1973-1982. Historical studies. ■Lindsay Kemp Company, with a biographic note. Related to Mime.

418 Temkine, Raymonde. "Théâtre: un entretien avec Françoise Kourilsky." (Theatre: A Conversation with Françoise Kourilsky.) *CF.* 1982 June-July; 110: 28-29.
France. 1982. Histories-sources. ■Director Françoise Kourilsky discusses the 1981 Nancy festival and the Hispanic theatre troupes imported from New York: The Family, El Teatro Campesino.

419 Rigg, Diana, comp. *No Turn Unstoned: The Worst Ever Theatrical Reviews.* London: Elm Tree; 1982. 192 pp. Index. Biblio. Illus. Dwg. B&W.
Great Britain. 1650-1982. Reviews of performances. ■Compilation of humorous unfavorable reviews.

420 Merschmeier, Michael. "Italien: Auf der Suche nach dem Theater..." (Italy: In Search of the Theatre...) *TH.* 1982; 13: 113-118. Illus.
Italy. 1981-1982. Reviews of performances. ■Notes on general situation of Italian theatre.

421 Anon. "Women in the Arts: A Cultural Explosion." *Ebony.* 1982 Aug.; 37(10): 150-152.
USA. 1982. Histories-sources. ■Black actresses' opportunities in 1980s.

422 Bailey, A. Peter. "Harlem Theatre: The Struggle Continues." *OvA.* 1982 Nov.; 10: 3-5. Illus.
USA. 1980-1982. Historical studies. ■Review of traditions and problems.

423 Pontbriand, Chantal; Parsons, C.R., transl. "The Eye Finds No Fixed Point on Which to Rest." *MD.* 1982 Mar.; 25(1): 54-162. Notes.
USA. Canada. Twentieth cent. Studies of theories/theorists. ■Discussion of theatrical performance based on writings by Michael Fried, Walter Benjamin and Richard Foreman.

424 Smith, Alan. "The Moscow Season." *NSEEDT.* 1982 June; 2(2): 8-15.
USSR. 1981-1982. Histories-sources. ■Highlights of theatrical season.

Performance/performers: Acting/actors

425 Bohn, Rainer. "Schauspieler und Schauspielen: Ein Forschungsbericht." (Actor and Acting: On the State of Research.) *Tzs.* 1982; 2: 43-62. Notes. Biblio.
1982. Studies of research/researchers. ■Criticizes present mostly unsystematic research and proposes systematic semiotic approach to development of acting theories based on psychological, psychoanalytic, social-psychological and sociological inquiry.

426 Lucignani, Luciano. *Intervista sul teatro.* (Interview on Theatre.) Bari: Laterza; 1982. 155 pp.
1922-1982. Biographical studies. ■Vittorio Gassman's experiences and theories about actor's role in theatre and cinema. Related to Media: Film.

427 Anon. "Theaterkritiker zur Saison 1981/82." (Theatre Critics on the 1981-82 Season.) *TZ.* 1982; 37(9): 7-12.
East Germany. 1981-1982. Histories-sources. ■Critics discuss important performances, trends and best actors.

428 Hill, Errol. "S. Morgan Smith: Successor to Ira Aldridge." *BALF.* 1982 Winter; 16(4): 132-135. Notes.
England. 1860-1869. Historical studies. ■S. Morgan Smith, an American Black actor, played roles in England similar to those played by Black actor Ira Aldridge.

429 Jones, Dorothy. "Du nouveau sur Françoise Raisin." (New Information about Françoise Raisin.) *RHT.* 1982; 34(3): 199-203. Notes.
France. 1661-1721. Biographical studies. ■New data about Comédie Française actress and her family.

430 Ulriksen, Solveig Schult. "Le théâtre parisien en 1788, vu par trois acteurs danois." (The Parisian Theatre in 1788, Viewed by Three Danish Actors.) *RHT.* ; 34(2): 169-185. Notes.
France. 1788. Historical studies. ■Reactions of Danish actors to performances at the Théâtre Italien, the Comédie Française and the Opéra. Published journals of Michael Rosing and Joachim Daniel Preisler.

431 Wennersten, Robert. "Remembering Lenya." *PArts.* 1982 Mar.; 16(3): 55. Illus.: Photo.
Germany. 1920-1949. Biographical studies. ■Lotte Lenya discusses early life and marriage.

432 Carrano, Patrizia. *La Magnani — Il romanzo di una vita.* (Magnani: The Story of a Life.) Milan: Rizzoli; 1982. 275 pp. Illus.
Italy. 1908-1973. Biographies. ■Italian actress Anna Magnani.

433 Tognoloni, Daniela. "Un torneo di improvvisazione." (An Improvisation Tournament.) *QT.* 1982 Nov.; 5(18): 49-54. Notes.
Italy. 1982. Histories-sources. ■Tournament organized in Turin, May 13-16.

434 Savarese, Nicola. "Un riflesso orientale." (An Oriental Reflection.) *QT.* 1982 Nov.; 5(18): 55-63.
Japan. 1913-1930. Biographical studies. ■Mori Ritsuko, one of the first Japanese actresses to interpret Western repertory.

435 Anon. "Black Women in Entertainment: The Talent That Refuses to Be Denied." *Ebony.* 1982 Aug.; 37(10): 102-108.
USA. Twentieth cent. Histories-sources. ■Backgrounds and careers of Debbie Allen, Madge Sinclair, Nell Carter, Bever-Leigh Banfield and Cheryl Lynn.

436 Bartow, Arthur. "Auditions via Video." *AmTh.* 1982 Feb.; 3(11): 1-4.
USA. 1982. Histories-sources. ■Discusses Theatre Communications Group's pilot project in which actors audition for directors via videotape. Related to Media: Video forms.

437 Berg, Shelley C. "Yours in Pain — Al." *PS.* 1982 Summer; 6(2): 5-7. Illus.
USA. 1911-1922. Histories-sources. ■Personal and professional relationship of J.J. Shubert and Al Jolson.

438 Haun, Harry. "Ellen Burstyn." *Pb.* 1982 Nov.; 1(2): 14. Illus.
USA. 1960-1982. Histories-sources. ■Work as actress in *84 Charing Cross Road*, president of Actors' Equity and co-artistic director of Actor's Studio.

439 Johnson, Herschel. "Howard Rollins Jr. Hits the Big Time in *Ragtime*." *Ebony.* 1982 Jan.; 12(9): 13.
USA. Twentieth cent. Histories-sources. ■Theatre background of Rollins, star of film *Ragtime*. Related to Media: Film.

440 Johnson, Herschel. "Behind the Scenes with Actor Adolph Caesar." *Ebony.* 1982 Dec.; 13(8): 12.
USA. Twentieth cent. Histories-sources. ■Professional history of actor Adolph Caesar, lead in *A Soldier's Play*.

441 Knutson, Joel. "Henry Fonda: Coming Home to Theatre." *ThNe.* 1982 Fall; 14(7): 1, 3. Illus. Photo. B&W. 3.
USA. 1925-1982. Histories-sources. ■Omaha Community Playhouse, Henry Fonda Theatre Center and The Nebraska Theatre Caravan: Dorothy Mcguire and Jane Fonda in relation to Henry Fonda's career. Related to Media: Film.

442 Litvinoff, Valentina. "Movement Specialist's Views on Actors and Stretching." *ThNe.* 1982 Nov.; 14(8): 10.

THEATRE IN GENERAL — cont'd

USA. 1982. Technical studies. ▪Appropriate placement of stretching in actors' exercises.

443 Norment, Lynn. "*Ragtime* Star Is Rich in Talent: Howard Rollins Steals Show As Leading Character in Movie." *Ebony*. 1982 Feb.; 37(4): 115-122.
USA. 1960-1982. Histories-sources. ▪Details of Rollins' career. Related to Media: Film.

444 Norment, Lynn. "Lou Gossett, Jr.: The Agony and Ecstasy of Success." *Ebony*. 1982 Dec.; 38(2): 142-146.
USA. 1950-1980. Histories-sources. ▪Personal history of Black actor Lou Gossett, Jr.

445 Nouryeh, Andrea J. "When the Lord Was a Black Man: A Fresh Look at the Life of Richard Berry Harrison." *BALF*. 1982 Winter; 16(4): 142-146. Notes. Illus.: Photo.
USA. 1864-1935. Biographical studies. ▪Brief biography, emphasizing role in *Green Pastures*.

446 Prideaux, James. "Pennies in Heaven." *Pb*. 1982 Dec.; 1(3): 100-101. Illus.
USA. Great Britain. 1890-1959. Historical studies. ▪Accounts of famous actors and theatre personalities who died in poverty.

447 Wilkerson, Margaret B. "Glynn Turman, The Committed Actor." *CAM*. 1982 June; 4(6): 35. [Column: Bay Area Arts Forum.]
USA. Twentieth cent. Histories-sources. ▪Interview prior to world premiere of *Proud*.

Performance/performers: Singing/singers

448 Keveanos, John. "Carmen Miranda on Broadway." *PS*. 1982 Summer; 6(2): 2-3. Illus.
USA. 1939-1941. Biographical studies. ▪Summary of early career. Related to Music-Drama: Musical theatre.

Personnel

449 Feldman, Laurence. "Are Volunteers Filling the Gap?" *AmTh*. 1982 June; 4(3): 6-7. Notes. Illus.: Photo. B&W. 2.
USA. 1982. Histories-sources. ▪Survey of resident theatres on volunteer help.

450 Langley, Stephen. "Arts Management in America Yesterday and Tomorrow: A Perspective." *TA*. 1982; 37: 15-27.
USA. 1750-1982. Historical studies. ▪Overview of arts management.

451 Rhodes, Crystal V. "Third World Actors on the Boards: Opportunity and Possibility." *CAM*. 1982 Sep.; 4(9): 20-21. [Column: Bay Area Arts Forum.]
USA. Twentieth cent. Histories-sources. ▪Profiles of minority theatre artists and managers.

Personnel: Health and safety

452 Pohlen, Peter. "Unfallverhütungsvorschrift — Bühnen und Studios." (Accident Prevention Regulations for Stage and Studios.) *BtR*. 1982 June; 3: 27-28.
West Germany. 1982. Technical studies. ▪Safety regulations and need for revisions.

453 Reinl, Heinz. "Die Arbeitssicherheit im Theaterbetrieb." (Work Safety at the Theatre.) *BtR*. 1982 Aug.; 4: 24-25.
West Germany. Twentieth cent. Technical studies. ▪Accident prevention in the theatre.

Personnel: Labor relations

454 Guibert, Noëlle; Razgonnikoff, Jacqueline. "L'Emploi en question." (Type-Casting in Question.) *CF*. 1982 Feb.; 106: 3-14.
France. 1650-1980. Historical studies. ▪Contract-controlled casting practices.

455 Bartow, Arthur. "Bay Area Actors, Theatres Confront a Changing Future." *AmTh*. 1982 Sep.; 5(6): 1-3. Notes. Illus.: Photo. pr. B&W.
USA. 1972-1982. Histories-sources. ▪Dispute between Equity and Bay Area theatres over 'waiver agreement' and 'letters of agreement'.

456 Berg, Shelley C. "Performers' Contracts." *PS*. 1982 Winter; 6(1): 7-9. Illus.
USA. 1900-1925. Histories-sources. ▪Nature and range of contractual arrangements and disputes between Shuberts and performers.

457 Munk, Erika. "Equity And Inequities." *VV*. 1982 Jan. 26; 27(4): 76.
USA. Twentieth cent. Histories-sources. ▪Non-traditional casting and Actors' Equity policy of equal employment opportunities.

458 Gruber, Birgit. "'Sie sollen nicht denken, sondern spielen!': Erfahrungen eines Schauspielers mit der Theater Institution." ('You Shall Not Think, But Act!': Experiences of an Actor with the Theatre as Institution.) *Tzs*. 1982; 2: 4-14. Illus.
West Germany. Twentieth cent. Histories-sources. ▪Interview with actor Wolfgang Mentzel about working conditions of an actor in subsidized municipal theatres and in free groups: independence, democratization in free group Dreckschleuder.

459 Schneider, Horst. "Arbeitszeit kontra Kultur." (Working Hours against Culture.) *BtR*. 1982 Apr.; 2: 21.
West Germany. 1982. Histories-sources. ▪Theatre and labor law.

Personnel: Top management/producers

460 Hirsch, John. "My Life In Canadian Art." *CTR*. 1982 Spring; 34: 39-45. Illus.
Canada. 1930-1982. Histories-sources. ▪Career of artistic director John Hirsch.

461 "Ralf Långbacka à la direction du théâtre municipal de Helsinki/Ralf Långbacka to Manage the Helsinki City Theatre." *NFT*. 1982; 34: 20. Illus.
Finland. 1982. Histories-sources. ▪Appointment of Ralf Långbacka to replace Paavo Liski as manager of the Helsingin Kaupunginteatteri in August 1983.

462 Cypkin, Diane. "Of Madame Kalich and *The Kreutzer Sonata*." *PS*. 1982 Winter; 6(1): 7. Loc.: The Shubert Archive, 149 W. 45th Street New York, NY 10036.
USA. 1910-1926. Histories-sources. ▪Madame Kalich's association with the Shuberts.

463 Fellom-McGibboney, Martie. "Glamorous Gaby." *PS*. 1982 Summer; 6(2): 9-10. Illus.
USA. 1911-1914. Histories-sources. ▪The Shuberts' financial arrangements with, and promotion of, Gaby Deslys.

464 Gilbert, Edes. "The Business of Boards: An Argument for Active Trustees, and for Brave Chairmen." *AmTh*. 1982 Apr.; 4(1): 3-4. Notes.
USA. Twentieth cent. Histories-sources. ▪Role of trustee in resident theatre.

465 Nelson, Steve; Malnig, Julie. "Ruth Gordon on Mr. Lee." *PS*. 1982 Summer; 6(2): 13-14. Illus. Loc.: The Shubert Archive, 149 W. 45th Street New York, NY 10036.
USA. 1982. Histories-sources. ▪Interview with emphasis on private 'Mr. Lee' (Shubert).

466 Odom, Leigh George. "Sammie Dear..." *PS*. 1982 Winter; 6(1): 4-5. Illus.
USA. 1902-1905. Histories-specific. ▪Women's correspondence to Sam Shubert.

467 Rosenthal, Judy C. "The International Shuberts." *PS*. 1982 Winter; 6(1): 9-10. Loc.: The Shubert Archive, 149 W. 45th St., New York, NY 10036.
USA. 1900-1925. Histories-sources. ▪Contracts and agreements between Shuberts and authors, composers and playwrights.

THEATRE IN GENERAL — cont'd

468 Hofmann, Jürgen. "Kultur im Widerspruch: Münchner Freiheit oder Alle freuen sich über die Koordination." (Culture in Contradiction: Munich Freedom or All Are Pleased with the Coordination.) *Tzs.* 1982; 1: 34-43.
West Germany. Twentieth cent. Histories-sources. ■Appointment of August Everding as General Manager of the Bavarian state theatres.

Plays/playwrights

469 Filewod, Alan. "Collective Creation: Process, Politics, and Poetics." *CTR.* 1982 Spring; 34: 46-58. Notes. Illus.
Canada. 1970-1982. Histories-sources. ■Collective creation as theatrical form.

470 Blau, Herbert. *Take Up the Bodies: Theater at the Vanishing Point.* Urbana: Univ. of Illinois P; 1982. xxv, 299 pp. Pref. Illus.: Photo. B&W. 28.
USA. 1960-1980. Histories-sources. ■Personal critical memoirs concerned particularly with the author's productions and their dramatic values.

471 McClintock, Ernie. "Published Criticism and Its Positive Effect on Black Theatre." *OvA.* ; 10: 9, 11.
USA. Twentieth cent. Critical studies. ■Reviews of plays help Black theatre, suggests methods of engendering reviews.

472 Rogoff, Gordon. "On Not Attending Theater." *VV.* 1982 Oct. 5; 27(40): 103.
USA. 1980-1982. Critical studies. ■Criticism of theatre's self-conscious attempts to be impressive.

473 Tanzman, Carol M. "The Young Playwrights' Festival: Serious Beginnings." *ChTR.* 1982 Summer; 31(3): 9-11.
USA. 1980-1982. Histories-sources. ■Gerald Chapman's workshops for eight- to eighteen-year-old playwrights.

474 "16 Kritiker beschreiben Höhepunkte der Spielzeit 1981/82." (Sixteen Theatre Critics Describe Highlights of the 1981-82 Season.) *TH.* 1982; 1(13): 5-64. Pref. Illus.
West Germany. 1981-1982. Reviews of performances. ■Includes interview with actor Bernhard Minetti about production of Goethe's *Faust*, directed by Klaus Michael Grüber at the Freie Volksbühne (Berlin).

Plays/playwrights: Adaptations

475 Schwanbom, Per. "Den undansmusslade dramatiken." (The Hidden Drama.) *Entre.* 1982; 9(1): 22-23. Illus.
Sweden. 1980-1981. Histories-sources. ■Negative response to adaptation of novels for stage: Franz Kafka's *Amerika* and Alexander Weiss' *Skårvor* at Dramaten.

Plays/playwrights: Genres

476 Swortzell, Lowell. "New Faces: Professional Playwrights Discover Young Audiences." *ChTR.* 1982 Summer; 31(3): 3-4.
USA. 1950-1982. Histories-sources. ■Contributions to children's theatre by important playwrights.

Plays/playwrights: Plot/subject/theme

477 Helbing, Terry. "Curtain Raisers." *GTAN.* 1982 Aug.; 4(1): 1-2.
USA. 1981-1983. Histories-sources. ■Survey of American consciousness of gays and lesbians in live performance, television and film. Winners of the Gay Theatre Alliance 1981-82 International Gay Playwriting Contest and guidelines for the 1982-83 contest. Related to Media.

Plays/playwrights: Structure/language

478 Knapp, Bettina L. "Collective Creation from Paris to Jerusalem: An Interview with Liliane Atlan." *ThM.* 1981-82 Winter ; 13(1): 43-50. Illus.
France. 1944-1980. Histories-sources. ■Interview on improvisation and collective creation in theatre and video.

479 Black, Sebastian. "Makers of Real Shapes: Christopher Hampton and His Story-tellers." *MD.* 1982 June; 25(2): 207-221. Notes.
Great Britain. Twentieth cent. Critical studies. ■Use of dramatic monologue as dominant stylistic device.

480 Davis, Jed H. "They're *Not* 'Writing Down' to Children." *ThNe.* 1982 Mar.; 14(3): 5-6. Biblio.
USA. 1982. Histories-sources. ■Subject matter, production styles and international dimensions of writing and producing plays for children.

Public relations: Advertising and development

481 Robinson, Vivian. "10th Annual Audelco Recognition Awards." *OvA.* 1982 Nov.; 10: 17-36. Illus.
USA. 1971-1982. Histories-sources. ■Listing of all Audelco (Audience Development Committee) awards, standards for selection and brief biographical material on selected winners.

Public relations: Community relations

482 Wallach, Susan Levi. "Mark Lamos and William Stewart: Art and Management at Hartford Stage." *ThCr.* 1982 Jan.; 16(1): 15, 32-38. Illus.
USA. 1982. Histories-sources. ■Discussion of artistic decisions that affect relation of theatre to community.

Public relations: Press relations

483 Abrams, Anne. "Press Agents and ATPAM." *ThCr.* 1982 Aug.-Sep.; 16(7): 36, 97-102.
USA. Twentieth cent. Critical studies. ■Interview with Merle Debuskey and Harvey Sabinson about training for press agents and ATPAM (Association of Theatrical Press Agents & Managers).

484 Levy, Suzanne. "A. Toxen Worm, 1910-1921." *PS.* 1982 Summer; 6(2): 7-9. Illus.
USA. 1910-1921. Histories-sources. ■Worm's responsibilities as press agent for the Shuberts.

485 Sobieski, Lynn; Nelson, Steve. "Reminiscences from the Shubert Press Department, 1922-1949." *PS.* 1982 Winter; 6(1): 11-12. Illus.
USA. Histories-sources. ■Impressions of the Shuberts and their press department.

Relation to other fields: Anthropology

486 Turner, Victor. *From Ritual to Theatre: The Human Seriousness of Play.* New York: Performing Arts Journal Publications; 1982. 127 pp. (Performance Studies Series 1.) Pref. Index.
Multi-period. Studies of theories/theorists. ■Social drama and dramatic ritual: acting in everyday life and everyday life in acting.

487 Barba, Eugenio. "Theatre Anthropology." *TDR.* 1982 Summer; 26(2): 5-32.
Asia. Twentieth cent. Studies of theories/theorists. ■Theoretical study of socio-cultural and physiological behavior of the theatrical performer as seen through various non-Western performance theorists.

488 Kidd, Ross. "Reclaiming Culture: Indigenous Performers Take Back Their Show." *Tk.* 1982 Nov.-Dec.; 3(1): 32-47. Illus.
Canada. 1982. Histories-sources. ■Report on the organization, achievements and frustrations of the second international Indigenous People's Theatre Celebration.

489 Joseph, Garnet. "Carifuna Cultural Group." *Tk.* 1982 Nov.-Dec.; 3(1): 48-49. Illus.
Dominica. 1978-1982. Historical studies. ■History of Caribs and efforts to reconstruct their culture.

490 Wakabayashi, Akira. "Ainu." *Tk.* 1982 Nov.-Dec.; 3(1): 51. Illus.

THEATRE IN GENERAL — cont'd

Japan. 1600-1982. Histories-sources. ■Remains of ancient Ainu culture, which is struggling to preserve its language, crafts and performance arts.

Relation to other fields: Education

491 Gressler, Thomas H. "Theatre in Liberal Arts/Liberal Arts Vs. Theatre." *ThNe.* 1982 Mar.; 14(3): 12.
USA. 1982. Critical studies. ■Argues that theatre programs are in crucial position in liberal arts programs because theatre provides both cognitive and affective experiences, thus educating both intellectually and emotionally.

Relation to other fields: Philosophy

492 Rapp, Uri. "Simulation and Imagination: Mimesis as Play." *MuK.* 1982; 28(2): 67-86. Notes.
Europe. Multi-period. Studies of theories/theorists. ■Discussion of concepts: simulation, mimesis, semblance, representation, fantasy, imagination, creativity and their relevance for the comprehension of the make-believe character of play. Discusses theories of Gregory Bateson, Roger Caillos, Erving Goffman, Ralph Barton Perry, William Stern, Eric Klinger and Rosemary Gordon.

493 Milosz, Czeslaw; Vallee, Lillian, transl. "Who is Gombrowicz?" *PerAJ.* 1982; 6(3): 7-22.
Poland. Studies of theories/theorists. ■Importance of Witold Gombrowicz's writings. Infl. by Fëdor Michajlovič Dostoevskij.

494 Blau, Herbert. *Blooded Thought: Occasions of Theatre.* New York: Performing Arts Journal Publications; 1982. 166 pp. Illus.: Photo. B&W.
USA. 1950-1982. Critical studies. ■Investigation of selected plays and their productions. Grp/movt: Postmodernism.

495 Fichandler, Zelda. "A Test of Resonance, A Test of Life." *AmTh.* 1982 Jan.; 3(10): 4-6. Notes.
USA. 1982. Histories-sources. ■Dramatic experience as relevant to the human experience.

Relation to other fields: Politics

496 Davies, Robertson. "Robertson Davies on the Young Vincent Massey." *THC.* 1982 Spring; 3(1): 97-100. Notes. Illus.
Canada. 1982. Histories-sources. ■A commentary on the late Vincent Massey, former Canadian Governor-General and noted patron.

497 Wendrich, Fritz. "Politisches Theater — Volkstheater. Fragen der Production und der Rezeption." (Political Theater, Popular Theater: Questions of Production and Reception.) *TZ.* 1982 Mar.; 37(3): 3-4.
East Germany. 1982. Histories-sources. ■Political values through theatre.

498 Cosgrove, Stuart; Mathers, Peter. "Urgent Theatre: And the Practices of Cultural Democracy." *Tk.* Sep.-Oct.; 2(6): 6-10. Notes.
England. Ireland. 1978-1982. Critical studies. ■Discussion of theatre's responses to demands of political immediacy as exemplified by playwright Trevor Griffiths.

499 Brookes, Chris. "Notes on Nicaragua: Two Theatres." *Tk.* 1982 Mar.-Apr.; 2(3): 18-20. Illus.
Nicaragua. 1970-1982. Historical studies. ■Los Alpes and Nistayalero, two companies serving illiterate audiences with social and political theatre.

500 Kidd, Ross. "Testimony from Nicaragua: An Interview with Nidia Bustos." *Tk.* 1982 Sep.-Oct.; 2(6): 32-40. Illus.
Nicaragua. 1970-1982. Histories-sources. ■Nidia Bustos, coordinator of MECATE (Nicaragua's Movement of Campesino Artistic and Theatrical Expression), answers questions about the rise and development of popular political theatre groups.

501 "Teatern i fängelse." (The Theatre in Prison.) *Entre.* 1982; 9(1): 5.

Poland. 1981. Histories-sources. ■List of actors, playwrights and other theatre people believed to be in prison.

502 Burian, Jarka. "Poland's Theatre in Crisis." *AmTh.* 1982 Nov.; 4(8): 1-4. Notes. Illus.: Photo. B&W. 6.
Poland. 1950-1982. Histories-sources. ■Brief history of recent Polish theatre, with emphasis on effects of martial law.

503 Englund, Claes. "Intervjuer." (Interviews.) *Entre.* 1982; 9(1): 6-8. Illus.
Poland. 1956-1982. Histories-sources. ■Katarzyna Hanuskiewicz, actress, and Leo Kantor, scholar, discuss trends in Polish theatre and politics.

504 Klimt, Jan; Gwozdz, Z.P. "Polen: *Kolas* werden weggeklatscht." (Poland: *Kolas* Gets the Hook.) *Bühne.* 1982 Oct.: 33-35.
Poland. 1981-1982. Histories-sources. ■Theatre after proclamation of martial law, 'inner migration' of artists, boycotting of conformist artists and governmental institutions.

505 Mellgren, Thomas. "Arbetarspelen: Dåtiden — samtiden — framtiden." (Labor Play: Past — Present — Future.) *Entre.* ; 9(4): 3-7. Illus.
Sweden. Twentieth cent. Histories-sources. ■Amateur theatre based upon local labor problems has impact, but genre faces uncertain future.

506 Adams, Don; Goldbard, Arlene. "Animation: What's In a Name?" *Tk.* 1982 May-June; 2(4): 11-13.
USA. Canada. 1950-1982. Studies of theories/theorists. ■Definition and function of community animation theatre programs.

507 Adams, Don; Goldbard, Arlene. "Disarming Art." *Tk.* 1982 May-June; 2(4): 38-39.
USA. 1982. Histories-sources. ■Plans for anti-nuclear protests by arts and community organizations.

508 Anon. "Leading Voices: Our Style of Protest." *Ebony.* 1982 Oct.; 13(6): 78-79, 132-136.
USA. Twentieth cent. Histories-sources. ■Interviews on Black protest theatre with leading figures, including Amiri Imamu Baraka (LeRoi Jones).

509 Benedetti, Robert. "American Assembly: How Valuable an Arts Overview?" *ThNe.* 1982 Apr.; 14(4): 4, 14.
USA. 1950-1982. Histories-sources. ■Efforts to garner financial support from Federal government and other constituencies and a plea for independence of arts policies from politics.

510 Fletcher, Winona L. "Let It Be Known: I Was There, a Report of the New Commissioner to the United States National Commission for UNESCO." *ThNe.* 1982 Mar.; 14(3): 3. Illus. Photo. B&W.
USA. 1982. Histories-sources. ■Report on American Theatre Association's role as a non-governmental organization, and on publications about UNESCO, including important addresses.

511 Malpede, Karen. "Arts Alive: Protest & Survive." *Tk.* 1982 May-June; 2(4): 37-39.
USA. 1982. Histories-sources. ■Plans for arts activities and public demonstrations during season of anti-nuclear protest.

512 Marranca, Bonnie. "Robert Jay Lifton: Art and the Imagery of Extinction." *PerAJ.* 1982; 6(3): 51-66. Illus.: Photo. [Interview.]
USA. Twentieth cent. Critical studies. ■Therapeutic values of death, extinction and violence in theatre.

513 Marranca, Bonnie. "Nuclear Theatre." *PerAJ.* 1982; 6(3): 46-50. Illus.: Photo.
USA. Twentieth cent. Linguistic studies. ■Application of theatrical terminology to nuclear war and weaponry.

514 Marranca, Bonnie. "Nuclear Theater." *VV.* 1982 June 29; 27(26): 103-104.
USA. Twentieth cent. Linguistic studies. ■Use of theatre metaphor by those who write about prospects of nuclear war.

THEATRE IN GENERAL — cont'd

515 Munk, Erika. "Cross Left." *VV*. 1982 Apr 20; 27(16): 92. [Editorial column appearing irregularly.]
USA. 1982. Histories-sources. ■First public meeting of Performing Artists for Nuclear Disarmament.

516 Rogoff, Gordon. "Making Distinctions." *VV*. 1982 Apr 20; 27(16): 93.
USA. 1982. Histories-sources. ■Boston Symphony Orchestra's refusal to permit Vanessa Redgrave to perform.

Relation to other fields: Psychology

517 Schaper, Karen K. "Psychological Research and Its Implication for Creative Drama." *ChTR*. 1982 Winter; 31(1): 16-18. Notes.
Twentieth cent. Studies of research/researchers. ■Involvement in creative dramatics aids development of role-taking skills and decreases egocentrism.

518 Volli, Ugo. "Pratiche in attesa di teoria." (Experiences Waiting for Theory.) *QT*. 1982 Nov.; 5(18): 83-88.
Italy. Twentieth cent. Histories-sources. ■Psychophysical training conducted at Volterra by international group L'Avventura. Infl. by Jerzy Grotowski.

519 Woodruff, Marci. "Erikson's Theory of Psycho-Social Development: The Socialization of Developmental Drama." *ChTR*. 1982 Spring; 31(2): 22-25. Notes.
USA. Twentieth cent. Studies of theories/theorists. ■Theories of Erik Erikson and Moses Goldberg related to creative dramatics and children's theatre.

Relation to other fields: Religion

520 Mazouer, Charles. "Théâtre et mission pendant la conquête du Chablais (1597-1598)." (Theatre and Mission during the Conquest of the Chablais, 1597-1598.) *DSS*. 1982 Oct.-Dec.; 137: 399-412.
France. Switzerland. 1597-1598. Historical studies. ■Didactic theatre and missionary work in Calvinist territory during the Counter-Reformation in Savoy.

521 Lombardi, Giovanni. "Il Francescanesimo e il teatro medievale." (Franciscanism and Medieval Theatre.) *QT*. 1982 Nov.; 5 (18): 168-171.
Italy. Medieval period. Histories-sources. ■Report on a national meeting on Franciscanism and medieval theatre.

Relation to other fields: Sociology

522 Rojas, Luis. "Ayni Ruway." *Tk*. 1982 Nov.-Dec.; 3(1): 49-50. Illus.
Bolivia. 1970-1982. Historical studies. ■Movement to organize and educate native communities for their economic and cultural advancement.

523 Anon. "Was erwartet die Gesellschaft vom Theater?" (What Does Society Expect from the Theatre?)*TZ*. 1982 Feb.; 37: 9.
East Germany. Twentieth cent. Critical studies. ■Industrial physicist's thoughts on socially responsible theatre.

524 John, Hans-Rainer. "Erkennen und Bekennen." (Discerning and Confessing.) *TZ*. 1982 Jan.; 37(1): 4-7. [First of a series.]
East Germany. Twentieth cent. Histories-sources. ■Interview with Hans-Peter Minetti on social value of theatre work after the Tenth Party Congress.

525 Lorenz, Siegfried. "Wechselwirkung von Theater und Publikum." (Interaction of Theater and Public.) *TZ*. 1982 Feb.; 37 (2): 5-6. [Official view from Administrative Secretary of Karl-Marx-Stadt.]
East Germany. 1982. Histories-sources. ■Place of government agencies in promoting theatre to instill appropriate social values.

526 Wekwerth, Manfred. *Theater in Diskussion: Notate, Gespräche, Polemiken.* (Theatre in Discussion: Notes, Discourses, Polemics.) Berlin: Henschel; 1982. 342 pp. Pref. Index.
East Germany. 1970-1980. Critical studies. ■Collection of essays on social aspects of theatre.

527 Schechner, Richard. "Ramlila of Ramnager." *NCPA*. 1982 Sep.-Dec.; 11(3-4): 67-98. Notes.
India. 1976-1978. Historical studies. ■Observations exploring Ramlila's theatrical, social and religious significance.

528 Abah, Oga S.; Etherton, Michael. "The Samaru Projects: Street Theatre in Northern Nigeria." *ThR*. 1982 Autumn; 7(3): 222-234. Notes.
Nigeria. Twentieth cent. Histories-sources. ■Street theatre performance about social problems in underdeveloped suburban areas required as project for first year students at Ahmadu Bello University, Zaria.

529 Barranger, Milly S. "Theatre Women Share Career Perspectives on Sex Bias." *ThNe*. 1982 Dec.; 14(9): 1, 10.
USA. 1980-1982. Histories-sources. ■Career problems of women in theatre. Grp/movt: Feminism.

530 Goldbard, Arlene. "The Challenge of Cultural Action." *Tk*. 1982 Mar.-Apr.; 2(3): 13.
USA. Nineteenth cent. Histories-sources. ■Methods of achieving cultural democracy with suggestions about how artists can interact with community for community's benefit.

531 Hazlett, John. "Casting for the Human Struggle." *CAM*. 1982 Nov.; 4(11): 21.
USA. 1982. Histories-sources. ■Charles Gordone's role in establishing American Stage in Berkeley, and casting Black actors in traditionally white roles.

532 Leavitt, Robert. "The Search for a New Poetic of Theatre." *AmTh*. 1982 Nov.; 4(8): 8-10. Notes. Illus.: Photo. B&W. 1.
USA. Europe. Multi-period. Critical studies. ■Examines developing relationship of theatre to culture since the 18th century.

533 Niemi, Loren. "Gypsy Geographer." *Tk*. 1982 Sep.-Oct.; 2(6): 18-19. [Irregular correspondence.]
USA. 1982. Histories-sources. ■Itinerant storyteller reports on Women's Theatre Project's investigation of the oppression of women by organized religions in *Women Arise!* and *Between Silence and Light II* by Yen Lu Wong.

534 Norris, Sababu C. "Waiting for Whitey: An Examination of the Reviews by White Critics of *Ceremonies in Dark Old Men.*" *Encore*. 1982 Apr.: 14-17.
USA. 1960-1969. Studies of criticism/critics. ■Racial biases are evident in white critics' reviews of *Ceremonies in Dark Old Men*.

535 Patterson, Douglas L. "The Living Story." *Tk*. 1982 Jan.-Feb.; 2(2): 21.
USA. 1981-1982. Studies of theories/theorists. ■Storytelling as self-identification, and collective playwriting. Related to Popular Entertainment.

536 Rosenblatt, Bernard S. "Ethics and Excellence: A Challenge to Children's Theatre Producers." *ThNe*. 1982 Nov.; 14(8): 15-16.
USA. 1970-1982. Critical studies. ■Developments of the past decade and future considerations: ethics, excellence, performance and education.

537 Dresen, Adolf; Neuenfels, Hans; Wendt, Ernst; Becker, Peter von; Iden, Peter; Rischbieter, Henning. "Theater und Gesellschaft — ein Gespräch." (Theatre and Society: A Conversation.) *TH*. 1982; 13: 67-82.
West Germany. Twentieth cent. Histories-sources. ■Discussion among directors and critics about theatre's relation to society and general policy, national theatre and national identity, pressure for legitimation, role of tradition.

THEATRE IN GENERAL — cont'd

Scores/composers

538 Dömling, Wolfgang. "Stilisierung und Spiel. Über Igor Strawinskys Bühnenwerke und ihren Zusammenhang mit dem Theaterkonzept W.E. Meyerholds." (Stylization and Play: On Igor Stravinsky's Works for the Theatre and Their Relation to the Theatre Concept of W.E. Meyerhold.) *MuK*. 1982; 28(1): 18-34. Notes.
USSR. 1900-1930. Critical studies. ■Stylization and alienation in anti-illusionistic theatre, applied by Stravinsky in his compositions of operas and ballets, and by Tairov and Diaghilev. Chapter on influence of Meyerhold. Related to Music-Drama: Opera.

Staging

539 Feral, Josette; Lyons, Terese, transl. "Performance and Theatricality: The Subject Demystified." *MD*. 1982 Mar.; 25(1): 170-181. Notes.
Twentieth cent. Studies of theories/theorists. ■Analysis of the fundamental characteristics of performance and theatricality.

540 "Les femmes finlandaises à l'étranger/Our Women Abroad." *NFT*. 1982; 34: 16.
Finland. Iceland. Sweden. Norway. Twentieth cent. ■Ritva Siikala taught acting in Iceland, Ritva Holmberg directed *Marathon Dance* in Sweden, Tytti Oittinen directed a play by Ionesco in Norway.

541 Aliverti, Maria Ines. "Note e documenti sulla *Santa Uliva* di Jacques Copeau (1932-1933)." (Notes and Documents on Jacques Copeau's production of *Santa Uliva*, 1932-1933.) *TArch*. 1982 Jan.; 6: 12-103. Notes. Illus.
Italy. 1932-1933. Histories-reconstruction. ■Annotated correspondence of Silvio d'Amico, Guido M. Gatti and Jacques Copeau on staging of *Santa Uliva*.

542 Tinterri, Alessandro. "Padova 1937. Restauro d'un 'Mistero'." (Padua 1937: Restoration of a 'Mystery'.) *TArch*. 1982 Jan.; 6: 104-109. Notes. Illus.
Italy. 1937. Histories-reconstruction. ■*Mistero della Natività, Passione e Resurrezione de Nostro Signore (Mystery of Nativity, Passion and Resurrection of Our Lord)* performed by students of Accademia Reale d'Arte Drammatica in Rome under direction of Tatiana Pavlova, based on text edited by Silvio d'Amico.

543 Trauth, Suzanne. "One on the Aisle." *CueM*. 1982 Fall-Winter; 61(1): 5.
USA. England. 1981-1982. Histories-sources. ■Imported English plays are bright spots in professional American theatre.

544 Stössel, Marleen. "Der unsichtbare Zauber oder Notizen aus der Werkstatt." (The Invisible Glamour or Notes from the Workshop.) *TH*. 1982 Aug.; 8: 4-18.
West Germany. 1982. Histories-sources. ■Rehearsals for *Macbeth*, produced at Bühnen der Stadt Köln, directed by Luc Bondy.

Staging: Directing/directors

545 Pietzsch, Ingeborg. "Gertrud-Elisabeth Zillmer." *TZ*. 1982 Mar.; 37(3): 15-17. [Conversation with a director.]
East Germany. 1982. Histories-sources. ■Zillmer discusses directing to emphasize social values.

546 Pietzsch, Ingeborg. "Mehr Phantasie! Gespräch mit dem Regisseur Karl-Friedrich Zimmermann, Magdeburg." (More Fantasy: A Conversation with the Director Karl-Friedrich Zimmermann of Magdeburg.) *TZ*. 1982 Nov.; 37(11): 57-59. Illus.
East Germany. Twentieth cent. Histories-sources. ■Zimmermann's work with children's theatre. Grp/movt: Theater für Junge Zuschauer.

547 Ullrich, Peter. "Denn nur der grosse Gegenstand..." (Only the Great Subject...)*TZ*. 1982 Mar.; 37(3): 4-5. Illus.: Photo. [Column.]
East Germany. 1982. Critical studies. ■Problems of presenting great historical themes on the modern stage.

548 Wolfram, Gerhard. "Vergangenheit als Horizont eigener Möglichkeiten. Beobachtungen in unserer jüngeren Theatergeschichte." (The Past as a Horizon of Future Possibilities: Observations on Our Recent Theatre History.) *TZ*. 1982 Sep.; 37(9): 12-15.
East Germany. Twentieth cent. Historical studies. ■Cultural heritage and its value for today's theatre.

549 Mellgren, Thomas. "Kalle Holmberg." *Entre*. 1982; 9(5): 25-33. Illus.
Finland. 1966-1982. Histories-sources. ■Interview with Holmberg on director as author, rehearsal process, and his work with theatre, opera and film.

550 Aslan, Odette; Strachan, Fiona, transl. "From Giorgio Strehler to Victor García." *MD*. 1982 Mar.; 25(1): 113-126. Notes. Illus.: Photo. B&W.
France. 1978. Historical studies. ■Discussion of production concept, rehearsals, and director's influence on the actors, using Strehler's production of *Holiday Trilogy (La Trilogia della Villeggiatura)* by Goldoni and Victor García's production of *Gilgamesh*.

551 Champagne, Lenora. "Armand Gatti: Toward Spectacle without Spectators." *ThM*. 1981-82 Winter; 13(1): 26-42. Illus.
France. 1955-1981. Historical studies. ■Major projects of collective leader: Paris, Brussels (non-theatre space), Brabant Wallon (open air procession), Saint-Nazaire (multi-media), Isle d'Abian (video, opera) and Derry, Northern Ireland (film).

552 Cohn, Ruby. "Benmussa's Planes." *ThM*. 1981-82 Winter; 13(1): 51-54. Illus.
France. England. 1976-1981. Reviews of performances. ■Descriptions of London productions of Renaud-Barrault Company directed by dramaturg Simone Benmussa.

553 Dort, Bernard. "Le mystère Grüber." (The Grüber Mystery.) *CF*. 1982 Sep.; 111: 19.
France. Germany. 1967-1982. Critical studies. ■Klaus Michael Grüber, director of Goethe's *Faust* at the Théâtre Odéon: an evocation of his past work and recurring images.

554 Hullberg, Inger. "Den 'Store' Vitez." (The 'Great' Vitez.) *Entre*. 1982; 9(3): 22-23. Illus.
France. 1968-1982. Histories-sources. ■Antoine Vitez's controversial productions of Goethe's *Faust*, Racine's *Britannicus* and Pierre Goyota's *Grave for Five Thousand Soldiers (Tombeau pour cinq mille soldats)* at Théâtre National de Chaillot focusing on hell and using violence and stylization.

555 Szafkó, Péter. "Sándor Hevesi and the Thália Society in Hungary." *THSt*. 1982; 2: 115-124. Notes. Illus.
Hungary. 1901-1939. Studies of theories/theorists. ■Career and contributions of major figure in modern Hungarian theatre as director, theorist, translator and playwright. Mentions Nemzeti Színház (National Theatre) and Thália Theatre of Budapest, Gordon Craig, Hungarian productions of Shakespeare, Shaw, Ibsen, Gorky and Chekhov.

556 Meldolesi, Claudio. "I Teatri possibili di Vito Pandolfi — Con un'appendice su Gadda." (The Possible Theatres of Vito Pandolfi — With An Appendix On Gadda.) *QT*. 1982 Nov.; 5(18): 5-31.
Italy. 1947-1955. Historical studies. ■Three productions by Vito Pandolfi: Cocteau's *The Eiffel Tower Wedding Party (Les Mariés de la Tour Eiffel)*, Toller's *Brokenbrow (Hinkemann)* and Gadda's *Skirt Buffoon (Gonnella buffone)*. In appendix, text of *Gonnella buffone*, Gadda's adaptation from Matteo Bandello's tales.

557 Braun, Edward. *The Director and the Stage: From Naturalism to Grotowski*. New York, NY: Holmes and Meier; 1982. 218 pp. Pref. Notes. Index. Illus.: Photo. B&W. 10.
Russia. Germany. England. France. Poland. 1890-1980. Histories-specific. ■Rise of the director, concentrating on Georg II of Saxe-Meiningen, André Antoine, Gordon Craig, Konstantin S. Stanislavski,

THEATRE IN GENERAL — cont'd

Max Reinhardt, Vsevolod E. Meyerhold, Erwin Piscator, Bertolt Brecht, Antonin Artaud, Jerzy Grotowski.

558 Golub, Spencer. "Mysteries of the Self: The Visionary Theatre of Nikolai Evreinov." *THSt.* 1982; 2: 15-35. Notes. Illus.
Russia. 1879-1953. Studies of theories/theorists. ■Theatrical theories, plays and productions, including *The Theatre of the Soul (V Kulisach Duši)*, and *The Storming of the Winter Palace (Shturm Zimnego dvoltsa)*.

559 Ödeen, Mats. "Agera, mina damer och herrar!" (Take Action, Ladies and Gentlemen!)*Entre.* 1982; 9(4): 16-17.
Sweden. 1968-1982. Histories-sources. ■After period of emphasis on actors, there is now demand for strong, effective directors. Infl. by Postmodernism.

560 Bartow, Arthur. "Home of the Freelance — and the Brave." *AmTh.* 1982 Dec.; 4(9): 6-7. Notes. Illus.: Photo. B&W. 4.
USA. 1982. Histories-sources. ■Roundtable discussion with directors Israel Hicks, Dean Irby, Jonas Jurasas, Stephen Katz, John Lane, Robert MacBeth and Julie Taymor.

561 Keating, Keith. "The Human Form as Dramatic Symbol: An Interview with G. Wilson Knight." *LPer.* 1982 Nov.; 3(1): 49-59. Notes. Illus.: Photo. [Held in October 1980, during Knight's recital tour in the USA.]
USA. Europe. 1980. Critical studies. ■Knight's use of nudity in character portrayal.

562 Parent, Jennifer. "Arthur Hopkin's Production of Sophie Treadwell's *Machinal*." *TDR.* 1982 Spring; 26(1): 87-100.
USA. 1928. Histories-reconstruction. ■Performance history of Arthur Hopkin's staging of *Machinal* by Sophie Treadwell at Plymouth Theatre in New York, 1928.

563 Rogoff, Gordon. "Malle Treatment." *VV.* 1982 Apr. 6; 27(14): 87-88. Illus.
USA. Twentieth cent. Critical studies. ■Suggests that Louis Malle confuses theatre with film in his stage direction. Related to Media: Film.

564 Roth, Martha. "An Interview with Martha Boesing." *Tk.* 1982 Jan.-Feb.; 2(2): 4-5. Illus.
USA. 1950-1982. Biographical studies. ■Playwright-director discusses her education as radical-feminist theatre worker.

565 Krengel-Strudthoff, Inge. "'... doch hart im Raume stossen sich die Sachen' Von der Einfachheit im Theater." (The Problem of Being Uncomplicated: On Simplicity in the Theatre.) *BtR.* 1982 June; 3: 24-26. B&W.
West Germany. Twentieth cent. Histories-sources. ■Difficulties of using an 'empty space' rather than realistic settings.

Training

566 Bandettini, Anna. "Improvvisazione teatrale e Theatre Sport." (Theatrical Improvisation and Theatre Sport.) *QT.* 1982 Nov.; 5(18): 40-48.
Canada. 1956-1981. Studies of theories/theorists. ■Improvisation in Keith Johnston's performance theory and realization by his group, Theatre Sport.

567 Doolittle, Joyce. "The Child: A Place in Life." *CTR.* 1982 Summer; 35: 50-56. Illus.
Canada. Twentieth cent. Critical studies. ■Creative drama teacher explains when and why theatre training begins.

568 Barba, Eugenio. "The Way of Opposites." *CTR.* 1982 Summer; 35: 12-37. Illus.
Denmark. Twentieth cent. Studies of theories/theorists. ■Experimental director discusses nature of training and its implications for future of theatre.

569 Guarino, Raimondo. "Memoria dell'improvvisazione." (Memory in Improvisation.) *QT.* 1982 Nov.; 5(18): 32-39. Notes.

Europe. Japan. Twentieth cent. Technical studies. ■Characteristics of improvisation in Occidental theatre and in classical Japanese theatre. Infl. by Konstantin Sergeevič Stanislavskij; Jerzy Grotowski; Eugenio Barba.

570 Aptekar, Sheldon I. "Director Training Profiled." *ThNe.* 1982 Jan.; 14(1): 5, 10.
USA. 1980-1982. Histories-sources. ■Philosophy of director training programs in degree-granting institutions.

571 Geiger, Ted. "Affiliate." *Encore.* 1982 Apr.: 10-12.
USA. Twentieth cent. Histories-sources. ■Technical internships for minorities in casino theatre.

572 Schechner, Richard. "The Performer: Training Interculturally." *CTR.* 1982 Summer; 35: 38-47. Illus.
USA. Canada. 1982. Studies of theories/theorists. ■Talk given by director and theorist on performer training.

573 Soviet Ministry of Culture. "The Critic: A Soviet Training Model." *CTR.* 1982 Summer; 35: 61-66. Pref.
USSR. 1970. Studies of criticism/critics. ■Outline for five year training period for drama critics.

574 Himstedt, Hellmut. "Lehrgang für Requisiteure." (Courses for Property Managers.) *BtR.* 1982 Aug.; 4: 18.
West Germany. 1982. Technical studies. ■Description of course offered in Frankfurt.

Training: Studies of theories/theorists

575 Latham, David. "The Performer: Let's Train the Actor, Let's Break the Rules." *CTR.* 1982 Summer; 35: 48-49. Illus.
Canada. Twentieth cent. ■Director of Vancouver's Playhouse Acting School calls for return to meaningful self-exploration in actor training.

Training: Teaching methods

576 Ritch, Pamela. "Pi — From the Editor." *ChTR.* 1982 Spring; 31(2): 2.
Twentieth cent. Studies of research/researchers. ■Goals of research in creative dramatics and children's theatre.

577 Barba, Eugenio; Blum, Lambert; Falke, Christoph. "Schauspieler-Training an Eugenio Barbas Odin Teatret (Holstebro/Dänemark)." (Actor-training at Eugenio Barba's Odin Teatret.) *Tzs.* 1982; 2: 63-84. Biblio. Illus.
Denmark. 1966-1982. Historical studies. ■Documentation of actor training with German translation of article published in Barba's *The Floating Islands*.

578 Schechner, Richard. "Défense et illustration de la formation mécanique (II)." (In Defense of Mechanical Training.) *PrTh.* 1982 Winter-Spring; 14-15: 56-76. Notes. [Second part of a transcribed lecture. The first part was published in volume 10 of *La Grande Réplique* (1980-81) — now *Pratiques Théâtrales*. For both articles Schechner prefers the title, 'Performer Training Interculturally'.]
Europe. Asia. North America. 1982. Studies of theories/theorists. ■Two contrasting methods of training performers: Euro-American method of interpretation and Asiatic method of direct transmission of a role using body as an instrument. Includes references to Brecht, Meyerhold, Foreman, Grotowski, *kathākali*, and *nō*. Related to Dance-Drama.

579 Coccheri, Paolo. "La formazione dell'attore negli Anni Ottanta: metodologia e ricerca." (Actor Training in the Eighties: Methodology and Research.) *QT.* 1982 Aug.; 5(27): 201-205.
Italy. 1980-1982. Technical studies. ■Adoption by Actor's International Laboratory of Florence of miming method created by Orazio Costa.

580 Mouton, Kobus. "Voorbereiding vir die vertolkingsaksie: herskep deur herskepping." (Preparation for Interpretation: Creation Through Re-creating.) *TF.* 1982 May; 3(1): 26-41. Illus.

THEATRE IN GENERAL — cont'd

South Africa, Republic of. 1981. Technical studies. ■Story translated into movement as basis for verbal work. Related to Dance.

581 Scheepers, Elize. "Prinsipiële vraagstukke met betrekking tot beroepsopleiding van spraak en teaterkundiges aan die Universiteite in die RSA." (Fundamental Problems Regarding Professional Training of Speech and Theatre Specialists at Universities in the RSA.) *TF.* 1982; 3(1): 45-64. Notes. Biblio.
South Africa, Republic of. Twentieth cent. Technical studies. ■Analysis and critique of current trends in theatre training in English, American and South African Universities.

582 Beam, Richard S. "Theatre: Specialty Enough?" *ThNe.* 1982 Jan.; 14(1): 12.
USA. Twentieth cent. Histories-sources. ■Educational theatres with degree programs should recognize that ability to deal with total theatre field may serve student and theatre better than a high degree of specialization.

583 Gross, Roger. "The Promise of the New Actor Training — A Professional Challenge for Teachers." *ThNe.* 1982 Dec.; 14(9): 14-15.
USA. 1980-1982. Textbooks/manuals/guides. ■Proposes new approaches to theatre training.

584 O'Farrell, Lawrence. "Origins of Drama." *ChTR.* 1982 Fall; 31(4): 3-7. Notes. Biblio.
USA. England. Twentieth cent. Studies of theories/theorists. ■Three approaches to creative dramatics: Brian Way, Winifred Ward and Dorothy Heathcote.

Other entries with significant content related to Theatre In General: 8, 10, 28, 65, 68, 271, 586, 591, 974, 1033, 1047, 1070.

DANCE

General

Choreography/choreographers

585 Luger, Eleanor Rachel. "Nancy Spanier's People Dances." *Dm.* 1982 July; 56(7): 47-49.
USA. 1960-1982. Biographical studies. ■Background and work of choreographer Nancy Spanier.

Design/technology: Costuming/costumers

586 Phaedre, Phyllis Saretta. "Costumes...By an Artist." *AbqN.* 1982 Mar.-Apr.; 7(6): 10-12.
USA. Twentieth cent. Technical studies. ■Costuming Oriental dances, with focus on fabrics, styles and headdresses. Related to Theatre in General: Multiple application.

Performance/performers: Dance/dancers

587 Trucco, Terry. "When West Meets East." *BaNe.* 1982 July; 4(1): 10-15. Illus.
Japan. 1982. Histories-sources. ■Japanese dance troupes visit USA. Related to Dance-Drama: *Kabuki.*

588 Barnes, Clive. "Barnes on the Plight of the Aging Dancer." *BaNe.* 1982 Apr.; 3(10): 46. Illus.
USA. Twentieth cent. Critical studies. ■Reflections inspired by Maxim Mazumdar's play *Invitation to the Dance*, based on career of dancer-turned-actor John Gilpin.

589 Stoop, Norma McLain. "Why Annie Isn't Annie Anymore." *Dm.* 1982 June; 56(6): 52-56. Illus.: Photo.
USA. 1982. Histories-sources. ■Ann Reinking, with emphasis on training and role in *Annie*. Related to Music-Drama: Musical theatre.

Public relations: Press relations

590 Siegel, Marcia B. "The Death of Some Alternatives." *BR.* 1982 Fall; 10(3): 76-80.
USA. 1974-1982. Histories-sources. ■Dance critic eulogizes defunct *Soho News*, an 'alternative' newspaper, and its influence on dance writing.

Relation to other fields: Other arts

591 Cash, Deborah. "Wiz Kid." *BaNe.* 1982 June; 3(12): 16, 18. Illus.
USA. 1950-1982. Histories-sources. ■Interview with performer, director, designer Geoffrey Holder about his activities in theatre and other arts. Related to Theatre in General.

Relation to other fields: Sociology

592 Lerman, Liz. "Seniors, Young Performers: Growing Together on Stage." *ThNe.* 1982 Nov.; 14(8): 7-8. Illus.: Photo. 2.
USA. 1970-1982. Histories-sources. ■Program for senior adults that combines old and young dancers.

Staging: Choreography/choreographers

593 Rawson, Deborah. "A New Laura Dean?" *BaNe.* 1982 Dec.; 4(6): 22. Illus.
USA. 1982. Histories-sources. ■Interview with choreographer Laura Dean about her new work for Joffrey Ballet in collaboration with architect/designer Michael Graves. Grp/movt: Joffrey Ballet.

594 Stoop, Norma McLain. "Dancing: On Broadway and Off." *Dm.* 1982 Sep.; 56(9): 100.
USA. Twentieth cent. Biographical studies. ■Short biography of dancer/choreographer Michael Peters emphasizing his role as co-choreographer of *Dreamgirls*.

Ballet

Choreography/choreographers

595 Terry, Walter. "Miss Birgit." *BaNe.* 1982 Nov.; 4(5): 18. Illus.
Sweden. 1940-1982. Biographical studies. ■Surveys career of Birgit Cullberg, founder of Cullberg Ballet.

Choreography/choreographers: Adaptations

596 Köllinger, Bernd. "Ballett zwischen Gestern und Morgen: Zur Interpretation von Werken der Vergangenheit(9)." (Ballet between Yesterday and Tomorrow: On the Problem of Adapting the Cultural Heritage in Ballet.) *TZ.* 1982; 37(11): 8-9.
East Germany. Twentieth cent. Critical studies. ■Discusses problems of continuity between classical and modern ballet.

597 Barnes, Clive. "Barnes on the Revival or Reconstruction of Ballet Classics." *BaNe.* 1982 Feb.; 3(8): 46. Illus.
USA. 1982. Critical studies. ■Commentary on restoring and maintaining the original choreography.

Choreography/choreographers: Biographical studies

598 Wechsler, Bert. "Survivor." *BaNe.* 1982 Apr.; 3(10): 20-22, 24. Illus.
USA. 1948-1981. Biographical studies. ■Career survey of Sallie Wilson, ballerina and choreographer with American Ballet Theatre and New York City Ballet, emphasizing relationship with Antony Tudor.

Choreography/choreographers: Genres

599 Cohen, Selma Jean. *Next Week, Swan Lake: Reflection on Dance and Dances.* Middletown, CT: Wesleyan UP; 1982.

DANCE — cont'd

xiii, 193 pp. Pref. Notes. Index. Biblio. Illus.: Photo. B&W. 15.
Multi-period. Critical studies. ∎Analysis of dance forms and styles using *Swan Lake* as basis.

Financial operations: Planning and accounting

600   Jacobson, Robert. "Viewpoint." *BaNe.* 1982 Mar.; 3(9): 5.
USA. 1981. Critical studies. ∎Editorial on Pennsylvania Ballet's suspension of activities.

Institutions: Producing/performing

601   Crabb, Michael. "Thirty Years of Accomplishment: The National Ballet of Canada Continues to Set New Record." *OC.* 1982 Spring; 23(1): 15-16, 49. Illus.
Canada. 1952-1982. Histories-sources. ∎Debate over Canadian content of repertory.

602   Anderson, Jack. "The Ballets Russes Saga." *BaNe.* 1982 Jan.; 3(7): 10-15, 45. Illus.
Europe. USA. 1929-1962. Historical studies. ∎History of various Ballets Russes companies formed after Diaghilev's death: their impresarios, choreographers and stars.

Performance/performers: Dance/dancers

603   Barnes, Clive. "Barnes on...What is Ballet Acting?" *BaNe.* 1982 June; 3(12): 46. Illus.
USA. 1950-1982. Critical studies. ∎Differences between theatre and dance acting, and revitalization of ballet mime. Related to Mime.

604   Cleveland, David. "No Gimmicks." *BaNe.* 1982 Apr.; 3(10): 26-29, 43. Illus.
USA. 1950-1981. Histories-sources. ∎Interview with Kevin McKenzie about his performances with American Ballet Theatre, National Ballet and Joffrey Ballet.

Scores/composers: Genres

605   Scherer, Barrymore Laurence. "Toast of the Czars." *BaNe.* 1982 Jan.; 3(7): 26-28.
Italy. Russia. 1846-1930. Biographical studies. ∎Life of Riccardo Drigo, composer and conductor for Russian Imperial Theatres in St. Petersburg.

Staging: Choreography/choreographers

606   Barker, Barbara. "Nijinsky's *Jeux*." *TDR.* 1982 Spring; 26(1): 51-60.
France. 1913. Histories-specific. ∎Performance history of Nijinsky's second ballet, *Jeux*, performed in Paris in 1913, with reference to Diaghilev, Bakst and Debussy.

607   Reiter, Susan. "His Own Man." *BaNe.* 1982 June; 3(12): 10-14, 45. Illus.
USA. 1960-1982. Histories-sources. ∎Interview with Eliot Feld about his ballet company, the New Ballet School, and the renovated Joyce Theatre. Related to Media.

608   Markard, Anna. "Kurt Jooss and His Work." *BR.* 1982 Spring; 10(1): 15-67. Illus.
West Germany. 1901-1982. Biographies. ∎Life and career of choreographer Kurt Jooss. Infl. on Modern dance.

Ethnic dance

609   Jenson, Gunilla. "Kandy-dansen i Sri Lanka." (Kandy Dance in Sri Lanka.) *Entre.* 1982; 9(3): 18-21. Illus.
Sri Lanka. Multi-period. Twentieth cent. Historical studies. ∎Commercialized dances for tourist audiences and long tradition of Buddhist ceremonial dances featured in August Perahera festival.

Institutions: Producing/performing

610   Luger, Eleanor Rachel. "Choreography as Geography: Guillermina Bravo's Dances of Mexico." *Dm.* 1982 Feb.; 56(2): 68-71. Illus.
Mexico. 1930-1982. Historical studies. ∎History of El Ballet Nacional de México and its director. Infl. by Martha Graham.

Performance/performers: Dance/dancers

611   Rosen, Lillie F. "Bhaskar's Dance Journey...A Spiritual Odyssey (Part I)." *AbqN.* 1982 July-Aug.; 8(2): 12-14, 17, 22, 25, 29. Illus.
India. 1950-1981. Histories-sources. ∎Part One of an interview with Roy Chowdhury Bhaskar, concerning his education, early career and spiritual recovery from a crippling accident.

612   Rosen, Lillie F. "Bhaskar's Dance Journey...A Spiritual Odyssey (Part II)." *AbqN.* 1982 Sep.-Oct.; 8(3): 6-9. Illus.
India. 1950-1981. Histories-sources. ∎Part Two of an interview with Roy Chowdhury Bhaskar concerning his career as a dancer and film star. Related to Media: Film.

Staging: Choreography/choreographers

613   Lewis, Julinda. "African Traditions, American Dancers: A Look at African Dance in the '80s." *AbqN.* 1982 Mar-Apr.; 7(6): 4-5, 23. Illus.
USA. 1980-1982. Histories-sources. ∎Performance styles and approaches of African dance companies.

Training: Teachers

614   Farrah, Ibrahim; Lahm, Adam. "Sizing Up Realities in Ethnic Dance." *AbqN.* 1982 July-Aug.; 8(2): 4-5, 20. Illus.
USA. Middle East. Twentieth cent. Studies of research/researchers. ∎Search for authenticity through travel, research and study with native teachers.

Training: Teaching methods

615   Farrah, Ibrahim. "Stretching for Dimension." *AbqN.* 1982 Mar.-Apr.; 7(6): 13, 17. Illus.
USA. Twentieth cent. Technical studies. ∎Discussion by leading Middle Eastern dancer: Posture and stance in oriental dance.

Modern dance

Institutions: Producing/performing

616   Temin, Christine. "New England Sampler." *BaNe.* 1982 July; 4(1): 16-20. Illus.
USA. 1931-1982. Historical studies. ∎History of Jacob's Pillow, Ted Shawn's farm turned dance festival and its relevance to the development of American dance.

Performance/performers: Dance/dancers

617   Harris, Dale. "Isadora." *BaNe.* 1982 Feb.; 3(8): 12-16, 45. Illus.
USA. Twentieth cent. Biographical studies. ∎Duncan's legacy to modern dance.

618   Haskins, James. *Katherine Dunham.* New York: Putnam; 1982. 158 pp. (The Dance Program 14.) Pref. Gloss. Index. Illus.
USA. Twentieth cent. Biographical studies. ∎Katherine Dunham's life, professional career, choreography and influence on contemporary dance.

619   Kendall, Elizabeth. "Victim of History." *BaNe.* 1982 Feb.; 3(8): 18-20, 42. Illus.
USA. 1970-1982. Critical studies. ∎Portrayals of Isadora Duncan.

620   Laine, Barry. "In Her Footsteps." *BaNe.* 1982 Feb.; 3(8): 22, 24. Illus.

DANCE — cont'd

USA. 1928-1981. Histories-reconstruction. ■Interview with Annabelle Gamson concerning her re-creation and interpretation of Isadora Duncan's dances.

621   Ostlere, Hilary. "Isadorable." *BaNe.* 1982 Feb.; 3(8): 26-27. Illus.

USA. 1894-1981. Histories-sources. ■Reminiscences of Maria-Theresa, one of six 'Isadorables' brought to U.S. by Isadora Duncan in the 1920s.

622   Terry, Walter. "Dancing Prince." *BaNe.* 1982 July; 4(1): 22-23. Illus.

USA. 1931-1982. Historical studies. ■Interview with Barton Mumaw, soloist with Ted Shawn and his Men Dancers: Shawn, Ruth St. Denis, and historic American dances.

Relation to other fields: Other arts

623   Sears, David. "A Trisha Brown-Robert Rauschenberg Collage." *BR.* 1982 Fall; 10(3): 47-51. Illus.

USA. 1963-1982. Histories-sources. ■Interview with choreographer and painter about their collaborative performances. Grp/movt: Postmodernism.

Relation to other fields: Psychology

624   Irwin, Eleanor C. "From Trauma to Mastery: A Lesson in Survival." *ThNe.* 1982 Mar.; 14(3): 1, 14.

USA. 1970-1982. Reviews of publications. ■Psychiatric evaluation of Agnes de Mille's *In Reprieve: A Memoir* with psychological, biological, medical and environmental factors responsible for recovery from trauma.

Training: Teaching methods

625   Potgieter, Brenda. "Rosalia Chladek: nDanseres, choreograaf en pedagoog." (Rosalia Chladek: Dancer, Choreographer and Pedagogue.) *TF.* 1982 May; 3(1): 42-44.

Austria. 1905-1981. Biographical studies. ■Chladek and her teaching practice.

Popular dance

Choreography/choreographers

626   Flatow, Sheryl. "Tune on Top." *BaNe.* 1982 Nov.; 4(5): 12-16. Illus.

USA. 1960-1982. Biographical studies. ■Surveys career of Tommy Tune.

Choreography/choreographers: Genres

627   Jones, Alan. "Morris Dancing — Tradition for Today." *AbqN.* 1982 May-June; 8(1): 18-19. Illus.

England. USA. Multi-period. Historical studies. ■Morris dancing's origins, history as an English folk dance and preservation by American folk dance groups.

Institutions: Producing/performing

628   Christiansen, Richard. "Good-Time Dancers." *BaNe.* 1982 Nov.; 4(5): 26-28, 30. Illus.

USA. 1970-1982. Histories-specific. ■Development of Hubbard Street Dance Company.

Performance/performers: Dance/dancers

629   Heymont, George. "Older and Wiser." *BaNe.* 1982 Aug.; 4(2): 28-30. Illus.

USA. 1950-1982. Histories-sources. ■Interview with musical comedy dancer Marge Champion. Related to Music-Drama: Musical theatre.

Other entries with significant content related to Dance: 13, 43, 185, 187, 274, 538, 580, 954, 975, 1015, 1076, 1077.

DANCE-DRAMA

General

Audience

630   Henry, Karen. "Wallflower Order." *Tk.* Sep.-Oct.; 2(6): 12-17. Notes. Illus.

USA. Nicaragua. 1975-1982. Histories-sources. ■Wallflower Dance Collective's reception in Nicaragua and impressions of tour.

Relation to other fields: Anthropology

631   Hanna, Judith Lynne. "Dance and the 'Women's War'." *DRJ.* 1981-82; 14(1-2): 25-28. Biblio. Notes. Illus.

Nigeria. 1929-1982. Histories-sources. ■Dance plays for births, deaths, female solidarity and political protest.

Kabuki

632   Brandon, James R., ed. *Chūshingura: Studies in Kabuki and the Puppet Theater.* Honolulu: Univ. of Hawaii P; 1982. xiii, 231 pp. Pref. Index. Illus.: Photo. Diagram. B&W. Color.

Japan. Tokugawa period. Eighteenth cent. ■Contains essays by Donald H. Shively, William P. Malm, James R. Brandon, and the text of a *kabuki* version of *Chūshingura (The Forty-Seven Samurai).*

633   Vaughan, David. "Reviews: Grand Kabuki." *Dm.* 1982 Dec.; 56(12): 124, 127-128, 138.

Japan. USA. 1982. Reviews of performances. ■Grand Kabuki theatre at Metropolitan Opera House. Noted are Nakamura Utaemon VI and Nakamura Kanzaburō XVII. Discusses acting styles, plots, use of *mie*, role of dance and contrast of stylization and naturalism.

Legal aspects: Licensing and regulation

634   Shively, Donald H. "Tokugawa Plays on Forbidden Topics." 23-57 in Brandon, James R., ed. *Chūshingura: Studies in Kabuki and Puppet Theater.* Honolulu, HI: Univ. of Hawaii P; 1982. xiii, 231 pp. Notes.

Japan. Eighteenth cent. Tokugawa period. Historical studies. ■Strict censorship in drama and playwrights' means of evading it.

Plays/playwrights: Adaptations

635   Brandon, James R. "The Theft of *Chūshingura*: or the Great Kabuki Caper." 111-146 in Brandon, James R., ed. Chūshingura: *Studies in Kabuki and the Puppet Theater.* Honolulu: Univ of Hawaii P; 1982. xiii, 231 pp. Notes.

Japan. Tokugawa period. Eighteenth cent. Historical studies. ■History of changes in *kabuki* play as a result of puppet theatre adaptations.

Plays/playwrights: Plot/subject/theme

636   Keene, Donald. "Variations on a Theme: Chūshingura." 1-21 in Brandon, James R., ed. *Chūshingura: Studies in Kabuki and the Puppet Theatre.* Honolulu, HI: Univ. of Hawaii P; 1982. xiii, 231 pp.

Japan. Eighteenth cent. Tokugawa period. Critical studies. ■Recent thematic variations in interpretation of *The Forty-Seven Samurai (Chūshingura).*

Staging: Directing/directors

637   John, Hans-Rainer. "Wesen und Form des Kabuki: Gespräch mit dem japanischen Regisseur Hironori Terasaki." (Nature and Form of *Kabuki*: Conversation with the Japanese Director Hironori Terasaki.) *TZ.* 1982 June; 37(6): 55-58. Illus.

Japan. Multi-period. Histories-sources. ■Interview on the nature and origin of *kabuki*, and comparisons with *nō* and *kyōgen*.

DANCE-DRAMA – cont'd

_____

Other entries with significant content related to Dance-Drama: 80, 578, 587, 725, 884, 988.

DRAMA

General

638 Volkmer, Rüdiger. "Dem Zufall nachhelfen." (Lending Chance a Hand.) *TZ.* 1982 Jan.; 37: 6-7. Notes. Illus.: Photo.
East Germany. 1982. Critical studies. ▪Problems in development of dramatic art.

639 Deák, Frantisek. "Meyerhold's Staging of *Sister Beatrice*." *TDR.* 1982 Spring; 26(1): 41-50.
Russia. 1906. Histories-reconstruction. ▪Performance history of Meyerhold's 1906 production of *Sister Beatrice*: discusses work as culmination of Meyerhold's symbolist period, effect on Vera Komissarzhevskaya's performance.

640 Law, Alma H. "Meyerhold's *The Magnanimous Cuckold*." *TDR.* 1982 Spring; 26(1): 61-86.
USSR. 1922. Histories-reconstruction. ▪Performance history of Meyerhold's 1922 production of *The Magnanimous Cuckold*, with discussion of constructivism, Popova and Aksyonov.

Audience

641 Werner, Hans-Georg. "Historizität plus Aktualität. Zur Interpretation von Dramen der Vergangenheit." (Historical Authenticity in the Present: On the Interpretation of Period Plays.) *TZ.* 1982 Jan.; 37(1): 31-32.
East Germany. 1982. Historical studies. ▪Current reception of period plays.

Audience: Reactions/comments

642 Kuckhoff, Armin-Gerd. "Zur Interpretation von Dramen der Vergangenheit (6): Anlässe Shakespeare zu spielen." (On the Interpretation of Period Plays (6): Occasions to Play Shakespeare.) *TZ.* 1982 July; 37(7): 13-15. Illus.
East Germany. 1982. Critical studies. ▪Modern audiences' reaction to Shakespeare. Related to Individuals: Shakespeare.

643 Mieth, Gunter. "Nutzt ein *magisches* Begriffspaar? Zur Interpretation von Dramas der Vergangenheit." (Is a *Magical* Comprehension Necessary? On the Interpretation of Period Plays.) *TZ.* 1982 Mar.; 37(3): 8-9. [Installment of a regular series.]
East Germany. Twentieth cent. Histories-sources. ▪Audience reception of period plays.

644 Rohmer, Rolf. "Drei Aspekte. Kommunikation, Schauspielkunst, Volkstheatertradition." (Three Aspects: Communication, Dramatic Art and Popular Theatre Tradition.) *TZ.* 1982 June; 37(6): 11-13.
East Germany. 1982. Historical studies. ▪Reception of classical drama in contemporary theatres.

645 Kahn, Jean-François. "Le paradoxe sur Victor Hugo." (The Paradox of Victor Hugo.) *CF.* 1982 Sep.; 111: 5-7.
France. Nineteenth cent. Twentieth cent. Historical studies. ▪Like other Hugo plays, *Marie Tudor*, acclaimed by the public at the Comédie Française, was rejected by the critics.

646 Amor, Edward; Nevin, John R.; Dorn, Dennis. "The *Out Cry* Questionnaire." *TWNew.* 1982 Spring-Fall; 3(2): 21-26.
USA. Twentieth cent. Histories-sources. ▪Analysis of audience responses to university production of Tennessee Williams' play.

647 Rensburg, Peet van. "Lewensbeskoulike boodskappersepsie in die toneel." (Lifeview and Perception of Message in Drama.) *TF.* 1982; 3(1): 73-90. Biblio.
USA. Multi-period. Technical studies. ▪How personal and religious beliefs influence reception.

Design/technology: Scenery/scene designers

648 Stauffacher, Paul K. "Designing Tennessee Williams' *Out Cry*." *TWNew.* 1982 Spring-Fall; 3(2): 17-20.
Twentieth cent. Histories-sources. ▪Design for Tennessee Williams' *Out Cry*.

Institutions: Producing/performing

649 Merin, Jennifer. "Mexico: The Cervantes Festival." *CTR.* 1982 Fall; 36: 120-123.
Mexico. 1982. Histories-sources. ▪Tenth anniversary of festival.

650 Brennan, Brian. "Louisville: The Canadian Experience." *CTR.* 1982 Summer; 35: 135-137. Illus.
USA. 1982. Histories-sources. ▪Jon Jory's New Play Festival.

651 Rogoff, Gordon. "Culture Shlock." *VV.* 1982 Mar. 23; 27(12): 89.
USA. Italy. 1982. Critical studies. ▪Contrasts production seasons of American and Italian regional theatres.

652 Rzhevsky, Nicholas. "Interview with Yuri Liubimov." *NSEEDT.* 1982 Mar.; 2(1): 11-19.
USSR. Twentieth cent. Histories-sources. ▪Covers Liubimov's career, history of the Taganka Theatre and political aspects of theatre in USSR.

Institutions: Service

653 Noonan, James. "Playwrights Canada, The First Ten Years." *THC.* 1982 Fall; 3(2): 209-213.
Canada. 1971-1981. Histories-sources. ▪Survey of activities and importance of Playwrights Canada.

Legal aspects: Performance rights

654 Horn, Pierre L. "Victor Hugo's Theatrical Royalties During his Exile Years." *ThR.* 1982 Spring; 7(2): 132-137. Notes.
France. 1851-1870. Historical studies. ▪Also deals with question of playwrights' royalties and theatre economics of the period.

Performance/performers

655 "La prima recita dell' *Ortensio* degli Intronati alla luce di testimonianze inedite." (The First Performance of *Ortensio* by the Intronati in the Light of Unpublished Testimonies.) *QT.* 1982 Nov.; 5(18): 201-211. Notes.
Italy. 1561. Historical studies. ▪Examination of previously unpublished testimonies about first performance of *Ortensio* at the Accademia degli Intronati in Siena.

656 Beaufort, John; Kroll, Jack; Rich, Frank; Watt, Douglas; Barnes, Clive; Cohen, Ron; Cunningham, Dennis; Siegel, Joel. "*Almost an Eagle*." *NYTCR.* 1982 Dec. 13; 43(17): 116-118.
USA. 1982. Reviews of performances. ▪Eight critics review Jacques Levy's production, presented at Longacre Theatre.

657 Cunningham, Dennis; Barnes, Clive; Rich, Frank; Beaufort, John; Wilson, Edwin; Watt, Douglas; Kalem, T.E.; Kroll, Jack. "*Foxfire*." *NYTCR.* 1982 Nov. 29; 43(16): 141-147.
USA. 1982. Reviews of performances. ▪Eight critics review David Trainer's production, presented at Ethel Barrymore Theatre.

658 Cunningham, Dennis; Rich, Frank; Watt, Douglas; Kissel, Howard; Barnes, Clive; Kroll, Jack; Beaufort, John; Wilson, Edwin. "*Twice Around the Park*." *NYTCR.* 1982 Nov. 1; 43(14): 172-176.
USA. 1982. Reviews of performances. ▪Eight critics review Arthur Storch's production, presented at Cort Theatre.

DRAMA — cont'd

659 Kissel, Howard; Watt, Douglas; Rich, Frank; Kroll, Jack; Kalem, T.E.; Barnes, Clive; Beaufort, John. *"Edmond."* *NYTCR.* 1982 Nov. 15; 43(15): 159-163. [Off-Broadway Supplement IV.]
USA. 1982. Reviews of performances. ▪Seven critics review Gregory Mosher's production, presented at Provincetown Playhouse.

660 Kroll, Jack; Watt, Douglas; Rich, Frank; Beaufort, John; Sharp, Christopher; Wilson, Edwin; Barnes, Clive; Siegel, Joel; Cunningham, Dennis. *"Steaming."* *NYTCR.* 1982 Dec. 13; 43(17): 128-132.
USA. 1982. Reviews of performances. ▪Nine critics review Roger Smith's production of Nell Dunn's play, presented at Brooks Atkinson Theatre.

661 Rich, Frank; Watt, Douglas; Barnes, Clive; Kissel, Howard; Beaufort, John; Kroll, Jack; Wilson, Edwin; Siegel, Joel; Cunningham, Dennis. *"Monday After the Miracle."* *NYTCR.* 1982 Dec. 13; 43(17): 123-127.
USA. 1982. Reviews of performances. ▪Nine critics review Arthur Penn's production of William Gibson's play, presented at Eugene O'Neill Theatre.

662 Rich, Frank; Beaufort, John; Kroll, Jack; Barnes, Clive; Kissel, Howard; Watt, Douglas; Clarke, Gerald; Cunningham, Dennis. *"Come Back to the Five & Dime Jimmy Dean, Jimmy Dean."* *NYTCR.* 1982 Feb. 15; 43(4): 333-337.
USA. 1982. Reviews of performances. ▪Eight critics review Robert Altman's production of Ed Graczyk's play.

663 Rich, Frank; Watt, Douglas; Kissel, Howard; Barnes, Clive; Beaufort, John; Cunningham, Dennis; Siegel, Joel. *"The Queen and the Rebels."* *NYTCR.* 1982 Oct. 4; 43(12): 202-206.
USA. 1982. Reviews of performances. ▪Seven critics review Waris Hussein's production, presented by Circle in the Square at Plymouth Theatre.

664 Rich, Frank; Wilson, Edwin; Watt, Douglas; Kissel, Howard; Barnes, Clive. *"The Wake of Jamey Foster."* *NYTCR.* 1982 Nov. 1; 43(14): 180-182.
USA. 1982. Reviews of performances. ▪Five critics review Ulu Grosbard's production, presented at Eugene O'Neill Theatre.

665 Rich, Frank; Watt, Douglas; Barnes, Clive; Kissel, Howard; Beaufort, John. *"The Holly and the Ivy."* *NYTCR.* 1982 Nov. 15; 43(15): 150-153. [Off-Broadway Supplement IV.]
USA. 1982. Reviews of performances. ▪Five critics review Lindsay Anderson's production presented by the Roundabout Theatre Company at the Susan Bloch Theatre.

666 Rich, Frank; Watt, Douglas; Beaufort, John; Barnes, Clive; Kroll, Jack; Kalem, T.E.; Sharp, Christopher. *"Some Men Need Help."* *NYTCR.* 1982 Nov. 15; 43(15): 156-159. [Off-Broadway Supplement IV.]
USA. 1982. Reviews of performances. ▪Seven critics review John Ferraro's production, presented at 47th Street Theatre.

667 Rich, Frank; Cohen, Ron; Beaufort, John; Watt, Douglas; Kroll, Jack; Barnes, Clive. *"Talking With."* *NYTCR.* 1982 Nov. 15; 43(15): 167-170. [Off-Broadway Supplement IV.]
USA. 1982. Reviews of performances. ▪Six critics review Jon Jory's production, presented by Manhattan Theatre Club.

668 Rich, Frank; Watt, Douglas; Cohen, Ron; Barnes, Clive; Siegel, Joel. *"Herman van Veen: All of Him."* *NYTCR.* 1982 Nov. 29; 43(16): 134-136.
USA. 1982. Reviews of performances. ▪Five critics review Michel La Faille's production at Ambassador Theatre.

669 Siegel, Joel; Kroll, Jack; Rich, Frank; Wilson, Edwin; Barnes, Clive; Sharp, Christopher; Watt, Douglas; Beaufort, John. *"Whodunnit."* *NYTCR.* 1982 Dec. 31; 43(18): 104-108.
USA. 1982. Reviews of performances. ▪Eight critics review Michael Kahn's production of Anthony Shaffer's play, presented at the Biltmore Theatre.

670 Siegel, Joel; Cunningham, Dennis; Rich, Frank; Beaufort, John; Watt, Douglas; Kissel, Howard; Barnes, Clive; Wilson, Edwin; Clarke, Gerald. *"Eighty-four Charing Cross Road."* *NYTCR.* 1982 Nov. 29; 43(16): 136-141.
USA. 1982. Reviews of performances. ▪Nine critics review James Roose's production, presented at Nederlander Theatre.

671 Watt, Douglas; Wilson, Edwin; Beaufort, John; Rich, Frank; Barnes, Clive; Kissel, Howard; Kroll, Jack; Cunningham, Dennis; Siegel, Joel. *"Alice in Wonderland."* *NYTCR.* 1982 Dec. 31; 43(18): 108-114.
USA. 1982. Reviews of performances. ▪Nine critics review Eva Le Gallienne's production, presented in association with WNET/Thirteen.

672 Watt, Douglas; Wilson, Edwin; Gussow, Mel; Cohen, Ron; Beaufort, John; Barnes, Clive. *"Geniuses."* *NYTCR.* 1982 Sep. 13; 43(11): 231-234. [Off-Broadway Supplement III.]
USA. 1982. Reviews of performances. ▪Six critics review Gerald Gutierrez's production, presented by Playwrights Horizons.

673 Watt, Douglas; Rich, Frank; Wilson, Edwin; Barnes, Clive; Beaufort, John; Kissel, Howard; Kalem, T.E.; Kroll, Jack; Cunningham, Dennis; Siegel, Joel. *"Good."* *NYTCR.* 1982 Oct. 18; 43(13): 184-190.
USA. 1982. Reviews of performances. ▪Ten critics review Howard Davies' production, presented at Booth Theatre.

674 Wilson, Edwin; Watt, Douglas; Rich, Frank; Barnes, Clive; Sharp, Christopher; Siegel, Joel; Cunningham, Dennis; Beaufort, John; Kroll, Jack. *"A Little Family Business."* *NYTCR.* 1982 Dec. 13; 43(17): 119-122.
USA. 1982. Reviews of performances. ▪Nine critics review Martin Charnin's production, presented at Martin Beck Theatre.

Performance/performers: Acting/actors

675 Anon. *"Heinrich Schweiger — Part 2."* *Bühne.* 1982 Feb.: 13-15. Illus.
Austria. Twentieth cent. Histories-sources. ▪Overview of career at Burgtheater and other Austrian and German theatres.

676 Böhm, Gotthard. *"Oskar Werner 60: 'Die Wahrheit ist unbequem'."* (Oskar Werner at 60: 'The Truth Is Uncomfortable'.) *Bühne.* 1982 Nov.: 4-5. Illus.
Austria. 1922-1982. Histories-sources. ▪Actor's reservations about today's theatre.

677 Lossmann, Hans. *"Guido Wieland."* *Bühne.* 1982 Jan.: 13-15. Illus.
Austria. 1945-1980. Biographical studies. ▪Biographical essay on actor Guido Wieland at Theatre in der Josefstadt.

678 Rismondo, Piero. *Leopold Rudolf.* Vienna, Munich: Jugend und Volk; 1982. 131 pp. (Wiener Themen.) Index. Illus.
Austria. 1911-1978. Biographies. ▪Actor Leopold Rudolf's career.

679 Heilmann, Annegudrun. *"Garderobengespräch mit Hermann Stövesand."* (Dressing Room Interview with Hermann Stövesand.) *TZ.* 1982; 37(2): 42-46. Illus.
East Germany. 1906-1981. Histories-sources. ▪Hermann Stövesand's stage career and interpretation of dramas.

680 Van Dijk, Maarten. *"John Phillip Kemble and the Critics."* *TN.* 1982; 36(3): 110-118.
England. 1800-1811. Studies of criticism/critics. ▪Kemble's relationship with critics.

681 Asholt, Wolfgang. *"Les Matinées caractéristiques et le Théâtre des Nations."* (The Characteristic Matinees and the Theatre of Nations.) *RHT.* 1982; 34(3): 211-236. Notes.
France. 1877-1880. Historical studies. ▪Matinee series by Marie Dumas and Gustave Bergrand develops Theatre of Nations. Production style

DRAMA — cont'd

anticipates naturalism of André Antoine and the repertoire of Lugné-Poë.

682 Guibert, Noëlle. "*Le Voyage de Monsieur Perrichon* de Labiche. Les voyages de la pièce." (*Monsieur Perrichon's Journey*, by Eugène Labiche: The Runs of the Play.) *CF.* 1982 Apr.; 108: 15-17. Illus.: Photo.
France. 1860-1982. Histories-sources. ■Summary of career of Eugène Labiche, particularly at Comédie Française, and brief history of various Paris runs. Photos of sets from various productions.

683 La Place, Roselyne. "René Arrieu." *CF.* 1982 June-July; 110: 3-4.
France. 1982. Histories-sources. ■Tribute to Comédie Française actor on his death.

684 La Place, Roselyne. "Trois engagements à la Comédie-Française." (Three Appointments at the Comédie Française.) *CF.* 1982 June-July; 110: 14-16.
France. 1982. Histories-sources. ■Background of three newly hired actors appearing in *The Vultures (Les Corbeaux).*

685 La Place, Roselyne. "Béatrice Bretty." *CF.* 1982 Dec.; 114: 18-19.
France. 1914-1982. Biographical studies. ■Tribute to Béatrice Bretty, actress at the Comédie-Française.

686 Winterstein, Eduard von. *Mein Leben und meine Zeit.* (My Life and My Time.) Berlin: Henschel; 1982. 456 pp. Illus.
Germany. 1889-1918. Biographies. ■Actor's memoirs. Infl. by Max Reinhardt.

687 Janzon, Leif. "Thommy Berggren." *Entre.* 1982; 9(6): 3-8. Illus.
Sweden. 1961-1982. Histories-sources. ■Interview with actor Thommy Berggren about his performances and his belief in rigorous self-discipline.

688 Löbl, Hermi. "Maria Bill: 'Ich bereue nichts...'." (Maria Bill: 'I regret nothing...'.) *Bühne.* 1982 Oct.: 8-10 . Illus.
Switzerland. Austria. 1982. Histories-sources. ■Interview with Swiss actress Maria Bill on receiving the Kainz-medal for her title role in Pam Gems' *Piaf* at Wiener Schauspielhaus.

689 "Ladies of the Chorus: An Acting Journal." *AmTh.* 1982 Mar.; 3(12): 14-16. Notes. Illus.: Photo. B&W. 3.
USA. 1982. Histories-sources. ■Life as chorus member in Hartford Stage Company's production of Greek drama entitled *The Greeks.*

690 Angelou, Maya. "The Heart of a Woman." *Ebony.* 1982 Jan.; 12(9): 76, 108-113.
USA. 1950-1960. Biographical studies. ■Excerpt from autobiography of poet, actress and playwright.

691 Duvall, Henry. "W. Montague Cobb Makes Acting Debut." *Crisis.* 1982 Aug.-Sep.; 89(7): 52.
USA. 1982. Histories-sources. ■Professor appears in *Without A Doubt,* a one-man show based on the life of Black philosopher W.E.B. Du Bois.

692 Fennema, David H. "The Popular Response to Tommaso Salvini in America." *THSt.* 1982; 2: 103-113. Notes.
USA. 1873-1890. Historical studies. ■Summarizes popular and critical reaction to acting and repertoire, and mentions his joint appearances with Clara Morris (1883) and Edwin Booth (1886).

693 Gura, Timothy. "An Interview with Zoe Caldwell." *LPer.* 1982 Nov.; 3(1): 60-74. Illus.
USA. 1982. Histories-sources. ■Classical actress/director Zoe Caldwell's views on importance of pre-performance research in preparing for roles.

694 Harris, Laurilyn J. "Charles Gilpin: Opening the Way for the American Black Actor." *THSt.* 1982; 2: 93-101. Notes. Illus.
USA. 1920-1925. Historical studies. ■Account of performance as Brutus Jones in Eugene O'Neill's *The Emperor Jones.*

695 Macnaughton, Bruce. "Center Stage: Father and Son Advise 'Act Now'." *ThNe.* 1982 Summer; 14(6): 9. Illus.: Photo. B&W.
USA. 1979-1982. Histories-sources. ■Comments on writing of *Act Now: An Actor's Guide for Breaking In.*

696 Rogoff, Gordon. "Uneasy Lie the Crowns." *VV.* 1982 Nov. 2; 27(44): 85-86.
USA. England. 1982. Critical studies. ■Criticizes superficial acting of visiting English actors.

697 Shafer, Yvonne. "Women in Ibsen." *AmTh.* 1982 Feb.; 3(11): 1-5. Notes. Illus.: Photo. B&W. 3.
USA. 1920-1982. Histories-sources. ■Interview with Eva Le Gallienne on acting Ibsen.

Plays/playwrights

698 Heresch, Elisabeth. *Schnitzler und Russland: Aufnahme, Wirkung, Kritik.* (Schnitzler and Russia: Reception, Influence, Criticism.) Vienna: Braumüller; 1982. viii, 208 pp. Notes. Index. Biblio. Illus.
Austria. Russia. 1895-1980. Historical studies. ■Reception of Arthur Schnitzler's plays. Includes dramatic and performance criticism.

699 Hüttner, Johann. "Dokumente zu Nestroys Werk auf der Bühne." (Documents Concerning Nestroy's Work on the Stage.) *Ns.* 1982; 4(2): 54-56.
Austria. 1800-1899. Histories-sources. ■Use of diary notes as sources for audience reception research. Includes reprint of review of Johann Nestroy's *Der Unbedeutende (A Man Without Importance)* in diary of Robert Hamerling.

700 Mayer, Gerhard. "Lieben Sie Klassik?" (Do You Love Classics?)*Bühne.* 1982 Sep.: 9-11. Illus.
Austria. 1982. Histories-sources. ■Interview with Achim Benning, manager of Burgtheater, about productions of German classical plays.

701 Mayer, Gerhard. "Wolfgang Bauer: Comeback eines Schockers." (Wolfgang Bauer: The Comeback of a Shocker.) *Bühne.* 1982 Dec.: 4-5. Illus.
Austria. West Germany. 1982. Histories-sources. ■Playwright Wolfgang Bauer's comeback with original productions of *Bathyscaphe 17-16* and *Woher kommen wir? Was sind wir? Wohin gehen wir? (Where Do We Come from? What Are We? Where Are We Going?).*

702 Roessler, Peter. "Vom Bau der Schweigemauer: Überlegungen zu den 'Reaktionen' auf Elfriede Jelineks Stück *Burgtheater.*" (On Building a Wall of Silence: Notes on the Reactions to Elfriede Jelinek's Play *Burgtheater.*) *Tzs.* 1982; 2: 85-91. Notes. Illus.
Austria. 1982. Studies of criticism/critics. ■Critical reaction to play, treating role of Vienna's Burgtheater during Nazism.

703 Serafini, Giuliano. "Thomas Bernhard: Incontro col convitato di pietra." (Thomas Bernhard: Meeting with the Stone Guest.) *QT.* 1982 Nov.; 5(18): 159-167.
Austria. 1982. Histories-sources. ■Summary of significant contributions at the conference on Thomas Bernhard's work (Sesto Fiorentino, September 11-12, 1982).

704 Anon. "Framing the Mysteries." *CTR.* 1982 Spring; 34: 165-172. Illus.
Canada. 1981. Histories-sources. ■Globe Theatre playwright-in-residence, Rex Deverell, is interviewed about his work.

705 Edwards, Murray D. "A Playwright from the Canadian Past: W.A. Tremayne (1864-1939)." *THC.* 1982 Spring; 3(1): 41-50. Notes.
Canada. 1864-1939. Biographical studies.

706 Hirsch, John. "Will the Classics Survive the '80's?" *AmTh.* 1982 Oct.; 4(7): 1-2. Notes. Illus.: Photo. B&W. 4.
Canada. 1982. Critical studies. ■Artistic director of Stratford Festival focuses on value of classical theatre in modern era.

DRAMA — cont'd

707 Knowles, Richard Paul. "The Maritimes: New Work."
CTR. 1982 Fall; 36: 111-112.
Canada. 1981. Histories-sources. ■Premiere of two plays by Maritime writers at Theatre New Brunswick.

708 Pollock, Sharon. "Canada's Playwrights: Finding Their Place." *CTR*. 1982 Spring; 34: 34-38. Illus.
Canada. Twentieth cent. Histories-sources. ■Playwright challenges Canadians to explore their own time and place.

709 Usmiani, Renate. "The Playwright as Historiographer: New Views of the Past in Contemporary Québeçois Drama."
CDr. 1982; 8(2): 117-128.
Canada. 1930-1980. Critical studies.

710 Hilton, Julian, ed. "The End of an Artistic Era." *Gambit*. 1982; 10(39-40): 1-32. [Appears at end of issue, and does not follow pagination.]
East Germany. West Germany. 1960-1980. Critical studies. ■Comments on forms, styles and function of German plays by Herbert Achternbusch, Thomas Bernhard, Tankard Dorst, Peter Hacks, Franz Xaver Krötz, Horst Laube, Heiner Müller, Maria Reinhard, Friederike Roth, Stefan Schütz and Peter Turrini.

711 Bliss, Lee. *The World's Perspective: John Webster and the Jacobean Drama*. New Brunswick, NJ: Rutgers UP; 1982. x, 246 pp. Pref. Notes. Index.
England. 1600-1620. Historical studies. ■Historical context for Webster's major plays.

712 Courtney, Richard. *Outline History of British Drama*. Totowa, NJ: Littlefield, Adams; 1982. ix, 336 pp. Pref. Index. Biblio.
England. 1400-1982. Histories-specific.

713 Jordon, R.L. "Congreve and the Drury Lane Playwrights, 1698." *MP*. 1982 May; 79(4): 402-407.
England. 1698. Textual studies. ■Refutation of Edmund Gosse's attribution of *Animadversions* to George Powell.

714 Mills, David. "Edward Gregorie — A 'Bunbury Scholar'."
REEDN. 1982; 1: 49-50. Notes.
England. 1591-1628. Histories-sources. ■Information about scribe of the Chester cycle of mystery plays.

715 Yates, W. Edgar. "Nestroy im Studienprogram an der Universität Exeter: Ein kleiner Beitrag zur Rezeptionsgeschichte Nestroys im Ausland." (Nestroy in the Curriculum of the University of Exeter: A Brief Look at the Reception of Nestroy Abroad.) *Ns*. 1982; 4(1): 25-30.
England. 1972-1982. Histories-sources.

716 Czarnecki, Marguerite. "*La Commère*, de Marivaux. L'éducation sentimentale de Jacob poli par l'amour." (*The Godmother*, by Marivaux: The Sentimental Education of Jacob, Refined by Love.) *CF*. 1982 May; 109: 14-16.
France. 1688-1763. Critical studies. ■Marivaux's play in relation to his novel, *Le Paysan Parvenu*, and other 18th century theatre.

717 Czarnecki, Marguerite. "Le Rire de Labiche." (The Humor of Labiche.) *CF*. 1982 Dec.; 114: 11-12.
France. Critical studies. ■Eugène Labiche's techniques for eliciting laughter in *Monsieur Perrichon's Journey (Le Voyage de Monsieur Perrichon)* and *An Italian Straw Hat (Un Chapeau de Paille d'Italie)*.

718 Derigny, Colette. "Exposition Giraudoux à la Bibliothèque Nationale." (Giraudoux Exhibit at the Bibliothèque Nationale.) *CF*. 1982 Dec.; 114: 6.
France. 1982. Histories-sources. ■Review of an exhibit marking centenary celebration of Jean Giraudoux's birth.

719 Fontenay, Elisabeth de. "*Dorval et moi*. La réconciliation de la sensibilité et de la moralité." (*Dorval and I*: The Reconciliation of Sensitivity and Morality.) *CF*. 1982 Jan.; 105: 29-30.

France. Eighteenth cent. Critical studies. ■Reflections on Diderot's theatrical imagination as evidenced through Jean Dautremay's adaptation.

720 Lindenberg, Daniel. "Un dissident théâtral: les luttes d'Henry Becque." (A Theatrical Dissident: The Struggles of Henry Becque.) *CF*. 1982 May; 109: 7-12.
France. 1837-1899. Biographical studies. ■Brief account of Becque's life, his struggle to remain independent of literary movements and to have *The Vultures (Les Corbeaux)* performed. Grp/movt: Théâtre Libre.

721 Lindenberg, Daniel. "*Les Corbeaux*. Henry Becque: morale et métaphysique." (*The Vultures*. Henry Becque: Morals and Metaphysics.) *CF*. 1982 June-July; 110: 9-13.
France. Nineteenth cent. Critical studies. ■Treatment of Becque as philosopher rather than in the usual context of naturalism. Grp/movt: Naturalism.

722 Rousseau, Josanne. "Sous les oripeaux du Boulevard." (Beneath the Glitter of the Boulevard.) *CF*. 1982 Oct.; 112: 20-21.
France. 1909-1982. Histories-sources. ■Director Jean Bouchaud comments on Roger Vitrac's *Victor ou Les enfants au pouvoir (Victor, or The Children in Power)*.

723 Aikin, Judith Popovich. *German Baroque Drama*. Boston: Twayne Publishers; 1982. xiv, 186 pp. (TWAS 634.) Pref. Notes. Index. Illus.
Germany. Austria. Baroque period. Seventeenth cent. Eighteenth cent. Historical studies.

724 Hilton, Julian. *Georg Büchner*. New York: Grove; 1982. xi, 167 pp. (Grove Press Modern Dramatist Series.) Pref. Notes. Index. Biblio. Illus.
Germany. 1750-1982. Critical studies. ■Büchner's life, society, literary background and stage history of plays. Analyses of *Danton's Death (Dantons Tod)*, *Leonce and Lena (Leonce und Lena)*, and *Woyzeck*.

725 Piretti Santangelo, Laura. *Il teatro indiano antico. Aspetti e problemi*. (Ancient Indian Theatre: Aspects and Problems.) Bologna: Clueb; 1982. 133 pp. Biblio.
India. Multi-period. Critical studies. ■Collected essays on characteristics of classic dramatic theatre. Related to Dance-Drama.

726 Bortignoni, Daniela. "Un caso 'Bertolazzi' nel Novecento." (A 'Bertolazzi' Case in the 20th Century.) *QT*. 1982 Aug.; 5 (17): 121-150. Notes.
Italy. 1870-1916. Historical studies. ■Playwright Carlo Bertolazzi's theatrical appeal and his rediscovery by Piccolo Teatro di Milano.

727 Guccini, Gerardo. "Domande sulla Sacra Rappresentazione e su Feo Belcari." (Questions about the *Sacra Rappresentazione* and Feo Belcari.) *QT*. 1982 Feb.; 4(15): 127-135. Notes.
Italy. Fifteenth cent. Historical studies. ■Feo Belcari, author of *sacre rappresentazioni*.

728 Heibert, Frank; Merschmeier, Michael. "Als Senator kann ich bei jeder Sitzung aus meinen Komödien zitieren." (As a Senator I Can Quote from My Comedies at Every Meeting.) *TH*. 1982 June; 6: 12-15. Illus.
Italy. Twentieth cent. Histories-sources. ■Interview with playwright and actor Eduardo de Filippo.

729 Innamorati, Isabella. "Due commedie morali del primo Cinquecento fiorentino." (Two Morality Plays of the Early 16th Century in Florence.) *QT*. 1982 Nov.; 5(18): 89-105. Notes.
Italy. Sixteenth cent. Critical studies. ■Analysis of two Florentine morality plays: the anonymous *Comedy of Opinion among the Gods (Commedia di opinione fra li dei)* and *Deceit (Inganno)* by Jacopo Bientina.

730 Padoan, Giorgio. *La commedia rinascimentale veneta*. (Venetian Renaissance Drama.) Vicenza: Neri Pozza; 1982.

DRAMA — cont'd

302 pp. (Studi e testi veneziani 9.) Notes. Index. Append. Illus.
Italy. 1433-1565. Histories-specific. ■History of Venetian drama. Infl. by Pietro Aretino.

731 Gibbs, James. "The Masks Hatched Out." *ThR.* 1982 Autumn; 7(3): 180-206. Notes. Illus.
Nigeria. 1958-1982. Historical studies. ■Production history and development of Wole Soyinka's plays.

732 Wennergren, Jan. "En särskild atmosfär." (A Distinctive Atmosphere.) *Entre.* 1982; 9(2): 35. Illus.
Norway. 1981-1982. Histories-sources. ■Tor Åge Bringsvaerd, playwright with state traveling theatre, Riksteatret, author of *The Great One Who Stops the Color (Den store Farvesluker)*, a children's play exemplifying his imaginative style.

733 Mellgren, Thomas. "Spelet on järnverket." (The Play about the Foundry.) *Entre.* 1982; 9(6): 13-16. Illus.
Sweden. 1982. Histories-sources. ■Collaboration of amateur theatre of Karlsvik and regional theatre of Norrbotten in producing a play based on local labor problems at mine and foundry. Infl. by Vsevolod Emil'evič Mejerchol'd.

734 Smedmark, Carl Reinhold. "Strindbergssymposium i Stockholm." (Strindberg Symposium in Stockholm.) *MfS.* 1982 Apr.; 66: 17-18.
Sweden. 1981. Histories-sources. ■Report on 'Strindberg On Stage,' a major international symposium: scenography, directing and reception abroad.

735 Amacher, Richard E. *Edward Albee.* New York: Twayne; 1982. vii, 219 pp. (TUSAS 141.) Pref. Notes. Index. Illus. [Revised edition.]
USA. 1928-1982. Critical studies. ■Biography and criticism of plays.

736 Anon. "The Living Langston: Eightieth Anniversary Celebrations Honor Poet Laureate of Black America." *Ebony.* 1982 May; 37(7): 53-55.
USA. 1902-1982. Histories-sources.

737 Anon. "Pinter, Williams: Common Wealth Winners." *ThNe.* 1982 Jan.; 14(1): 1. Illus.: Photo.
USA. 1981. Histories-sources. ■Harold Pinter and Tennessee Williams receive the Third Annual Common Wealth Award for Distinguished Service in Dramatic Arts, presented by the American Theatre Association.

738 Atkinson, Brooks; Lowery, Robert G., ed. *Sean O'Casey: From Times Past.* Totowa, NJ: Barnes and Noble; 1982. x, 175 pp. Pref. Index. Biblio.
USA. Ireland. 1926-1964. Reviews of performances. ■Atkinson's reviews of O'Casey's plays.

739 Auerbach, Doris. *Sam Shepard, Arthur Kopit, and the Off Broadway Theater.* Boston: Twayne Publishers; 1982. xiv, 145 pp. (TUSAS 432.) Pref. Notes. Index. Biblio.
USA. Twentieth cent. Critical studies. ■Study of major plays, exploring similarities and differences.

740 Bailey, A. Peter. "Charles Fuller, Pulitzer Prize Playwright." *BlC.* 1982 Aug.-Sep.; 13: 16, 21. Illus.
USA. 1980. Histories-sources. ■Fuller's philosophy of theatre, his plays and his career.

741 Bailey, A. Peter. "The Ties That Bind." *Ebony.* 1982 Jan.; 12(9): 78-79, 102, 107-8.
USA. 1960-1969. Histories-sources. ■Personal history and background of daughters of Martin Luther King and Malcolm X and their collaboration on production of a play, *Of One Mind*, about their fathers' similar goals.

742 Bigsby, C.W.E. *A Critical Introduction to Twentieth-Century American Drama: 1900-1940.* Vol. l. New York: Cambridge UP; 1982. ix, 342 pp. Pref. Notes. Index. Biblio.

USA. 1900-1940. Histories-specific. ■Survey of dramatic developments.

743 Foreman, Farrell J. "Coming Home: Confessions of a Playwright." *Encore.* 1982 Apr.: 18-19.
USA. Twentieth cent. Histories-sources. ■Problems of Black playwrights.

744 Frazer, Winifred L. "A Day in the Life of Tennessee Williams." *TWNew.* 1982 Spring-Fall; 3(2): 30-37.
USA. 1979. Histories-sources. ■Description of visit to University of Florida in conjunction with a production of *Tiger Tail.*

745 Gagliano, Frank. "The American Theatre Today: From the Eyes of a Practicing Playwright, Part One." *ThNe.* 1982 Jan.; 14 (1): 1, 4, 6, 8. [Revision of a paper read as part of Benedum/Centennial Lectures, March 1981.]
USA. 1920-1982. Historical studies. ■Problems playwrights face in having plays produced as exemplified in Frank Gagliano's *Night of the Dunce.*

746 Landes, Brigitte. "Eine lebende Legende." (A Living Legend.) *TH.* 1982 July; 7: 15-17. Illus.
USA. 1892-1982. Histories-sources. ■Commemorating novelist/playwright Djuna Barnes.

747 Leverett, James. "Holiday without Scrooge." *AmTh.* 1982 Dec.; 4(9): 1. Notes. Illus.: Photo. B&W. 1.
USA. 1981-1982. Histories-sources. ■Examines decrease in *A Christmas Carol* productions at TCG (Theatre Communications Group) theatres.

748 Leverett, James. "New Plays USA 1: A Literature in the Making." *AmTh.* 1982 Apr.; 4(1): 12-14. Notes. Illus.: Photo. B&W. 12.
USA. 1982. Histories-sources. ■Summary of *New Plays U.S.A. 1* with Tom Cole, Lee Breuer, David Hwang, Emily Mann, Oyam O and Adele Shank discussing their works.

749 Miller, Tice L. "Fitz-James O'Brien: Irish Playwright and Critic in New York, 1851-1862." *NCTR.* 1982 Summer; 10(1): 19-36. Notes. Illus.
USA. 1851-1862. Biographical studies. ■Career and contributions, with particular attention to work as a dramatic critic, playwright and essayist.

750 Molette, Barbara. "They Speak: Who Listens? Black Women Playwrights." *OvA.* 1982 Nov.; 10: 13-16.
USA. 1920-1979. Historical studies. ■Survey of published Black women playwrights with analysis of why there were so few and what they have to contribute.

751 Patterson, Douglas L. "Playmaking with the Dakota Theatre Caravan." *Tk.* 1982 Mar.-Apr.; 2(3): 7-9. Illus.
USA. USA. 1980-1982. Histories-sources. ■Describes process of collective playwriting through combined rehearsals and interviews used by Dakota Theatre Caravan.

752 Phillips, Jerrold A. "Imagining *I Can't Imagine Tomorrow.*" *TWNew.* 1982 Spring-Fall; 3(2): 27-29.
USA. Twentieth cent. Critical studies. ■Discussion of Tennessee Williams' play.

753 Powers, Dennis. "Whose Play Is It, Anyway?" *AmTh.* 1982 Jan.; 3(10): 1-3. Notes.
USA. 1982. Histories-sources. ■Focuses on financial relationship between resident theatres and playwrights — Hartford Stage Company, Mark Taper Forum, Circle Repertory, Milwaukee Repertory, Yale Repertory and Magic Theatre.

754 Schechter, Joel. "Notes from under My Desk: On the End of the World and Other Spectacles." *ThM.* 1982 Summer-Fall; 13 (3): 38-39.
USA. 1980. Histories-sources. ■*Dead End Kids: A History of Nuclear Power*, first play competition organized by *Theater*, with analysis and commentary.

755 Shewey, Don. "The True History of *True West.*" *VV.* 1982 Nov. 30; 27(48): 115. Illus.: Photo.
USA. 1982. Histories-sources. ■Brief production history of Sam Shepard's play.

DRAMA — cont'd

756   Smith, Yvonne. "Ntozake Shange: A 'Colored Girl' Considers Success." *Ebony*. 1982 Feb.; 12(10): 12, 14.
USA. 1980-1982. Histories-sources. ■Reflections on her play, *for colored girls who have considered suicide/when the rainbow is enuf*, five years after its opening and just prior to its TV adaptation. Related to Media: Video forms.

757   Williams, Tennessee. "Notes for *The Two Character Play*." *TWNew*. 1982 Spring-Fall; 3(2): 3-4.
USA. Twentieth cent. Histories-sources.

758   Witham, Barry B. "Images of America: Wilson, Weller and Horovitz." *TJ*. 1982 May; 34(2): 223-232. Notes. Illus.
USA. 1977-1979. Plot/subject/theme. ■Examines *Fifth of July* by Lanford Wilson, *Loose Ends* by Michael Weller and *Alfred Dies* by Israel Horovitz as plays that use July 4th setting to define American consciousness.

759   Iversen, Fritz. "Mit viel Geduld und Liebe zum Theater: Ein Gespräch mit dem Schriftsteller Dieter Kühn über seine Theaterstücke." (With Great Patience and Love toward Theatre: Conversation with Author Dieter Kühn about His Plays.) *Tzs*. 1982(2): 92-102. Illus.
West Germany. Twentieth cent. Histories-sources. ■Interview with author Dieter Kühn on his recent radio and stage plays, including brief summaries of *Ten Thousand Trees (Zehntausend Bäume)*, *Conversations with the Executioner (Gespräche mit dem Henker)*, *Separate Performance (Separatvorstellung)*.

760   Naumann-Will, Cornelia. "Mülheim im verflixten 7. Jahr: Von der Schwierigkeit, junge deutsche Dramatik zu fördern." (Mülheim in the 7th year: On the Difficulties of Supporting New German Drama.) *Tzs*. 1982; 1: 114-123. Illus.
West Germany. 1976-1982. Histories-sources. ■Seven years of drama festival at Mülheim, awards for best play produced in previous season, commentary on prize winning plays and criteria of competition.

761   Rischbieter, Henning. "Peter Weiss, Rechercheur." (Peter Weiss, Investigator.) *TH*. 1982 June; 6: 1.
West Germany. Twentieth cent. Histories-sources. ■Brief obituary of Peter Weiss.

Plays/playwrights: Adaptations

762   Senelik, Laurence. "Bringing *Dead Souls* to Life." *NSEEDT*. 1982 Nov.; 2(3): 16-17.
Europe. Twentieth cent. Histories-sources. ■Problems of adapting fiction to dramatic form: Laurence Senelik's adaptation of Gogol's *Dead Souls*.

763   Delmas, Christian. "Mythologie et Mythe: *Électre* de Giraudoux, *Les Mouches* de Sartre, *Antigone* d'Anouilh." (Mythology and Myth: Giraudoux's *Electra*, Sartre's *The Flies*, Anouilh's *Antigone*.) *RHT*. 1982; 34(3): 249-263. Notes.
France. 1930-1945. Critical studies. ■Mythological material versus personal myth.

764   Derigny, Colette. "Un Entretien avec Jean-Claude Brisville." (A Conversation with Jean-Claude Brisville.) *CF*. 1982 Sep.; 111: 23-24.
France. 1982. Histories-sources. ■Playwright contrasts the play *Le Fauteil à Bascule (The Rocking Chair)* with the novel.

765   Mordillat, Gérard. "Réfléchir à neuf dans chaque situation nouvelle." (Thinking Afresh in Each New Situation.) *CF*. 1982 Mar.; 107: 23.
France. Twentieth cent. Histories-sources. ■Note about relationship between Geneviève Serreau's play *Vous avez dit oui, ou bien vous avez dit non? (Did You Say Yes, Or Rather Did You Say No?)* and two short Brecht operas.

766   Wennergren, Jan. "På jakt efter Ibsen." (Hunting for Ibsen.) *Entre*. 1982; 9(2): 11-13. Illus.

Norway. China. 1923-1982. Histories-sources. ■Tormod Skagestad's play *Nora Helmer* continues themes and action of *A Doll's House (Et Dukkehjem)*. Lu Hsun's 1923 report on reaction to *A Doll's House* in China.

767   Le Gallienne, Eva. "The Joy of *Alice*." *Pb*. 1982 Nov.; 1(2): 20. Illus. [*Alice in Wonderland*, revival of stage adaptation of Lewis Carroll's *Alice* books, New York, 1982.]
USA. 1932-1982. Histories-sources. ■Eva Le Gallienne discusses her 1932 and 1982 Broadway productions of *Alice in Wonderland*. Infl. by John Tenniel.

768   Salzmann-Čelan, Marija. "Eine unbekannte Bearbeitung der Sage von Gyges und seinem Ring in der kroatischen Literatur." (An Unknown Adaptation of the Legend of Gyges and His Ring in Croatian Literature.) *MuK*. 1982; 28(1): 1-17. Notes.
Yugoslavia. 1924. Critical studies. ■Brief interpretation of Božo Lovriś' *The King and the Artist (Kralj i umjetnik)*, comparison of adaptations, excerpts from Croatian text, with emphasis on character of Gyges.

Plays/playwrights: Characters/roles

769   Hughes, Leo. "Redating Two Eighteenth Century Theatrical Documents." *MP*. 1982 Aug.; 80(1): n.p. Notes.
England. 1786-1792. Historical studies. ■Investigates true dates for role of Falstaff in *Henry IV, Part 1* and promptbook for Garrick's *Harlequin's Invasion* at Boston Public Library.

770   Czarnecki, Marguerite. "Hugo Misogyne?" (Was Hugo a Misogynist?)*CF*. 1982 Oct.; 112: 11-13.
France. Nineteenth cent. Critical studies. ■Victor Hugo's attitude toward women is revealed by the characters of Jane and the queen in his play *Marie Tudor*.

771   Marie, Charles P. "Dans l'ombre de 'l'arbre aux fées': Anouilh et Montherlant." (In the Shade of 'The Fairy Tree': Anouilh and Montherlant.) *RHT*. 1982; 34(3): 264-294. Notes.
France. 1940-1960. Critical studies. ■Character attitude and definition of self as role in plays.

772   Wells, Stanley. "Shakespeare in Hazlitt's Theatre Criticism." *ShS*. 1982; 35: 43-55. Notes.
Great Britain. 1812-1828. Studies of criticism/critics. ■Analysis of Hazlitt's theatre criticism, especially his preference for character analysis. Infl. on Edmund Kean. Related to Individuals: Shakespeare.

773   Bhat, G.K. "The Vidushaka in Sanskrit Drama." *NCPA*. 1982 June; 11(2): 1-7. Notes.
India. Multi-period. Historical studies. ■Discussion of origins, characteristics and function of comic character *vidūṣaka* in classical plays.

774   Gibson, William. "The Miracle is Annie." *Pb*. 1982 Dec.; 1(3): 25. Illus.
USA. 1950-1982. Histories-sources. ■Discusses *The Miracle Worker* as a comedy, and *Monday After the Miracle* as a darker work.

Plays/playwrights: Editions

775   Derigny, Colette. "Le Centénaire de Giraudoux." (The 100th Anniversary of Giraudoux.) *CF*. 1982 Dec.; 114: 3-5.
France. 1982. Histories-sources. ■Interview with Jacques Body, editor of the Pléiade edition of Giraudoux's complete works.

776   Dahlbäck, Lars. "Presentation av den nya Strindbergsupplagan på Strindbergssymposiet den 22 maj 1981." (Presentation of the New Strindberg Edition at the Strindberg Symposium, May 22, 1981.) *MfS*. 1982 Apr.; 66: 19-24.
Sweden. 1981-1982. Textual studies. ■72-volume edition of Strindberg's work, published by Almqvist & Wiksell, as basis for new research and translations.

777   Alexander, Robert. "Center Stage: An Anthology of 21 Contemporary Black American Plays." *CAM*. 1982 Mar.; 4(3): 39. [Column: Bay Area Arts Forum.]

DRAMA — cont'd

USA. 1982. Histories-sources. ∎Chronicles gathering of plays for anthology, published by Eileen Ostrow of Sea Urchin Press. Comments on Black theatre community, funding for publishing and use of theatre community as a resource.

Plays/playwrights: Genres

778 Bourassa, André. "Étude historique: vers la modernité de la scène québécois (III), Les contre-courants, 1901-1951." (Historical Study: Towards Modernism in Québec Drama, Part 3: Counter-currents, 1901-1951.) *PrTh.* 1982 Winter-Spring; 14-15: 1-31. Notes.
Canada. 1901-1951. Historical studies. ∎Consideration of avant-garde from Impressionism through Surrealism.

779 Davenport, W.A. *Fifteenth-Century English Drama: The Early Moral Plays and Their Literary Relations.* Totowa, NJ: Rowman and Littlefield; 1982. vii, 152 pp. Pref. Notes. Index. Biblio.
England. 1300-1559. Critical studies. ∎Comparison of selected morality plays with other literary types.

780 Pettitt, Thomas. "English Folk Drama and the Early German *Fastnachtspiele.*" *RenD.* 1982; n.s. 13: 1-34. Notes.
England. Germany. 1400-1899. Historical studies. ∎Analogous traditions in medieval folk play: mode of presentation and dramaturgy, possible institutional context. Characteristics of folk plays preserved in regular drama.

781 Shafer, Yvonne. "Center Stage: Peter Barnes and the Theatre of Disturbance." *ThNe.* 1982 Dec.; 14(9): 7-9. Illus.: Photo. B&W. 4.
England. 1968-1982. Histories-sources. ∎Interview with playwright/screenwriter/adapter Peter Barnes, in which he eschews naturalism in favor of the 'theatre of disturbance'. Infl. by Naturalism.

782 Pettitt, Thomas. "Early English Traditional Drama: Approaches and Perspectives." *RORD.* 1982; 25: 1-30. Notes.
Great Britain. Medieval period. Renaissance period. Critical studies. ∎Medieval and Renaissance antecedents of modern folkdrama.

783 Clarke, Brenda Katz. *The Emergence of the Irish Peasant Play at the Abbey Theatre.* Ann Arbor, MI: UMI Research P; 1982. xi, 223 pp. (Theater and Dramatic Studies 12.) Notes. Index. Append. Biblio. Illus.
Ireland. 1902-1908. Historical studies. ∎Analysis of peasant drama as a genre. Playwrights discussed: W.B. Yeats, Lady Gregory, J.M. Synge, Padraic Colum, William Boyle, James Cousins and George Fitzmaurice. Leadership of Frank and William G. Fay also discussed.

784 Alexander, Robert. "Ed Bullins, The Prodigal Son." *CAM.* 1982 Sep.; 4(9): 19.
USA. 1982. Histories-sources. ∎Discussion of New Lafayette Theatre, and collaboration with John Doyle, Joe Papp and Public Theatre and status of Blacks in theatre.

785 Bank, Rosemarie K. "The Naturalistic Bias in Criticism at the Turn of the Century vs. Lillian Mortimer." *THSt.* 1982; 2 : 61-68. Notes.
USA. 1890-1910. Studies of criticism/critics. ∎Shift in public taste leads to decline of melodrama, rise of naturalism.

Plays/playwrights: Plot/subject/theme

786 Berghaus, Günter. "Quellen zu Nestroys Weltanschauung und Lebensphilosophie." (Sources of Nestroy's Philosophy of Life.) *Ns.* 1982; 4(1): 3-24. Notes.
Austria. Nineteenth cent. Critical studies. ∎Influence of philosophy of order, Austrian school-philosophy and Josephinian popular philosophy on background of Johann Nestroy's plays.

787 Mautner, Franz H. "Nestroy als Philosoph." (Nestroy as Philosopher.) *Ns.* 1982; 4(2): 38-49.
Austria. Nineteenth cent. Critical studies. ∎Examples of Johann Nestroy's dialectic view of life, his pessimism, scepticism and cynicism.

788 Černý, František. "Die Bühnenwerke Karel Čapeks." (The Plays of Karel Čapek.) *MuK.* 1982; 28(2) : 125-142. Notes. Illus.
Czechoslovakia. 1910-1928. Critical studies. ∎Interpretations and short references to performances, mainly in Prague. Grp/movt: Expressionism.

789 Fischborn, Gottfried. "Dramatik in Druck: Beim Lesen von Stück-Veröffentlichungen in TdZ notiert." (Drama in Print: Reading Plays Published in *Theater der Zeit.*) *TZ.* 1982 May; 37: 58-60. Illus. [Third in a series of three articles.]
East Germany. 1982. Histories-sources. ∎Problems of contemporary socialist drama.

790 Fischborn, Gottfried. "Dramatik im Druck: Beim Lesen von Stück-Veröffentlichungen in TdZ notiert." (Drama in Print: Reading Plays Published in *Theater der Zeit.*) *TZ.* 1982 Mar.; 37: 64. Illus. [First in a series of three articles.]
East Germany. 1982. Histories-sources. ∎Problems of contemporary socialist drama.

791 Fischborn, Gottfried. "Dramatik in Druck: Beim Lesen von Stück-Veröffentlichungen in TdZ notiert." (Drama in Print: Reading Plays Published in *Theater der Zeit.*) *TZ.* 1982 Apr.; 37(4): 61-63. Illus. [Second in a series of three articles.]
East Germany. 1982. Critical studies. ∎Problems of socialist drama observed in the plays printed in *Theater der Zeit.*

792 Bigsby, C.W.E. *Joe Orton.* New York: Methuen; 1982. 79 pp. (Contemporary Writers Series.) Pref. Notes. Biblio.
England. Twentieth cent. Critical studies. ∎Brief biography followed by extensive exegesis of work.

793 Cohn, Ruby. "Modest Proposals of Modern Socialists." *MD.* 1982 Dec.; 25(4): 457-468. Notes.
England. 1970-1979. Critical studies. ∎Grotesque comedy in socialist plays.

794 Dukore, Bernard F. *Harold Pinter.* New York: Grove Press; 1982. x, 139 pp. (Grove Press Modern Dramatists.) Pref. Index. Biblio. Illus.
England. Twentieth cent. Critical studies. ∎Critical treatment of Pinter's career, combining chronological development with broader thematic framework.

795 Hinden, Michael. "To Verify a Proposition in *The Homecoming.*" *TJ.* 1982 Mar.; 34(1): 27-39. Notes.
England. 1930-1982. Critical studies. ∎Play as an example of logical positivism, with characters' main actions as attempts to determine truth of various propositions. Parallels difficulty of verifying truth in general world to difficulty of achieving or believing in sexual fidelity in Pinter's world. Infl. by Ludwig Wittgenstein; *Tractatus logico-philosophicus.*

796 Innes, Christopher. "The Political Spectrum of Edward Bond: From Rationalism to Rhapsody." *MD.* 1982 June; 25(2): 189-206. Notes.
England. Twentieth cent. Critical studies. ∎Social analysis of use of violence and comparison with works of Brecht.

797 Jordan, William Chester. "Approaches to the Court Scene in the Bond Story: Equity and Mercy or Reason and Nature." *SQ.* 1982 Spring; 33(1): 49-59. Notes.
England. Elizabethan period. Sixteenth cent. Critical studies. ∎Conditions of acquittal in bond stories examined through use of words and meanings. Related to Individuals: Shakespeare.

798 Morley, Sheridan. "*Steaming.*" *Pb.* 1982 Dec.; 1(3): 36. Illus.
England. USA. 1960-1980. Histories-sources. ∎Interview with playwright Nell Dunn on *Steaming*, and its origins in women's conversations in steam bath.

DRAMA — cont'd

799　Reinhold, Heinz. *Das englische Drama, 1580-1642: Aspekte zeitgenössischer Aktualität.* (The English Drama, 1580-1642: Aspects of Its Contemporary Topical Interest.) Stuttgart: Kohlhammer; 1982. 190 pp. (Sprache und Literatur 118.) Index. Biblio.
England. 1580-1642. Critical studies. ■Shakespeare and his contemporaries: topical aspects of their plays.

800　Lossmann, Hans; Wilk, Gerard H. "Spiel mit dem Feuer." (Playing With Fire.) *Bühne.* 1982 Dec.: 33-35. Illus.
Europe. USA. Twentieth cent. Critical studies. ■Treatment of Nazi themes in productions.

801　Ring, Lars. "Canetti: en dramatiker att spela." (Canetti: A Dramatist to Play.) *Entre.* 1982; 9(4): 25-27. Illus.
Europe. 1932-1982. Critical studies. ■Three plays treat themes of individuality, self-deception and death. Infl. by Expressionism.

802　Valle, Outi. "Paavo Haavikko: Le rire noir à l'adresse du monde qui a la forme d'une pièce de monnaie/Paavo Haavikko: Black Laughter at a World Shaped Like a Piece of Money." *NFT.* 1982; 34: 4-5. Illus.
Finland. 1982. Critical studies. ■Paavo Haavikko's eight plays combine myths, irony and epic elements, using both modern and historic themes such as finance and power.

803　Cooper, Barbara T. "Exploitation of the Body in Vigny's *Chatterton*: The Economics of Drama and the Drama of Economics." *TJ.* 1982 Mar.; 34(1): 20-26. Notes.
France. 1835. ■Play deals primarily with economic issues, plight of poverty-stricken poet reflecting triumph of mercantile and physical over humanistic and spiritual values.

804　Czarnecki, Marguerite. "De *l'Échange* à *Partage de Midi*." (From *The Exchange* to *Break of Noon*.) *CF.* 1982 Sep.; 111: 20-21.
France. Belgium. 1894-1906. Critical studies. ■Paul Claudel's *l'Échange*, though an early play, contains many of the poetic and religious elements of *Partage de midi*.

805　Czarnecki, Marguerite. "*Les Caprices de Marianne*, pièce romantique?" (*The Follies of Marianne*: A Romantic Play?) *CF.* 1982 Feb.; 106: 8-9.
France. Nineteenth cent. Romantic period. Critical studies. ■Play expresses author Alfred de Musset's individuality more than influence of Romanticism.

806　Dumur, Guy. "Un Fantôme en Limousin ou L'impromptu de Bellac." (A Phantom in Limousin, or The Bellac Impromptu.) *CF.* 1982 Nov.; 113: 3-6.
France. Twentieth cent. Biographical studies. ■*Intermezzo* owes certain elements to Jean Giraudoux's native province of Limousin.

807　Knapp, Bettina L. *Paul Claudel.* New York: Frederick Ungar; 1982. vi, 287 pp. Pref. Notes. Index. Biblio. Illus.
France. 1868-1955. Biographies. ■Biography followed by thematic analysis of Claudel's major dramas.

808　Nores, Dominique. "*Le Voyage de Madame Knipper à travers la Prusse-Orientale*, l'abandon, l'exil, la fuite." (*Mrs. Knipper's Journey through Eastern Prussia*: Abandon, Exile, Flight.) *CF.* 1982 Feb.; 106: 17-18.
France. Twentieth cent. Histories-sources. ■Brief discussion with author and director about meaning of play.

809　Nores, Dominique. "Une Mise à Mort." (An Execution.) *CF.* 1982 Dec.; 114: 15-16.
France. 1982. Critical studies. ■Yves-Fabrice Lebeau, playwright, and Jean-Luc Boutté, director, examine the meaning of Lebeau's play, *Comptine*.

810　Pieiller, Evelyne. "La mise en crise des silences." (Silences in Crisis.) *CF.* 1982 Nov.; 113: 18-19.
France. Germany. Twentieth cent. Critical studies. ■Analysis and commentary on *Grand et Petit (Gross und Klein)* by Botho Strauss.

811　Hartigan, Karelisa V., ed. *To Hold a Mirror to Nature: Dramatic Images and Reflections.* Univ. of Florida Dept. of Classics & Comparative Literature Conference Papers 1980. Washington, DC: UP of America; 1982. viii, 164 pp. Pref. Notes. [Vol. I.]
Greece. Great Britain. France. West Germany. USA. 400 B.C.-1982 A.D. Critical studies. ■Ten papers on Greek tragedy, Restoration comedy, Marivaux, Goering, New York productions of *Phèdre*, modern German drama and *King Lear*.

812　Johnson, Toni O'Brien. *Synge: The Medieval and the Grotesque.* Totowa, NJ: Barnes and Noble; 1982. viii, 209 pp. (Irish Literary Studies Series 11.) Pref. Notes. Index. Biblio.
Ireland. Twentieth cent. Critical studies. ■Use of medieval material and grotesque elements in his translations and in *The Well of the Saints*, *The Playboy of the Western World* and *Deirdre of the Sorrows*.

813　Puppa, Paolo. "Rosso di San Secondo e Pirandello: la cultura dei morti." (Rosso di San Secondo and Pirandello: The Culture of the Dead.) *QT.* 1982 Nov.; 5(18): 106-120. Notes.
Italy. Twentieth cent. Critical studies. ■Topic of death in some works by Rosso di San Secondo and Luigi Pirandello.

814　Obafemi, Olu. "Political Perspectives and Popular Theatre in Nigeria." *ThR.* 1982 Autumn; 7(3): 235-244. Notes.
Nigeria. Twentieth cent. Critical studies. ■Social revolution, spectacle and oral tradition in contemporary plays.

815　"Plays from the Proletariat." *Tk.* 1982 July-Aug.; 2(5): 45-48.
South Africa, Republic of. 1970-1982. Histories-sources. ■Discussion of plays, actors and companies developed by and about life as lived by South African Blacks.

816　Izakowitz, David. "The Heresy of Athol Fugard." *AmTh.* 1982 June; 4(3): 1-3. Notes. Illus.: Photo. B&W. 4.
South Africa, Republic of. USA. 1982. Critical studies. ■Discusses Fugard as a writer and as director of his own work.

817　Mshengu. "Political Theatre in South Africa and the Work of Athol Fugard." *ThR.* 1982 Autumn; 7(3): 160-179. Notes.
South Africa, Republic of. 1950-1982. Critical studies. ■Influence of traditional and experimental South African Black theatre on Fugard's work.

818　Hepburn, Katharine. "Hepburn on Thompson." *Pb.* 1982 Nov.; 1(2): 12. Illus. [Reprint of introduction to *The West Side Waltz* by Ernest Thompson, Dodd, Mead & Co., 1982.]
USA. 1982. Histories-sources. ■Playwright Ernest Thompson's use of 'ordinary man' as his subject.

819　Lewiton, Margo; Chambers, Jane; Maiorisi, Catherine; Fierstein, Harvey. "Chambers/Fierstein: Award Winners of Merit." *GTAN.* 1982 Aug.; 4(1): 3-5.
USA. 1982. Histories-sources. ■Transcripts of acceptance speeches by Jane Chambers and Harvey Fierstein at the fifth annual National Gay Task Force Fund for Human Dignity Awards Dinner.

820　Pawley, Thomas D. "Three Views of the Returning Black Veteran." *BALF.* 1982 Winter; 16(4): 163-167. Notes. Illus.
USA. 1945-1946. Critical studies. ■Three contemporary portrayals of returning Black servicemen: *Deep Are the Roots*, *Job*, *On Whitman Avenue*.

821　Reif, Robin. "The Double Life of Harvey Fierstein." *Pb.* 1982 Oct.; 1(1): 26. Illus.
USA. 1977-1982. Histories-sources. ■Evolution and significance of *Torch Song Trilogy* as gay play and Fierstein's career including roles as playwright and principal actor.

822　Stephens, Judith L. "*Why Marry?* The 'New Woman' of 1918." *TJ.* 1982 May; 34(2): 183-196. Notes. Illus.
USA. 1918. Critical studies. ■Play as representative of post-World War I interest in the 'New Woman.' Surveys common images of women in

DRAMA — cont'd

literature, and poses a four-step evaluative scale for judging female characters' emancipation: motivation, deliberation, decision and action.

823 Watt, Stephen. "The 'Formless Fears' of O'Neill's *Emperor* and Tennyson's *King*." *EON*. 1982 Winter; 6(3): 14-15.
USA. Twentieth cent. Critical studies. ■Alfred Tennyson's *Idylls of the King* as a source for *The Emperor Jones*. Related to Individuals: O'Neill.

Plays/playwrights: Structure/language

824 Schaefer, James F., Jr. "An Explanation of Language as Gesture in a Play by Gertrude Stein." *LPer*. 1982 Nov.; 3(1): 1-14. Notes.
Twentieth cent. Linguistic studies. ■Using language as gesture is key to understanding *Doctor Faustus Lights the Lights* by Gertrude Stein.

825 Bortenschlager, Wilhelm. *Tiroler Drama und Dramatiker im 20. Jahrhundert*. (Tyrolean Drama and Dramatists in the Twentieth Century.) St. Michael: Bläschke; 1982. 259 pp. (Schrifttum der Gegenwart, 17.) Pref. Notes. Index. Biblio.
Austria. Twentieth cent. Critical studies.

826 Miller, Mary Jane. "The Use of Stage Metaphor in *The Donnellys*." *CDr*. 1982; 8(1): 34-41.
Canada. 1975-1977. Critical studies. ■Analysis of play by James Reaney.

827 Sherrill, Grace. "A Northern Quality: Herman Voaden's Canadian Expressionism." *CDr*. 1982; 8(1): 1-14.
Canada. 1905-1937. Critical studies. ■Analysis of work by playwright Herman Voaden.

828 Savran, David. "The Girardian Economy of Desire: *Old Times* Recaptured." *TJ*. 1982 Mar.; 34(1): 40-54. Notes.
England. 1930. Critical studies. ■Broadens imitative desire pattern to include triangle formed by Pinter's play, the audience and the audience's expectations of a traditional psychological play. Infl. by René Girard.

829 Tener, Robert L. "Edward Bond's Dialectic: Irony and Dramatic Metaphors." *MD*. 1982 Sep.; 25(3): 423-434. Notes.
England. Twentieth cent. Critical studies. ■Ironic interplay of scenic images and dramatic metaphors creates social dialectic.

830 Matzat, Wolfgang. *Dramenstruktur und Zuschauerrolle: Theater in der französischen Klassik*. (The Structure of Drama and the Role of the Spectator: Theatre in French Classicism.) Munich: Fink; 1982. 336 pp. (Theorie und Geschichte der Literatur und der schönen Künste 62.) Notes. Index. Biblio.
France. French classicism. Seventeenth cent. Critical studies. ■Structuralist approach to drama as a complex communication system.

831 Picart, Hervé. "Théâtre, Langage, Vérité." (Theatre, Language, Truth.) *CF*. 1982 Nov.; 113: 9-11.
France. Nineteenth cent. Linguistic studies. ■Henry Becque's realistic language stripped of rhetorical device in *The Vultures (Les Corbeaux)*. Grp/movt: Realism.

832 Hoff-Purviance, Linda. "The Form of Kleist's *Penthesilea* and the *Iliad*." *GQ*. 1982 Jan.; 55(1): 39-48. Notes.
Germany. 1808. Critical studies. ■Scene structure of *Penthesilea* follows that of *The Iliad*'s 24 books in complication and denouement. Infl. by Johann Wolfgang von Goethe; William Shakespeare.

833 Tendulkar, Vijay. "My Drama Education." *NCPA*. 1982 Sep.-Dec.; 11(3-4): 41-52.
India. Twentieth cent. Histories-sources. ■Dramatist recalls his progress into theatre, including journalistic descriptions of influential performances and productions.

834 Botha, Bet. "Enkele gedagtes oor 'n 'blitskursus' in toneelskryf." (Some Thoughts on a 'Crash Course' in Playwriting.) *TF*. 1982 May; 3(1): 1-10.

South Africa, Republic of. 1980-1982. Studies of theories/theorists. ■Nature of playwriting and dialogue, course structure and sample exercises.

835 Janzon, Leif. "Lars Norén." *Entre*. 1982; 9(1): 24-27. Illus.
Sweden. 1973-1981. Histories-sources. ■Interview with playwright Lars Norén about character, structure and rhetoric in his plays. Infl. by Harold Pinter; Edward Albee.

836 Berg, Shelley C.; Davis, Rick; Schechter, Joel. "Rip Van Winkle Our Contemporary: An Interview with Richard Nelson." *ThM*. 1982 Spring; 13(2): 6-8.
USA. 1981. Histories-sources. ■Dramaturgy of Nelson's play, produced at Yale Repertory Theatre.

837 Debusscher, Gilbert. "French Stowaways on an American Milk Train: Williams, Cocteau and Peyrefitte to Jacques Guicharnaud." *MD*. 1982 Sep.; 25(3): 399-408. Notes.
USA. Twentieth cent. Critical studies. ■Proposes that Williams took most of his inspiration for *The Milk Train Doesn't Stop Here Anymore* from Ronald Duncan's adaptation of Jean Cocteau's *The Eagle Has Two Heads (L'Aigle à deux têtes)*.

838 Miller, Jane. "Writing in a Second Language." *Raritan*. 1982 Summer; 2(1): 115-132.
USA. Great Britain. USSR. Twentieth cent. Linguistic studies. ■Reasons writers choose to compose in their second languages.

839 Miller, Jeanne-Marie A. "Three Theatre Pieces by Ntozake Shange." *ThNe*. 1982 Apr.; 14(4): 8. [The second of four brief articles in *The Black Theatre Bulletin* included as part of *Theatre News*.]
USA. 1970-1982. Critical studies. ■Comments on controversial themes and new form (choreopoem) of Shange's three pieces: *Spell #7, A Photograph: Lovers in Motion* and *Boogie Woogie Landscapes*.

840 Parder, Brian. "The Composition of *The Glass Menagerie*: An Argument for Complexity." *MD*. 1982 Sep.; 25(3): 409-422. Notes.
USA. 1965-1982. Critical studies. ■Analyzes genesis of Tennessee Williams' play based on material at the Humanities Research Center of the University of Texas.

Relation to other fields: Politics

841 Hilton, Julian. "Four Walls." *Gambit*. 1982; 10(39-40): 3-14.
East Germany. West Germany. 1960-1980. Historical studies. ■Political theatre.

842 Kröplin, Wolfgang. "Mass und Möglichkeit: Zum Einfluss europäischer sozialistischer Theaterkulturen auf unseren Theater." (Measure and Possibility: Influence of European Socialist Theatre Cultures on Theatre in East Germany.) *TZ*. 1982 May; 37: 5-8.
East Germany. 1982. Histories-sources.

843 Davison, Peter. *Contemporary Drama and the Popular Democratic Tradition in England*. Totowa, NJ: Barnes and Noble; 1982. xi, 193 pp. Pref. Index. Illus.
England. 1900-1982. Historical studies.

844 Weitz, Hans J. "Im Schatten der Nazis." (In the Shadow of the Nazis.) *TH*. 1982 Sep.; 9: 20-25. Illus.
Germany. 1932-1933. Historical studies. ■Summary of season at Düsseldorfer Schauspielhaus. Reviews work of Leopold Lindtberg at Schillertheater, Berlin.

845 Temkine, Raymonde. "Théâtre à l'étranger, le dernier festival dans la Pologne de Solidarité." (Theatre Abroad: The Last Festival in Poland of the Solidarity Era.) *CF*. 1982 Feb.; 106: 19-20.
Poland. 1981. Reviews of performances. ■Political ramifications of festival.

DRAMA — cont'd

846 Gray, Garry. "What Direction Black Theatre?" *ThNe.* 1982 Apr.; 14(4): 9. [The third of four brief articles in *The Black Theatre Bulletin* included as part of *Theatre News.*]
USA. 1920-1982. Histories-sources. ■Samuel A. Hay, Black critic, professor and playwright, comments on Black theatre in an era fraught with social and economic problems.

847 Wertheim, Albert. "The McCarthy Era and the American Theatre." *TJ.* 1982 May; 34(2): 211-222. Notes.
USA. 1947-1954. Historical studies. ■Discusses McCarthy era plays that attacked HUAC (House Un-American Activities Committee) investigations or protested author's innocence of communist sympathies in works by John Druten, Sidney Kingsley, Maxwell Anderson, William Saroyan, James Thurber, Elliot Nugent, Lillian Hellman, Arthur Miller, Robert Anderson, Jerome Laurence, Robert E. Lee, Albert Matz and Robert Audrey.

Relation to other fields: Psychology

848 Huntsman, Karla Hendricks. "Improvisational Dramatic Activities: Key to Self-Actualization?" *ChTR.* 1982 Spring; 31(2): 3-9. Notes.
Twentieth cent. Technical studies. ■Effects of creative drama course on participants' confidence, spontaneity and interpersonal relations.

849 Rosenberg, Helene S.; Castellano, Rose; Chrein, Geraldine; Pinciotti, Patricia. "Answering a Research Need: Developing an Imagery-Based Theory for the Field of Creative Drama." *ChTR.* 1982 Spring; 31(2): 16-20. Notes. Illus.: Diagram.
Twentieth cent. Studies of theories/theorists. ■Research in cognitive development as a theoretical basis for creative drama.

Relation to other fields: Sociology

850 Wayne, Don E. "Drama and Society in the Age of Jonson: An Alternative View." *RenD.* ; n.s. 13: 103-129. Notes.
England. 1500-1642. Historical studies. ■Challenges L.C. Knights' *Drama and Society in the Age of Jonson*. Plays reflect tension between two conceptions of individualism: as root of social disorder and as poet's assertion of individuality. Tension is related to rise of contract law as means of social control, in lieu of order based on faith.

851 Ventrone, Paola. "Aspetti della società fiorentina nella Sacra Rappresentazione dei secoli XV e XVI." (Aspects of Florentine Society in the *Sacra Rappresentazione* of the 15th and 16th Centuries.) *QT.* 1982 Feb.; 4(15): 81-126. Notes.
Italy. Fifteenth cent. Sixteenth cent. Renaissance period. Critical studies. ■Depiction of Florentine society through sociological analysis of *sacre rappresentazioni*, with selection of texts.

852 McCaslin, Nellie. "The Quest for New Heroines: Sexism and Children's Theatre." *ThNe.* 1982 Fall; 14(7): 1.
USA. Twentieth cent. Histories-sources. ■Points to importance of children's plays providing girls as well as boys with admirable roles with which they can identify.

853 Vorenberg, Bonnie. "New Plays for Seniors: What the Playwright Needs to Know." *ThNe.* 1982 Nov.; 14(8): 8-9. Illus. Photo.
USA. 1981-1982. Histories-sources. ■Requirements for plays with senior adults: plot, dialogue and setting.

Staging

854 Berg, Jean. "Werktreue: eine Kategorie geht fremd: Über Klassikeraufführungen." (Fidelity to Original Work Creates Obsolescence: On Performing Classics.) *Tzs.* 1982; 1: 93-100. Notes. Illus.
Multi-period. Critical studies. ■Discussion of the principle of fidelity to the original work in performance of classical plays.

855 Clark, Georgina A. "Gordon Craig and the Paradox of Shakespeare." *MuK.* 1982; 28(2): 113-119. Notes.

England. 1885-1911. Studies of theories/theorists. ■Craig's reflections on staging Shakespeare: *Hamlet, Macbeth, Richard III*. Shakespeare's unactable plays as challenge for Craig's impossible theatre, projects for union of 'Three Arts'. Related to Individuals: Shakespeare.

856 Planson, Claude. "Jean Vilar et *Le Prince De Hombourg*." (Jean Vilar and *The Prince of Homburg*.) *CF.* 1982 Mar.; 107 : 21-22.
France. 1951. Histories-sources.

857 "Hartford Hosts Ward, Walcott and a New Idea." *AmTh.* 1982 May; 4(2): 1-3. Notes. Illus.: Photo. B&W. 4.
USA. 1982. Histories-sources. ■Collaboration of Negro Ensemble Co. and Hartford Stage Co. on production of *The Isle is Full of Noises*.

858 Johnson, Stephen. "Joseph Jefferson's *Rip Van Winkle*." *TDR.* 1982 Spring; 26(1): 3-20.
USA. Nineteenth cent. Histories-reconstruction. ■Recreation of Joseph Jefferson's *Rip Van Winkle* based on information found in diaries, reviews, photographs, films and Edison cylinders dating as far back as 1865.

Staging: Directing/directors

859 Böhm, Gotthard. "Hans Jaray: Verpönt wie Schulschwänzen." (Interview with Hans Jaray.) *Bühne.* 1982 Dec.: 16-18. Illus.
Austria. 1930-1982. Histories-sources. ■Interview with actor and director on his career, productions at Theater in der Josefstadt and his opinion of entertainment's role in theatre.

860 Dahnke, Hans-Dietrich. "Dimensionen der Geschichtlichkeit. Zur Interpretation von Dramen der Vergangenheit (7)." (Dimensions of Historicity: On the Interpretation of Period plays, Part 7.) *TZ.* 1982 Sep.; 37(9): 22-23.
East Germany. Twentieth cent. Historical studies. ■Discussion on harmonizing historical content and present interpretation.

861 Görne, Dieter. "'Ich will schon vorkommen in dem Werk': Erfahrungen mit dem Erbe." (Experiences with the Cultural Heritage.) *TZ.* 1982 June; 37(6): 14-16.
East Germany. Twentieth cent. Histories-sources. ■Round-table talk with directors on their adaptations of historical dramas.

862 Kuckhoff, Armin-Gerd. "Zur Interpretation von Dramen der Vergangenheit (10 und Schluss): Erben-Erwerben über einige 'Parameter'." (On the Interpretation of Period Plays, Part 10: Inherit and Acquire.) *TZ.* 1982; 37(12): 31-33.
East Germany. Twentieth cent. Critical studies. ■Responsibility of actors to period plays.

863 Leistner, Bernd. "Zum Beispiel *Torquato Tasso*. Zur Interpretation von Dramen der Vergangenheit (8)." (*Torquato Tasso*: On the Interpretation of Period Plays, Part 8.) *TZ.* 1982; 37(10): 26-27. Illus.
East Germany. 1982. ■Description of the Friedrich Solter's production of Goethe's *Torquato Tasso* at Deutsches Theater, East Berlin: a compromise between historical accuracy and creative license.

864 Lorenzen, Richard L. "The Bancroft-Robertson Collaboration on *Caste*." *NCTR.* 1982 Summer; 10(1): 1-17. Notes. Illus.
England. 1867-1883. Histories-reconstruction. ■Description of business and composition in T.W. Robertson's *Caste* as originally staged and revived by Squire and Marie Bancroft at the Prince of Wales Theatre, London.

865 Rajala, Panu. "Kalle Holmberg." *NFT.* 1982; 34: 2-3. Illus.
Finland. 1982. Histories-sources. ■Theatre director Kalle Holmberg's direction of television film, *The Iron Age*, an adaptation of the *Kalevala* by Paavo Haavikko, and Aleksis Kivi's *Kullervo* at KOM Theatre.

866 Gasc, Yves. "*Le Plaisir de rompre*. Jules Renard: cruauté instinctive ou pudeur?" (*The Pleasure of Breaking* by Jules Renard: Instinctive Cruelty or Modesty?) *CF.* 1982 Feb.; 106: 7.

DRAMA — cont'd

France. Twentieth cent. Histories-sources. ■Yves Gasc, director of the Renard play at the Comédie Française, discusses its interpretation.

867 Guibert, Noëlle. "*Marie Tudor* de Victor Hugo. L'histoire de la pièce." (*Marie Tudor* by Victor Hugo: The History of the Play.) *CF*. 1982 May; 109: 18-23.
France. Nineteenth cent. Twentieth cent. Historical studies. ■Personal factors in casting of first performance: Juliette Drouet and Mademoiselle George. Listing of satires of play.

868 Pascaud, Fabienne. "*Palais de Justice*. Un entretien avec Jean-Pierre Vincent." (*Palace of Justice:* A Conversation with Jean-Pierre Vincent.) *CF*. 1982 Jan.; 105: 14-16.
France. 1982. Histories-sources. ■Jean-Pierre Vincent, director of Théâtre National de Strasbourg, describes how the group developed a play based on observations of courtroom trials.

869 Poulet, Jacques. "*Les Corbeaux* d'Henry Becque. Un Entretien avec Jean-Pierre Vincent." (*The Vultures* by Henry Becque: A Conversation with Jean-Pierre Vincent.) *CF*. 1982 May; 109: 3-5.
France. 1982. Histories-sources. ■Director discusses his interpretation of *Les Corbeaux* for the Comédie Française.

870 Rousseau, Josanne. "Un entretien avec Jean-Paul Roussillon." (A Conversation with Jean-Paul Roussillon.) *CF*. 1982 Nov. ; 113: 21-22.
France. 1982. Histories-sources. ■Jean-Paul Roussillon, director of *Vacation (Vacances)* and *Riot (Rixe)* by Jean-Claude Grumberg, discusses their staging at the Comédie Française.

871 Surgers, Anne. "Un entretien avec Jean-Pierre Vincent à propos du décor des *Corbeaux*." (A Conversation with Jean-Pierre Vincent about the Setting of *The Vultures*.) *CF*. 1982 Sep.; 111: 3-4.
France. 1982. Histories-sources. ■Director of the Becque play explains the unexpected stage setting used at the Comédie Française.

872 Tarkiel, Jacqueline. "*Les Caprices de Marianne*. Un entretien avec François Beaulieu." (*The Follies of Marianne:* A Conversation with François Beaulieu.) *CF*. 1982 Jan.; 105: 3-4.
France. 1982. Histories-sources. ■Director discusses his understanding of Alfred de Musset's play.

873 Heap, Carl. "On Performing *Mankind*." *MET*. 1982; 4(2): 93-103.
Great Britain. 1982. Histories-sources. ■Analysis by director of a production of *Mankind*.

874 Benedetti, Jean. *Stanislavski: An Introduction*. New York: Theatre Arts Books; 1982. xii, 81 pp. Pref. Index. Biblio.
Russia. 1899-1936. Critical studies. ■Analysis of selected issues in life and work of director K.S. Stanislavsky.

875 Chesler, S. Alan. "An Interview with Eve Adamson." *TWNew*. 1982 Spring-Fall; 3(2): 38-45. [Includes July 1981 note by Tennessee Williams about his work with Eve Adamson.]
USA. 1982. Histories-sources. ■Interview with director of three of Tennessee Williams' plays at Jean Cocteau Repertory Theatre.

876 Colt, Jay Leo. "Dancing in Red Hot Shoes." *TWNew*. 1982 Spring-Fall; 3(2): 6-8.
USA. 1976. Histories-sources. ■Director's notes to 1976 San Francisco production of *The Two Character Play* by Tennessee Williams.

877 Jones, Betty Jean. "Tennessee Williams' *Out Cry*: Studies in Production Form at the University of Wisconsin-Madison, Part II." *TWNew*. 1982 Spring-Fall; 3(2): 9-16. Illus.: Photo.
USA. Twentieth cent. Histories-sources. ■Discussion of preparatory work.

878 Rabkin, Gerald; Loney, Glenn; Coco, William. "Styles in Production." *PerAJ*. 1982; 6(3): 67-86.

USA. Austria. Germany. Twentieth cent. Critical studies. ■Various productions examined for differences in style: *Don Juan (Dom Juan)*, *Ghosts (Gengangere)*, *Faust, Summer Vacation Madness, Parsifal, Richard II, Twelfth Night, Above the Villages (Über die Dörfer)*.

879 Schechner, Richard. "Genet's *The Balcony*: A 1951 Perspective on a 1979/80 Production." *MD*. 1982 Mar.; 25(1): 82-104 . Illus.: Photo. Diagram. B&W.
USA. 1979-1980. Histories-sources. ■Schechner explains his deconstruction-reconstruction of the author's text.

880 Shafer, Yvonne. "Strasberg's Recollections Highlight Ibsen Society Activities This Year." *ThNe*. 1982 Nov.; 14(8): 11-12. Illus. Photo. B&W. 2.
USA. 1930-1982. Histories-sources. ■Productions of *Peer Gynt* and *Ghosts (Gengangere)* and founding of Ibsen Theatre in America.

881 Shyer, Laurence. "Andrei Serban Directs Chekhov: *The Seagull* in New York and Japan." *ThM*. 1981-82 Winter; 13(1): 56-66. Illus.
USA. Japan. 1980. Critical studies. ■Minimalist stagings of Chekhov's *The Seagull (Čajka)*.

882 Böhm, Gotthard. "Ins Zentrum des Taifuns." (Into the Middle of the Typhoon.) *Bühne*. 1982 Sep.: 11-12.
West Germany. Austria. 1970-1982. Histories-sources. ■Interview with director Peter Palitzsch about his concept of staging classical plays, especially Goethe's *Egmont* at Burgtheater.

883 Marker, Lisa-Lone; Marker, Frederick J. "Of Winners and Losers: A Conversation with Ingmar Bergman." *ThM*. 1982 Summer-Fall; 13(3): 42-52. Illus.
West Germany. 1981. Histories-sources. ■Conflation of conversations before and after opening of Bergman Project, a four-hour production combining *A Doll's House (Et Dukkehjem)*, *Miss Julie (Fröken Julie)* and a stage version of Bergman's film *Scenes from a Marriage*, at Residenztheater, Munich.

884 Skasa, Michael; Strauss, Botho. "Fassbinders Anfänge." (The Beginnings of Fassbinder.) *TH*. 1982(8): 24-27. Illus.
West Germany. 1967-1969. Biographical studies. ■Early career of film director Rainer Werner Fassbinder at Münchner Anti-Theater. Related to Dance-Drama.

Training

885 Corrigan, Mary, ed. "Learning to 'Speak the Speech': A Directors' Survey on Shakespeare and the American Actor." *ThNe*. 1982 Fall; 14(7): 5, 10. Illus. Dwg. 1.
USA. 1979-1980. Histories-sources. ■Reports directors' answers to the question, 'Have you encountered distinctive problems when directing actors in Shakespeare?' posed by a twenty question survey regarding adequacy of actor training for Shakespearean roles. Related to Individuals: Shakespeare.

Training: Teaching methods

886 Ratliff, Gerald Lee. "Reader's Theatre: Beginning Exercises to Promote a Theatrical Mind in Performance." *CueM*. 1982 Fall-Winter; 61(1): 19-21.
USA. Twentieth cent. Textbooks/manuals/guides.

Comedy

887 Bareiss, Karl-Heinz. *Comoedia: Die Entwicklung der Komödien-diskussion von Aristoteles bis Ben Jonson*. (Comedia: The Discussion of Comedy from Aristotle to Ben Jonson.) Frankfurt a.M., Bern: Lang; 1982. 525 pp. (Europäische Hochschulschriften, Reihe 14/100.) Notes. Biblio.
Europe. 380 B.C.-1700 A.D. Studies of theories/theorists. ■Study of documents on comic theory from antiquity through the English Renaissance.

888 Blair, Herbert. "Comedy Since the Absurd." *MD*. 1982 Dec.; 25(4): 545-568. Notes.

DRAMA — cont'd

USA. Twentieth cent. Critical studies. ■Meaning and language of comedy, which has become painful and grotesque.

Institutions: Producing/performing

889 Jackson, Russell. "The Royal Shakespeare Company in *Money.*" *NCTR.* 1982 Summer; 10(1): 39-42. Illus.
England. 1981. Reviews of performances. ■Review. article on Royal Shakespeare Company's production of Edward Bulwer-Lytton's Victorian comedy, directed by Bill Alexander at The Other Place in Stratford-upon-Avon.

Performance/performers: Acting/actors

890 de Rosbo, Patrick. "Un Entretien avec José-María Flotats." (A Conversation with José-María Flotats.) *CF.* 1982 October; 112: 17-18.
France. 1982. Histories-sources. ■Interview with actor playing Don Juan in the Comédie Française production of Molière's play.

Plays/playwrights

891 Duckworth, Colin. "Jean Tardieu and Comedy: So Frolic Music Wards Off the Gathering Dark." *MD.* 1982 Dec.; 25(4): 514-533. Notes.
France. Twentieth cent. Critical studies. ■Director's examination of comedy in playwright's works.

892 Borsellino, Nino, ed. *L'interpretazione goldoniana: critica e messinscena.* (Interpretation of Goldoni: Criticism and Staging.) Rome: Officina Edizioni; 1982. 270 pp. (Collana del Teatro di Roma 16.) Illus.
Italy. 1950-1980. Studies of criticism/critics. ■Essays on modern staging and literary criticism of Carlo Goldoni's works.

Plays/playwrights: Genres

893 Charney, Maurice. "What Did the Butler See in Orton's *What the Butler Saw*?" *MD.* 1982 Dec.; 25(4): 496-504. Notes.
England. Twentieth cent. Critical studies. ■Study of new farce which reflects an image of the world gone mad.

894 Milhous, Judith; Hume, Robert D. "*The Beaux' Stratagem:* A Production Analysis." *TJ.* 1982 Mar.; 34(1): 77-95. Notes. Illus.
England. 1707. Critical studies. ■Play as light romp or serious satire.

Plays/playwrights: Plot/subject/theme

895 Diamond, Elin. "Parody Play in Pinter." *MD.* 1982 Dec.; 25(4): 477-488. Notes.
England. Twentieth cent. Critical studies. ■Definition of parody in Pinter's plays.

896 Hunter, Jim. *Tom Stoppard's Plays.* New York: Grove; 1982. 217 pp. Pref. Index. Biblio.
England. Twentieth cent. Critical studies. ■Biography followed by chapters analyzing different aspects of his plays — theatricalism, comic elements, thought, language, parody, the sense of values.

897 Kennedy, Andrew K. "Tom Stoppard's Dissident Comedies." *MD.* 1982 Dec.; 25(4): 469-476. Notes.
England. Twentieth cent. Critical studies. ■Development in Stoppard's style from parody to comedy of moral and political commitment.

898 Miller, Terry. "The Politics of Gay Romantic Comedy." *GTAN.* 1982 Aug.; 4(1): 13.
USA. Twentieth cent. Critical studies. ■Homosexuality as a subject for romantic comedy with references to *Pines '79* and TV soap operas. Related to Media: Video forms.

Plays/playwrights: Structure/language

899 Krauss, Cornelia. "Vom 'Wert-Vakuum' und seinen dramaturgischen Folgen: Ödön von Horváths Leitmotivtechnik und Peter Handkes Psychodrama." (On the 'Vacuum of Values' and Its Dramaturgical Consequences: Ödön von Horváth's Technique of Leitmotifs and Peter Handke's Psychodrama.) *MuK.* 1982; 28(3-4): 195-289. Notes. Biblio.
Austria. 1920-1932. Critical studies. ■Analysis of Horváth's dialogue, use of leitmotif as means of character development and as reaction to loss of values in Austrian society between the wars, including influence on Peter Handke's *Kaspar.*

900 Hart, Steven. "Professional Profiles: Cruelty in the Comedy of George Bernard Shaw." *Cue.* 1982 Fall-Winter; 61(1): 7-8, 15-16, 19.
England. Twentieth cent. Critical studies. ■Shaw's use of structure to emphasize paradox and examine social issues in *The Doctor's Dilemma, Pygmalion,* and *Great Catherine.*

901 Kleiman, Carol. *Sean O'Casey's Bridge of Vision: Four Essays on Structure and Perspective.* Toronto: Univ. of Toronto P; 1982. xiv, 148 pp. Pref. Notes. Index. Biblio. Illus.
Ireland. 1914-1982. Critical studies. ■*The Silver Tassie* and *Red Roses for Me* as visionary dramas and bridges between expressionist theatre and absurdism.

Staging: Directing/directors

902 Evenden, Michael. "False Talismans in a Genuine *Talisman.*" *ThM.* 1981-82 Winter; 13(1): 72-76. Illus.
Austria. 1980. Reviews of performances. ■Critic re-examines comic form in a review of Johann Nestroy's *Der Talisman* at the Theater in der Josefstadt, Vienna. Staging by Fritz Zecha.

903 McDonald, Jan. "An Unholy Alliance: William Poel, Martin Harvey and *The Taming of the Shrew.*" *TN.* 1982; 36(2): 64-72 . Illus.: Photo. B&W. 2.
England. 1912-1913. Histories-reconstruction. ■Based on correspondence between Poel and Harvey, reconstructs production of *The Taming of the Shrew.*

904 Tarkiel, Jacqueline. "*Le Voyage de Monsieur Perrichon,* un entretien avec Jean Le Poulain." (*Monsieur Perrichon's Journey:* A Conversation with Jean Le Poulain.) *CF.* 1982 Feb.; 106: 5-6.
France. Twentieth cent. Histories-sources. ■Director discusses his interpretation.

905 Heard, Doreen B. "*Pinocchio*: An Examination of the Productions by Yasha Frank for the Federal Theatre Project." *ChTR.* 1982 Spring; 31(2): 10-15. Notes. Biblio.
USA. 1933-1939. Historical studies.

Experimental forms

906 Carpenter, Charles A. "'E'Victims of Duty?' The Critics, Absurdity, and *The Homecoming.*" *MD.* 1982 Dec.; 25(4): 489-495. Notes.
Europe. North America. Twentieth cent. Studies of criticism/critics. ■Critics accept absurdity of Pinter's play.

907 Guidotti, Mario. "L'autodramma." (Autodrama.) *QT.* 1982 Aug.; 1(1): 59-61.
Italy. 1969-1980. Historical studies. ■Historical notes on the 'Poor Theatre' of Montichiello.

Audience: Relationship to performer

908 Jones, Claire. "Levels of Audience Involvement in Participation Theatre." *ChTR.* 1982 Summer; 31(3): 5-7. Illus.: Photo.
USA. 1965-1982. Critical studies. ■Eight levels of audience participation in children's theatre.

DRAMA — cont'd

Institutions: Producing/performing

909   Friedl, Peter. "Schauplatz Wien: Dramatisches Zentrum." (Scene Vienna: Dramatisches Zentrum.) *TH*. 1982 Apr.; 4: 26-29 . Illus.
Austria. 1982. Histories-sources. ■Repertory and economic conditions at Vienna's only institutionalized alternative theatre, Dramatisches Zentrum Wien.

910   Sircar, Badal. "A Letter from Badal Sircar." *TDR*. 1982 Summer; 26(2): 51-58.
India. 1975-1982. Histories-sources. ■Overview of the history and philosophy of Satabdi, an experimental Indian theatre group founded by Badal Sircar in Calcutta.

911   Schaefer, Gabriele. "Das japanische Underground-Theater heute und die Studentenbewegung von gestern: Zum Beispiel: Satō Makoto und das 'Zentrum 68/71-Schwarzes Zelt'." (The Japanese Underground Theatre of Today and Yesterday's Student Movement: Satō Makoto and the 'Centre 68/71-Black Tent'.) *MuK*. ; 28(2): 154-162.
Japan. 1968-1981. Critical studies. ■Influence of 1960s student movement — as well as of *nō*, *kabuki* and European dramatists such as Brecht — on Japanese underground political theatre. Emphasis on work of Satō Makoto. Infl. by Bertolt Brech.

Performance/performers

912   Van Kleef, Deborah. "Pillbox Hats, White Gloves, and Ladies Against Women." *ThM*. 1982 Summer-Fall; 13(3): 74-75. Illus.
USA. 1982. Histories-sources. ■Journalistic account of guerrilla theatre actions of feminists greeting Phyllis Schlafly in Cleveland.

Performance/performers: Acting/actors

913   Grotowski, Jerzy. "Spannung und Entspannung müssen zusammenspielen." (Tension and Relaxation Have to Go Together.) *TH*. 1982 Sep.; 9: 13-14. Illus.
Europe. Asia. Twentieth cent. Critical studies. ■Anthropological aspects of acting. Relation between Theatre of Sources, Oriental theatre and body-language.

914   Pasquier, Pierre. "Athlétisme affectif et ascèse blanche chez Antonin Artaud." (Affective Athleticism and White Asceticism in Antonin Artaud.) *RHT*. 1982; 34(3): 237-248. Notes.
France. 1920-1935. Studies of theories/theorists. ■Theory of acting in articles by Camille Sauton and René Guénon in periodical, *La Voile d'Isis*.

915   Bartenieff, George; O'Reilly, Terry; Maleczech, Ruth; Cowing, Charles; Schofield, B. St. John. "Performing *Dead End Kids*: Statements by Mabou Mines Actors." *ThM*. 1982 Summer-Fall; 13(3): 35-37. Illus.
USA. 1980. Histories-sources. ■Statements by Mabou Mines performers. Related to Mixed Performances: Performance art.

Plays/playwrights: Plot/subject/theme

916   Kantor, Leo. "Mrożeks pjäs *Till fots*." (Mrożek's Play *On Foot*.) *Entre*. 1982; 9(1): 2-4. Illus.
Poland. 1944-1981. Critical studies. ■Sławomir Mrożek's use of social problems in 1944-45 sheds light on Polish developments in 1980-81.

917   Maderna, Maria. "Botho Strauss, malessere di una generazione." (Botho Strauss, Uneasiness of a Generation.) *QT*. 1982 Aug.; 5(17): 191-199. Notes.
West Germany. Twentieth cent. Critical studies. ■Analysis of works, with reference to the theme of 'uneasiness'.

Plays/playwrights: Structure/language

918   Calimani, Dario. "Harold Pinter: la realtà e il linguaggio delle Voci." (Harold Pinter: Reality and Language of the Voices.) *QT*. 1982 Feb.; 4(15): 225-239. Notes.

England. Twentieth cent. Critical studies. ■Language in *Family Voices* compared to language in other Pinter plays.

919   Lamont, Rosette C. "Roger Planchon's *Gilles de Rais*: A Liturgy of Evil." *MD*. 1982 Sep.; 25(3): 363-373. Notes.
USA. 1980-1981. Critical studies. ■Analysis of structure occasioned by 1980-81 Canadian Stage Company production.

Relation to other fields: Politics

920   Anon. "Tunnel Vision." *VV*. 1982 Oct. 19; 27(42): 41. Illus.: Photo.
USA. 1982. Histories-sources. ■Describes informal performance on a subway train and arrest of members of Dinosaur Theatre.

Staging: Directing/directors

921   Clarke, B. Elizabeth. "Grotowski Speaks Again." *ThM*. 1982 Summer; 13(2): 86-87.
USA. 1981. Histories-sources. ■Account of remarks at showing of film, *Vigil*.

922   Pasquier, Marie-Claire. "Richard Foreman: Comedy Inside Out." *MD*. 1982 Dec.; 25(4): 534-544. Notes.
USA. Twentieth cent. Critical studies. ■Analysis of comedy that forces audience to observe.

Melodrama

Plays/playwrights

923   Molin, Sven Eric; Goodefellowe, Robin. "Dion Boucicault, the Shaughraun — Part Two: Up and Down in Paris and London." *GSTB*. 1982 Summer; 4(2): 1-88. Pref. Notes. Append. Illus.
England. France. 1845-1853. Biographical studies. ■Nine years in the life of Dion Boucicault, from documents, will, contemporary journalistic reports and production reviews.

Plays/playwrights: Adaptations

924   McConachie, Bruce A. "H.J. Conway's Dramatization of *Uncle Tom's Cabin*: A Previously Unpublished Letter." *TJ*. 1982 May; 34(2): 149-154. Notes.
USA. Nineteenth cent. Histories-sources. ■Adaptation of Harriet Beecher Stowe's novel to produce a more cheerful and pro-Southern play.

Plays/playwrights: Plot/subject/theme

925   Richardson, Gary A. "Boucicault's *The Octoroon* and American Law." *TJ*. 1982 May; 34(2): 155-164. Notes. Illus.
USA. Nineteenth cent. Critical studies. ■Play deals with legal issues, questioning law's efficacy to deal with issues like motivation: suggests that law is necessary but imperfect.

Tragedy

926   Döring, Jürgen. *Tragödie: Notwendigkeit und Zufall im Spannungsfeld tragischer Prozesse*. (Tragedy: Necessity and Chance in the Tragic Process.) Stuttgart: Klett-Cotta; 1982. 398 pp. Gloss. Notes. Index. Biblio.
Europe. Multi-period. Studies of theories/theorists. ■Analysis of tragedy: necessity and contingency, motivation for the tragic fall.

Institutions: Producing/performing

927   Munk, Erika. "Merely Wounding the Messenger." *VV*. 1982 Apr. 13; 27(15): 82.
USA. 1982. Histories-sources. ■Circle Repertory Company's withdrawal of *Richard II*.

DRAMA — cont'd

Legal aspects: Licensing and regulations

928   Hume, Robert D. "*The Maid's Tragedy* and Censorship in the Restoration Theatre." *PQ.* 1982 Fall; 61(4): 484-490.
England. 1660-1687. Historical studies. ▪Dates prohibition of Beaumont and Fletcher's *The Maid's Tragedy* and other regicide dramas.

Performance/performers: Acting/actors

929   Watermeier, Daniel J. "Edwin Booth's Performances: New Documentation." *THSt.* 1982; 2: 125-128. Notes.
USA. 1880-1899. Histories-reconstruction. ▪Description of manuscript in Harvard Theatre Collection known as the *M. Isabella Stone...Commentaries on Edwin Booth*, an eyewitness account of Booth's performances in *Hamlet*, *Othello*, and *King Lear*.

Plays/playwrights

930   Davis, Bertram H., ed. *Thomas Otway.* Boston: Twayne Publishers; 1982. (TEAS, 335.) Pref. Index. Biblio. Illus.: Photo. B&W.
England. Seventeenth cent. Restoration period. Biographies. ▪Critical assessment of plays.

931   Mályusz, Edith. "*Prinz Berchtold von Mähren*, eine Banus Bánk-Tragödie aus dem Jahr 1794." (*Prince Berchtold von Mähren*, a Tragedy about Banus Bánk from the Year 1794.) *MuK.* 1982; 28(2): 105-112. Notes.
Hungary. 1794. Historical studies. ▪Notice of unpublished and never performed play by Ionnes Endrödy, dealing with story of Banus Bánk, famous in national literature. Background of story and statements by censor, including biographical survey on author.

932   *Studi sul teatro classico italiano tra Manierismo ed età dell'Arcadia.* (Studies on Italian Classic Theatre between Mannerism and the Arcadian Age.) Rome: Ateneo; 1982. 117 pp. (NS 4.) Notes.
Italy. 1627-1713. Critical studies. ▪Analysis of three tragedies: *Ester* by Federico della Valle, *Aristodemo* by Carlo Dottori and *Merope* by Scipione Maffei.

Plays/playwrights: Characters/roles

933   McDavid, Raven I., Jr. "Rosenkrantz and Guildenstern Are Alive and Prospering." *MP.* 1982 May; 79(4): 400-402.
Denmark. 1300-1982. Histories-sources. ▪Lineage of true Rosenkrantz and Guildenstern families. Related to Individuals: Shakespeare.

Plays/playwrights: Genres

934   Barnwell, H.T. *The Tragic Drama of Corneille and Racine.* Oxford: Clarendon Press; 1982. 288 pp. Pref. Notes. Index. Biblio.
France. French classicism. Seventeenth cent. Critical studies. ▪History, criticism and interpretation.

Plays/playwrights: Plot/subject/theme

935   Perloff, Eveline; Clergé, Claude. "Théâtre et folie." (Theatre and Madness.) *CF.* 1982 Jan.; 105: 17-27. [Part I.]
Europe. 500 B.C.-1610 A.D. Critical studies. ▪Aspects of madness in theatre. Excerpts from Aeschylus' *Orestes*, Sophocles' *Ajax*, Euripides' *Bacchants*, Shakespeare's *Hamlet*, *Macbeth* and *King Lear*.

936   Fairchild, Sharon L. "Les théories de Victor Hugo appliquées à son théâtre." (Victor Hugo's Theories Applied to His Plays.) *RHT.* 1982; 34(2): 157-168. Notes.
France. 1827-1843. Studies of theories/theorists.

937   Ubersfeld, Anne. "Le rire noir de Hugo." (Hugo's Black Humor.) *CF.* 1982 Apr.; 108: 5-9.
France. 1802-1885. Critical studies. ▪Black humor in *Marie Tudor*.

938   Rey, William H. *Georg Büchner's* Dantons Tod: Revolutions-tragödie und Mysterienspiel. (Georg Büchner's *Danton's Death*: Tragedy of Revolution and Mystery Play.) Bern, Frankfurt a.M.: Lang; 1982. 121 pp. Notes.
Germany. France. 1835. Critical studies. ▪Marxist and Christian approaches.

Relation to other fields: Sociology

939   Greenblatt, Stephen. "The Cultivation of Anxiety: *King Lear* and His Heirs." *Raritan.* 1982 Summer; 2(1): 92-114. Notes.
Great Britain. USA. Seventeenth cent. Nineteenth cent. Critical studies. ▪Parallels between *King Lear* and 19th century familial relationships: discusses parental withholding of love, parental authority and disinheritance of the elderly. Related to Individuals: Shakespeare.

Staging: Directing/directors

940   LaPorte, Michel. "Langage Scénique: *Médée* par la Kaléidoscope." (Stage Talk: *Medea* by the Kaléidoscope.) *PrTh.* 1982 Winter-Spring(14-15): 32-36. Illus.: Photo. B&W.
Canada. 1981. Critical studies. ▪Production focuses on theatrical aspects rather than traditional story.

Other entries with significant content related to Drama: 2, 16, 34, 37, 63, 950, 1131, 1143, 1154, 1161, 1194, 1202, 1206, 1216, 1217, 1218, 1221, 1225, 1227, 1228, 1230, 1233, 1240, 1233.

MEDIA

General

Performance/performers: Acting/actors

941   Hickethier, Knut. "Mit Zucken im Mundwinkel: Schauspielen in den Medien." (The Quiver at the Corners of the Mouth: Acting in the Media.) *Tzs.* 1982; 2: 15-31. Notes. Illus.
Twentieth cent. Critical studies. ▪Acting styles in film, radio and television: relation to acting styles in theatre, impact of media on acting and perception, different styles and movements in television.

Plays/playwrights: Adaptations

942   Leverett, James. "Allies: Playwrights at Work in the Electronic Media." *AmTh.* 1982 Sep.; 4(6): 18-22. Notes. Illus.: Photo. B&W. 4.
USA. 1982. Histories-sources. ▪Writers Toni Cole, Corinne Jacker, Steve Lawson and Michael Weller discuss experiences in TV and film.

Audio forms

943   Cook, Michael. "The Last Refuge of the Spoken Word." *CTR.* 1982 Fall; 36: 49-51. IL.
Canada. Twentieth cent. Histories-sources. ▪Responsibilities of radio in arresting decline of literacy.

944   Corbeil, Carole. "Walking a Thin Line." *CTR.* 1982 Fall; 36: 43-48. Illus.
Canada. 1976-1982. Histories-sources. ▪Discussion of current radio drama on CBC networks.

945   Fink, Howard. "Canadian Radio Drama and the Radio Drama Project." *CTR.* 1982 Fall; 36: 12-22. Illus.
Canada. 1930-1982. Histories-reconstruction. ▪Head of Concordia University radio archives discusses attempts to retrieve and maintain radio drama heritage.

946   Peterson, Leonard. "With Freedom in Their Eye..." *CTR.* 1982 Fall; 36: 23-29. Pref. Illus.
Canada. 1930-1982. Histories-sources. ▪Memories of radio producers Andrew Allan and Esse Ljungh by a playwright who worked closely with them.

MEDIA — cont'd

947 Russell, Lawrence. "The DNA Tape Exchange: Quantum Perturbations and Altered Structures." *CTR.* 1982 Fall; 36: 57-59. Illus.
Canada. 1971-1982. Histories-sources. ■Creator of DNA audio tape exchange discusses developments in dramaturgy occasioned by new technology.

Design/technology: Sound

948 Ready, Patrick. "The Luxe Radio Players: Eliciting 'The Third Man'." *CTR.* 1982 Fall; 36: 60-65. IL. Illus.
Canada. 1975. Histories-sources. ■Personal diary of soundman's experience with live radio.

Personnel: Top management/producers

949 Blanchard, Sharon. "Esse Ljungh and the Stage Series." *CTR.* 1982 Fall; 36: 107-111. Notes. Illus.
Canada. 1955-1969. Histories-sources. ■Style and approach of a radio producer.

Plays/playwrights

950 Ryga, George. "Memories and Some Lessons Learned." *CTR.* 1982 Fall; 36: 40-42. IL.
Canada. Twentieth cent. Histories-sources. ■Playwright Ryga is influenced by radio. Related to Drama.

Relation to other fields: Other arts

951 Miller, Mary Jane. "Radio's Children." *CTR.* 1982 Fall; 36: 30-39. Notes. Illus.
Canada. 1960-1970. Historical studies. ■Influence of radio drama on theatre.

Film

952 Giordano, Frank. "The Movies Go to the Theatre." *PArts.* 1982 Jan.; 16(1): 6. Illus.: Photo.
USA. Twentieth cent. Histories-sources. ■Motion picture versions of Broadway backstage scene.

Performance/performers: Acting/actors

953 Benayoun, Robert. *Le Regard de Buster Keaton.* (Buster Keaton's Gaze.) Paris: Herscher; 1982. 205 pp. Pref. Biblio. Illus.: Photo.
USA. 1895-1966. Biographies. ■Description of films and work methods.

Staging: Directing/directors

954 Bradburn, Donald. "Dancebiz: A Greaser Named Birch." *Dm.* 1982 July; 56(7): 76. Illus.
USA. 1959-1982. Biographical studies. ■Choreographer Patricia Birch discusses her approach to directing the film *Grease II.* Related to Dance.

Video forms

955 Szyszkowitz, Gerald. "Ein Beitrag zur Geschichte des Fernsehspiels in Österreich in den Jahren 1978-1981." (A Contribution to the History of the Television Play in Austria, 1978-1981.) *MuK.* 1982; 28(1): 43-50.
Austria. 1972-1981. Histories-sources. ■Listing of television plays produced on television (ORF). Related to Reference Material: Lists.

Design/technology: Lighting/lighting designers

956 Humphrey, L.F. "Lanterns to Luxor." *Tabs.* 1982 Nov.; 39(2): 18-19.
Egypt. 1980-1982. Technical studies. ■Design and construction of three remote television lighting trucks for Egyptian Broadcasting Federation.

Legal aspects

957 Fantel, Hans. "Is Copying Right?" *BaNe.* 1982 July; 4(1): 24.
USA. 1976-1982. Technical studies. ■Discussion of copyright infringement by users of home video recording systems.

Performance spaces: Planning/design

958 Futers, Steve. "Suspense Story." *Tabs.* 1982 Nov.; 39(2): 29.
1982. Technical studies. ■Available automated rigging systems for television studios, concentrating on improved mobility and flexbility.

Performance/performers: Acting/actors

959 Greenbaum, Everett. "How to Act." *PArts.* 1982 Feb.; 16(2): 8. Illus.
USA. Twentieth cent. Histories-sources. ■Humorous account of writer's attempts at television acting.

960 Marshall, Marilyn. "Prime Time for Michael Warren: Actor Is Riding High on TV's Award-winning *Hill Street Blues.*" *Ebony.* 1982 Apr.; 37(6): 48, 50.
USA. Twentieth cent. Histories-sources. ■Background as theatre student, and role as part of ensemble.

Plays/playwrights: Adaptations

961 Greene, Alexis. "TV & Theatre Strike a New Bargain." *AmTh.* 1982 Oct.; 4(7): 8-10. Notes. Illus.: Photo. B&W. 2.
USA. Twentieth cent. Histories-sources. ■Shirley Clarke's effort to transform Sam Shepard's and Joseph Chaikin's *Tongues* and companion piece *Savage/Love* from stage to video.

———

Other entries with significant content related to Media: 40, 49, 156, 188, 231, 410, 412, 426, 436, 439, 441, 443, 477, 563, 607, 612, 756, 898, 972, 1109, 1205, 1272.

MIME

General

Institutions: Training

962 Balsimelli, Rossano; Negri, Livio. *Guida al mimo e al clown.* (Guide Book to Mime and Clowning.) With the collaboration of Ineichen Rose. Milan: Rizzoli; 1982. 205 pp. Biblio. Illus.
Twentieth cent. Textbooks/manuals/guides. ■Survey of mime schools and important performers with chapter on mask construction.

Performance/performers

963 Löschke, Maravene Sheppard. *All About Mime: Understanding and Performing the Expressive Silence.* Englewood Cliffs, NJ: Prentice-Hall; 1982. viii, 184 pp. Pref. Index. Biblio. Illus.
Twentieth cent. Critical studies. ■Discussion of literal and abstract mime, Oriental, Italian and French schools, mime acting and techniques, with appendices on performing, teaching and critiquing mime.

964 Cunningham, Kitty. "Niels Bjørn Larsen: A Life in Mime." *BR.* 1982 Summer; 10(2): 88-94. Illus.
Denmark. 1919-1982. Biographies. ■The education and career of character mime Niels Bjørn Larsen. Grp/movt: Kongelige Danske Ballet (Royal Danish Ballet).

MIME — cont'd

Training: Training aids

965 Pecknold, Arnold. *Mime, The Step Beyond Words.* Toronto: NC Press; 1982. 144 pp. Pref. Gloss. Biblio. Illus.: Photo. B&W.
1900-1982. Textbooks/manuals/guides. ■Exercises and mime plays.

Pantomime

966 Tessari, Roberto. "Il corpo silente del pantomimo: archetipi e autopsie." (The Silent Body of the Pantomimist: Archetypes and Autopsies.) *QT.* 1982 Aug.; 5(17): 5-29. Notes.
Multi-period. Critical studies. ■History of the figure of the mime from origins of the genre through the 18th century.

Other entries with significant content related to Mime: 417, 603, 1102.

MIXED PERFORMANCES

Court Masque

Design/technology

967 Streitberger, W.R. "Court Entertainments, 1601-1603: The Extraordinary Works Account." *REEDN.* 1982; 2: 1-8. Notes.
England. 1601-1603. Historical studies. ■Records of carpentry and other work for royal entertainments.

Performance art

968 Crispolti, Enrico. "Definire il 'Teatro d'artista'." (Defining 'Artist's Theatre'.) *TeatrC.* 1982 May-Sept; 1(1): 19-37. Illus.
Italy. Twentieth cent. Studies of theories/theorists. ■Theoretical presuppositions and practical realization of multi-media performance.

969 Robertson, Allen. "Clever Cookie." *BaNe.* 1982 Mar.; 3(9): 26-27. Illus.
USA. 1981-1982. Histories-sources. ■Postmodern dancer David Gordon discusses multimedia performance developed for loft concert.

970 Weiner, Bernard. "Performance Art into Theatre." *AmTh.* 1982 Mar.; 3(12): 1-3. Notes. Illus.: Photo. B&W.
USA. Twentieth cent. Histories-sources. ■Snake Theatre's use of environmental theatre defined as performance art.

Performance/performers

971 Coe, Robert. "Four Performance Artists." *ThM.* 1982 Spring; 13(2): 76-85. Illus.
USA. 1968-1981. Reviews of performances. ■Commentary on work of Joan Jonas, Robert Ashley, Julia Heyward and Laurie Anderson.

Performance/performers: Acting/actors

972 Monk, Philip. "Common Carrier: Performance by Artists." *MD.* 1982 Mar.; 25(1): 163-169. Notes. B&W. 2.
Canada. 1978. Critical studies. ■Examination of performance artist Elizabeth Chitty's *Demo Model* at the 'Fifth Network' video conference. Grp/movt: Minimalist art. Related to Media.

Other entries with significant content related to Mixed Performances: 915.

MUSIC-DRAMA

General

973 Serafini, Giuliano. "Dall'intermedio al melodramma." (From *Intermedio* to *Melodramma*.) *QT.* 1982 Aug.; 5(17): 84-92.
Italy. 1500-1650. Historical studies. ■Evolution of form from 16th century *intermedio* to early 17th century *melodramma*.

974 Otto, Werner. "Theatergeschichte(n) Folge 9: Komponisten, Dirigenten und Theaterleute über ihre Eindrücke in der Sowjetunion (1924-1932)." (Theatre History/9: Composers, Conductors, and Theatre Experts on Their Impressions in the Soviet Union, 1924-1932.) *TZ.* 1982 Oct.; 37: 15-17. Illus. [Installment of an irregular series.]
USSR. 1924-1932. Histories sources. ■Musical theatre commentary. Related to Theatre in General: Multiple application.

Institutions: Special

975 Frede, Matthias; Fritzsche, Dietmar; Katzer, Georg; Lang, Joachim Robert; Lange, Wolfgang; Rank, Mathias; Reglin, Norbert; Saz, Natalja. "Dresdner Musikfestspiele '82." (Music Festival of Dresden, 1982.) *TZ.* 1982 Aug.; 37(8): 24-38. Illus.
East Germany. 1982. Reviews of performances. ■Reports from fifth festival, plus two articles on children's musical theatre and a report on the ballet in Dresden. Related to Dance.

Performance/performers

976 Carlitschek, Gesine. "Zwischenbilanz. Zu Ergebnissen im 2. Leistungsvergleich der Schauspiel- und Musiktheaterensembles der DDR 1980/81." (Interim Balance: Results of the Second Comparison of Accomplishments of Dramatic and Music Theatre Ensembles of the German Democratic Republic 1980-81.) *TZ.* 1982 June; 37: 6-8.
East Germany. 1980-1981. Histories-sources.

Personnel: Top management/producers

977 De Angelis, Marcello. *Le carte dell'impresario — Melodramma e costume teatrale nell'Ottocento.* (Manager's Papers: *Melodramma* and Theatrical Custom in the 19th Century.) Florence: Sansoni; 1982. 283 pp. Notes. Illus.
Italy. 1820-1852. Historical studies. ■Music theatre organization reconstructed through archives of manager Alessandro Lanari, with chronological inventory of his activity.

Scores/composers: Characters/roles

978 Rienäcker, Gerd. "Soziales Rollenspiel: Zu einigen Vorgängen und Figuren in Igor Strawinskis Musiktheater — anlässlich seines 100. Geburtstages." (Social Role-Playing: On Some Episodes and Characters in Igor Stravinsky's Musical Theatre, on Occasion of His 100th Birthday.) *TZ.* 1982 Sep.; 37(9): 41-44. Illus.
Twentieth cent. Critical studies.

Staging

979 "Musikalische Aufführungenpraxis heute: Zur Interpretation von Werken der Vergangenheit." (Contemporary Musical Performance Praxis: Interpretation of Period Works.) *TZ.* 1982 May; 37: 33-36. [Irregular series on historical works.]
Europe. 1982. Critical studies. ■Problems in presenting classical music on today's stage.

980 Verdone, Mario; Vlad, Roman. "*L'Opera dello straccione* di John Gay (un documento d'epoca, 15 febbraio 1943)." (*The Beggar's Opera* by John Gay (Document of an Epoch, February 15, 1943).) *TeatrC.* 1982 May-Sept; 1(1): 63-72.

MUSIC-DRAMA — cont'd

Italy. 1943. Reviews of performances. ▪Reprinted review of Vito Pandolfi's production, with preliminary note on its political significance and appendix on incidental music.

Musical theatre

981   Arkatov, Janice. "The Musicals Man." *PArts*. 1982 Mar.; 16(3): 7. Illus.: Photo.
USA. Twentieth cent. Histories-sources. ▪Interview with Lehman Engel about his workshops for composers and lyricists.

982   Bordman, Gerald. *American Musical Comedy: From* Adonis *to* Dreamgirls. New York: Oxford UP; 1982. vii, 244 pp. Pref. Index. Illus.: Photo. B&W. 20.
USA. 1884-1980. Histories-specific. ▪Developments in form, style and subject matter.

Audience: Reactions/comments

983   Anon. "A Religious Experience at the Vatican: Pope John Paul II is Thrilled by Music of Langston Hughes' *Black Nativity*." *Ebony*. 1982 Apr.; 37(6): 63, 65-66. Illus.
Vatican. USA. 1982. Reviews of performances. ▪Production by Richard Allen Center for Culture and Art New York City, first such group to appear at Vatican.

Design/technology: Costuming/costumers

984   Wallach, Susan Levi. "William Ivey Long Dressed to the Nines." *ThCr*. 1982 Aug.-Sep.; 16(7): 17-19, 86-92. Illus.
USA. 1982. Histories-sources. ▪Problems of designing costumes for *Nine*.

Design/technology: Scenery/scene designers

985   Smith, Ronn. "Putting *Dreamgirls* on Broadway." *ThCr*. 1982 May; 16(5): 13, 49-52. Illus.
USA. 1982. Histories-sources. ▪Interviews with Robin Wagner and Peter Feller, Jr., on evolution of *Dreamgirls* set.

Financial operations: Planning and accounting

986   Sacheli, Robert. "Harold Prince on Money and the Musical Theatre." *ThNe*. 1982 Dec.; 14(9): 1, 3. Illus.: Photo. B&W.
USA. 1980-1982. Critical studies. ▪Economic realities make it necessary to re-think musical theatre.

Legal aspects: Performance rights

987   Golden, Peter. "A Technicolor Dream Come True." *Pb*. 1982 Oct.; 1(1): 20. Illus.
USA. 1979-1982. Histories-sources. ▪Producers discuss problems of obtaining rights to *Joseph and the Amazing Technicolor Dreamcoat*.

Librettos/librettists: Genres

988   Bussey, William M. *French and Italian Influence on the Zarzuela: 1700-1770*. Ann Arbor, MI: UMI Research P; 1982. xiii, 297 pp. (Studies in Musicology Series 53.) Pref. Index.
Spain. Italy. France. 1700-1770. Critical studies. ▪Analysis of international contributions to musical comedies. Related to Dance-Drama.

Performance/performers

989   Siegmund-Schultze, Annette. "Garderobengespräch mit Rosl Schönfeld." (An Interview in the Dressing-Room with Rosl Schönfeld.) *TZ*. 1982 Sep.; 37(9): 50-53. Illus.
East Germany. 1922-1982. Histories-sources. ▪Discussion of musical theatre career. Infl. by Ive Becker; Carl Riha.

990   Allen, Bonnie. "*Dreamgirls* Lights Up Broadway." *Ebony*. 1982 May; 13(1): 15-18, 157-8.

USA. 1982. Histories-sources. ▪Compares musical to facts on the Supremes, Motown Recording Company, actress/singer Diana Ross and producer Berry Gordy.

991   Allen, Bonnie. "Patti LaBelle: Out Here on Her Own." *Ebony*. 1982 Sep.; 13(5): 60-62, 139-145.
USA. 1982. Histories-sources. ▪Personal/professional history of star of *Your Arms Too Short to Box with God*.

992   Bailey, A. Peter. "Dreams Come True on Broadway for Young Stars in *Dreamgirls*." *Ebony*. 1982 May; 37(7): 90-92, 94-96 .
USA. 1982. Histories-sources. ▪Backgrounds of cast members.

993   Corliss, Richard; Rich, Frank; Nelson, Don; Kissel, Howard; Wilson, Edwin; Beaufort, John; Stasio, Marilyn. "*Little Shop of Horrors*." *NYTCR*. 1982 Sep. 13; 43(11): 219-223. [Off-Broadway Supplement III.]
USA. 1982. Reviews of performances. ▪Seven critics review Howard Ashman's production, presented at Orpheum Theatre.

994   Corry, John; Henry, William A., III; Cohen, Ron; Beaufort, John; Barnes, Clive; Stasio, Marilyn; Wilson, Edwin. "*Charlotte Sweet*." *NYTCR*. 1982 Sep. 13; 43(11): 234-236. [Off-Broadway Supplement III.]
USA. 1982. Reviews of performances. ▪Eight critics review Edward Stone's production of musical by Michael Colby presented at the Chernuchin Theatre.

995   Cypkin, Diane. "The Shubert-Cantor Interlude." *PS*. 1982 Summer; 6(2): 4-5. Illus.
USA. 1919-1923. Histories-sources. ▪Eddie Cantor's involvement in Equity strike forced him to leave Ziegfeld and sign with Shuberts.

996   Haun, Harry. "New Woman in Town: Raquel Welch Loves Broadway...and Vice Versa." *Pb*. 1982 Oct.; 1(1): 14. Illus.
USA. 1981-1982. Histories-sources. ▪Interview with comments on *Woman of the Year*.

997   Holden, Stephen; Cohen, Ron; Clarke, Gerald; Sterritt, David; Barnes, Clive; Kroll, Jack; Nelson, Don. "*Pump Boys and Dinettes*." *NYTCR*. 1982 Feb. 15; 43(4): 338-341.
USA. 1982. Reviews of performances. ▪Seven critics review a collective theatre work, presented at the Westside Arts Theatre.

998   Johnson, Herschel. "Once More for *One Mo' Time!* New York Honors Lively Jazz Musical After 1,150th Performance in City." *Ebony*. 1982 Nov.; 38(1): 69-72.
USA. 1982. Histories-sources. ▪Production history of *One Mo' Time*, musical based on T.O.B.A. (Theatre Owners' Booking Agency circuit) also known as 'Tough On Black Actors'.

999   Palmer, Robert; Barnes, Clive; Spina, James; Nelson, Don. "*Your Arms Too Short to Box with God*." *NYTCR*. 1982 Oct. 4; 43(12): 212-214.
USA. 1982. Reviews of performances. ▪Four critics review Vinette Carroll's production, produced by Anita MacShanes and The Urban Arts Theatre at Alvin Theatre.

1000   Palmer, Robert; O'Haire, Patricia; Barnes, Clive; Sharp, Christopher; Sterritt, David. "*Rock 'n Roll! The First 5000 Years*." *NYTCR*. 1982 Nov. 1; 43(14): 176-179.
USA. 1982. Reviews of performances. ▪Five critics review Joe Layton's production, presented at St. James Theatre.

1001   Reif, Robin. "Making Broadway Magic." *Pb*. 1982 Dec.; 1(3): 6. Illus.
USA. 1976-1982. Histories-sources. ▪Interview with Doug Henning: integrated use of magic in *Merlin*, parallels between Henning and Merlin as character. Related to Popular Entertainment.

1002   Rich, Frank; Watt, Douglas; Barnes, Clive; Cohen, Ron; Beaufort, John; Kalem, T.E.; Ansen, David. "*The Death of von Richtofen as Witnessed from Earth*." *NYTCR*. 1982 Sep. 13; 43(11): 223-228.
USA. 1982. Reviews of performances. ▪Eight critics review Des McAnuff's production, presented by Joseph Papp at Public Theatre.

MUSIC-DRAMA — cont'd

1003   Rich, Frank; Wilson, Edwin; Barnes, Clive; Beaufort, John; Kalem, T.E.; Kissel, Howard; Watt, Douglas; Kroll, Jack; Guthrie, Constance; Cunningham, Dennis; Siegel, Joel. "*Cats.*" *NYTCR.* 1982 Oct. 18; 43(13): 191-199.
USA. 1982. Reviews of performances. ■Eleven critics review Trevor Nunn's production at Winter Garden Theatre.

1004   Rich, Frank; Watt, Douglas; Kissel, Howard; Beaufort, John; Barnes, Clive; Siegel, Joel; Cunningham, Dennis. "*A Doll's Life.*" *NYTCR.* 1982 Oct. 4; 43(12): 207-211.
USA. 1982. Reviews of performances. ■Seven critics review Harold Prince's production, presented at the Mark Hellinger Theatre.

1005   Sanders, Charles L. "Stephanie Mills: The Painful Education of A Young Superstar." *Ebony.* 1982 Feb.; 37(4): 36-40, 44.
USA. 1980-1982. Histories-sources. ■Effect of stardom on personal and professional life of star of Broadway musical, *The Wiz.*

1006   Watt, Douglas; Rich, Frank; Barnes, Clive; Kissel, Howard; Cunningham, Dennis. "*Little Johnny Jones.*" *NYTCR.* 1982 Feb. 15; 43(4): 330-333.
USA. 1982. Reviews of performances. ■Five critics review Gerald Gutierrez's production of musical by George M. Cohan, presented at the Alvin Theatre.

1007   Watt, Douglas; Rich, Frank; Beaufort, John; Kissel, Howard; Barnes, Clive. "*Lennon.*" *NYTCR.* 1982 Nov. 15; 43(15): 164-166. [Off-Broadway Supplement.]
USA. 1982. Reviews of performances. ■Five critics review Bob Eaton's production, presented at Entermedia Theatre.

Plays/playwrights

1008   Eyen, Tom. "Tom Eyen's Unedited Speech on the Winning of the 1982 Tony Award for Writing the Best Musical Book." *VV.* 1982 June 22; 27(25): 109.
USA. 1982. Histories-sources. ■Tony award acceptance speech by Tom Eyen.

Plays/playwrights: Plot/subject/theme

1009   Bailey, A. Peter. "*Dreamgirls*, the Serious Musical." *BlC.* 1982 Apr.-May; 12(5): 18, 20. Illus.
USA. 1980. Reviews of performances. ■Comment on Black musicals.

Relation to other fields: Sociology

1010   Anderman, Gunilla. "Musikalen — 82." (The Musical, '82.) *Entre.* 1982; 9(5): 19-24. Illus.
USA. England. 1982. Critical studies. ■The year's musicals tend toward escapism and musical collage with revivals predominating.

Scores/composers

1011   Jarman, Douglas. *Kurt Weill: An Illustrated Biography.* Bloomington: Indiana UP; 1982. 160 pp. Notes. Index. Biblio. Illus.
Germany. USA. Twentieth cent. Biographies. ■A study in two parts: A biography of Weill and an analysis of his instrumental, dramatic and vocal works.

1012   Botto, Louis. "Lucky *Nine.*" *Pb.* 1982 Nov.; 1(2): 6. Illus.
USA. 1963-1982. Histories-sources. ■Interview with Maury Yeston, composer/lyricist of *Nine.*

Staging

1013   Morley, Sheridan. "Here Comes *Cats.*" *Pb.* 1982 Oct.; 1(1): 6. Illus.
England. USA. 1980-1982. Histories-sources. ■Concept, evolution and creative components.

1014   Anon. "The Dream Team on Collaboration, or Five Designers in Search of an Author." *ThCr.* 1982 Aug.-Sep.; 16(7): 13-15, 40-43. Illus.

USA. 1982. Histories-sources. ■Round-table discussion by the creators of *Dreamgirls:* Michael Bennett, Robin Wagner, Tharon Musser and Theoni V. Aldredge.

1015   Jacobson, Robert. "Viewpoint." *BaNe.* 1982 Nov.; 4(5): 6. [Monthly editorial column.]
USA. 1982. Critical studies. ■Dominance of visual effects over scripts and scores of recent Broadway musicals. Related to Dance.

Staging: Choreography/choreographers

1016   Barnes, Clive. "Barnes on the Broadway Musical Since Jerome Robbins." *BaNe.* 1982 Nov.; 4(5): 46. Illus.
USA. 1940-1982. Historical studies. ■Evolution of choreographer/director in Broadway musicals.

1017   Philip, Richard. "Transatlantic Crossing: Keeping Company with *Cats.*" *Dm.* 1982 Dec.; 56(12): 92-97. Illus.
USA. England. 1982. Histories-sources. ■Discussion of two productions, emphasizing choreography.

Staging: Directing/directors

1018   Kiziuk, Len. "The New Musical." *ThNe.* 1982 Jan.; 14(1): 2-3.
USA. 1982. Histories-sources. ■Changes needed in production and direction.

1019   Maschio, Geraldine. "Directing the Musical: Some Important Considerations." *ThNe.* 1982 Feb.; 14(2): 17.
USA. Twentieth cent. Technical studies. ■Eight considerations for directors of musicals.

1020   Pikula, Joan. "Tommy Tune." *Dm.* 1982 Sep.; 56(9): 52-57.
USA. 1973-1982. Biographical studies. ■Tommy Tune's Broadway career.

1021   Quander, Georg. "Schauplätze für Musik: Tendenzen im amerikanischen Musiktheater der Gegenwart." (Performance Spaces for Music: Trends in Contemporary American Musical Theatre.) 105-121 in Kühn, Hellmut, ed. *Musiktheater heute.* Mainz: Schott; 1982. 121 pp. (Veröffentlichungen des Instituts für Neue Musik und Musikerziehung Darmstadt 22.)
USA. 1975. Historical studies. ■Outlines recent developments in the relationship of musical theatre to environmental theatre and performance art.

1022   Rich, Frank; Nelson, Don; Beaufort, John; Cohen, Ron; Kroll, Jack; Barnes, Clive. "*Herringbone.*" *NYTCR.* 1982 Sep. 13 ; 43(11): 228-230. [Off-Broadway Supplement III.]
USA. 1982. Reviews of performances. ■Six critics review Ben Levit's production, presented by Playwrights Horizons.

1023   Sacheli, Robert. "Harold Prince is Common Wealth Winner." *ThNe.* 1982 Nov.; 14(8): 1, 14. Illus. Photo.
USA. 1950-1982. Biographical studies. ■Harold Prince's career, including shows and people. As producer and director, he changed musical comedy to musical theatre.

Opera

1024   "Calendar." *OC.* 1982 Spring; 23(1): 42-45. Illus.
1982. Histories-sources. ■Forthcoming events in international opera world.

1025   Mercer, Ruby. "People Are Talking About..." *OC.* 1982 Spring; 23(1): 6-10. Illus.
1982. Histories-sources. ■Tidbits about personalities in international opera world.

1026   Mercer, Ruby. "People Are Talking About..." *OC.* 1982 Summer; 23(2): 4-7. Illus.
1982-1983. Histories-sources. ■Tidbits about personalities in opera world.

MUSIC-DRAMA — cont'd

1027　Mercer, Ruby. "People Are Talking About..." *OC*. 1982 Summer; 23(3): 4-7. Illus.
1982. Histories-sources. ■Tidbits about personalities in world of opera.

1028　Mercer, Ruby. "People Are Talking About..." *OC*. 1982 Dec.; 23(4): 4-7. Illus.
1982. Histories-sources. ■Tidbits about personalities in opera world.

1029　Steane, John. "Newman of *The Sunday Times*: The World of Opera." *Opera*. 1982 Feb.; 33(2): 126-131. Illus.
England. 1920-1939. Critical studies. ■Ernest Newman, music critic for *The Sunday Times*, advocates better production standards, and expresses the opinion that Britain can never have a national opera.

1030　Staud, Géza. "Haydn's *Armida* oder die unerschlossenen Quellen der Theaterforschung." (Haydn's *Armida* or The Unrevealed Sources of Theatre Research.) *MuK*. 1982; 28(2): 87-104. Notes. Illus.
Hungary. 1784. Histories-reconstruction. ■Sources for the reconstruction of the original performance at court theatre at Eszterházy, using additional material from various collections and original designs.

1031　Bonnenberg, Henry. "Why Not Go for Baroque?" *OC*. 1982 Summer; 23(2): 16-18. Illus.
Italy. 1600-1750. Historical studies. ■Survey of baroque opera with special reference to Händel's *Rinaldo*.

Design/technology: Costuming/costumers

1032　Ananoff, Alexandre. "Propos sur trois dessins de François Boucher." (Remarks on Three Designs by François Boucher.) *GdBA*. 1982 May-June; 99(5): 211-213. Notes. Illus.
France. 1748-1753. Historical studies. ■Notes three costume designs by François Boucher, one for *Tancrède et Herminie* (1748), two for *Titon et l'Aurore* (1753).

1033　Kahane, Martine. "Costumes from the Paris Opera." *EHN*. 1982 June; 9(2): 31-39. Illus.
France. 1930-1981. Histories-sources. ■Costume exhibition from Paris Opera productions. Related to Theatre in General.

1034　Bovard, Jeannette. "Costuming Falstaff." *PArts*. 1982 Mar.; 16(3): 26. Illus.
Great Britain. Italy. USA. 1982. Histories-sources. ■Michael Stennett describes costume designs for tri-national production of Verdi's *Falstaff* by Los Angeles Philharmonic, conducted by Carlo Maria Giulini at L.A. Music Center, April, 1982.

1035　Campbell, Patton. "A Second Ride on the Beloved War-Horse." *ThCr*. 1982 Oct.; 16(8): 19-21, 52-55. Illus.
USA. 1982. Technical studies. ■Costume design research for *La Traviata*.

Design/technology: Masks/wigs

1036　McClelland, John. "Mozart et les Masques." (Mozart and Masks.) *OC*. 1982 Summer; 23(3): 16, 44-47. Illus.
Europe. 1750-1799. Histories-sources. ■Use of masks in Mozart's operas.

Design/technology: Scenery/scene designers

1037　Shyer, Laurence. "John Dexter at the Met: Reflections of a Director of Production." *ThCr*. 1982 Nov.-Dec.; 16(9): 29-38. Illus.
USA. 1982. Histories-sources. ■Struggle to simplify scenery at Metropolitan Opera.

1038　Geleng, Ingvelde. "*Die Meistersinger von Nürnberg* in Bayreuth 1981 als komische Oper." (*Die Meistersinger von Nürnberg* as Comic Opera at Bayreuth, 1981.) *BtR*. 1982 Feb.; 1: 14-17. Plan.
West Germany. 1945-1981. Critical studies. ■Discussion of new scenery and comparison with other postwar productions.

Financial operations: Planning and accounting

1039　Grosser, Hellmut. "Muss Oper so Teuer sein?" (Must Opera Be So Expensive?) *BtR*. 1982 Aug.; 4: 20-22. Plan.
West Germany. 1982. Histories-sources. ■Technical director explains and defends production expenses of opera at Nationaltheater München.

Institutions: Producing/performing

1040　McCann, John. "The New Regime Launched." *Opera*. 1982 Jan.; 33(1): 46-48, 64. Illus.
Belgium. 1981. Histories-sources. ■Belgian National Opera opens new season at Théâtre de la Monnaie with *Don Carlos*, directed by Gérard Mortier and conducted by John Pritchard.

1041　Cherniavsky, Felix. "A Remarkable Story: Edmonton Opera's 20 Years." *OC*. 1982; 23(4): 18, 42-43. Illus.
Canada. 1952-1982. Histories-sources.

1042　Fraser, Hugh. "Opera Comes to Hamilton." *OC*. 1982 Summer; 23(3): 14, 47. Illus.
Canada. 1976-1982. Histories-sources. ■How Opera Hamilton grew out of city's Festitalia.

Institutions: Special

1043　Rosenthal, Harold. "A 'Club' for Administrators." *Opera*. 1982 Dec.; 33(12): 1224-1228. Illus.
1982. Histories-sources. ■Sir John Tooley, General Director of Covent Garden, discusses International Association of Opera Directors.

Institutions: Training

1044　Dyson, Peter; Sirett, Mark. "Hope for the Future." *OC*. 1982 Summer; 23(2): 20-23, 43. Illus.
Canada. Twentieth cent. Histories-sources. ■The Canadian Opera Company Ensemble's devotion to training young singers. Edmonton's School-and-Community Opera brings opera to several rural communities in Alberta.

Librettos/librettists: Adaptations

1045　Descotes, Maurice. "Du drame à l'opéra: les transpositions lyriques du théâtre de Victor Hugo." (From Drama to Opera: Musical Transpositions of Victor Hugo's Plays.) *RHT*. 1982; 34(2): 103-156. Notes.
France. Italy. 1830-1876. Critical studies. ■Operatic adaptations considered dramaturgically: Donizetti's *Lucrezia Borgia*, Verdi's *Ernani* and *Rigoletto*, Ponchielli's *La Gioconda*.

1046　Henderson, Robert. "Busoni, Gozzi, Prokofiev and *The Oranges*." *Opera*. 1982 May; 33(5): 458-464. Illus.
Italy. Russia. Eighteenth cent. Twentieth cent. Historical studies. ■Use of Gozzi's play, *L'amore delle tre melarance*, with historical background material.

Librettos/librettists: Genres

1047　Forsyth, Karen. Ariadne auf Naxos *by Hugo von Hofmannsthal and Richard Strauss: Its Genesis and Meaning.* New York: Oxford UP; 1982. ix, 291 pp. Pref. Index. Biblio.
Austria. 1912-1916. Critical studies. ■Analysis of collaborative process for the 1912 and 1916 versions. Related to Theatre in General.

Librettos/librettists: Plot/subject/theme

1048　Howard, Patricia. "*Armide*, A Forgotten Masterpiece." *Opera*. 1982 June; 33(6): 572-576. Illus.
France. 1777. Critical studies. ■Brief analysis of Gluck's *Armide* from Quinault's libretto, compared with Lully's version and analysis of action.

Performance spaces: Theatres

1049　"Covent Garden's 250th Birthday." *Opera*. 1982 Dec.; 33(12): 1234-1237. Illus.: Photo. Poster. Print. B&W. 9.

MUSIC-DRAMA — cont'd

England. 1732-1982. Histories-sources. ▪Pictures relating to history of Covent Garden Opera house.

1050   Modi, Sorab. "La Scala: Theatre of the People." *OC.* 1982 Summer; 23(3): 13, 48-49. Illus.
Italy. 1776-1982. Histories-sources. ▪Brief history of opera house.

Performance/performers

1051   Bharucha, Rustom. "*Satyagraha*: A World Outside of Time." *ThM.* 1982 Spring; 13(2): 64-69. Illus.
USA. 1981. Reviews of performances. ▪Polemic on mystification of history in Philip Glass's *Satyagraha: M.K. Gandhi in South Africa 1893-1914*, libretto by Constance DeJong, produced at the Brooklyn Academy of Music.

1052   Harris, David. "The Original *Four Saints in Three Acts*." *TDR.* 1982 Spring; 26(1): 101-130.
USA. 1934. Histories-reconstruction. ▪Historical study of 1934 production of *Four Saints in Three Acts* by Gertrude Stein and Virgil Thomson, with reference to John Houseman, Maurice Grosser, Florine Stettheimer and 'Freddie' Ashton.

Performance/performers: Acting/actors

1053   Cannon, Robert. "Stanislavski and the Opera." *Opera.* 1982 Nov.; 33(11): 1112-1117. Illus.
Russia. 1900. Historical studies. ▪Stanislavski's training of opera singers.

Performance/performers: Singing/singers

1054   Cairns, David. "Jon Vickers." *OC.* 1982 Summer; 23(3): 18-21. Illus.
1927-1982. Biographical studies. ▪Analysis of tenor's personality and performance style.

1055   Löbl, Hermi. "Ein Tenor aller Klassen." (A World Class Tenor.) *Bühne.* 1982 Sep.: 23-24. Illus.
1982. Histories-sources. ▪Interview with Placido Domingo about his career and forthcoming roles.

1056   Lossmann, Hans. "Jewgenij Nesterenko." *Bühne.* 1982 Apr.: 13-15. Illus.
1963-1982. Histories-sources. ▪Career of Soviet opera singer.

1057   Lossmann, Hans. "Heinz Zednik." *Bühne.* 1982 July-Aug.: 13-15. Illus.
1964-1982. Histories-sources. ▪Career of Austrian opera singer.

1058   Morra, Louis A. "Teresa Stratas." *OC.* 1982 Dec.; 23(4): 14-17, 38-39. Illus.
Twentieth cent. Histories-sources. ▪Interview with and biographical sketch of soprano, with focus on her relationship with Lotte Lenya.

1059   Lossmann, Hans. "Luis Lima." *Bühne.* 1982 May: 13-15. Illus.
Argentina. 1973-1982. Histories-sources. ▪Career of opera singer Luis Lima.

1060   Blyth, Alan. "Lucia Popp." *Opera.* 1982 Feb.; 33(2): 132-138. Illus.
Austria. Germany. England. 1963-1982. Histories-sources. ▪Interview about her career and approach to roles.

1061   Anon. "Spotlight: Diane Loeb." *OC.* 1982 Spring; 23(1): 4-5. Illus.
Canada. 1982. Histories-sources. ▪Interview with young mezzo-soprano Diane Loeb.

1062   Anon. "Spotlight: Alan Woodrow." *OC.* 1982 Dec.; 23(4): 8, 10. Illus.
Canada. 1982. Histories-sources. ▪Interview with young tenor Alan Woodrow.

1063   Potvin, Gilles. "Emma Albani." *OC.* 1982 Dec.; 23(4): 20-21. Illus.

Canada. 1847-1950. Biographical studies. ▪Soprano Emma Albani's career.

1064   Forbes, Elizabeth. "Pauline Tinsley." *Opera.* 1982 Mar.; 33(3): 258-267. Illus.
England. 1961-1982. Biographical studies. ▪Brief biography of soprano Tinsley.

1065   Olivier, Michael. "Jon Vickers in Conversation with Michael Olivier." *Opera.* 1982 Apr.; 33(4): 362-367. Illus.
England. Twentieth cent. Histories-sources. ▪Jon Vickers' approach to roles, specifically Tristan, Peter Grimes, Otello and Samson.

1066   Reilly, Joan. "Winston's Brahm Scrapbook." *TN.* 1982; 36(2): 52-55.
England. 1787-1839. Histories-sources. ▪Citations from opera tenor's scrapbook. Related to Music-Drama: Opera.

1067   Steane, John. "English Opera Criticism in the Interwar Years: 4. Herman Klein of *The Gramophone*." *Opera.* 1982 Oct.; 33(10): 1002-1007. Illus.
England. 1920-1939. Studies of criticism/critics. ▪Survey of critic Herman Klein's work, with special emphasis on his comparison of singers' performances on stage and on recordings.

1068   Segalini, Sergio. "Gabriel Bacquier." *Opera.* 1982 June; 33(6): 577-583. Illus.
France. 1924-1982. Biographical studies. ▪Baritone Bacquier's career.

1069   Baldridge, Charlene. "Brecknock: At Breakneck Pace Noted British Tenor Discusses His Career." *OC.* 1982 Spring; 23(1): 20-21. Illus.
Great Britain. 1938-1982. Histories-sources. ▪Brief interview with tenor John Brecknock.

1070   Borovsky, Victor. "The Art of Chaliapin." *Opera.* 1982 Jan.; 33(1): 27-34. Illus.
Russia. 1873-1917. Biographical studies. ▪Chaliapin as an actor. His relationship to theatre of his time, Mamontov and Stanislavsky. His early struggles, first successes in Russia and his acting technique. Related to Theatre in General.

1071   Lossmann, Hans. "Patricia Wise." *Bühne.* 1982 Mar.: 13-15. Illus.
USA. Twentieth cent. Histories-sources. ▪Overview of career with reference to recent roles at European festivals and opera houses.

1072   Lossmann, Hans. "Siegfried Jerusalem." *Bühne.* 1982 June: 13-15. Illus.
West Germany. 1976-1982. Histories-sources. ▪Career of tenor and recent parts in Wagner's operas.

Personnel: Top management/producers

1073   Anon. "Ich glaube an die Total-Oper." (I Believe in Total Opera.) *Bühne.* 1982 Sep.: 4-7. Illus.
Austria. USA. 1982. Histories-sources. ▪Interview with Lorin Maazel about preparations and plans as new manager of Vienna's Staatsoper.

1074   Livio, Antoine. "L'Opéra de Paris, tangue, tangue." (L'Opéra de Paris: The Boat is Rocking.) *OC.* 1982 Summer; 23(2): 19, 48. Illus.
France. 1973-1982. Histories-sources. ▪Discusses administrations of Rolf Liebermann and Bernard Lefort on occasion of Massimo Bogianchino's assumption of artistic direction.

Scores/composers

1075   Lamb, Andrew. "Emmerich Kalman — A Centenary Tribute." *Opera.* 1982 Oct.; 33(10): 1009-1015. Illus.
Austria. 1883-1953. Histories-sources. ▪Summary of operetta composer's life including a brief description of major works.

1076   Cenni, Anna. "Leggenda e inquietudine: note sulla produzione teatrale di Béla Bartók." (Legend and Restlessness: Notes on Béla Bartók's Theatrical Productions.) *QT.* 1982 Aug.; 5(17): 93-114. Notes.

MUSIC-DRAMA — cont'd

Hungary. Twentieth cent. Critical studies. ■Analysis of *A Kékszakallu Hereeg Varó* and two ballets, *A fobol faragott Kiralyfi* and *A csodalatos Mandarino*, by Béla Bartók. Related to Dance: Ballet.

1077 Staud, Géza. "Béla Bartóks Bühnenwerke." (Béla Bartók's Works for the Stage.) *MuK*. 1982; 28(1) : 35-42. Notes. Illus.
Hungary. 1910-1981. Historical studies. ■Creation, production and reception of operas and ballets. Grp/movt: Art nouveaux. Related to Dance.

1078 Morey, Carl. "Donizetti Revised the Rules." *OC*. 1982 Summer; 23(2): 24-26. Illus.
Italy. 1797-1848. Biographical studies. ■Brief account of Gaetano Donizetti's reception in Canada with brief biography.

1079 Otto, Werner. "Theatergeschichte(n) Folge 5: Giuseppe Verdi — Erinnerungen, Betrachtungen." (Theatre History/ 5: Giuseppe Verdi — Reminiscences and Reflections.) *TZ*. 1982 Feb.; 37(2): 26-28. Illus. [Installment of an irregular series.]
Italy. 1813-1901. Biographical studies. ■Reflections on Verdi and his work.

Scores/composers: Adaptations

1080 Glover, Jane. "Cavalli and *L'Egisto*." *Opera*. 1982 Jan.; 33(1): 19-26. Illus.
Italy. 1637. Critical studies. ■Analysis of Cavalli's *L'Egisto* with comments on Raymond Leppard's version as performed by the Scottish Opera.

Scores/composers: Plot/subject/theme

1081 Howarth, Elgar. "Ligeti's *Le Grand Macabre*." *Opera*. 1982 Dec.; 33(12): 1229-1233. Illus.
Hungary. Twentieth cent. Histories-sources. ■Description of György Ligeti's Breughelesque comedy with strongly sexual themes, written by conductor of first British performance.

Scores/composers: Structure/language

1082 Blyth, Alan. "*Igor* at Last." *Opera*. 1982 Sep.; 33(9): 901-904. Illus.
Russia. 1870-1879. Histories-sources. ■Interview with artistic director of Opera North in connection with production of *Prince Igor*, including genesis of score and libretto and description of adaptations.

Staging

1083 Kretzschmann, Hartmut; Lange, Wolfgang; Pfützner, Klaus; Rienäcker, Gerd; Riha, Carl. "II. Werkstatt-Tage des Musiktheaters." (Second Workshop on Music Theater.) *TZ*. 1982 Feb.; 37(2): 16-23. Illus.
East Germany. 1981. Histories-sources. ■Includes notes on difficulties of staging today's operas, problems with librettos and role of ensemble.

Staging: Conducting/conductors

1084 Bernheimer, Martin. "Giulini and *Falstaff*." *Opera*. 1982 July; 33(7): 680-684. Illus.
USA. England. 1982. Histories-sources. ■Conductor Carlo Maria Giulini explains why he conducts so little opera and his cooperation with stage director.

Staging: Directing/directors

1085 Anon. "Spotlight: Robert Carsen." *OC*. 1982 Summer; 23(2): 8-10.
Canada. 1982. Histories-sources. ■Interview with young opera stage director.

1086 McClelland, John. "Splendeurs et misères de la mise en scène." (Pains and Pleasures of Staging.) *OC*. 1982 Spring; 23(1): 22-23. Illus.

Canada. Twentieth cent. Critical studies. ■Directors' and designers' interpretations of operas.

1087 De Bosio, Gianfranco; Stetka, Boris; Messinis, Mario, ed. Aida *1913, 1982. Diario per una regia all'Arena.* (*Aida* 1913 and 1982: Diary for a Production at the Arena.) Milan: Il Saggiatore; 1982. 213 pp. (Politeama 6.) Illus.
Italy. 1913-1982. Historical studies. ■Gianfranco De Bosio's new staging at Arena of Verona of 1913 edition.

1088 Yohalem, John. "Directing Opera, Making Theatre." *AmTh*. 1982 July-Aug.; 4(4-5): 1-4. Notes. Illus.: Photo. B&W. 5.
USA. 1982. Histories-sources. ■Why theatre directors are doing opera productions, and impact of theatre techniques on opera audiences and singers.

Operetta

Performance/performers: Singing/singers

1089 O'Connor, Patrick. "Fritzi Massary — A Centenary Tribute." *Opera*. 1982 May; 33(5): 467-473. Illus.
Austria. Germany. 1904-1930. Biographical studies. ■Leading operetta singer Fritzi Massary's career.

Scores/composers

1090 Citron, Paula. "The Two Sides of Offenbach." *OC*. 1982 Summer; 23(4): 12, 40-41. Illus.
France. Nineteenth cent. Biographical studies.

Other entries with significant content related to Music-Drama: 48, 72, 397, 448, 538, 589, 629, 1066, 1269, 1270.

POPULAR ENTERTAINMENT

General

1091 Testaverde, Anna Maria. "Il ruolo della soprintendenza granducale nell'organizzazione delle feste fiorentine del 1589." (The Role of Grand-ducal Supervision in the Organization of the Florentine Festivities in 1589.) *QT*. 1982 Aug.; 5(17): 69-83.
Italy. 1589. Historical studies. ■Changing relationship between artists and political figures.

1092 Valenti, Cristina. "Le egloghe rusticali dello Strascino e la multiformità attorica. In margine al 'teatro popolare' del primo Cinquecento." (Strascino's Rustic Eclogues and the Actor's Multi-faceted Skills in the Popular Theatre of the Early 16th Century.) *QT*. 1982 Aug.; 5(17): 56-68. Notes.
Italy. 1511-1520. Historical studies. ■Figure of Niccolò Campani, called Lo Strascino: information on his life and analysis of his works: *The Street Vendor (Lo Strascino)*, *The Thin Guy (Il Magrino)*, *The Pocketknife (Il Coltellino)*.

Audience: Composition

1093 Calore, Marina. *Pubblico e spettacolo nel Rinascimento — Indagine sul territorio dell'Emilia Romagna.* (Audience and Performance During the Renaissance: Research on the Emilia Romagna Area.) Bologna: Forni; 1982. 179 pp. Notes. Illus.
Italy. Renaissance period. Fifteenth cent. Sixteenth cent. Historical studies. ■Characteristics, organization, popular participation in festivities and performances.

POPULAR ENTERTAINMENT — cont'd

Institutions: Producing/performing

1094 Eckey, Lorelie F.; Schoyer, Maxine Allen; Schoyer, William T. *1,001 Broadways: Hometown Talent on Stage.* Ames, IA: Iowa State UP; 1982. xiv, 143 pp. Pref. Illus.
USA. 1928-1935. Historical studies. ■Universal Producing Company viewed as small-town show business.

Performance/performers

1095 Haddad, Youssef Rachid. "Art du conteur: Art de l'acteur." (The Art of the Storyteller: The Art of the Actor.) *CTL.* 1982; 47: 3-141. Notes. Biblio. Illus.: Photo. B&W. 10.
Arabic-speaking countries. 100-1982. Historical studies. ■Book-length study of the storyteller as performer in Arab culture. Sociological as well as religious and aesthetic aspects are examined.

1096 Coldwey, John C. "Some Nottinghamshire Waits: Their History." *REEDN.* 1982; 1: 40-48. Notes.
England. 1400-1642. Historical studies. ■Activities of 'waits' or liveried town musicians described from contemporary records.

1097 Fresta, Mariano; Venturelli, Gastone. "Togno e Catera vecchia secondo il testo adottato dalla Compagnia di Torrita di Siena." (Togno and Catera Vecchia According to the Text Chosen by the Company of Torrita of Siena.) *QT.* 1982 Nov.; 5(18): 173-200 . Notes.
Italy. 1974. Histories-reconstruction. ■Reconstruction of *Segalavecchia*, a folk festivity in Valdichiara, by the Company of Torrita of Siena in 1974, from a manuscript edited in appendix.

1098 Bliss, Shepherd. "Ken Feit: 'Presente'." *Tk.* 1982 July-Aug.; 2(5): 40-41.
USA. 1981-1982. Histories-sources. ■Response to death of Ken Feit, itinerant storyteller.

1099 Feit, Ken. "A Letter to My Friends on the Occasion of My Fortieth Birthday." *Tk.* July-Aug.; 2(5): 24-31. Illus.
USA. 1940-1982. Histories-sources. ■Education and memoirs of itinerant storyteller.

1100 Feit, Ken. "Reflections of a Foolish Storyteller." *Tk.* 1982 July-Aug.; 2(5): 32-37. Illus.
USA. 1970-1982. Histories-sources. ■Memoirs of an itinerant storyteller.

1101 Niemi, Loren. "Gypsy Geographer." *Tk.* 1982 July-Aug.; 2(5): 22-23. Illus. [Irregular correspondence.]
USA. 1981-1982. Histories-sources. ■Experiences of itinerant storyteller Loren Niemi.

Performance/performers: Acting/actors

1102 Ross, Janice. "Bill Irwin, Getting Physical with Comedy." *Dm.* 1982 June; 56(6): 68-72. Illus.: Photo.
USA. 1968-1982. Histories-sources. ■Background and career of dancer/clown. Related to Mime.

Relation to other fields: Anthropology

1103 Hagher, Iyorwuese. "Kwagh-Hir." *Tk.* 1982 Nov.-Dec.; 3(1): 52.
Nigeria. 1960-1982. Historical studies. ■*Kwagh-Hir*, performance technique combining storytelling, puppets, masks, songs and dances, provides Tiv villagers with outlet for native language expression.

Relation to other fields: Sociology

1104 Niemi, Loren. "Gypsy Geographer." *Tk.* 1982 Nov.-Dec.; 3(1): 28-30. [Irregular correspondence.]
USA. 1982. Histories-sources. ■Itinerant storyteller's experiences at conferences and political theatres.

Staging: Directing/directors

1105 Brown, Langdon. "Gémier and Baty's *La Grande Pastorale*: A Medieval Mystery Play for the Twentieth Century." *THSt.* 1982; 2: 69-82. Notes. Illus.
France. 1920. Historical studies. ■Account of spectacular dramatic entertainment, based on medieval sources, created by Firmin Gémier and Gaston Baty at the Cirque d'Hiver.

Training: Non-formal training

1106 Feder, Happy Jack. *The Independent Entertainer.* Englewood Cliffs, NJ: Prentice-Hall; 1982. 154 pp. Pref. Index. Illus.: Dwg. B&W.
USA. Twentieth cent. Textbooks/manuals/guides. ■How to be a successful clown, juggler, mime, magician or puppeteer.

Cabaret

1107 Di Giulio, Maria. "Il cabaret nella Russia del primo Novecento — Dagli albori ai maggiori successi." (Cabaret in Russia in the Early 20th Century: From Beginnings to Success.) *QT.* 1982 Nov.; 5(18): 129-158. Biblio.
Russia. 1882-1921. Historical studies.

Performance/performers: Acting/actors

1108 Schumacher, Ernst. "Valentins Tag." (Valentin's Day.) *TZ.* 1982; 37: 22-26. Illus.
East Germany. 1882-1982. Biographical studies. ■On the 100th anniversary of Karl Valentin's birth, Schumacher evaluates the comedian and presents Valentin's 1928 curriculum vitae.

1109 Case, Sue-Ellen. "Introducing Karl Valentin." *ThM.* 1981-82, Winter; 13(1): 6-11. Notes. Illus.
Germany. 1908-1948. Historical studies. ■Analysis of Valentin's acting style and verbal wit. Related to Media: Film.

Plays/playwrights: Genres

1110 Goldstein, Imre. "Karinthy's *Kabaré*." *PerAJ.* 1982; 6(3): 87-90.
Hungary. 1887-1938. Historical studies. ■Works, reputation and interpretation of Frigyes Karinthy, who anticipated absurdism.

Carnival

1111 Marino, Massimo E. "Messa in opera della Giostra di San Giovanni." (Construction of the Carnival at San Giovanni.) *QT.* 1982 Aug.; 5(17): 207-223.
Italy. 1979. Historical studies. ■Detailed account of a theatrical experience.

Performance/performers: Acting/actors

1112 Gardy, Philippe. "Les limites du jeu carnavalesque? (La Carrièra, 1976-1982)." (The Limits of Carnival Acting? — La Carrièra, 1976-1982.) *RHT.* 1982; 34(1): 89-91. Notes.
France. 1976-1982. Histories-sources. ■Teatre de la Carrièra's developments away from carnival sources.

Plays/playwrights: Characters/roles

1113 Mathieu, Guy. "Théâtre et carnaval en Provence du XVIIIe au XXe siècles." (Theatre and Carnival in Provence from the 18th to the 20th Centuries.) *RHT.* 1982; 34(1): 66-72. Notes.
France. Multi-period. Histories-reconstruction. ■Development of theatrical farces involving characters of Carême and Caramentrant in 18th century carnival festivities, in literary form in 19th century and in contemporary adaptation.

Plays/playwrights: Genres

1114 Gardy, Philippe. "Naissances du théâtre en pays occitan: les célébrations carnavalesques." (Origins of Theatre in Regions Where Provençal is Spoken: Carnival-like celebrations.) *RHT.* 1982; 34(1): 10-30. Notes. Illus. Photo. Print. B&W. 2.

POPULAR ENTERTAINMENT — cont'd

France. 1530-1640. Historical studies. ■Development of theatrical farces in the religious carnival season: Provençal language farces by Benoet du Lac, Claude Brueys and Gaspard Zerbin. Related to Ritual and Ceremony: Religious.

Scripts/scriptwriters

1115   Scabia, Giuliano. "La Giostra di San Giovanni." (The Carnival at San Giovanni.) *QT*. 1982 Aug.; 5(17): 224-231. Notes.
Italy. Twentieth cent. Histories-sources. ■Discusses setting up the carnival and text of the performance.

Circus acts

Performance/performers

1116   Guccini, Gerardo. "Teatro e violenza nelle azioni e nelle riflessioni di Leo Bassi." (Theatre and Violence in Leo Bassi's Actions and Considerations.) *QT*. 1982 Nov.; 5(18): 64-70.
Twentieth cent. Biographical studies. ■Training and significant experiences in artistic life of clown Leo Bassi.

Commedia dell'arte

Plays/playwrights: Characters/roles

1117   Taviani, Ferdinando. "La composizione del dramma nella Commedia dell'Arte." (Play Composition in *Commedia dell'Arte*.) *QT*. 1982 Feb.; 4(15): 151-171. Notes.
Italy. Multi-period. Historical studies. ■Composition of *scenari*, and origin of roles.

Relation to other fields: Other arts

1118   Sito Alba, Manuel. "The *Commedia dell'Arte*: Key to the Source of *Don Quijote*." *TA*. 1982; 37: 1-13. Notes. Illus.
Spain. 1547-1587. Critical studies. ■Influence of *commedia dell'arte*, especially Alberto Naselli's character Zan Ganassa, on Miguel de Cervantes.

Pageants

1119   Kipling, Gordon. "The London Pageants for Margaret of Anjou." *MET*. 1982; 4(1): 5-27. Notes. Illus.
England. 1445. Historical studies. ■Examines the evidence for the Royal Entry, with text clarification and specification of locale.

1120   Klotz, Roger. "Un Théâtre populaire à Marseille: la Pastorale." (Popular Theatre in Marseilles: The Pastorale.) *RHT*. 1982; 34(1): 53-65. Notes.
France. Nineteenth cent. Historical studies. ■Popular development of the pastorale after its standardization by Antoine Maurel in the *Pastorale Maurel* of 1844.

1121   Meffre, Joel. "Le Théâtre de la Nativité en Provence." (Nativity Plays in Provence.) *RHT*. 1982; 34(1): 32-52. Notes. Illus. Diagram. Chart.
France. Nineteenth cent. Historical studies. ■Development of popular Provençal pastorales in the 19th century, and origins in religious nativity songs.

Staging

1122   Zarrilli, Phillip; Neff, Deborah. "Performance in 'America's Little Switzerland': New Glarus, Wisconsin." *TDR*. 1982 Summer; 26(2): 111-124.
USA. 1845-1981. Histories-specific. ■Description and history of annual *Wilhelm Tell* pageant performed in New Glarus, Wisconsin.

Parades

1123   Bell, John. "The Fight Against the End of the World." *Tk*. 1982 Sep.-Oct.; 2(6): 20-27. Illus.

USA. 1982. Histories-sources. ■Participation of Bread and Puppet Theatre in March for Nuclear Disarmament, and preparations for their parade and pageant.

———

Other entries with significant content related to Popular Entertainment: 21, 69, 230, 319, 381, 535, 1001.

PUPPETRY

General

1124   Poli, Paola. "Gaston Baty: il teatro della morte del teatro." (Gaston Baty: Theatre of Theatre's Death.) *QT*. 1982 Feb. ; 4(15): 200-213. Notes.
France. Twentieth cent. Studies of theories/theorists. ■Baty's theatrical poetics, with special focus on puppet theatre.

Design/technology: Scenery/scene designers

1125   Brendenal, Silvia. "Szenographie national (8)." (National Scenography, 8.) *TZ*. 1982 Jan.; 37(1): 19-23. [One of a series of conversations with theatre artists.]
East Germany. 1982. Histories-sources. ■Interview with puppet player Konstanza Kavrakova-Lorenz about realization of concept and design of scenery.

Institutions: Producing/performing

1126   Brendenal, Silvia; Kratochwil, Ernst-Frieder; Mechtel, Hartmut; Schreiber, Hans Peter. "Anliegen — Vermögen — Wirkung: Versuch einer Standortbestimmung nach dem III. Puppentheaterfestival der DDR." (Concern — Ability — Effect: Orientation after the Third Festival of Puppet Theatre of East Germany.) *TZ*. 1982 July; 37(7): 40-45. Illus.
East Germany. 1982. Reviews of performances. ■Report on Festival, including performance reviews.

Staging: Directing/directors

1127   Kratochwil, Ernst-Frieder. "Regisseure im Gespräch: Hans-Dieter Stäcker, Direktor des Puppentheaters Zwickau." (Directors in Conversation: Hans-Dieter Stäcker, Director of the Puppet Theatre in Zwickau.) *TZ*. 1982 June; 37(6): 44-46. Illus.
East Germany. 1938-1982. Histories-sources. ■Career survey of director Stäcker and cooperation of Puppentheater Zwickau with other forms of theatre.

Shadow puppets

Plays/playwrights: Characters/roles

1128   Long, Roger. *Javanese Shadow Theatre: Movement and Characterization in Ngayogyakarta Wayang Kulit*. Ann Arbor, MI: UMI Research P; 1982. xi, 195 pp. Pref. Notes. Gloss. Index. Biblio. Illus.
Indonesia. Twentieth cent. Technical studies. ■Examination of traditional movements of *wayang kulit* puppets in relation to character types.

RITUAL AND CEREMONY

General

Relation to other fields: Anthropology

1129   Turner, Victor. "Performing Ethnography." *TDR*. 1982 Summer; 26(2): 33-50.

RITUAL AND CEREMONY — cont'd

Studies of theories/theorists. ▪Performance ethnography aids actors in understanding how ritual and ceremonial structures are cognitively represented.

Staging: Choreography/choreographers

1130 Shea, Ann Marie; Citron, Atay. "The Powwow of the Thunderbird American Indian Dancers." *TDR*. 1982 Summer; 26(2): 73-88.
USA. 1981. Histories-sources. ▪Evaluation and description of annual event in New York.

Civic

Relation to other fields: Politics

1131 Hatley, Barbara. "Indonesian Ritual, Javanese Drama — Celebrating Tujubelasan." *I*. 1982 Oct.; 34: 55-65. Notes.
Indonesia. 1977-1981. Critical studies. ▪Celebration of independence day. Related to Drama.

Religious

1132 Anderson, Michelle. "Authentic Voodoo is Synthetic." *TDR*. 1982 Summer; 26(2): 89-110.
Haiti. 1980. Histories-specific. ▪Study of contermporary voodoo practices in Haiti and their relationship to dramatic presentation.

1133 Lourie, Elena. "Jewish Participation in Royal Funeral Rites: An Early Use of the *Representatio* in Aragón." *JWCI*. 1982; 45: 192-194. Notes.
Spain. 1291. Historical studies. ▪Funeral rites for Alfonso III: earliest known instance of *representatio* (simulated bier) by Jews. Includes another example from Cervera in 1473.

Relation to other fields: Anthropology

1134 Metzger, Deena. "Returning: The Eleusinian Mysteries." *Tk*. 1982 July-Aug.; 2(5): 42-44.
Greece. 1980. Histories-reconstruction. ▪Workshop recreation of the Eleusinian Mysteries, the sacred rites of Demeter, at the original sites.

1135 Yousof, Ghulam-Sarwar. "Nora Chatri in Kedah: A Preliminary Report." *JRASM*. 1982 July; 55(242): 53-61. Notes. Illus.
Malaysia. Twentieth cent. Histories-sources. ▪Ritual performances, stage, orchestra, costumes, possession by spirits, Manora story, repertoire, singing, mythic origin.

Other entries with significant content related to Ritual And Ceremony: 1114.

INDIVIDUALS

Beckett

Plays/playwrights: Plot/subject/theme

1136 Memola, Massimo Marino. "Crisi e frantumazione del soggetto nell'opera di Samuel Beckett." (Crisis and Fragmentation of the Subject in Samuel Beckett's Work.) *QT*. 1982 Aug.; 5(17): 151-178.
Twentieth cent. Critical studies. ▪Ego, body and word in Beckett's plays.

Plays/playwrights: Structure/language

1137 Astier, Pierre. "Beckett's *Ohio Impromptu*: A View from the Isle of Swans." *MD*. 1982 Sep.; 25(3): 331-341. Notes.
Twentieth cent. Critical studies. ▪Analysis of play and meaning of title.

1138 Fehsenfeld, Martha. "Beckett's Late Works: An Appraisal." *MD*. 1982 Sep.; 25(3): 355-362. Notes.

1977-1981. Critical studies. ▪Brief examination of later works shows Beckett's continuing development as a playwright.

1139 Morrison, Kristin. "The Rip Word in *A Piece of Monologue*." *MD*. 1982 Sep.; 25(3): 349-354. Notes.
Twentieth cent. Critical studies. ▪Verbal play with the term 'rip word' in *A Piece of Monologue*.

1140 Simon, Richard Keller. "Dialectical Laughter: A Study of *Endgame*." *MD*. 1982 Dec.; 25(4): 505-513. Notes.
Twentieth cent. Critical studies. ▪Samuel Beckett's study of laughter, onstage and in audience.

1141 Brater, Enoch. "Light, Sound, Movement, and Action in Beckett's *Rockaby*." *MD*. 1982 Sep.; 25(3): 342-348. Notes.
USA. Twentieth cent. Critical studies. ▪Complexities in *Rockaby*.

Brecht

Plays/playwrights

1142 Guarino, Raimondo. "L'acquisto della carne, ovvero del tragico in Bertolt Brecht." (The Purchase of Flesh, or On the Tragic in Bertolt Brecht.) *QT*. 1982 Feb.; 4(15): 214-224. Notes.
Germany. Twentieth cent. Study of theories/theorists. ▪Comparison of Brechtian tragedy, as exemplified by *Die Massnahme (The Measures Taken)*, with Nietzsche's definition of tragedy in *Die Geburt der Tragödie (The Birth of Tragedy)*.

Plays/playwrights: Characters/roles

1143 Fenn, Bernard. *Characterization of Women in the Plays of Bertolt Brecht*. Frankfurt a.M., Bern: Lang; 1982. 241 pp. (European University Studies 1, v. 383.) Pref. Notes. Biblio. [Dissertation, Kerala University, 1979.]
Germany. 1918-1954. Critical studies. ▪Women in Brecht's plays: history of changing images, role in theory of epic theatre, interpretation of female characters. Function of women in Brecht's life and in realization of the utopian character of his plays. Related to Drama.

Plays/playwrights: Plot/subject/theme

1144 Walser, Martin; Honegger, Gitta, trans. "A Beautiful Life: A Sermon on the Occasion of the 25th Anniversary of the Death of Bertolt Brecht." *PerAJ*. 1982; 6(2): 37-45.
Germany. 1918-1979. Historical studies. ▪Development of moral concerns in poetry and comparison with later writers.

Calderón

Staging: Directing/directors

1145 Satgé, Alain. "Lavelli et le théâtre: 'Sur le fil'." (Lavelli and the Theatre: 'On the Edge'.) *CF*. 1982 Oct.; 112: 3-7.
France. 1975-1982. Critical studies. ▪Jorge Lavelli's poetic approach to directing Calderón's *Life is a Dream (La vida es sueño)* at the Comédie Française.

1146 Satgé, Alain. "Le Rêve Hyperbolique: Calderón Interpreté par Lavelli." (The Hyperbolic Dream: Calderón Interpreted by Lavelli.) *CF*. 1982 Dec.; 114: 7-9.
France. 1982. Reviews of performances. ▪Dream-like atmosphere of *Life is a dream (La vida es sueño)* by Calderón in Jorge Lavelli's staging at the Comédie Française.

Chekhov

Staging

1147 Bristow, Eugene K. "Let's Hear It from the Losers: or Chekhov, Komissarzhevskaya, and *The Seagull* at St. Petersburg in 1896." *THSt*. 1982; 2: 1-13. Notes.
Russia. 1896. Histories-reconstruction. ▪Revisionist account of first production of *The Seagull (Čajka)*: presents evidence that it was not a

INDIVIDUALS — cont'd

complete failure. Discusses performers, Chekhov's contributions and other successful productions prior to Moscow Art Theatre production in 1898.

Corneille

Design/technology: Scenery/scene designers

1148   Guarino, Raimondo. *La tragedia e le macchine* — Andromède *di Corneille e Torelli.* (Tragedy and Machines: *Andromède* by Corneille and Torelli.) Rome: Bulzoni; 1982. 180 pp. Notes. Illus.
France. 1650. Histories-reconstruction. ■Performance of *Andromède*: union of classical dramaturgy and baroque scenery.

Plays/playwrights: Characters/roles

1149   Kowsar, Mohammad. "In Defense of Desire: Chimène's Role in *Le Cid* Reconsidered." *TJ.* 1982 Oct.; 34(3): 289-301. Notes. Illus.
France. 1636. Critical studies. ■Relation to themes of passion, revenge and feudal order.

Goethe

1150   Otto, Werner. "Theatergeschichte(n) Folge 6: Der Theaterdirektor Johann Wolfgang von Goethe." (Theatre History/6: Goethe as a Theatre Manager.) *TZ.* 1982 Mar.; 37(3): 5-8. Illus. [Installment of an irregular series.]
Germany. 1790-1817. Histories-sources. ■Documents concerning Johann Wolfgang von Goethe as manager of theatre in Weimar, with commentary.

Performance/performers

1151   Gussow, Mel; Barnes, Clive; Kissel, Howard; Skerritt, David. "*Faust, Parts I and II.*" *NYTCR.* 1982 Nov. 15; 43(15): 153-156. [Off-Broadway Supplement IV.]
USA. 1982. Reviews of performances. ■Four critics review Christopher Martin's production, presented by Classic Stage Company, New York.

Plays/playwrights: Plot/subject/theme

1152   Hölzel, Alfred. "The Conclusion of Goethe's *Faust*: Ambivalence and Ambiguity." *GQ.* 1982 Jan.; 55(1): 1-12. Notes.
Germany. 1797-1801. Critical studies. ■Reinterpretation denying Christian fulfillment and emphasizing ambiguity and inscrutability.

Plays/playwrights: Structure/language

1153   Bennett, Benjamin. "Levels and Movements of Consciousness in Goethe's *Faust.*" *TJ.* 1982 Mar.; 34(1): 5-19. Notes.
Germany. 1769-1831. Critical studies. ■Substitutes 'level of consciousness' for 'reality' or 'unreality' and suggests that play moves between levels of consciousness, for characters and audience. Infl. by *Über die ästhetische Erziehung des Menschen (On the Aesthetic Educati.*

Ibsen

Plays/playwrights: Characters/roles

1154   Dukore, Bernard F. "Kristine Linde and Gregers Werle." *ET.* 1982 Nov.; 1(1): 45-51. Notes.
Norway. 1879-1885. Critical studies. ■Gregers Werle in *The Wild Duck (Vildanden)* seen as development of the character of Kristine Linde in *A Doll's House (Et Dukkehjem).* Related to Drama.

1155   Sprinchorn, Evert. "Honoring the *Ghosts* Centennial: Pastor Manders." *INC.* 1981; 2: 4-6.
Norway. 1882. Critical studies. ■Character study of Pastor Manders in *Ghosts (Gengangere).*

Plays/playwrights: Plot/subject/theme

1156   Hanson, Katherine. "Ibsen's Women Characters and Their Feminist Contemporaries." *THSt.* 1982; 2: 83-91. Notes.
Norway. 1870-1899. Historical studies. ■Relationship between Ibsen and several important Norwegian feminist authors and critics: *A Doll's House (Et Dukkehjem), Hedda Gabler* and *Rosmersholm.*

Plays/playwrights: Structure/language

1157   Chamberlain, John S. *Ibsen: The Open Vision.* Distributed by Humanities. London: Athlone; 1982. vii, 223 pp. Pref. Notes. Index. Biblio.
Norway. Nineteenth cent. Critical studies. ■Examination of *Peer Gynt, Ghosts (Gengangere), The Wild Duck (Vildanden)* and *The Master Builder (Bygmester Solness)*, with a discussion of Ibsen's vision and dramatic forms.

1158   Edwards, Angela B. "Water in the Landscape Symbolism of Ibsen's Late Outdoor Plays." *IÅ.* 1981-1982: 23-46. Notes. Biblio.
Norway. Nineteenth cent. Critical studies.

Staging

1159   Rudler, Roderick. "Ibsen i Bergen." (Ibsen in Bergen.) *IÅ.* 1981-82: 80-85. Notes.
Norway. Nineteenth cent. Histories-sources. ■Productions of Ibsen's plays in Bergen and influences on the playwright during his lifetime. Infl. by Ole Bull.

Ionesco

Librettos/librettists: Plot/subject/theme

1160   Lamont, Rosette C. "Ionesco's First Opera: An Introduction." *PerAJ.* 1982; 6(2): 29-31.
France. 1941-1982. Histories-sources. ■Ionesco's religious, philosophical and political beliefs in relation to opera on holocaust.

Plays/playwrights

1161   Kott, Jan. "Ionesco und der schwangere Tod: Über das Tragikomische im Werk des Dramatikers." (Ionesco and the Pregnant Death: On the Tragicomic in the Work of the Dramatist.) *TH.* 1982(13): 108-111.
France. Twentieth cent. Critical studies. Related to Drama.

Plays/playwrights: Plot/subject/themes

1162   Lazar, Moshe, ed. *The Dream and the Play: Ionesco's Theatrical Quest.* Malibu, CA: Undena; 1982. viii, 176 pp. (Interplay Series 1.) Illus.
France. Twentieth cent. Critical studies. ■Essays on theatre of Eugène Ionesco by Richard N. Coe, Martin Esslin, George E. Wellworth, Robert W. Corrigan, Emmanuel Jacquart, David I. Grossvogel, Rosette C. Lamont, and Jan Kott. With three hitherto unpublished 'dream scenes' excised from Ionesco's *Voyages chez les morts (Journeys to the Land of the Dead).*

Molière

Plays/playwrights

1163   Howarth, W.D. *Molière: A Playwright and His Audience.* New York: Cambridge UP; 1982. xiii, 325 pp.
France. 1650-1699. Critical studies. ■Influence of stage experience and need for broad popular appeal on Molière's style as a playwright.

Plays/playwrights: Characters/roles

1164   Beck, William John. "Tartuffe — La Fouine de Séville ou simplement une belette de La Fontaine." (Tartuffe — The Marten of Seville or Simply a Weasel from La Fontaine.) *RHT.* 1982; 34(3): 204-210. Notes.

INDIVIDUALS — cont'd

France. 1660-1669. Historical studies. ■Possible sources for character of Tartuffe: La Fontaines' *Fables* (in particular, *Weasel in the Granary*) and Castillo y Solórzano's *The Marten of Seville (La Garduña de Sevilla).*

1165 Peacock, N.A. "The Comic Ending of *George Dandin.*" *FS.* 1982 Apr.; 36(2): 144-153. Notes.
France. 1668. Critical studies. ■Character of Dandin as parody of contemporary tragedy.

1166 Planson, Claude. "*Dom Juan* de Molière. Dom Juan ou l'aventurier de l'Eros." (*Don Juan* by Molière: Don Juan or the Adventurer of Eros .) *CF.* 1982 June-July; 110: 17-19.
France. Seventeenth cent. Critical studies. ■Don Juan as libertine symbol of pagan energy, outside human and religious law.

1167 Schérer, Jacques. "La Statue du Commandeur." (The Statue of the Commander.) *CF.* 1982 Sep.; 111: 12-14.
France. 1665. Critical studies. ■Analysis of Molière's use of the statue of the commander in *Don Juan (Dom Juan).*

Plays/playwrights: Plot/subject/theme

1168 Gross, Nathan. *From Gesture to Idea: Esthetics and Ethics in Molière's Comedy.* New York: Columbia UP; 1982. xi, 159 pp. Pref. Index.
France. Seventeenth cent. Critical studies. ■Ethical values in Molière's *Tartuffe, Le Misanthrope, George Dandin* and *Le Bourgeois Gentilhomme,* drawing upon patterns of physical movement as well as plot and language.

Staging

1169 Berkowitz, Janice. "The Where and the Wherefore: A Study of Spatiality in Molière's Theatre." *FrF.* 1982 Jan.; 7(1) : 37-44.
France. 1658-1673. Critical studies. ■Implications for staging and design in texts.

O'Neill

Plays/playwrights

1170 Ben-Zvi, Linda. "Susan Glaspell and Eugene O'Neill." *EON.* 1982 Summer-Fall; 6(2): 21-29.
USA. 1916-1922. Historical studies. ■Discusses close personal relationship between O'Neill and Susan Glaspell, and analyzes Glaspell's plays, including *Bernice, Inheritors, The Verge,* and *Alison's House.*

1171 Berlin, Normand. *Eugene O'Neill.* New York: Grove Press; 1982. xiv, 178 pp. (Grove Press Modern Dramatists Series.) Pref. Index. Biblio.
USA. Twentieth cent. Biographies. ■A biography of Eugene O'Neill.

1172 Egri, Peter. "*The Iceman Cometh*: European Origins and American Originality (Part 2)." *EON.* 1982 Spring; 6(1): 16-24.
USA. Ireland. Twentieth cent. Critical studies. ■O'Neill's play compared to works by J.M. Synge and Joseph Conrad.

1173 Egri, Peter. "*The Iceman Cometh*: European Origins and American Originality (Part 3)." *EON.* 1982 Summer-Fall; 6(2): 30-36.
USA. Twentieth cent. Critical studies. ■Joseph Conrad's influence on O'Neill.

1174 Timár, Esther. "Possible Sources for Two O'Neill One-Acts: *Recklessness* and *In the Zone.*" *EON.* 1982 Winter; 6 (3): 20-23.
USA. 1910-1913. Critical studies. Infl. by Edgar Allen Poe; Giovanni Boccaccio.

Plays/playwrights: Characters/roles

1175 Mandl, Bette. "Absence and Presence: The Second Sex in *The Iceman Cometh.*" *EON.* 1982 Summer-Fall; 6(2): 10-15.
USA. Twentieth cent. Critical studies. ■Feminist analysis: misogynist O'Neill's female characters are presented as means for men's enacting of their destinies.

1176 Nelson, Doris. "O'Neill's Women." *EON.* 1982 Summer-Fall; 6(2): 3-7.
USA. Twentieth cent. Critical studies. ■Inferior position of female characters in O'Neill's plays mirror his personal relationship with wives.

1177 Tuck, Susan. "O'Neill and Frank Wedekind." *EON.* 1982 Summer-Fall; 6(2): 17-21. [Part Two.]
USA. Germany. Twentieth cent. Critical studies.

1178 Wertheim, Albert. "Eugene O'Neill's *Days Without End* and the Tradition of the Split Character in Modern American and British Drama." *EON.* 1982 Winter; 6(3): 5-9.
USA. Great Britain. Twentieth cent. Critical studies. ■O'Neill's influence on contemporary playwrights Hugh Leonard, Sam Shepard, Adrienne Kennedy, Peter Nichols and Marsha Norman.

1179 Young, William. "Mother and Daughter in *Mourning Becomes Electra.*" *EON.* 1982 Summer-Fall; 6(2): 15-17.
USA. Twentieth cent. Critical studies. ■Argues that Christine, not Lavinia, is the central tragic figure of the trilogy.

Plays/playwrights: Editions

1180 Coppenger, Royston. "The Incomplete Plays of Eugene O'Neill: Floyd's *Eugene O'Neill at Work.*" *ThM.* 1982 Summer-Fall; 13(3): 65-69. Illus.
USA. 1918-1943. Reviews of publications. ■Annotated edition of Eugene O'Neill's unpublished notebooks.

Plays/playwrights: Plot/subject/theme

1181 Manheim, Michael. "Dialogue Between Mother and Son in Chekhov's *The Sea Gull* and O'Neill's *Long Day's Journey into Night.*" *EON.* 1982 Spring; 6(1): 24-29.
USA. Russia. Twentieth cent. Critical studies. ■Suggests similarities in vision of life and dramatization of close emotional relationships.

1182 Manheim, Michael. *Eugene O'Neill's New Language of Kinship.* Syracuse, NY: Syracuse UP; 1982. xiii, 240 pp. Pref. Notes. Index.
USA. Twentieth cent. Critical studies. ■Final dramas: a vision of human kinship as existential answer to world devoid of ideals.

1183 Ratliff, Gerald Lee. "*Fog:* An O'Neill Theological Miscellany." *EON.* 1982 Winter; 6(3): 15-20.
USA. 1913-1914. Critical studies. ■O'Neill and theology.

1184 Tuck, Susan. "O'Neill and Frank Wedekind." *EON.* 1982 Spring; 6(1): 29-35. [Part One.]
USA. West Germany. Twentieth cent. Critical studies. ■Similarities in personality and artistic aims between Frank Wedekind and Eugene O'Neill. Influence of *Frühlings Erwachen (Spring's Awakening)* on *Ah, Wilderness.*

Plays/playwrights: Structure/language

1185 Perrin, Robert. "O'Neill's Use of Language in *Where the Cross Is Made.*" *EON.* 1982 Winter; 6(3): 12-13.
USA. Twentieth cent. Critical studies.

Relation to other fields: Other arts

1186 Linney, Romulus. "About O'Neill." *EON.* 1982 Winter; 6(3): 3-5.
USA. Twentieth cent. Biographical studies. ■O'Neill's autobiographical work compared to that of other writers.

INDIVIDUALS — cont'd

Staging: Directing/directors

1187 Sarlós, Robert K. "Nina Moise Directs Eugene O'Neill's *The Rope*." *EON*. 1982 Winter; 6(3): 9-12.
USA. 1918. Historical studies. ■First production of *The Rope*.

Pirandello

Performance/performers

1188 Tamberlani, Carlo. *Pirandello nel 'teatro che c'era'*. (Pirandello in the 'Theatre ... That Was'.) Rome: Bulzoni; 1982. xiii, 176 pp.
Italy. Twentieth cent. Historical studies. ■Author's memories of Pirandellian productions and actors of his time.

Racine

Plays/playwrights

1189 "Sur le jeune Racine: Culture et Découverte de Soi." (On Young Racine: Culture and Self-Discovery.) *DSS*. 1982 Jan.-Mar.; 134: 3-18.
France. 1639-1670. Biographical studies. ■Racine's early years based on his correspondence, poetry, book annotations and other writings.

Shakespeare

1190 Bradbrook, Muriel C. *The Artist and Society in Shakespeare's England: The Collected Papers of Muriel Bradbrook*. Vol. 1. Totowa, NJ: Barnes and Noble; 1982. x, 177 pp. Pref. Notes.
England. 1564-1616. Historical studies. ■Essays and lectures on Shakespeare and his drama.

1191 Jackson, Russell. "Before the Shakespeare Revolution: Developments in the Study of Nineteenth-Century Shakespearean Production." *ShS*. 1982; 35: 1-12. Notes.
England. Nineteenth cent. Studies of history/historians. ■Discussion of 19th century's contribution to Shakespearean production, review of major historians of the 19th century stage, listings of stage histories, biographies of actor-managers, editions of promptbooks and possibilities for future research.

1192 Salgādo, Gāmini. "The Year's Contribution to Shakesperian Study: Shakespeare's Life, Times and Stage." *ShS*. 1982; 35: 174-179. Notes.
England. USA. 1980-1981. Reviews of publications.

1193 Sherbo, Arthur. "A Neglected Critic of Shakespeare's Poetry." *SQ*. 1982 Spring; 33(1): 102-105. Notes.
England. Elizabethan period. Eighteenth cent. Textual studies. ■Late 18th century critic identified only as 'W.' made useful notes on difficult words or passages (some of which were included by Malone in his 1790 edition), and published them in the *European Magazine*, June 1787, pages 414-416. All notes reprinted.

Audience: Reactions/comments

1194 "Zur Shakespeare-Rezeption auf der Bühne der DDR (1945-1980)." (Shakespeare's Reception on the Stages of the German Democratic Republic, 1945-1980.) *SJH*. 1982; 118: 107-119. Notes. [Contribution to Congress of the International Shakespeare Association, Stratford-upon-Avon, 1981.]
East Germany. 1945-1980. Critical studies. ■Reception of Shakespeare productions in principal cities, including productions by worker groups. Related to Drama.

Institutions: Producing/performing

1195 Booth, Michael R. "The Meininger Company and English Shakespeare." *ShS*. 1982; 35: 13-20. Notes. Illus.: Photo. 2.
England. Germany. 1874-1900. Historical studies. ■Touring company from Saxe-Meiningen had little if any direct influence on English productions of Shakespeare.

Institutions: Research

1196 Klatz, Günther. "Die Shakespeare-Tage 1981 in Weimar." (Shakespeare Conference, Weimar, 1981.) *SJW*. 1982; 118: 198-208.
East Germany. 1981. Histories-sources. ■Report of German Shakespeare Society meeting on 'Shakespeare and Peace'.

Performance/performers

1197 Bartholomeusz, Dennis. "Shakespeare on the Melbourne Stage, 1843-1861." *ShS*. 1982; 35: 31-41. Notes.
Australia. 1843-1861. Reviews of performances. ■Survey of productions.

1198 Bains, Yashdip Singh. "Shakespeare on the Canadian Stage: The First Sixty Years." *CDr*. 1982; 8(1): 66-73.
Canada. 1768-1826. Historical studies.

Performance/performers: Acting/actors

1199 Cerasano, S.P. "More on Edward Alleyn's 'Shakespearean' Portrait of Richard III." *SQ*. 1982 Autumn; 33(3): 342-344. Notes.
England. Elizabethan period. Jacobean period. Sixteenth cent. Seventeenth cent. Historical studies. ■Refutes previously published note by R.M. Frye indicating that a portrait of King Richard III owned by Edward Alleyn portrayed Burbage in the role.

1200 Hallinan, Tim; Andrew, John F. "Ian McKellen on Acting Shakespeare." *SQ*. 1982 Summer; 33(2): 135-141. Illus. [From two different interviews.]
England. Twentieth cent. Histories-sources. ■Comments on history of *Acting Shakespeare* program and on relationship between academics and professionals.

1201 Rosenberg, Marvin. "Macbeth and Lady Macbeth in the Eighteenth and Nineteenth Centuries." 73-86 in Brown, John Russell, ed. *Focus on* Macbeth. Boston, MA: Routledge and Kegan Paul; 1982. viii, 258 pp. Notes.
Great Britain. USA. 1745-1890. Historical studies. ■Various actors and actresses in the roles.

Plays/playwrights

1202 Park, Roy. "Lamb, Shakespeare, and the Stage." *SQ*. 1982 Summer; 33(2): 164-177. Notes.
England. 1790-1820. Studies of criticism/critics. ■Study of Charles Lamb's essay 'On the Tragedies of Shakespeare'. Related to Drama: Tragedy.

1203 Blinn, Hansjürgen, ed. "Shakespeare-Rezeption: Die Diskussion um Shakespeare in Deutschland." (The Reception of Shakespeare: Shakespeare in Germany.) Pref. Notes. Index. Biblio. [Band 1, Ausgewählte Texte von 1741 bis 1788.]
Germany. 1741-1788. Studies of criticism/critics. ■Volume I of selected texts related to reception of Shakespeare by German critics.

Plays/playwrights: Adaptations

1204 Pedicord, Harry William. "Shakespeare, Tate and Garrick: New Light on Alterations of *King Lear*." *TN*. 1982; 36(1): 14-21.
England. 1741-1774. Textual studies. ■Comparison of Garrick's 1741 *King Lear*, his alterations for the 1756 production and the 1773-1774 Bell edition.

1205 Wells, Stanley. "Television Shakespeare." *SQ*. 1982 Autumn; 33(3): 261-277. Notes.

INDIVIDUALS — cont'd

England. Twentieth cent. Histories-sources. ■History and comment on the BBC series, enumerating problems in producing Shakespeare on TV. Related to Media: Video forms.

1206 Dean, Paul. "Shakespeare's *Henry VI* Trilogy and Elizabethan 'Romance' Histories: The Origins of a Genre." *SQ.* 1982 Spring; 33(1): 34-48. Notes.
Great Britain. 1580-1600. Histories-reconstruction. ■Possible sources for style and treatment of historical material. Related to Drama.

Plays/playwrights: Characters/roles

1207 Davis, Derek D. "Hurt Minds." 210-228 in Brown, John Russell, ed. *Focus on* Macbeth. Boston: Routledge and Kegan Paul; 1982. viii, 258 pp. Notes.
England. 1605-1606. Critical studies. ■'Systems theory' analysis of psychopathology as determinant of action and character.

1208 Everett, Barbara. "'Spanish' Othello: The Making of Shakespeare's Moor." *ShS.* 1982; 35: 101-112. Notes.
England. 1604-1605. Critical studies. ■Othello seen as Spanish Moor in context of Shakespeare's view of Spanish culture and politics.

1209 Foakes, R.A. "Images of Death: Ambition in *Macbeth.*" 7-29 in Brown, John Russell, ed. *Focus on* Macbeth. Boston: Routledge and Kegan Paul; 1982. viii, 258 pp. Notes.
England. 1605-1606. Critical studies. ■Effect of ambition in *Macbeth.*

1210 Gaudet, Paul. "The 'Parasitical' Counselors in Shakespeare's *Richard II:* A Problem in Dramatic Interpretation." *SQ.* 1982 Summer; 33(2): 142-154. Notes.
England. 1596-1597. Critical studies. ■Study shows the characters of Bushy, Bagot and Green to be loyal subjects defamed by Northumberland and Bolingbroke.

1211 Kimbrough, Robert. "Androgyny Seen through Shakespeare's Disguise." *SQ.* 1982 Spring; 33(1): 17-33. Notes.
England. Sixteenth cent. Seventeenth cent. Critical studies. ■Androgyny defined not as sexual blending, but as total 'humanhood', illustrated through Julia, Portia, Rosalind, Imogen and Viola.

1212 Stansbury, Joan. "Characterization of the Four Young Lovers in *A Midsummer Night's Dream.*" *ShS.* 1982; 35: 57-63. Notes.
England. 1592-1596. Critical studies. ■Analysis of Shakespeare's characterization of Hermia, Helena, Lysander and Demetrius by means of distinctive language.

Plays/playwrights: Editions

1213 Connell, Charles. *They Gave Us Shakespeare: John Heminge and Henry Condell.* Distributed by Routledge and Kegan Paul. Stocksfield, Northumberland, England: Oriel Press; 1982. xiii, 110 pp. Notes. Biblio. Illus.: Photo. B&W. 15.
England. 1600-1623. Historical studies. ■Circumstances surrounding publication of Shakespeare's plays in 1623.

1214 Kerrigan, John. "*Love's Labour's Lost* and Shakespearean Revision." *SQ.* 1982 Autumn; 33(3): 337-339. Notes.
England. 1594-1595. Textual studies. ■*Love's Labour's Lost* in Quarto was printed from foul papers and not revised by Shakespeare.

Plays/playwrights: Plot/subject/theme

1215 Appel, Libby; Flachmann, Michael. *Shakespeare's Lovers.* Carbondale: Southern Illinois UP; 1982. 156 pp. Pref.
England. Elizabethan period. Sixteenth cent. Seventeenth cent. Textual studies. ■Discusses scenes featuring lovers from several plays.

1216 Boose, Lynda E. "The Father and the Bride in Shakespeare." *PMLA.* 1982 May; 97(3): 325-347. Notes. Biblio.

England. 1564-1616. Critical studies. ■Fathers' possessive love for daughters, despite economic burden, resolved in marriage ceremony. Related to Drama.

1217 Brown, John Russell, ed. *Focus on* Macbeth. Boston: Routledge and Kegan Paul; 1982. viii, 258 pp. Pref. Index.
England. Jacobean period. Seventeenth cent. Critical studies. ■Essays on literary and theatrical facets of the tragedy. Related to Drama: Tragedy.

1218 Erickson, Peter B. "Patriarchal Structures in *The Winter's Tale.*" *PMLA.* 1982 Oct.; 97(5): 819-829. Notes. Biblio.
England. 1610-1611. Critical studies. ■Women's roles and power generate multiple responses. Related to Drama: Comedy.

1219 Erlich, Bruce. "Queenly Shadows: On Meditation in Two Comedies." *ShS.* 1982; 35: 65-77. Notes.
England. 1595-1597. Critical studies. ■Social paradoxes examined in *The Merchant of Venice* and *A Midsummer Night's Dream.* Infl. by Claude Lévi-Strauss.

1220 Kuckhoff, Armin-Gerd. "Was sagen die Volksgestalten in den Werken Shakespeares zum Krieg?" (What Do the Common People in Shakespeare's Plays Say About War?) *SJW.* 1982; 118: 30-36. Notes. [Contribution to Weimar Shakespeare Colloquium, 1981.]
England. Elizabethan period. Sixteenth cent. Seventeenth cent. Textual studies. ■Lower-class characters' ideas on war, peace and violence. Quotations from *Romeo and Juliet, Cymbeline, Troilus and Cressida, Coriolanus,* with support argument from Goethe's *Faust.*

1221 Landry, D.E. "Dreams as History: The Strange Unity of *Cymbeline.*" *SQ.* 1982 Spring; 33(1): 68-79. Notes.
England. 1609-1610. Critical studies. ■Dreams reveal characters' pasts and motives, and stress logic of chronicle-history in the play. Related to Drama.

1222 Loughrey, Bryan; Taylor, Neil. "Ferdinand and Miranda at Chess." *ShS.* 1982; 35: 113-118. Notes.
England. 1611-1612. Critical studies. ■Chess game in *The Tempest* reflects play's political action and concern with idea of government.

1223 Metscher, Thomas. "Krieg und Frieden bei Shakespeare im Weltliterarischen Kontext." (Shakespeare's Views of War and Peace in the Context of World Literature.) *SJW.* 1982; 118: 37-66. Notes. [Abstract from Weimar Shakespeare Colloquium, 1981.]
England. Elizabethan period. Multi-period. Critical studies. ■Shakespeare's treatment of humanity and power, based on references to Greek antiquity, Virgil, Dante and Erasmus of Rotterdam. Quotations from *Hamlet, Macbeth, Richard III, Henry V, As You Like It* and *Twelfth Night.*

1224 Morris, Brian. "The Kingdom, the Power and the Glory in *Macbeth.*" 30-53 in Brown, John Russell, ed. *Focus on* Macbeth. Boston: Routledge and Kegan Paul; 1982. viii, 258 pp. Notes.
England. 1605-1606. Critical studies. ■Investigation of dramatic themes.

1225 Schleiner, Louise. "Providential Improvisation in *Measure for Measure.*" *PMLA.* 1982 Mar.; 97(2): 227-236. Illus.
England. 1601-1602. Critical studies. ■Biblical and theological allusions evoke comic parallel between God and Duke. Related to Drama: Comedy.

1226 Schlösser, Anselm. "Der Friedengedanke bei Shakespeare." (Shakespeare's Thoughts on Peace.) *SJW.* 1982; 118: 9-29. Notes. [Revision of a speech given at Weimar Shakespeare Colloquium, 1981.]
England. 1590-1613. Critical studies. ■Marxist interpretation of Shakespeare's ideas on war and peace, with quotations from *Henry VIII, King John, The Tempest, Henry V, Henry IV, Parts 1 and 2, Julius Caesar, Henry VI, Parts 1, 2 and 3, Timon of Athens* and *King Lear.*

1227 Seehose, Georg. "*Macbeth* und der gesellschaftliche Fortschritt." (*Macbeth* and Social Progress.) *SJW.* 1982; 118: 75-82. Notes. [Contribution to Weimar Shakespeare Colloquium, 1981.]

INDIVIDUALS — cont'd

England. 1605-1606. Critical studies. ■Treatment of rights of succession. Related to Drama.

1228 Soellner, Rolf. "Coriolan zwischen Krieg und Frieden." (Coriolanus Between War and Peace.) *SJW.* 1982; 118: 67-74. Notes.
England. 1607-1608. Critical studies. ■Comparison of scenes that develop Coriolanus' attitudes towards war. Related to Drama.

1229 Stallybrass, Peter. "*Macbeth* and Witchcraft." 189-209 in Brown, John Russell, ed. *Focus on* Macbeth. Boston: Routledge and Kegan Paul; 1982. viii, 258 pp. Notes.
England. 1605-1606. Critical studies. ■Effects of witches and witchcraft on action and characterization.

1230 Waddington, Raymond B. "Moralizing the Spectacle: Dramatic Emblems in *As You Like It.*" *SQ.* 1982 Summer; 33(2): 155-163. Notes. Illus.
England. 1599-1600. Historical studies. ■Elizabethan audiences' understanding of emblematic meanings in *As You Like It.* Related to Drama.

1231 Wolf, William D. "'New Heaven, New Earth': The Escape from Mutability in *Antony and Cleopatra.*" *SQ.* 1982 Autumn; 33 (3): 328-335. Notes.
England. 1606-1607. Critical studies. ■Stability of their love allows Antony and Cleopatra to escape change of their worlds.

1232 Yearling, Elizabeth M. "Language, Theme, and Character in *Twelfth Night.*" *ShS.* 1982; 35: 79-86. Notes.
England. 1600-1602. Critical studies. ■Truth and illusion examined through vocabulary and syntax.

1233 Zanderová, Adĕla. "Recht und Gnade in *The Merchant of Venice.*" (Justice and Mercy in *The Merchant of Venice.*) *SJW.* 1982; 118: 100-106. Notes. [Abstract from a dissertation, 'Shakespeares Drama *The Merchant of Venice* im Kontext seiner Zeit und als ein Beistandteil des Kulturellen Erbes hier und heute,' Ernst-Moritz-Arndt Universität, Greifswald, 1980.]
Great Britain. 1600-1604. Critical studies. ■Historical background and present cultural heritage of play. Related to Drama.

Plays/playwrights: Structure/language

1234 Andrews, Michael Cameron. "His Mother's Closet: A Note on Hamlet." *MP.* 1982 Nov.; 80(2): 164-166. Notes.
England. 1600-1601. Textual studies. ■Alternative reading of Gertrude's closet.

1235 Bate, Jonathan A. "An Herb by Any Other Name: *Romeo and Juliet*, IV.iv.5-6." *SQ.* 1982 Autumn; 33(3): 336. Notes.
England. 1594-1595. Textual studies. ■Angelica as a proper name. 'Looke to the bakte meates, good *Angelica,*/Spare not for cost'.

1236 Binns, J.W. "Shakespeare's Latin Citations: The Editorial Problem." *ShS.* 1982; 35: 119-128. Notes.
England. Elizabethan period. Sixteenth cent. Seventeenth cent. Linguistic studies. ■Editors' mistrust of Shakespeare's Latin citations.

1237 Blythe, David-Everett. "Ox-eyed Phebe." *SQ.* 1982 Spring; 33(1): 101-102. Notes.
England. Elizabethan period. Linguistic studies. ■Reference to Phebe's 'bugle eye-balls' in *As You Like It* has source in Greek and Latin words meaning bovine.

1238 Bradbrook, Muriel C. "Tu-whit, To-who, a Merry Note." *SQ.* 1982 Spring; 33(1): 94-95. Notes. Illus.
England. 1594-1595. Linguistic studies. ■Closing lines of *Love's Labour's Lost*, though ostensibly referring to owl and cuckoo, are shown to be a pun drawn from hunting terminology encouraging continuation of lover's wooing.

1239 Fabry, Frank. "Shakespeare's Witty Musician: *Romeo and Juliet*, IV.v.114-117." *SQ.* 1982 Summer; 33(2): 182-183. Notes.
England. 1595-1596. Linguistic studies. ■Series of puns with sexual innuendos in musician's exchange with Peter.

1240 Goldman, Michael. "Language and Action in *Macbeth.*" 140-152 in Brown, John Russell, ed. *Focus on* Macbeth. Boston: Routledge and Kegan Paul; 1982. viii, 258 pp. Notes.
England. Jacobean period. Critical studies. ■Dramatic action and language from actor's point of view. Related to Drama: Tragedy.

1241 Hawkins, Michael. "History, Politics and *Macbeth.*" 155-188 in Brown, John Russell, ed. *Focus on* Macbeth. Boston: Routledge and Kegan Paul; 1982. viii, 258 pp. Notes.
England. Jacobean period. Seventeenth cent. Critical studies. ■Dramatic structure as reflection of contemporary perceptions of history and politics. Related to Drama: Tragedy.

1242 Hawkins, Sherman H. "*Henry IV:* The Structural Problem Revisited." *SQ.* 1982 Autumn; 33(3): 278-301. Notes.
England. 1597-1598. Textual studies. ■Reconsideration of Henry Jenkins' assertion that the work is composed of two individual plays intended as a single unit.

1243 Holmer, Joan Ozark. "'Runnawayes Eyes': A Fugitive Meaning." *SQ.* 1982 Spring; 33(1): 97-99. Notes.
England. 1594-1595. Linguistic studies. ■Term 'runnawayes eyes' in Juliet's soliloquy in III.ii may be taken to mean 'fugitive eyes' or 'vagabond's eyes'.

1244 Horn, R.L. "*Hamlet*, III.ii.376: A Defense of Q2's 'The Bitter Day'." *SQ.* 1982 Summer; 33(2): 179-181. Notes.
England. 1600-1601. Linguistic studies. ■Medieval use of 'bitter' as descriptive of doomsday supports correctness of Q2 reading.

1245 Levin, Richard. "The Indian/Iudean Crux in *Othello.*" *SQ.* 1982 Spring; 33(1): 60-67. Notes.
England. 1604-1605. Textual studies. ■Evidence supports 'base Indian' reading in Othello's last speech in the First Quarto.

1246 Marder, Louis. "Shakespeare's Art of Manipulating the Audience." *ShN.* 1982 Feb.; 32(1): 3. [International Shakespeare Association Conference (1981).]
England. Elizabethan period. Critical studies. ■Summary of a seminar dealing with Shakespeare's playwriting techniques.

1247 Marsh, Derrick R.C. "A Note on Hamlet's 'I Am Most Dreadfully Attended' (II.ii.266)." *SQ.* 1982 Summer; 33(2): 181-182. Notes.
England. 1600-1601. Linguistic studies. ■'Dreadfully attended' interpreted as oblique reference to the Ghost, whom Hamlet feels is always attendant upon him until he kills Claudius.

1248 Parker, Douglas H. "'Lysander' and 'Helen' in *A Midsummer Night's Dream.*" *SQ.* 1982 Spring; 33(1): 99-101. Notes.
England. 1595-1596. Critical studies. ■Pyramus and Thisbe's 'Lysander' and 'Helen' reference in the play-within-a-play scene as Shakespeare's ironic reference to inconstant Lysander and the faithful Helena of the play's own dramatis personae.

1249 Taylor, Gary. "Humfrey Hower." *SQ.* 1982 Spring; 33(1): 95-97. Notes.
England. 1592-1593. Linguistic studies. ■Richard's joking reference to Humfrey Hower can be shown by orthographic research to be variant or misprint referring to a table or house servant whose surname comes from his calling, (h)ewer.

1250 Walker, Alice. "Six Notes on *All's Well That Ends Well.*" *SQ.* 1982 Autumn; 33(3): 339-342. Notes.
England. 1602-1603. Linguistic studies. ■Six obscure words or phrases that have caused editorial confusion in Acts I, II, IV and V.

1251 Warren, Michael. "*King Lear*, V.iii.265: Albany's 'Fall and Cease'." *SQ.* 1982 Summer; 33(2): 178-179. Notes.
England. 1605-1606. Linguistic studies. ■Albany's line is not a troubled invocation to heaven, but a simple instruction to Kent and Edgar to kneel and be silent before their king.

1252 Wilcher, Robert. "The Art of Comic Duologue in Three Plays by Shakespeare." *ShS.* 1982; 35: 87-100. Notes.

INDIVIDUALS — cont'd

England. 1589-1603. Critical studies. ■Comic 'duologue' from early comedies to *Hamlet*.

1253 Williams, George Walton. "The Year's Contribution to Shakespearean Study: Textual Studies." *ShS*. 1982; 35: 179-191. Notes.
England. USA. 1980-1981. Textual studies. ■Review of Shakespearean textual studies with special attention to *King Lear* and *Henry IV, Part 2*.

Plays/playwrights: Translations

1254 Hamburger, Maik. "Volkssprache, Theatersprache, Übersetzung." (Popular Speech, Theatre Speech, Translation.) *TZ*. 1982 Jan.; 37: 9-10.
East Germany. Twentieth cent. Textual studies. ■Problems of translating Shakespeare for modern audiences.

Relation to other fields: Other arts

1255 Marder, Louis. "New Major Shakespeare in Music Project." *ShN*. 1982 Fall; 32(4): 18.
Canada. Twentieth cent. Histories-sources. ■Announcement of *The Shakespeare Music Catalogue*, including statement of scope and funding sources.

Relation to other fields: Sociology

1256 Berger, Harry Jr. "Against the Sink-a-Pace: Sexual and Family Politics in *Much Ado About Nothing*." *SQ*. 1982 Autumn; 33(3): 301-313. Notes.
England. 1598-1599. Critical studies. ■Explication of Beatrice's speech and attitude, showing that women and particularly marriage were exploited.

1257 Coursen, H.R. *The Leasing Out of England: Shakespeare's Second Henriad*. Washington DC: UP of America; 1982. vii, 222 pp. Pref. Notes. Index. Biblio. Illus.: Photo. B&W. 16.
England. 1300-1499. Historical studies. ■Analysis of historical background.

Staging

1258 Palmer, D.J. "A New Gorgon: Visual Effects in *Macbeth*." 54-69 in Brown, John Russell, ed. *Focus on* Macbeth. Boston: Routledge and Kegan Paul; 1982. viii, 258 pp. Notes.
1605-1606. Historical studies. ■Survey and analysis of visual effects in the play.

1259 Ripley, John. "Shakespeare on the Montreal Stage, 1805-1826." *THC*. 1982 Spring; 3(1): 3-20. Notes.
Canada. 1805-1826. Historical studies. ■Analysis of productions with calendar of performances.

1260 Smith, Mary Elizabeth. "Shakespeare in Atlantic Canada During the Nineteenth Century." *THC*. 1982 Fall; 3(2): 126-136. Notes.
Canada. Nineteenth cent. Historical studies. ■Actors and companies who presented adaptations of Shakespearean plays and audience reaction via newspaper reviews.

1261 Mennerich, Karl. "Shakespeares Stücke in Dessau." (Shakespeare's Plays in Dessau.) *SJH*. 1982; 118: 161-163. Notes. [Contribution to Weimar Shakespeare Colloquium, 1981.]
East Germany. 1794-1982. Historical studies. ■Regional history of Shakespeare productions.

1262 Bartholomeusz, Dennis. The Winter's Tale *in Performance in England and America, 1611-1976*. New York: Cambridge UP; 1982. xv, 279 pp. Pref. Notes. Index. Biblio. Illus.: Photo. B&W. 55.
England. USA. 1611-1976. Histories-specific. ■Survey of selected productions.

1263 Berry, Ralph. "Shakespeare in England." *CTR*. 1982 Winter; 33: 105-108.
England. 1981. Histories-sources. ■Special report on World Shakespeare Congress and some recent productions.

1264 Evans, Gareth L. "*Macbeth*: 1940-80 at Stratford-upon-Avon." 87-110 in Brown, John Russell, ed. *Focus on* Macbeth. Boston: Routledge and Kegan Paul; 1982. viii, 258 pp. Notes.
England. 1940-1980. Historical studies. ■Study of eight productions.

Staging: Directing/directors

1265 Williams, Simon. "Shakespeare at the Burgtheater: From Heinrich Auschütz to Josef Kainz." *ShS*. 1982; 35: 21-29. Notes.
Austria. 1812-1899. Historical studies. ■Discussion of Burgtheater directors Joseph Schreyvogel and Heinrich Laube, and actors Adolf von Sonnenthal, Heinrich Auschütz, Carl Ludwig Constenoble, Anton Friedrich Mitterwurzer and Joseph Kainz.

1266 Kuckhoff, Armin-Gerd. "Shakespeare auf den Bühnen der DDR im Jahre 1980." (Shakespeare on the Stages of the German Democratic Republic in 1980.) *SJH*. 1982; 118: 142-167. Notes.
East Germany. 1980. Critical studies. ■Romantic tradition compared with contemporary approaches to Shakespeare production.

1267 Brown, John Russell. "Directing *Macbeth*: An Interview with Peter Hall." 225-248 in Brown, John Russell, ed. *Focus on* Macbeth. Boston: Routledge and Kegan Paul; 1982. viii, 258 pp.
England. 1981. Histories-sources. ■Directorial conception, methodology and techniques.

1268 Gussow, Mel; O'Haire, Patricia; Tallmer, Jerry; Beaufort, John; Kissel, Howard; Schickel, Richard. "*A Midsummer Night's Dream*." *NYTCR*. 1982 Sep. 13; 43(11): 216-219. [Off-Broadway Supplement III.]
USA. 1982. Reviews of performances. ■Six critics review James Lapine's production, presented by Joseph Papp at Delacorte Theatre.

Wagner

1269 Nietzsche, Friedrich; Bartolotto, Mario, ed. *Scritti su Wagner — Richard Wagner a Bayreuth — Il caso Wagner — Nietzsche contro Wagner*. (Writings on Wagner: Wagner in Bayreuth — The Wagner Case — Nietzsche Against Wagner.) With an essay by Mario Bartolotto. Milan: Adelphi; 1982. 265 pp. (Piccola Biblioteca Adelphi 80.) Notes.
Germany. Nineteenth cent. Critical studies. ■Nietzsche's reflections on Richard Wagner's art, with essay by Mario Bartolotto that reconstructs Nietzsche-Wagner relationship. Related to Music-Drama: Opera.

Scores/composers

1270 Kröplin, Eckart. "Richard Wagner und das Theater: Thesen." (Richard Wagner and Theatre: Theses.) *TZ*. 1982; 37(10): 49.
Germany. 1848. Studies of theories/theorists. ■Social revolution in life and works. Related to Music-Drama.

1271 Wagner, Richard. *La mia vita*. (My Life.) Turin: E.D.T. Musica; 1982. xxx, 579 pp. (Biblioteca di cultura musicale — Documenti.)
Germany. 1813-1864. Biographies.

Scores/composers: Adaptations

1272 Friedl, Peter. "Richard Wagners Erlösung." (The Redemption of Richard Wagner.) *TH*. 1982 July; 7: 3-7. Illus.
France. 1982. Histories-sources. ■Hans-Jürgen Syberberg's film-opera *Parsifal*. Related to Media: Film.

INDIVIDUALS — cont'd

Scores/composers: Structure/language

1273   Borchmeyer, Dieter. *Das Theater Richard Wagners: Idee — Dichtung — Wirkung.* (The Theatre of Richard Wagner: Idea — Poetry — Effects.) Stuttgart: Reclam; 1982. 430 pp. Notes. Index. Biblio. Illus.

Germany. Nineteenth cent. Studies of theories/theorists. ■Analysis of Wagner's musical and theatrical theory, his operas and their reception.

1274   Sutcliffe, James Helme. "*Parsifal:* Summation of a Musical Lifetime." *Opera.* 1982 July-Aug.; 33(7-8): 685-692, 805-812. Illus.

Germany. 1850-1899. Critical studies. ■Wagner's score and its relationship to earlier operatic works, especially emphasis on leitmotif.

Staging: Directing/directors

1275   Kunze, Stefan. "Richard Wagners imaginäre Szene: Gedanken zu Musik und Regie im Musikdrama." (Richard Wagner's Imaginary Scene: Thoughts on Music and Directing in Musical Drama.) 35-44 in Lüthi, Hans Jürg, ed. *Dramatisches Werk und Theaterwirklichkeit.* Bern: Haupt; 1982. 72 pp. (Berner Universitätsschriften 28.)

West Germany. Twentieth cent. Critical studies.

———

Other entries with significant content related to Individuals: 6, 7, 33, 70, 141, 642, 772, 797, 823, 855, 885, 933, 939.

SUBJECT INDEX

SUBJECT INDEX

White critics' reviews of *Ceremonies in Dark Old Men*. USA. 1960-1969.   534

Excerpt from autobiography of poet, actress and playwright Maya Angelou. USA. 1950-1960.   690

One-man show on life of Black philosopher W.E.B. Du Bois. USA: Washington, DC. 1982.   691

Tribute to Langston Hughes. USA. 1902-1982.   736

Charles Fuller's philosophy of theatre. USA. 1980.   740

Daughters of Martin Luther King and Malcolm X collaborate on a play about their fathers. USA. 1960-1969.   741

Problems of Black playwrights. USA. Twentieth cent.   743

Survey of Black women playwrights. USA. 1920-1979.   750

Notes on publishing anthology of contemporary Black American plays. USA: San Francisco, CA. 1982.   777

Ed Bullins on status of Blacks in theatre. USA: San Francisco, CA. 1982.   784

Influence of South African Black theatre on Athol Fugard. South Africa, Republic of. 1950-1982.   817

Form and themes of plays by Ntozake Shange. USA. 1970-1982.   839

Playwright and critic Samuel A. Hay comments on Black theatre. USA. 1920-1982.   846

Performance of *Black Nativity* for Pope John Paul II. Vatican. USA: New York, NY. 1982.   983

Personal/professional history of actress Patti LaBelle. USA. 1982.   991

Backgrounds of *Dreamgirls* cast. USA. 1982.   992

Production history of *One Mo' Time*. USA: New York, NY. 1982.   998

Effect of stardom on performer in Broadway musical *The Wiz*. USA. 1980-1982.   1005

Boal, Augusto

History of Latin American theatre. South America. 1500-1982.   104

Third Festival of Fools. Denmark: Copenhagen. 1982.   291

Boccaccio, Giovanni

O'Neill influenced by other writers. USA. 1910-1913.   1174

Body, Jacques

Interview with editor of Giraudoux's complete works. France. 1982.   775

Boesing, Martha

Martha Boesing, playwright-director, discusses her education as radical-feminist theatre worker. USA: Minneapolis, MN. 1950-1982.   564

Bogianchino, Massimo

Summary of preceding administrations of L'Opéra de Paris. France: Paris. 1973-1982.   1074

Bol'šoj

Comparison of acting in theatre and dance. USA: New York, NY. 1950-1982.   603

Bolshoi. SEE: Bol'šoj.

Bond, Edward

Socialist playwrights' use of grotesque comedy. England. 1970-1979.   793

Comparison of Edward Bond and Brecht. England. Twentieth cent.   796

Edward Bond's technique for creating social dialectic. England. Twentieth cent.   829

Bondy, Luc

Luc Bondy's production of *Macbeth*. West Germany: Cologne. 1982.   544

Boogie Woogie Landscapes

Form and themes of plays by Ntozake Shange. USA. 1970-1982.   839

Booth, Edwin

Italian actor Tommaso Salvini's reception on American tours. USA. 1873-1890.   692

Edwin Booth's performances. USA: Boston, MA. 1880-1899.   929

Boston Metropolitan Theatre Center

Transformation of film-vaudeville house into modern theatre road-house. USA: Boston, MA. 1982.   381

Boston Symphony Orchestra

Boston Symphony Orchestra's refusal to permit Vanessa Redgrave to perform. USA: Boston, MA. 1982.   516

Bouchaud, Jean

Director Jean Bouchaud discusses Vitrac's *Victor, or The Children in Power*. France. 1909-1982.   722

Boucher, François

Three costume designs by François Boucher. France: Paris. 1748-1753.   1032

Boucicault, Dion

Nine years in the life of Dion Boucicault, from contemporary sources. England: London. France: Paris. 1845-1853.   923

Motivation and law in Dion Boucicault's *The Octoroon*. USA. Nineteenth cent.   925

Bourgeois Gentilhomme, Le

Plays by Molière examined for ethical values. France. Seventeenth cent.   1168

Boutté, Jean-Luc

Textual and staging analysis of Lebeau's *Comptine*. France: Paris. 1982.   809

Boyle, William

Abbey Theatre peasant drama. Ireland. 1902-1908.   783

Boys' companies

Rebuttal of W.R. Cair's article 'La Compagnie des Enfants de St. Paul'. England: London. 1575-1600.   116

Interaction between boys' company and political forces. England: London. 1553-1608.   292

Nine critics review Roger Smith's production of *Steaming*. USA: New York, NY. 1982. 660

Nine critics review Arthur Penn's production of *Monday After the Miracle*. USA: New York, NY. 1982. 661

Eight critics review Robert Altman's production of *Come Back to the Five & Dime Jimmy Dean, Jimmy Dean*. USA: New York, NY. 1982. 662

Seven critics review Waris Hussein's production of *The Queen and the Rebels*. USA: New York, NY. 1982. 663

Five critics review Michel La Faille's production of *Herman van Veen: All of Him*. USA: New York, NY. 1982. 668

Eight critics review Michael Kahn's production of *Whodunnit*. USA: New York, NY. 1982. 669

Nine critics review Eva Le Gallienne's production of *Alice in Wonderland*. USA: New York, NY. 1982. 671

Ten critics review Howard Davies' production of *Good*. USA: New York, NY. 1982. 673

Nine critics review Martin Charnin's production of *A Little Family Business*. USA: New York, NY. 1982. 674

Origins of Nell Dunn's *Steaming*. England: London. USA: New York, NY. 1960-1980. 798

Playwright Ernest Thompson uses 'ordinary man' as subject. USA. 1982. 818

Set designs for *Dreamgirls*. USA: New York, NY. 1982. 985

The musical *Dreamgirls* and the Supremes. USA: New York, NY. 1982. 990

Personal/professional history of actress Patti LaBelle. USA. 1982. 991

Backgrounds of *Dreamgirls* cast. USA. 1982. 992

Eddie Cantor's involvement with the Shuberts and Ziegfeld. USA: New York, NY, Philadelphia, PA. 1919-1923. 995

Raquel Welch comments on *Woman of the Year*. USA: New York, NY. 1981-1982. 996

Seven critics review collective theatre presentation *Pump Boys and Dinettes*. USA: New York, NY. 1982. 997

Four critics review Vinette Carroll's production of *Your Arms Too Short to Box with God*. USA: New York, NY. 1982. 999

Use of magic in *Merlin*. USA: New York, NY. 1976-1982. 1001

Eleven critics review Trevor Nunn's production of *Cats*. USA: New York, NY. 1982. 1003

Seven critics review Harold Prince's production of *A Doll's Life*. USA: New York, NY. 1982. 1004

Effect of stardom on performer in Broadway musical *The Wiz*. USA. 1980-1982. 1005

Comment on Black musicals and review of *Dreamgirls*. USA. 1980. 1009

Analysis of season's musicals. USA: New York, NY. England: London. 1982. 1010

Evolution of *Nine*. USA: New York, NY. 1963-1982. 1012

Creation of *Cats*. England: London. USA: New York, NY. 1980-1982. 1013

Round-table discussion by the creators of *Dreamgirls*. USA: New York, NY. 1982. 1014

Visual effects in Broadway musicals. USA: New York, NY. 1982. 1015

Evolution of choreographer/director in Broadway musicals. USA: New York, NY. 1940-1982. 1016

Two productions of *Cats*. USA: New York, NY. England: London. 1982. 1017

Tommy Tune's Broadway career. USA: New York, NY. 1973-1982. 1020

Brodal, Svein Erik

Artistic direction of repertory theatre. Norway: Oslo. 1980-1981. 306

Brokenbrow. SEE: *Hinkemann*.

Brook, Peter

Interview with designer Gunilla Palmstierna-Weiss. Sweden: Stockholm, Gothenburg. Germany. Twentieth cent. 216

Brooke, Gustavus

Shakespeare productions. Australia: Melbourne. 1843-1861. 1197

Brown, Trisha

Interview with Trisha Brown and Robert Rauschenberg about their collaborations. USA: New York, NY. 1963-1982. 623

Brown, Wynyard

Five critics review Lindsay Anderson's production of *The Holly and the Ivy*. USA: New York, NY. 1982. 665

Brueys, Claude

Development of theatrical farces. France. 1530-1640. 1114

Brustein, Robert

Interview concerning American Repertory Theatre. USA: Cambridge, MA. 1982. 342

Büchner, Georg

Analysis of Georg Büchner's life and work, with stage history of plays. Germany. 1750-1982. 724

Marxist and Christian approaches to Georg Büchner. Germany. France. 1835. 938

Budapest State Opera. SEE: Magyar Operház.

Buenaventura, Enrique

History of Latin American theatre. South America. 1500-1982. 104

Bühnen der Stadt Köln

Luc Bondy's production of *Macbeth*. West Germany: Cologne. 1982. 544

Bühnentechnische Rundschau

Celebration of 75th anniversary of *Bühnentechnische Rundschau*. Germany. 1907-1982. 155

Bull, Ole

Productions of Ibsen in Bergen. Norway: Bergen. Nineteenth cent. 1159

Bullins, Ed

Annotated bibliographies of playwrights. USA. Twentieth cent. 20

Ed Bullins on status of Blacks in theatre. USA: San Francisco, CA. 1982.   784

Bulwer-Lytton, Edward

Review article on Royal Shakespeare Company's production of Edward Bulwer-Lytton's *Money.* England. 1981.   889

Bunraku

Kabuki and puppet theatre. Japan. Tokugawa period. Eighteenth cent.   632

Influence of *jōruri* on *kabuki.* Japan. Tokugawa period. Eighteenth cent.   635

Burbage, Richard

Debate over actor portrayed in portrait of Richard III. England. Elizabethan period. Jacobean period. Sixteenth cent. Seventeenth cent.   1199

Burgtheater

Critical reaction to *Burgtheater*, about Nazi period. Austria: Vienna. 1982.   702

Burgtheater

Comprehensive season yearbook. Austria: Vienna. 1980-1981.   67

Career of actor Heinrich Schweiger. Austria: Vienna. Twentieth cent.   675

Interview with manager of Burgtheater on producing classical plays. Austria: Vienna. 1982.   700

Critical reaction to *Burgtheater*, about Nazi period. Austria: Vienna. 1982.   702

Interview with director Peter Palitzsch on staging classics. West Germany. Austria: Vienna. 1970-1982.   882

Major interpreters of Shakespeare at Vienna's Burgtheater. Austria: Vienna. 1812-1899.   1265

Burstyn, Ellen

Ellen Burstyn's role as actress, president of Actors' Equity Association and co-artistic director of Actor's Studio. USA: New York, NY. 1960-1982.   438

Nine critics review James Roose's production of *84 Charing Cross Road.* USA: New York, NY. 1982.   670

Busoni, Ferruccio Benvenuto

Adaptations of drama for opera. Italy. Russia. Eighteenth cent. Twentieth cent.   1046

Bustos, Nidia

Development of popular political theatre groups. Nicaragua. 1970-1982.   500

Bygmester Solness (Master Builder, The)

Critical study of Ibsen's work. Norway. Nineteenth cent. Twentieth cent.   1157

Cabaret

Acting style of cabaret performer Karl Valentin. Germany: Munich. 1908-1948.   1109

Caesar, Adolph

Actor Adolph Caesar's professional history. USA: New York, NY. Twentieth cent.   440

Caillos, Roger

Discussion of concepts related to mimesis and representation. Europe. Multi-period.   492

Cair, W.R.

Rebuttal of W.R. Cair's article 'La Compagnie des Enfants de St. Paul'. England: London. 1575-1600.   116

Čajka (Seagull, The)

Andrei Serban's production of *The Seagull.* USA: New York, NY. Japan. 1980.   881

Revisionist account of first production of *The Seagull.* Russia: Leningrad (St. Petersburg). 1896.   1147

Similarities in plays of O'Neill and Chekhov. USA. Russia. Twentieth cent.   1181

Calderón de la Barca, Pedro

Analysis of tragedy using examples of significant Western drama. Europe. Multi-period.   926

Jorge Lavelli's staging of Calderón's *Life is a Dream* at the Comédie Française. France: Paris. 1982.   1146

Caldwell, Zoe

Actress/director Zoe Caldwell's views on preparing for roles. USA: New York, NY. 1982.   693

Caletti Bruni, Pietro Francesco. SEE: Cavalli.

Calvinism

Theatre as missionary tool during Counter-Reformation. France. Switzerland: Thonon. 1597-1598.   520

Cambellotti, Duilio

Designer Duilio Cambellotti's writings on theatre, activity as a critic and an autobiography. Italy. 1933-1954.   212

Campani, Niccolò (*Lo Strascino*)

Life and works of Niccolò Campani, called *Lo Strascino.* Italy. 1511-1520.   1092

Campaspe

Possible sources for style and treatment of historical material in Shakespeare's plays. Great Britain. 1580-1600.   1206

Canada Council

Achievements of the Canada Council. Canada. Twentieth cent.   259

Achievements in theatre of the Canada Council. Canada. 1957-1982.   354

Canadian Broadcasting Corporation

Discussion of current radio drama on CBC networks. Canada. 1976-1982.   944

Canadian National Arts Centre

Interview with Mario Bernardi on occasion of his resignation from Canadian National Arts Centre. Canada. 1982.   280

Canadian Opera Company Ensemble

Groups promote opera training and performance. Canada. Twentieth cent.   1044

Candide

Altering theatre interiors for specific productions. USA: New York, NY. 1924-1982.   223

Canetti, Elias

Themes of three plays by Elias Canetti. Europe. 1932-1982.   801

Cantor, Eddie

Eddie Cantor's involvement with the Shuberts and Ziegfeld. USA: New York, NY, Philadelphia, PA. 1919-1923.   995

Čapek, Josef

Interpretations of Karel Čapek's plays. Czechoslovakia. 1910-1928. 788

Čapek, Karel

Organization and management of city theatre. Finland: Lappeenranta. 1980-1981. 373

Interpretations of Karel Čapek's plays. Czechoslovakia. 1910-1928. 788

Caprices de Marianne, Les (Follies of Marianne, The)

The Follies of Marianne as expression of Musset's individuality. France. Nineteenth cent. Romantic period. 805

Director discusses production concepts of Musset's The Follies of Marianne. France: Paris. 1982. 872

Caribs

Efforts to restore native Dominican culture. Dominica. 1978-1982. 489

Carifuna Cultural Group

Efforts to restore native Dominican culture. Dominica. 1978-1982. 489

Carnival

The Gran Teatre del Liceo and its carnival dances. Spain: Barcelona. 1837-1839. 309

Carrier, Mabel

Women's correspondence to Sam Shubert. USA: New York, NY. 1902-1905. 466

Carroll, Vinette

Four critics review Vinette Carroll's production of Your Arms Too Short to Box with God. USA: New York, NY. 1982. 999

Carsen, Robert

Interview with director Robert Carsen. Canada. 1982. 1085

Carter, Nell

Careers of Black women performers. USA. Twentieth cent. 435

Case of Rebellious Susan, The

Playtexts by Henry Arthur Jones with introduction. England. 1882-1897. 75

Cash, Rosalind

Vignettes of Black stars. USA. Twentieth cent. 136

Casketmaker, The. SEE: Cofanaria, La.

Caste

Business and composition in T.W. Robertson's Caste. England: London. 1867-1883. 864

Castillo y Solórzano, Alonso de

Possible sources for character of Tartuffe. France. 1660-1669. 1164

Casting

Contract-controlled casting practices. France. 1650-1980. 454

Casting Black actors in traditionally white roles. USA. 1982. 531

Cats

Altering theatre interiors for specific productions. USA: New York, NY. 1924-1982. 223

English theatre imported to America. USA: New York, NY. England: London. 1981-1982. 543

Eleven critics review Trevor Nunn's production of Cats. USA: New York, NY. 1982. 1003

Analysis of season's musicals. USA: New York, NY. England: London. 1982. 1010

Creation of Cats. England: London. USA: New York, NY. 1980-1982. 1013

Two productions of Cats. USA: New York, NY. England: London. 1982. 1017

Cavalli (Caletti Bruni, Pietro Francesco)

Scottish Opera production of L'Egisto. Italy: Venice. 1637. 1080

Čechov, Anton Pavlovič

Sándor Hevesi as major director, theorist, translator and playwright. Hungary. 1901-1939. 555

Andrei Serban's production of The Seagull. USA: New York, NY. Japan. 1980. 881

Revisionist account of first production of The Seagull. Russia: Leningrad (St. Petersburg). 1896. 1147

Similarities in plays of O'Neill and Chekhov. USA. Russia. Twentieth cent. 1181

Censorship

Theatre under martial law. Poland. 1981-1982. 504

Evasion of censorship by Japanese dramatists. Japan. Eighteenth cent. Tokugawa period. 634

Discussion of McCarthy era plays. USA. 1947-1954. 847

Center in the Square

Transforming theatre from concert hall to intimate auditorium. Canada: Kitchener, ON. Twentieth cent. 376

Ceremonies In Dark Old Men

White critics' reviews of Ceremonies in Dark Old Men. USA. 1960-1969. 534

Cervantes Festival

Tenth Anniversary of Cervantes Festival. Mexico: Guanajuato. 1982. 649

Cervantes, Miguel de

Influence of commedia dell'arte on writing of Miguel de Cervantes. Spain. 1547-1587. 1118

Chaikin, Joseph

Adaptations of Tongues and Savage/Love from stage to video. USA. Twentieth cent. 961

Chaliapin, Feodor (Chaliapine, Feodor)

Feodor Chaliapin as an actor. Russia. 1873-1917. 1070

Chambers, Jane

Playwrights' acceptance speeches, National Gay Task Force Fund for Human Dignity Awards. USA: New York, NY. 1982. 819

Champion, Gower

Interview with Marge Champion. USA. 1950-1982. 629

Champion, Marge

Interview with Marge Champion. USA. 1950-1982. 629

Einstein on the Beach

Relationship of musical theatre to environmental theatre and performance art. USA. 1975.   1021

Electra. SEE: *Électre*.

Électre (Electra)

Mythological material versus personal myth. France. 1930-1945.   763

Eleusinian Mysteries

Sacred rites of Demeter recreated in workshop. Greece. 1980.   1134

Eliot, T.S.

English theatre imported to America. USA: New York, NY. England: London. 1981-1982.   543

Eleven critics review Trevor Nunn's production of *Cats*. USA: New York, NY. 1982.   1003

Creation of *Cats*. England: London. USA: New York, NY. 1980-1982.   1013

Elizabethan period

Rebuttal of W.R. Cair's article 'La Compagnie des Enfants de St. Paul'. England: London. 1575-1600.   116

Scenic metamorphoses of Elizabethan stage. England. 1590-1610.   208

Interaction between boys' company and political forces. England: London. 1553-1608.   292

Estimates of Globe Theatre's size. England: London. 1576-1647.   399

Evidence that Henry Laneman owned Curtain Theatre. England: London. 1582.   402

Conditions of acquittal in bond stories. England. Elizabethan period. Sixteenth cent.   797

Topical references in drama. England. 1580-1642.   799

Essays and lectures on Shakespeare and his times. England. 1558-1603.   1190

Reprint of 18th century critic's notes on Shakespeare. England. Elizabethan period. Eighteenth cent.   1193

Debate over actor portrayed in portrait of Richard III. England. Elizabethan period. Jacobean period. Sixteenth cent. Seventeenth cent.   1199

Possible sources for style and treatment of historical material in Shakespeare's plays. Great Britain. 1580-1600.   1206

Study of character relationships in Shakespeare's *Richard II*. England. 1596-1597.   1210

Characterization of lovers in *A Midsummer Night's Dream*. England. 1592-1596.   1212

Textual study of *Love's Labour's Lost*. England. 1594-1595.   1214

Scenes featuring lovers from Shakespearean plays. England: London. Elizabethan period. Sixteenth cent. Seventeenth cent.   1215

Fathers and daughters in Shakespeare. England. 1564-1616.   1216

Women's roles in *The Winter's Tale*. England. 1610-1611.   1218

Social paradoxes in two Shakespeare comedies. England: London. 1595-1597.   1219

Ideas of lower-class characters in Shakespeare on war, peace and violence. England. Elizabethan period. Sixteenth cent. Seventeenth cent.   1220

Shakespeare's treatment of humanity and power. England. Elizabethan period. Multi-period.   1223

Biblical and theological allusions for comic effect in *Measure for Measure*. England. 1601-1602.   1225

Shakespeare's ideas on war and peace. England. 1590-1613.   1226

Spectators' understanding of emblematic meanings in *As You Like It*. England. 1599-1600.   1230

Truth and illusion examined through vocabulary and syntax in *Twelfth Night*. England. 1600-1602.   1232

Cultural heritage of *The Merchant of Venice*. Great Britain. 1600-1604.   1233

Alternative reading of Gertrude's closet in *Hamlet*. England. 1600-1601.   1234

Interpretation of *Romeo and Juliet*, IV.iv.5-6. England. 1594-1595.   1235

Editors judge Shakespeare's use of Latin. England: London. Elizabethan period. Sixteenth cent. Seventeenth cent.   1236

Origin and meaning of phrase 'bugle eye-balls' in *As You Like It*. England: London. Elizabethan period.   1237

Puns in *Love's Labour's Lost*. England. 1594-1595.   1238

Interpretation of *Romeo and Juliet*, IV.v.114-117. England. 1595-1596.   1239

Reconsideration of structural problems in *Henry IV*. England. 1597-1598.   1242

Double meanings of phrase in Juliet's soliloquy, *Romeo and Juliet* III.ii. England. 1594-1595.   1243

Interpretation of *Hamlet*, III.ii.376. England. 1600-1601.   1244

Shakespeare's art of manipulating audience. England. Elizabethan period.   1246

Interpretation of *Hamlet*, II.ii.266. England. 1600-1601.   1247

Reference to Leander and Hero within Pyramus and Thisbe segment. England: London. 1595-1596.   1248

Pun on Hower in *Richard III*. England. 1592-1593.   1249

Linguistic study of *All's Well That Ends Well*. England. 1602-1603.   1250

Comic 'duologue' from Shakespeare's early comedies to *Hamlet*. England. 1589-1603.   1252

Women and marriage as commodities in *Much Ado About Nothing*. England. 1598-1599.   1256

Emperor Jones, The

Controversy over award to Black actor Charles Gilpin. USA: New York, NY. 1921.   356

Charles Gilpin in Eugene O'Neill's *The Emperor Jones*. USA. 1920-1925.   694

Tennyson's influence on O'Neill. USA. Twentieth cent.   823

Garrick, David

Redating Falstaff's role, and a Garrick promptbook. England: London. 1786-1792. 769

Comparison of Garrick's *King Lear* and the Bell edition. England: London. 1741-1774. 1204

Gasc, Yves

Interpretation of Jules Renard's *The Pleasure of Breaking* by director Yves Gasc. France: Paris. Twentieth cent. 866

Gassman, Vittorio

Vittorio Gassman on actor's role in theatre and cinema. 1922-1982. 426

Gathering, The

Storytelling as self-identification, and collective playwriting. USA: St. Peter, MN. 1981-1982. 535

Gatti, Armand

Armand Gatti's major projects. France: Paris. 1955-1981. 551

Gatti, Guido M.

Correspondence S. d'Amico/G.M. Gatti/J. Copeau on staging of *Representation of Santa Uliva*. Italy: Florence. 1932-1933. 541

Gauvreau, Claude

Avant-garde from Impressionism through Surrealism. Canada. 1901-1951. 778

Gay theatre

Alphabetical listing of gay and lesbian theatre companies. USA. Europe. Australia. 1982. 63

Reports of gay theatre activities. USA. 1981-1982. 134

Subscription series promotion. USA. Twentieth cent. 277

Survey of gay and lesbian presence in culture. USA. 1981-1983. 477

Playwrights' acceptance speeches, National Gay Task Force Fund for Human Dignity Awards. USA: New York, NY. 1982. 819

Interview with playwright and actor Harvey Fierstein. USA: New York, NY. 1977-1982. 821

Homosexuality in romantic comedy. USA. Twentieth cent. 898

Gay Theatre Alliance

Survey of gay and lesbian presence in culture. USA. 1981-1983. 477

Gay, John

Review of Vito Pandolfi's production of *The Beggar's Opera*. Italy: Rome. 1943. 980

Geburt der Tragödie, Die (Birth of Tragedy, The)

Aesthetic theories of tragedy. Germany. Twentieth cent. 1142

Gelber, Jack

Annotated bibliographies of playwrights. USA. Twentieth cent. 20

Gémier, Firmin

Account of spectacle at Cirque d'Hiver. France: Paris. 1920. 1105

Genet, Jean

Richard Schechner's production of Genet's *The Balcony*. USA: New York, NY. 1979-1980. 879

Gengangere (Ghosts)

Various productions examined for differences in style. USA: New York, NY, Minneapolis, MN. Austria: Salzburg. Germany: Berlin. Twentieth cent. 878

Productions of *Peer Gynt* and *Ghosts* and founding of Ibsen Theatre in America. USA. 1930-1982. 880

Character and textual study of Pastor Manders in Ibsen's *Ghosts*. Norway. 1882. 1155

Critical study of Ibsen's work. Norway. Nineteenth cent. Twentieth cent. 1157

Geniuses

Six critics review Gerald Gutierrez's production of *Geniuses*. USA: New York, NY. 1982. 672

George a Green

Possible sources for style and treatment of historical material in Shakespeare's plays. Great Britain. 1580-1600. 1206

George Dandin

Character of Molière's George Dandin as parody of contemporary tragedy. France: Paris. 1668. 1165

Plays by Molière examined for ethical values. France. Seventeenth cent. 1168

Georgian period

Henry Thornton's management of provincial theatres. England: Oxford, Reading, Newbury, Windsor. 1787-1817. 296

German Shakespeare Society. SEE: Deutsche Shakespeare Gesellschaft.

Gespräche mit dem Henker (Conversations with the Executioner)

Interview with playwright Dieter Kühn. West Germany. Twentieth cent. 759

Gesture

Semiotic analysis of gestural codes. Germany. Baroque period. Eighteenth cent. 120

Ghosts. SEE: Gengangere.

Gibson, William

Nine critics review Arthur Penn's production of *Monday After the Miracle*. USA: New York, NY. 1982. 661

Discussion of themes in two plays by William Gibson. USA. 1950-1982. 774

Gilgamesh

Production approaches to *Holiday Trilogy* and *Gilgamesh*. France: Paris. 1978. 550

Gill, Bob

Five critics review Joe Layton's production of *Rock 'n Roll! The First 5000 Years*. USA: New York, NY. 1982. 1000

Gilles de Rais

Structural analysis of *Gilles de Rais*. USA: New York, NY. 1980-1981. 919

Gilpin, Charles

Controversy over award to Black actor Charles Gilpin. USA: New York, NY. 1921. 356

Charles Gilpin in Eugene O'Neill's *The Emperor Jones*. USA. 1920-1925. 694

Intensivstation (Intensive Care, or An Endless Vegetable-like Existence)

Text with commentary of *Intensive Care, or An Endless Vegetable-like Existence*. West Germany. 1980.　　82

Intermedio

Evolution of form from *intermedio* to *melodramma*. Italy. 1500-1650.　　973

Intermezzo

Relation between Giraudoux's *Intermezzo* and author's native province. France. Twentieth cent.　　806

International Association of Opera Directors

Semi-annual meeting of opera directors. 1982.　　1043

International Federation for Theatre Research

Report on FIRT's 9th World Congress. East Germany: Leipzig. 1981.　　352

International Theatre School of Anthropology (ISTA)

Report on theatre festival, research and theory of Eugenio Barba. Italy. Poland. Denmark: Holstebro. 1970-1981.　　124

Internships

Technical internships for minorities in casino theatre. USA: Atlantic City, NJ. Twentieth cent.　　571

Invitation to the Dance

On the plight of the aging dancer. USA. Twentieth cent.　　588

Ionesco, Eugène

Tragicomic elements in the plays of Ionesco. France. Twentieth cent.　　1161

Essays on Ionesco plus three scenes excised from *Journeys to the Land of the Dead*. France. Twentieth cent.　　1162

Iphigénie

English translations of four plays by Racine. France. Seventeenth cent. French classicism.　　76

Irby, Dean

Roundtable discussion with directors. USA. 1982.　　560

Iron Age, The. SEE: Järntiden.

Irwin, Bill

Career of dancer/clown Bill Irwin. USA: San Francisco, CA. 1968-1982.　　1102

Isadora

Portrayals of Isadora Duncan. USA. 1970-1982.　　619

Isadorables

Reminiscences of Maria Theresa, protégée of Isadora Duncan. USA. 1894-1981.　　621

Isle is Full of Noises, The

Collaboration of Negro Ensemble Co. and Hartford Stage Co. on production of *The Isle is Full of Noises*. USA. 1982.　　857

Italian Straw Hat, An. SEE: Chapeau de Paille d'Italie, Un.

Iwering, Tommy

English repertory companies in Sweden. Sweden: Stockholm. 1974-1981.　　312

Jacker, Corinne

Playwrights working in film and television. USA. 1982.　　942

Jackson, Anne

Eight critics review Arthur Storch's production of *Twice Around the Park*. USA: New York, NY. 1982.　　658

Jacob's Pillow Dance Festival

History of Jacob's Pillow Dance Festival. USA: Becket, MA. 1931-1982.　　616

Jacobean period

Part of the scholarly edition of the Beaumont and Fletcher canon. England: London. 1600-1625.　　74

Interaction between boys' company and political forces. England: London. 1553-1608.　　292

Design and arrangements in the hall of Christ Church. England: Oxford. 1605.　　385

Historical context for John Webster's major plays. England. 1600-1620.　　711

Topical references in drama. England. 1580-1642.　　799

Debate over actor portrayed in portrait of Richard III. England. Elizabethan period. Jacobean period. Sixteenth cent. Seventeenth cent.　　1199

Psychopathology as determinant of action and character in *Macbeth*. England: London. 1605-1606.　　1207

Othello seen as Spanish Moor. England. 1604-1605.　　1208

Ambition in *Macbeth*. England. 1605-1606.　　1209

Involvement with publication of Shakespeare's plays. England: London. 1600-1623.　　1213

Fathers and daughters in Shakespeare. England. 1564-1616.　　1216

Essays on literary and theatrical facets of *Macbeth*. England. Jacobean period. Seventeenth cent.　　1217

Women's roles in *The Winter's Tale*. England. 1610-1611.　　1218

Effect of dream motif in *Cymbeline*. England. 1609-1610.　　1221

Politics and chess in *The Tempest*. England: London. 1611-1612.　　1222

Dramatic themes in *Macbeth*. England. 1605-1606.　　1224

Shakespeare's ideas on war and peace. England. 1590-1613.　　1226

Treatment of rights of succession in *Macbeth*. England. 1605-1606.　　1227

Attitudes towards war in Shakespeare's *Coriolanus*. England. 1607-1608.　　1228

Effects of witchcraft in *Macbeth*. England. 1605-1606.　　1229

Stability of love as escape from social mutability in *Antony and Cleopatra*. England. 1606-1607.　　1231

Language and action in *Macbeth*. England. Jacobean period.　　1240

Dramatic structure and politics in *Macbeth*. England. Jacobean period. Seventeenth cent.　　1241

Evidence supports 'base Indian' reading in Othello's last speech in the First Quarto. England. 1604-1605.　　1245

Interpretation of *King Lear*, V.iii.265. England. 1605-1606.　　1251

SUBJECT INDEX

Jotuni, Maria

Organization and management of city theatre. Finland: Lappeenranta. 1980-1981. 373

Journeys to the Land of the Dead. SEE: *Voyages chez les morts.*

Joyce Theatre

Interview with Eliot Feld. USA: New York, NY. 1960-1982. 607

Judaica

Cultural heritage of *The Merchant of Venice.* Great Britain. 1600-1604. 1233

Judson Dance Theatre

Review of off-off Broadway movement. USA: New York, NY. 1950-1970. 129

Juggling

How to be a successful clown, juggler, mime, magician or puppeteer. USA. Twentieth cent. 1106

Julius Caesar

Shakespeare's ideas on war and peace. England. 1590-1613. 1226

Junction Avenue Theatre Company

Theatre reflecting Black life. South Africa, Republic of: Johannesburg. 1970-1982. 815

Jurasas, Jonas

Roundtable discussion with directors. USA. 1982. 560

Just Us Theatre

Atlanta's Black theatre companies. USA: Atlanta, GA. 1930-1982. 313

Kabuki

Translation and adaptation of *The Forty-Seven Samurai.* Japan. Tokugawa period. Eighteenth cent. 80

Influence of student movement on underground political theatre. Japan. 1968-1981. 911

Kafka, Franz

Interview with designer Gunilla Palmstierna-Weiss. Sweden: Stockholm, Gothenburg. Germany. Twentieth cent. 216

Adaptation of novels to stage. Sweden: Stockholm. 1980-1981. 475

O'Neill's autobiographical work compared to that of other writers. USA. Twentieth cent. 1186

Kahn, Michael

Eight critics review Michael Kahn's production of *Whodunnit.* USA: New York, NY. 1982. 669

Kainz, Josef

Major interpreters of Shakespeare at Vienna's Burgtheater. Austria: Vienna. 1812-1899. 1265

Kaiser, Bob

Interview with Bob Kaiser on building offbeat scenery. USA: New York, NY. 1982. 240

Kalevala

Interview with director Kalle Holmberg. Finland: Helsinki, Turku. 1966-1982. 549

Director Kalle Holmberg's activities. Finland. 1982. 865

Kalman, Emmerich

Career of composer Emmerich Kalman. Austria: Vienna. 1883-1953. 1075

Kandy dance

Commercialized ceremonial dances for tourist audiences. Sri Lanka. Multi-period. Twentieth cent. 609

Kani, John

Theatre reflecting Black life. South Africa, Republic of: Johannesburg. 1970-1982. 815

Kantor, Leo

Trends in theatre and politics. Poland: Warsaw. 1956-1982. 503

Kantor, Tadeusz

History of New York Street Theatre Caravan. Europe. USA: New York, NY. 1969-1981. 297

Trends in theatre and politics. Poland: Warsaw. 1956-1982. 503

Karinthy, Frigyes

Examination of Frigyes Karinthy. Hungary. 1887-1938. 1110

Karlsson, Sture

Collaborative play based on local labor problems. Sweden. 1982. 733

Karlstadt, Liesl

Acting style of cabaret performer Karl Valentin. Germany: Munich. 1908-1948. 1109

Karlsviks Teater

Collaborative play based on local labor problems. Sweden. 1982. 733

Kaspar

Composition and influences of Horváth's plays. Austria. 1920-1932. 899

Katz, Stephen

Roundtable discussion with directors. USA. 1982. 560

Katzelmacher (Cock-Artist)

Playtext with commentary of R.W. Fassbinder's *Cock-Artist.* West Germany: Munich. 1968-1979. 81

Kavrakova-Lorenz, Konstanza

Interview with puppet player about concept and scenery. East Germany: East Berlin. 1982. 1125

Kean, Edmund

Analysis of Hazlitt's theatre criticism. Great Britain: London. 1812-1828. 772

Keaton, Buster

Buster Keaton's films and work methods. USA. 1895-1966. 953

Kékszakállu Hereeg, A

Analysis of Bartók's opera and ballets. Hungary. -1945. Twentieth cent. 1076

Kemble, John Phillip

John Philip Kemble's relationship with critics. England: London. 1800-1811. 680

Kemp, Lindsay

Account of Lindsay Kemp company. England. 1973-1982. 417

Meininger, Die

Saxe-Meiningen touring company and English productions of Shakespeare. England: London. Germany. 1874-1900.　　1195

Meistersinger von Nürnberg, Die

New scenery for *Die Meistersinger von Nürnberg*. West Germany: Bayreuth. 1945-1981.　　1038

Meistersinger, The. SEE: *Meistersinger von Nürnberg, Die.*

Mejerchol'd, Vsevolod Emil'evič

Stylization and alienation in Stravinsky's ballets and operas. USSR. 1900-1930.　　538

Rise of the director from Naturalism to Grotowski. Russia. Germany. England. France. Poland. 1890-1980.　　557

Nikolai Evreinov's theories, plays and productions. Russia. 1879-1953.　　558

Alternative methods of performer training. Europe. Asia. North America. 1982.　　578

Meyerhold's production of *Sister Beatrice*. Russia: Moscow. 1906.　　639

Meyerhold's production of *The Magnificent Cuckold*. USSR: Moscow. 1922.　　640

Collaborative play based on local labor problems. Sweden. 1982.　　733

Melodrama

Career of Fitz-James O'Brien, playwright, critic, essayist. USA: New York, NY. 1851-1862.　　749

Shift in public taste leads to decline of melodrama, rise of naturalism. USA. 1890-1910.　　785

Melodramma

Evolution of form from *intermedio* to *melodramma*. Italy. 1500-1650.　　973

Memoirs

Bibliographical listing of theatre people's memoirs and autobiographies. USA. England. Nineteenth cent.　　18

Herbert Blau's memoirs. USA. 1960-1980.　　470

Mentzel, Wolfgang

Actor's working conditions with free group and with municipal theatres. West Germany: West Berlin. Twentieth cent.　　458

Merchant of Venice, The

Conditions of acquittal in bond stories. England. Elizabethan period. Sixteenth cent.　　797

Social paradoxes in two Shakespeare comedies. England: London. 1595-1597.　　1219

Cultural heritage of *The Merchant of Venice*. Great Britain. 1600-1604.　　1233

Mercier, Jean

Avant-garde from Impressionism through Surrealism. Canada. 1901-1951.　　778

Mercure, Marthe

Statements by theatre companies on fiscal conditions and government funding policies. Canada: Quebec, PQ. 1970-1982.　　258

Theatrical aspects of production of *Medea*. Canada: Quebec, PQ. 1981.　　940

Merlin

Use of magic in *Merlin*. USA: New York, NY. 1976-1982.　　1001

Merope

Analysis of three tragedies. Italy. 1627-1713.　　932

Mërtvyje duši (Dead Souls)

Problems of adapting fiction to dramatic form. Europe. Twentieth cent.　　762

Metropolitan Opera

Struggle to simplify scenery at the Metropolitan Opera. USA: New York, NY. 1982.　　1037

Meyer, Jimmy

Description of work in costume shops. USA: New York, NY. 1982.　　173

Meyerhold, Vsevolod. SEE: Mejerchol'd, Vsevolod Emil'evič.

Mickiewicz, Adam

Trends in theatre and politics. Poland: Warsaw. 1956-1982.　　503

Midnight Rounders, The

Eddie Cantor's involvement with the Shuberts and Ziegfeld. USA: New York, NY, Philadelphia, PA. 1919-1923.　　995

Midsummer Night's Dream, A

Shakespeare productions in principal cities. East Germany. 1945-1980.　　1194

Characterization of lovers in *A Midsummer Night's Dream*. England. 1592-1596.　　1212

Social paradoxes in two Shakespeare comedies. England: London. 1595-1597.　　1219

Reference to Leander and Hero within Pyramus and Thisbe segment. England: London. 1595-1596.　　1248

Contemporary Shakespeare productions. East Germany. 1980.　　1266

Six critics review James Lapine's production of *A Midsummer Night's Dream*. USA: New York, NY. 1982.　　1268

Midwest Area Theatre Conference

Paper calling for study of theatre history in Midwest. USA. 1930-1982.　　95

Milk Train Doesn't Stop Here Anymore, The

Influence of Cocteau on Tennessee Williams' *The Milk Train Doesn't Stop Here Anymore*. USA. Twentieth cent.　　837

Miller, Arthur

Discussion of McCarthy era plays. USA. 1947-1954.　　847

Mills, Stephanie

Effect of stardom on performer in Broadway musical *The Wiz*. USA. 1980-1982.　　1005

Milne, A.A.

Descriptive bibliography of A.A. Milne. Great Britain. Twentieth cent.　　12

Milwaukee Repertory Theatre

Financial relationship between resident theatres and playwrights. USA. 1982.　　753

SUBJECT INDEX

Mime

Buster Keaton's films and work methods. USA. 1895-1966.   953

Exercises in mime. 1900-1982.   965

How to be a successful clown, juggler, mime, magician or puppeteer. USA. Twentieth cent.   1106

Minetti, Bernhard

Theatre critics describe highlights of 1981-82 season. West Germany. 1981-1982.   474

Minetti, Hans-Peter

Theatre training at Hochschule für Schauspielkunst. East Germany: East Berlin. 1981.   363

Interview with Hans-Peter Minetti on social value of theatre work. East Germany. Twentieth cent.   524

Minimalist art

Performance at 'Fifth Network' video conference. Canada: Toronto, ON. 1978.   972

Miracle Worker, The

Discussion of themes in two plays by William Gibson. USA. 1950-1982.   774

Miranda, Carmen

Carmen Miranda's early career. USA: New York, NY. 1939-1941.   448

Misanthrope, Le

Plays by Molière examined for ethical values. France. Seventeenth cent.   1168

Miss Julie. SEE: *Fröken Julie*.

Mission, or Memory of a Revolution. SEE: *Auftrag oder Erinnerung einer Revolution, Der*.

Mistero della Natività, Passione e Resurrezione de Nostro Signore (Mystery of Nativity, Passion and Resurrection of Our Lord)

Reconstruction of a nativity play. Italy: Padua, Rome. 1937.   542

Mitterwurzer, Anton Friedrich

Major interpreters of Shakespeare at Vienna's Burgtheater. Austria: Vienna. 1812-1899.   1265

Modern dance

Life and career of choreographer Kurt Jooss. West Germany. 1901-1982.   608

History of Jacob's Pillow Dance Festival. USA: Becket, MA. 1931-1982.   616

Re-creation and interpretation of Isadora Duncan's dances. USA: New York, NY. 1928-1981.   620

Reminiscences of Maria Theresa, protégée of Isadora Duncan. USA. 1894-1981.   621

Moeser, Patricia

Interview with scene designer Patricia Moeser. USA: Bogota, NJ. 1982.   238

Molière

Different origins of drama and theatre. Greece. France. Multi-period.   92

Structuralist approach to French neoclassical drama. France. French classicism. Seventeenth cent.   830

Interview with José-María Flotats, playing Don Juan with the Comédie Française. France. 1982.   890

Character of Molière's George Dandin as parody of contemporary tragedy. France: Paris. 1668.   1165

Staging and designing Molière's plays. France: Paris. 1658-1673.   1169

Möller, Helen

Large collection of Shubert letters. USA: New York, NY. 1920-1923.   38

Monday After the Miracle

Nine critics review Arthur Penn's production of *Monday After the Miracle*. USA: New York, NY. 1982.   661

Discussion of themes in two plays by William Gibson. USA. 1950-1982.   774

Money

Review article on Royal Shakespeare Company's production of Edward Bulwer-Lytton's *Money*. England. 1981.   889

Monk, Debra

Seven critics review collective theatre presentation *Pump Boys and Dinettes*. USA: New York, NY. 1982.   997

Monsieur Perrichon's Journey. SEE: *Voyage de Monsieur Perrichon, Le*.

Monster Has Stolen The Sun, A

Productions of the New Cycle Theatre. USA. Twentieth cent.   332

Montel, Michael

Phoenix Theatre from founding to closing. USA: New York, NY. 1953-1982.   325

Montherlant, Henri de

Character attitude and self-definition in dramas by Anouilh and Montherlant. France. 1940-1960.   771

Montigny, Louvigny de

Avant-garde from Impressionism through Surrealism. Canada. 1901-1951.   778

Montresor, Beni

Survey of Beni Montresor's lighting designs and lighting for film. USA. Europe. 1982.   188

Morality plays

Analysis of two morality plays. Italy: Florence. Sixteenth cent.   729

Literary influences on morality plays. England. 1300-1559.   779

Morgan, Cass

Seven critics review collective theatre presentation *Pump Boys and Dinettes*. USA: New York, NY. 1982.   997

Mori, Ritsuko

Mori Ritsuko, an early interpreter of Western plays. Japan. 1913-1930.   434

Morris dance

Description of Morris dancing. England. USA. Multi-period.   627

Morris, Clara

Italian actor Tommaso Salvini's reception on American tours. USA. 1873-1890.   692

Mortier, Gérard

Belgian National Opera opens season. Belgium: Brussels. 1981. 1040

Mortimer, Lillian

Shift in public taste leads to decline of melodrama, rise of naturalism. USA. 1890-1910. 785

Moscow Art Theatre. SEE: Chudožestvennyj teatr.

Mosher, Gregory

Seven critics review Gregory Mosher's production of *Edmond.* USA: New York, NY. 1982. 659

Mott, Robert

First professional Black theatre company. USA: Chicago, IL. 1905-1911. 337

Mouches, Les (Flies, The)

Mythological material versus personal myth. France. 1930-1945. 763

Mourning Becomes Electra

Finding the tragic heroine in *Mourning Becomes Electra.* USA. Twentieth cent. 1179

Movement

Stretching in actors' exercises. USA. 1982. 442

Mozart, Wolfgang Amadeus

Karl Friedrich Schinkel's designs for *The Magic Flute.* Germany: Berlin. 1815-1816. 210

Use of masks in Mozart's operas. Europe. 1750-1799. 1036

Mr. Peepers

Humorous account of writer Everett Greenbaum's acting experiences. USA. Twentieth cent. 959

Mrożek, Sławomir

Social problems in 1944-45 as seen in Sławomir Mrożek's *On Foot* shed light on developments in 1980-81. Poland: Warsaw. 1944-1981. 916

Mrs. Knipper's Journey Through Eastern Prussia. SEE: Voyage de Madame Knipper à Travers la Prusse-Orientale, Le.

Much Ado About Nothing

Women and marriage as commodities in *Much Ado About Nothing.* England. 1598-1599. 1256

Müller, Harald

Text of Harald Müller's *Flotsam.* West Germany. 1974. 85

Müller, Heiner

Text of *The Mission, or Memory of a Revolution.* East Germany. 1981. 78

Forms, styles and function of plays. East Germany. West Germany. 1960-1980. 710

Multi-media

Collective creation in theatre and video. France. 1944-1980. 478

Artist's Theatre and multi-media performance. Italy. Twentieth cent. 968

Postmodern dancer David Gordon on development of performance. USA: New York, NY. 1981-1982. 969

Multi-period

Performing arts bibliography. Multi-period. 3

Bibliography of German books on theatre and drama. Multi-period. 5

Annotated bibliography of *Cymbeline* criticism. 1609-1982. 6

Shakespeare bibliography for 1980. Multi-period. 7

Annual theatre bibliography. Multi-period. 8

Catalogue of Italian books and journals on theatre and dance. Italy. Multi-period. 13

Annotated bibliography of popular culture. USA. Multi-period. 21

Exhibition catalogue of historical theatres. Italy. 1600-1982. 27

Records of medieval productions. England: Newcastle upon Tyne. 500-1559. 30

Compendium of acting terms. France. 1650-1982. 32

Biographical dictionary of dance. Europe. North America. South America. 1550-1982. 43

Guinness Record Book for theatre. Multi-period. 50

Dictionary of Comédie Française's actors and actresses, Auge to Beaubour. France: Paris. 1680-1982. 55

Dictionary of Comédie Française's actors and actresses, Chaumette to Delvair. France: Paris. 1680-1982. 56

Survey of world theatre history. Multi-period. 87

Essays on various subjects from Canadian and American theatre history. Canada. USA. 1700-1980. 88

Different origins of drama and theatre. Greece. France. Multi-period. 92

Brief history of American theatre. USA. 1700-1969. 96

General history of American theatre. USA. 1665-1982. 97

History of Latin American theatre. South America. 1500-1982. 104

Physical and social evolution of people in relationship to art. Europe. USA. Multi-period. 106

Historical involvement of women in theatre from ancient ritual to present. Multi-period. 110

Three hitherto unreported allusions to medieval drama. Great Britain. 1180-1621. 122

Contributions of Black artists. USA. 1700-1982. 132

Audience composition and sense of text in Shakespeare. England. 1594-1610. 141

Historical overview of the Comédie Française audience. France. 1600-1950. 142

Descriptive history of headgear in Western civilization. Europe. Multi-period. 164

Historical survey of handwear, primarily in Western civilization. Europe. Multi-period. 165

Clothing worn by farmers and laborers. Europe. Multi-period. 166

Costumes at Fashion Institute of Technology. USA: New York, NY. Twentieth cent. Multi-period. 172

SUBJECT INDEX

Mumaw, Barton

Mummer's plays

Münchner Anti-Theater

Munich National Theatre. SEE: Nationaltheater München.

Museums

Musical revues

Musical theatre

Nistayalero

Nō

Non-profit theatres

Nora chatri

Nora Helmer

Norén, Lars

Norman, Marsha

Norrbottensteatern

Norske Teatret

Ntshona, Winston

Old Times

Pattern of imitative desire in Pinter's *Old Times*. England. 1930. 828

Olsen and Johnson

Carmen Miranda's early career. USA: New York, NY. 1939-1941. 448

Omaha Community Playhouse

Various theatres and personalities in relation to Henry Fonda's career. USA: Omaha, NE. 1925-1982. 441

Omotoso, Kole

Social revolution and dramatic techniques in work of young playwrights. Nigeria. Twentieth cent. 814

On Foot. SEE: *Pieszo*.

On the Aesthetic Education of Man. SEE: *Über die ästhetische Erziehung des Menschen, in einer Reihe von Briefen*.

On Whitman Avenue

Returning Black servicemen on stage. USA: New York, NY. 1945-1946. 820

One Day More

O'Neill's *The Iceman Cometh* compared to works by J.M. Synge and Joseph Conrad. USA. Ireland. Twentieth cent. 1172

One Mo' Time

Production history of *One Mo' Time*. USA: New York, NY. 1982. 998

Open Theatre

Europeans examine subsidies of American groups. France. Netherlands. Italy. USA. Twentieth cent. 260

Opera

Interview with director Kalle Holmberg. Finland: Helsinki, Turku. 1966-1982. 549

Biography of Riccardo Drigo. Italy. Russia: Leningrad (St. Petersburg). 1846-1930. 605

Analysis of Wagner's musical and theatrical theory, his operas and their reception. Germany. Nineteenth cent. 1273

Opéra de Paris

Reactions of Danish actors to performances at theatres. France: Paris. 1788. 430

Costumes exhibition from L'Opéra de Paris. France: Paris. 1930-1981. 1033

Summary of preceding administrations of L'Opéra de Paris. France: Paris. 1973-1982. 1074

Opera dello Straccione. SEE: *Beggar's Opera, The*.

Opera Hamilton

History of Opera Hamilton. Canada: Hamilton, ON. 1976-1982. 1042

Opera North

Genesis of score and libretto for *Prince Igor*. Russia. 1870-1879. 1082

Operetta

Career of composer Emmerich Kalman. Austria: Vienna. 1883-1953. 1075

Orchard, Robert

Interview concerning American Repertory Theatre. USA: Cambridge, MA. 1982. 342

Orell, John

Estimates of Globe Theatre's size. England: London. 1576-1647. 399

Orestes

Aspects of madness in drama. Europe. 500 B.C.-1610 A.D. 935

Orff, Carl

Nature and function of masks. Multi-period. 201

Origins

Social drama and dramatic ritual. Multi-period. 486

Ortensio

Testimonies of first performance of *Ortensio* at the Accademia degli Intronati. Italy: Siena. 1561. 655

Orton, Joe

Brief biography and critical study of Joe Orton. England. Twentieth cent. 792

Study of Joe Orton's farce *What the Butler Saw*. England. Twentieth cent. 893

Oskarson, Peter

Court case over repertory and management of Göteborg Stadsteater. Sweden: Gothenburg. 1981-1982. 370

Oslo Nye Teater

Publicly funded theatre under economic pressure. Norway: Oslo. Twentieth cent. 304

Osofisan, Femi

Social revolution and dramatic techniques in work of young playwrights. Nigeria. Twentieth cent. 814

Österreichisches Theatermuseum (Austrian Theatre Museum)

Notice on costume exhibition at Austrian Theatre Museum. Austria: Vienna. 1982. 163

Othello

Audience composition and sense of text in Shakespeare. England. 1594-1610. 141

Edwin Booth's performances. USA: Boston, MA. 1880-1899. 929

Othello seen as Spanish Moor. England. 1604-1605. 1208

Evidence supports 'base Indian' reading in Othello's last speech in the First Quarto. England. 1604-1605. 1245

Otrabanda Company

Otrabanda Company's history. USA. 1970-1982. 341

Otway, Thomas

Biography and critical assessment of Thomas Otway's plays. England. Seventeenth cent. Restoration period. 930

Out Cry

Audience responses to Tennessee Williams' *Out Cry*. USA: Madison, WI. Twentieth cent. 646

Design for Tennessee Williams' *Out Cry*. Twentieth cent. 648

Preparatory work on Tennessee Williams' *Out Cry*. USA: Madison, WI. Twentieth cent. 877

Porter, Bruce

Bruce Porter and Bruce Rayvid's scene shop and working habits. USA: New York, NY. 1982.   239

Porter, Stephen

Phoenix Theatre from founding to closing. USA: New York, NY. 1953-1982.   325

Postmodernism

Critical investigation of theatre. USA. 1950-1982.   494

Transition from emphasis on actors to emphasis on directors. Sweden. 1968-1982.   559

Interview with Trisha Brown and Robert Rauschenberg about their collaborations. USA: New York, NY. 1963-1982.   623

Postmodern dancer David Gordon on development of performance. USA: New York, NY. 1981-1982.   969

Powell, George

Refutation of Edmund Gosse's attribution of *Animadversions* to George Powell. England: London. 1698.   713

Pöysti, Lasse

Rising costs demand new policies for box-office income. Sweden. Twentieth cent.   261

Preisler, Joachim Daniel

Reactions of Danish actors to performances at theatres. France: Paris. 1788.   430

Premieres

Survey of theatre information. USA. England. 1900-1982.   65

Press agents

Training for press agents. USA: New York, NY. Twentieth cent.   483

Price, Georgie

Large collection of Shubert letters. USA: New York, NY. 1920-1923.   38

Primitive theatre

Nature and function of masks. Multi-period.   201

Prince Berchtold von Mähren. SEE: *Prinz Berchtold von Mähren.*

Prince de Hombourg, Le. SEE: *Prinz von Homburg, Der.*

Prince Igor

Genesis of score and libretto for *Prince Igor*. Russia. 1870-1879.   1082

Prince of Homburg, The. SEE: *Prinz von Homburg, Der.*

Prince of Wales Theatre

Business and composition in T.W. Robertson's *Caste*. England: London. 1867-1883.   864

Prince, Harold

Phoenix Theatre from founding to closing. USA: New York, NY. 1953-1982.   325

Economics of musical theatre. USA. 1980-1982.   986

Seven critics review Harold Prince's production of *A Doll's Life*. USA: New York, NY. 1982.   1004

Role of Harold Prince in musical theatre. USA. 1950-1982.   1023

Prinz Berchtold von Mähren (Prince Berchtold von Mähren)

Unpublished, unperformed manuscripts on story of Banus Bánk. Hungary. 1794.   931

Prinz von Homburg, Der (Prince of Homburg, The)

Jean Vilar and *The Prince of Homburg*. France: Avignon. 1951.   856

Pritchard, John

Belgian National Opera opens season. Belgium: Brussels. 1981.   1040

Production histories

List of international Strindberg productions. 1981.   51

List of German productions of Strindberg plays. Germany. 1981.   57

Production of *The Black Crook*. USA: New York, NY. 1866.   135

Performance of *Sree Muchilot Bhagavathi* by Natana Kala Kshetram. India. 1981.   300

Luc Bondy's production of *Macbeth*. West Germany: Cologne. 1982.   544

Arthur Hopkin's production of Sophie Treadwell's *Machinal*. USA: New York, NY. 1928.   562

Production of Nijinsky's ballet *Jeux*. France: Paris. 1913.   606

Becque's life and production of *The Vultures*. France. 1837-1899.   720

Production history and development of Wole Soyinka's plays. Nigeria. 1958-1982.   731

Production history of *True West*. USA. 1982.   755

Recreation of Joseph Jefferson's *Rip Van Winkle*. USA. Nineteenth cent.   858

Personal factors involved in casting of *Marie Tudor*. France: Paris. Nineteenth cent. Twentieth cent.   867

Analysis of *Mankind* by director of recent production. Great Britain. 1982.   873

Preparatory work on Tennessee Williams' *Out Cry*. USA: Madison, WI. Twentieth cent.   877

Richard Schechner's production of Genet's *The Balcony*. USA: New York, NY. 1979-1980.   879

Reconstruction of a production of *The Taming of the Shrew*. England: London. 1912-1913.   903

Production history of *One Mo' Time*. USA: New York, NY. 1982.   998

Costume designs for a production of *Falstaff*. Great Britain. Italy. USA: Los Angeles, CA. 1982.   1034

Production of G. Stein/V. Thomson Opera *Four Saints in Three Acts*. USA. 1934.   1052

Revisionist account of first production of *The Seagull*. Russia: Leningrad (St. Petersburg). 1896.   1147

Discussion of 19th century contributions to Shakespearean production. England: London. Nineteenth cent.   1191

Production history of *The Winter's Tale*. England. USA. 1611-1976.   1262

SUBJECT INDEX

Radio drama

Responsibilities of radio in arresting decline of literacy. Canada. Twentieth cent. 943

Discussion of current radio drama on CBC networks. Canada. 1976-1982. 944

Efforts to retrieve early radio drama scripts. Canada. 1930-1982. 945

Memories of radio producers Andrew Allan and Esse Ljungh. Canada. 1930-1982. 946

Technology influences dramaturgy for radio. Canada. 1971-1982. 947

Diary of soundman's experience with live radio. Canada: Vancouver, BC. 1975. 948

Style and approach of radio producer Esse Ljungh. Canada. 1955-1969. 949

Influence of radio on playwright George Ryga. Canada. Twentieth cent. 950

Influence of radio drama on theatre. Canada. 1960-1970. 951

Ragtime

Howard Rollins Jr.'s theatrical background. USA. Twentieth cent. 439

Details of actor Howard Rollins Jr.'s career. USA. 1960-1982. 443

Raisin, Françoise

New biographical data about French actress Françoise Raisin. France. 1661-1721. 429

Ramlila

Exploration of Ramlila's theatrical, social and religious significance. India: Ramnager. 1976-1978. 527

Rappresentazione di Santa Uliva (Representation of Santa Uliva)

Correspondence S. d'Amico/G.M. Gatti/J. Copeau on staging of *Representation of Santa Uliva*. Italy: Florence. 1932-1933. 541

Rauschenberg, Robert

Interview with Trisha Brown and Robert Rauschenberg about their collaborations. USA: New York, NY. 1963-1982. 623

Rayvid, Bruce

Bruce Porter and Bruce Rayvid's scene shop and working habits. USA: New York, NY. 1982. 239

Reader's theatre

Classroom exercises based on reader's theatre. USA. Twentieth cent. 886

Realism

Trends in designs and designers' working conditions. USA: New York, NY. 1970-1980. 222

Henry Becque's use of language in *The Vultures*. France. Nineteenth cent. 831

Business and composition in T.W. Robertson's *Caste*. England: London. 1867-1883. 864

Reaney, James

Use of stage metaphor in James Reaney's *The Donnellys*. Canada. 1975-1977. 826

Recklessness

O'Neill influenced by other writers. USA. 1910-1913. 1174

Reconstruction

Adapting classical ballet repertory. East Germany. Twentieth cent. 596

Restoring, maintaining or changing classical choreography. USA. 1982. 597

Actors' responsibility to dramatic history. East Germany. Twentieth cent. 862

Red Roses for Me

Analyses of two O'Casey plays seen as visionary drama. Ireland. 1914-1982. 901

Redgrave, Vanessa

Boston Symphony Orchestra's refusal to permit Vanessa Redgrave to perform. USA: Boston, MA. 1982. 516

Regional Organization of Theatres-South (ROOTS)

Report on ROOTS Southern theatre conference festivals. USA: Atlanta, GA. 1982. 334

Regional theatre

Paper calling for study of theatre history in Midwest. USA. 1930-1982. 95

Trends in designs and designers' working conditions. USA: New York, NY. 1970-1980. 222

Set construction for Arena Stage production of *K2*. USA: Washington, DC. 1982. 228

Critical survey of regional theatres. USA. 1950-1980. 317

Report on ROOTS Southern theatre conference festivals. USA: Atlanta, GA. 1982. 334

History of Provincetown Players. USA: Provincetown, MA, New York, NY. 1912-1929. 339

Interview concerning American Repertory Theatre. USA: Cambridge, MA. 1982. 342

History of San Diego Shakespeare Festival and Old Globe Theatre. USA: San Diego, CA. Twentieth cent. 380

Survey on use of volunteers. USA. 1982. 449

Relation of regional theatre to community. USA: Hartford, CT. 1982. 482

Collaborative play based on local labor problems. Sweden. 1982. 733

Reid, John

Description of work in costume shops. USA: New York, NY. 1982. 173

Reindeer Werk (Reindeer Work)

Interviews with spectators to determine methodology for analyzing perception. Europe. Twentieth cent. 149

Reinhard, Maria

Forms, styles and function of plays. East Germany. West Germany. 1960-1980. 710

Reinhardt, Max

Rise of the director from Naturalism to Grotowski. Russia. Germany. England. France. Poland. 1890-1980. 557

Actor Eduard von Winterstein's memoirs. Germany: Berlin. 1889-1918. 686

Reinking, Ann

Ann Reinking's training and role in *Annie*. USA: New York, NY. 1982.   589

Religion

How personal and religious beliefs influence reception. USA. Multi-period.   647

Storyteller as performer in Arab culture. Arabic-speaking countries. 100-1982.   1095

Religious dance

Commercialized ceremonial dances for tourist audiences. Sri Lanka. Multi-period. Twentieth cent.   609

Religious theatre

Development of Provençal pastorales. France. Nineteenth cent.   1121

Renaissance period

Renaissance drama research opportunities. England. 1500-1700.   44

List of Tudor and Stuart entertainments. England: London. 1485-1558.   54

Discrepancies in Serlio's drawings. Italy. 1545.   213

Forerunners of folk drama. Great Britain. Medieval period. Renaissance period.   782

Sociological analysis of *Sacre rappresentazioni*. Italy: Florence. Fifteenth cent. Sixteenth cent. Renaissance period.   851

Characteristics, organization, popular participation in festivities and performances. Italy. Renaissance period. Fifteenth cent. Sixteenth cent.   1093

The Royal Entry for Margaret of Anjou and its text. England: London. 1445.   1119

Renard, Jules

Interpretation of Jules Renard's *The Pleasure of Breaking* by director Yves Gasc. France: Paris. Twentieth cent.   866

Renaud, Madeleine

Commentary on productions by Renaud-Barrault Company. France: Paris. England: London. 1976-1981.   552

Repertory theatre

Publicly funded theatre under economic pressure. Norway: Oslo. Twentieth cent.   304

Artistic direction of repertory theatre. Norway: Oslo. 1980-1981.   306

Rebuilt Old Globe Theatre with resident company. USA: San Diego, CA. Twentieth cent.   324

Court case over repertory and management of Göteborg Stadsteater. Sweden: Gothenburg. 1981-1982.   370

Organization and management of city theatre. Finland: Lappeenranta. 1980-1981.   373

Interview with manager of Burgtheater on producing classical plays. Austria: Vienna. 1982.   700

Decrease in *A Christmas Carol* productions at TCG theatres. USA. 1981-1982.   747

Financial relationship between resident theatres and playwrights. USA. 1982.   753

Representatio

Use of simulated bier in early Jewish funeral rites. Spain. 1291.   1133

Representation of Santa Uliva. SEE: *Rappresentazione di Santa Uliva*.

Research

Resources for 19th century scholars. Nineteenth cent.   36

Renaissance drama research opportunities. England. 1500-1700.   44

Call for theatre scholars to participate in mainstream journals. USA. 1970-1982.   133

Costumes at Fashion Institute of Technology. USA: New York, NY. Twentieth cent. Multi-period.   172

Techniques of researching historic theatres and theatre history. USA: Sacramento, CA. 1900-1940.   414

Goals of research in creative dramatics and children's theatre. Twentieth cent.   576

Review of Shakespeare scholarship. England. USA. 1980-1981.   1192

Restoration period

Reconstructing the finances of the United Company. Great Britain: London. 1682-1692.   276

Conjectural reconstruction of theatres. England: London. 1661-1674.   403

Prohibitions on regicide drama. England: London. 1660-1687.   928

Biography and critical assessment of Thomas Otway's plays. England. Seventeenth cent. Restoration period.   930

Revels

List of Tudor and Stuart entertainments. England: London. 1485-1558.   54

Revivals

Survey of theatre information. USA. England. 1900-1982.   65

Reynolds, Jonathan

Six critics review Gerald Gutierrez's production of *Geniuses*. USA: New York, NY. 1982.   672

Richard II

Various productions examined for differences in style. USA: New York, NY, Minneapolis, MN. Austria: Salzburg. Germany: Berlin. Twentieth cent.   878

Circle Repertory Company's withdrawal of *Richard II*. USA: New York, NY. 1982.   927

Shakespeare productions in principal cities. East Germany. 1945-1980.   1194

Study of character relationships in Shakespeare's *Richard II*. England. 1596-1597.   1210

Richard III

Gordon Craig's views on staging Shakespeare. England. 1885-1911.   855

Debate over actor portrayed in portrait of Richard III. England. Elizabethan period. Jacobean period. Sixteenth cent. Seventeenth cent.   1199

Shakespeare's treatment of humanity and power. England. Elizabethan period. Multi-period.   1223

Pun on Hower in *Richard III*. England. 1592-1593.   1249

Rigoletto

Operatic adaptations of plays by Victor Hugo. France. Italy. 1830-1876.   1045

Riha, Carl

Rosl Schönfeld's musical theatre career. East Germany: Karl-Marx-Stadt. 1922-1982.   989

Riksteatret

The Great One Who Stops the Color, a children's play by Tor Åge Bringsvaerd. Norway. 1981-1982.   732

Rinaldo

Survey of baroque opera with special reference to Händel's *Rinaldo*. Italy: Venice, Naples. 1600-1750.   1031

Ringling Brothers and Barnum and Bailey Clown College

Education and memoirs of storyteller Ken Feit. USA. 1940-1982.   1099

Career of dancer/clown Bill Irwin. USA: San Francisco, CA. 1968-1982.   1102

Ringtheater

Ringtheater's fire and its effects on subsequent theatre construction. Austria: Vienna. 1881-1981.   387

Riot. SEE: *Rixe*.

Rip Van Winkle

Recreation of Joseph Jefferson's *Rip Van Winkle*. USA. Nineteenth cent.   858

Rise and Fall of the City of Mahagonny. SEE: *Aufstieg und Fall der Stadt Mahagonny*.

Ritual theatre

Different origins of drama and theatre. Greece. France. Multi-period.   92

Performance of *Sree Muchilot Bhagavathi* by Natana Kala Kshetram. India. 1981.   300

Social drama and dramatic ritual. Multi-period.   486

Commercialized ceremonial dances for tourist audiences. Sri Lanka. Multi-period. Twentieth cent.   609

Use of simulated bier in early Jewish funeral rites. Spain. 1291.   1133

Sacred rites of Demeter recreated in workshop. Greece. 1980.   1134

Ritual performances of *nora chatri* in Kedah. Malaysia. Twentieth cent.   1135

Rixe (Riot)

Interview with director Jean-Paul Roussillon. France: Paris. 1982.   870

Robbins, Jerome

Evolution of choreographer/director in Broadway musicals. USA: New York, NY. 1940-1982.   1016

Robertson, T.W.

Business and composition in T.W. Robertson's *Caste*. England: London. 1867-1883.   864

Robinson, Vivian

Harlem's theatre traditions and problems. USA: New York, NY. 1980-1982.   422

Rock 'n Roll! The First 5000 Years

Script to *Rock 'n Roll! The First 5000 Years* and interview with author John Gray. Canada. 1981.   72

Five critics review Joe Layton's production of *Rock 'n Roll! The First 5000 Years*. USA: New York, NY. 1982.   1000

Rockaby

Analysis of Beckett's *Rockaby*. USA. Twentieth cent.   1141

Rocking Chair, The. SEE: *Fauteil à Bascule, Le*.

Rolland, Romain

Cultural politics during Popular Front. France. Twentieth cent.   107

Rollins, Howard Jr.

Howard Rollins Jr.'s theatrical background. USA. Twentieth cent.   439

Details of actor Howard Rollins Jr.'s career. USA. 1960-1982.   443

Romances

Possible sources for style and treatment of historical material in Shakespeare's plays. Great Britain. 1580-1600.   1206

Romantic period

Economic themes in Alfred de Vigny's *Chatterton*. France. 1835.   803

The Follies of Marianne as expression of Musset's individuality. France. Nineteenth cent. Romantic period.   805

Parallels in scene structure between *Penthesilea* and *The Iliad*. Germany. 1808.   832

Dramatic theories of Victor Hugo. France. 1827-1843.   936

Operatic adaptations of plays by Victor Hugo. France. Italy. 1830-1876.   1045

Levels of consciousness in Goethe's *Faust*. Germany. 1769-1831.   1153

Romeo and Juliet

Ideas of lower-class characters in Shakespeare on war, peace and violence. England. Elizabethan period. Sixteenth cent. Seventeenth cent.   1220

Interpretation of *Romeo and Juliet*, IV.iv.5-6. England. 1594-1595.   1235

Interpretation of *Romeo and Juliet*, IV.v.114-117. England. 1595-1596.   1239

Double meanings of phrase in Juliet's soliloquy, *Romeo and Juliet* III.ii. England. 1594-1595.   1243

Roose, James

Nine critics review James Roose's production of *84 Charing Cross Road*. USA: New York, NY. 1982.   670

Rope, The

First production of O'Neill's *The Rope*. USA. 1918.   1187

Rose, Susan

Obtaining performance rights to *Joseph and the Amazing Technicolor Dreamcoat*. USA: New York, NY. 1979-1982.   987

SUBJECT INDEX

SUBJECT INDEX

Stadt- und Landesbibliothek (Vienna)

Johann Nestroy manuscripts acquired at City Library. Austria: Vienna. 1982. 37

Stadttheater Konstanz

Repertory and business changes at Stadttheater Konstanz under new manager. West Germany: Constance. 1980-1982. 348

Staging

Theatricality expressed in space, time and character. Japan. Twentieth cent. 125

Performance theory according to M. Fried, W. Benjamin and R. Foreman. USA. Canada. Twentieth cent. 423

Stanislavskij, Konstantin Sergeevič

Interview with Jacques Lasalle on his various theatrical theories. France. 1981. 118

Rise of the director from Naturalism to Grotowski. Russia. Germany. England. France. Poland. 1890-1980. 557

Use of 'empty space' compared to realistic settings. West Germany. Twentieth cent. 565

Improvisation in Occidental and classical Japanese theatre. Europe. Japan. Twentieth cent. 569

Critical analysis of the works of Stanislavsky. Russia: Moscow. 1899-1936. 874

Stanislavski's training of opera singers. Russia. 1900. 1053

Feodor Chaliapin as an actor. Russia. 1873-1917. 1070

Revisionist account of first production of *The Seagull*. Russia: Leningrad (St. Petersburg). 1896. 1147

Stanislavsky, Konstantin. SEE: Stanislafskij, Konstantin Sergeevič.

State Theatre of Württemberg. SEE: Württembergische Landesbühne.

Stavis, Barrie

Accomplishments of American Theatre Association Fellows Mordecai Gorelik, Barrie Stavis and Robert Corrigan. USA. 1982. 128

Steaming

Nine critics review Roger Smith's production of *Steaming*. USA: New York, NY. 1982. 660

Origins of Nell Dunn's *Steaming*. England: London. USA: New York, NY. 1960-1980. 798

Stein, Gertrude

Word as gesture is key to understanding play by Gertrude Stein. Twentieth cent. 824

Production of G. Stein/V. Thomson Opera *Four Saints in Three Acts*. USA. 1934. 1052

Stennett, Michael

Costume designs for a production of *Falstaff*. Great Britain. Italy. USA: Los Angeles, CA. 1982. 1034

Sterijino Pozorje (Yugoslav Festival Theatre)

History of Yugoslav Festival Theatre and 1982 festival work of Drago Putnikovic. Yugoslavia. 1958-1982. 351

Stern, William

Discussion of concepts related to mimesis and representation. Europe. Multi-period. 492

Stettheimer, Florine

Production of G. Stein/V. Thomson Opera *Four Saints in Three Acts*. USA. 1934. 1052

Stewart, Ellen

Professionals relate experiences with Ellen Stewart. USA: New York, NY. 1960-1980. 131

Pictorial essay on Ellen Stewart and La Mama. USA: New York, NY. 1960-1980. 316

Brief history of Ellen Stewart and La Mama ETC. USA: New York, NY. 1962-1982. 327

Ellen Stewart's experiences with La Mama. USA: New York, NY. 1960-1980. 329

Stewart, William

Relation of regional theatre to community. USA: Hartford, CT. 1982. 482

Stone, Edward

Eight critics review Edward Stone's production of *Charlotte, Sweet*. USA: New York, NY. 1982. 994

Stoppard, Tom

Tom Stoppard biography with critical analyses. England. Twentieth cent. 896

Development in Tom Stoppard's comedy. England. Twentieth cent. 897

Storch, Arthur

Eight critics review Arthur Storch's production of *Twice Around the Park*. USA: New York, NY. 1982. 658

Store Alfredo, Den (Great Alfredo, The)

Repertory of oldest theatre in Bergen. Norway: Bergen. 1876-1981. 305

Store Farvesluker, Den (Great One Who Stops the Color, The)

The Great One Who Stops the Color, a children's play by Tor Åge Bringsvaerd. Norway. 1981-1982. 732

Storming of the Winter Palace, The. SEE: Shturm Zimnego dvoltsa.

Storytelling

Children's stories collected by Ken Feit. USA: Milwaukee, WI. 1971-1972. 71

Origins of Inuit theatre company. Greenland: Holstebro. 1975-1982. 299

Dramatic monologue as stylistic device. Great Britain. Twentieth cent. 479

Storytelling as self-identification, and collective playwriting. USA: St. Peter, MN. 1981-1982. 535

Storyteller as performer in Arab culture. Arabic-speaking countries. 100-1982. 1095

Itinerant storyteller Ken Feit. USA. 1981-1982. 1098

Education and memoirs of storyteller Ken Feit. USA. 1940-1982. 1099

Memoirs of itinerant storyteller Ken Feit. USA. 1970-1982. 1100

Experiences of storyteller Loren Niemi. USA. 1981-1982. 1101

SUBJECT INDEX

SUBJECT INDEX

Claudel's *The Exchange* compared to *Break of Noon*. France: Paris. Belgium: Louvain. 1894-1906.   804

Theatre of Disturbance

Plays and theories of Peter Barnes. England. 1968-1982.   781

Theatre of Nations

Report on ITI-sponsored Theatre of Nations festival. Bulgaria: Sofia. 1982.   284

Theatre of Nations Festival

Reports on Theatre of Nations festival. Bulgaria: Sofia. 1982.   111

Theatre of Sources

Anthropological aspects of acting. Europe. Asia. Twentieth cent.   913

Theatre of the Soul, The. SEE: *V Kulisach Duši.*

Theatre Sport

Improvisation in Keith Johnston's Theatre Sport. Canada: Calgary, AB, Vancouver, BC. 1956-1981.   566

Theatre Without Walls

Atlanta's Black theatre companies. USA: Atlanta, GA. 1930-1982.   313

Théâtre-Italien

Reactions of Danish actors to performances at theatres. France: Paris. 1788.   430

Theatricality

Concept of theatre as theatrical. Sweden. Twentieth cent.   94

Interview with Jacques Lasalle on his various theatrical theories. France. 1981.   118

Theatricality expressed in space, time and character. Japan. Twentieth cent.   125

Fundamental characteristics in performance. Twentieth cent.   539

Tom Stoppard biography with critical analyses. England. Twentieth cent.   896

Themes

Prohibitions on regicide drama. England: London. 1660-1687.   928

Theory

Different origins of drama and theatre. Greece. France. Multi-period.   92

Concept of theatre as theatrical. Sweden. Twentieth cent.   94

Coordination of critical approaches to theatre research. West Germany: Cologne, Berlin, Munich. 1800-1982.   99

How theatre can provide alternative images of community and social relationships. USA: St. Peter, MN. 1981-1982.   108

Criticism conference at Queen's University. Canada: Kingston, ON. 1982.   112

Western dramaturgy model crisis: separate analysis of its constituent elements. Europe. Twentieth cent.   117

Semiotic analysis of gestural codes. Germany. Baroque period. Eighteenth cent.   120

Collection of theatre professionals' opinions about critics. Italy. Twentieth cent.   123

Theoretical basis of theatre research. USA. Twentieth cent.   130

Performance theory according to M. Fried, W. Benjamin and R. Foreman. USA. Canada. Twentieth cent.   423

Study of current approaches to acting theory. 1982.   425

Social drama and dramatic ritual. Multi-period.   486

Non-Western perspectives on performance theory. Asia. Twentieth cent.   487

Discussion of concepts related to mimesis and representation. Europe. Multi-period.   492

Relationship of theatre to culture. USA. Europe. Multi-period.   532

Discussion among directors and critics. West Germany. Twentieth cent.   537

Sándor Hevesi as major director, theorist, translator and playwright. Hungary. 1901-1939.   555

Eugenio Barba discusses his theory of actor training. Denmark. Twentieth cent.   568

Director/theorist discusses performer training. USA. Canada: Toronto, ON, Montreal, PQ. 1982.   572

Alternative methods of performer training. Europe. Asia. North America. 1982.   578

Artistic director of Stratford Festival discusses value of classical theatre. Canada: Stratford, ON. 1982.   706

Theory for creative drama. Twentieth cent.   849

Discussion of fidelity to original work in performance of classical plays. Multi-period.   854

Comic theory. Europe. 380 B.C.-1700 A.D.   887

Anthropological aspects of acting. Europe. Asia. Twentieth cent.   913

Sources for the acting theory of Antonin Artaud. France. 1920-1935.   914

Social revolution in Wagner's life and works. Germany. 1848.   1270

Analysis of Wagner's musical and theatrical theory, his operas and their reception. Germany. Nineteenth cent.   1273

Thin Guy, The. SEE: *Magrino, Il.*

Thompson, Alfred

Career of writer/designer/costumer Alfred Thompson. USA: New York, NY. England: London. 1831-1895.   226

Thompson, Ernest

Playwright Ernest Thompson uses 'ordinary man' as subject. USA. 1982.   818

Thompson, Lauren

Eight critics review Michael Kahn's production of *Whodunnit*. USA: New York, NY. 1982.   669

Thompson, Liz

History of Jacob's Pillow Dance Festival. USA: Becket, MA. 1931-1982.   616

SUBJECT INDEX

SUBJECT INDEX

SUBJECT INDEX

SUBJECT INDEX

SUBJECT INDEX

SUBJECT INDEX

SUBJECT INDEX

SUBJECT INDEX

SUBJECT INDEX

SUBJECT INDEX

SUBJECT INDEX

SUBJECT INDEX

Seven critics review Harold Prince's production of *A Doll's Life*.
USA: New York, NY. 1982.   1004

Effect of stardom on performer in Broadway musical *The Wiz*. USA.
1980-1982.   1005

Five critics review *Little Johnny Jones*. USA: New York, NY. 1982.
                                                                            1006

Five critics review Bob Eaton's production of *Lennon*. USA: New
York, NY. 1982.   1007

Tony award acceptance speech by Tom Eyen. USA: New York, NY.
1982.   1008

Comment on Black musicals and review of *Dreamgirls*. USA. 1980.
                                                                            1009

Analysis of season's musicals. USA: New York, NY. England:
London. 1982.   1010

A biography of Weill and an analysis of his works. Germany:
Berlin. USA: New York, NY. Twentieth cent.   1011

Evolution of *Nine*. USA: New York, NY. 1963-1982.   1012

Creation of *Cats*. England: London. USA: New York, NY. 1980-
1982.   1013

Round-table discussion by the creators of *Dreamgirls*. USA: New
York, NY. 1982.   1014

Visual effects in Broadway musicals. USA: New York, NY. 1982.
                                                                            1015

Evolution of choreographer/director in Broadway musicals. USA:
New York, NY. 1940-1982.   1016

Two productions of *Cats*. USA: New York, NY. England: London.
1982.   1017

Changes needed in production and direction of musicals. USA. 1982.
                                                                            1018

Eight considerations for directors of musicals. USA. Twentieth cent.
                                                                            1019

Tommy Tune's Broadway career. USA: New York, NY. 1973-1982.
                                                                            1020

Relationship of musical theatre to environmental theatre and
performance art. USA. 1975.   1021

Six critics review Ben Levit's production of *Herringbone*. USA: New
York, NY. 1982.   1022

Role of Harold Prince in musical theatre. USA. 1950-1982.   1023

Forthcoming events in international opera world. 1982.   1024

Personalities of international opera world. 1982.   1025

Tidbits about personalities in opera world. 1982-1983.   1026

Tidbits about personalities in world of opera. 1982.   1027

Tidbits about personalities in opera world. 1982.   1028

Music critic's thoughts on opera. England: London. 1920-1939.   1029

Costumes exhibition from L'Opéra de Paris. France: Paris. 1930-
1981.   1033

Costume designs for a production of *Falstaff*. Great Britain. Italy.
USA: Los Angeles, CA. 1982.   1034

Costume design research for *La Traviata*. USA: New York, NY.
1982.   1035

Struggle to simplify scenery at the Metropolitan Opera. USA: New
York, NY. 1982.   1037

New scenery for *Die Meistersinger von Nürnberg*. West Germany:
Bayreuth. 1945-1981.   1038

Production expenses at Munich National Theatre. West Germany:
Munich. 1982.   1039

Belgian National Opera opens season. Belgium: Brussels. 1981.   1040

Brief history of the Edmonton Opera Company. Canada: Edmonton,
AB. 1952-1982.   1041

History of Opera Hamilton. Canada: Hamilton, ON. 1976-1982.   1042

Semi-annual meeting of opera directors. 1982.   1043

Groups promote opera training and performance. Canada. Twentieth
cent.   1044

Adaptations of drama for opera. Italy. Russia. Eighteenth cent.
Twentieth cent.   1046

The Richard Strauss/Hugo von Hofmannsthal collaboration on
Ariadne auf Naxos. Austria. 1912-1916.   1047

Mystification of history in Philip Glass's *Satyagraha*. USA: New
York, NY. 1981.   1051

Production of G. Stein/V. Thomson Opera *Four Saints in Three
Acts*. USA. 1934.   1052

Stanislavski's training of opera singers. Russia. 1900.   1053

Jon Vicker's performance style and personality. 1927-1982.   1054

Interview with Placido Domingo. 1982.   1055

Overview of singer Jewgenij Nesterenko's career. 1963-1982.   1056

Austrian opera singer Heinz Zednik's career. 1964-1982.   1057

Soprano Teresa Stratas' relationship with Lotte Lenya. Twentieth
cent.   1058

Career of opera singer Luis Lima. Argentina. 1973-1982.   1059

Interview about Lucia Popp's career. Austria: Vienna. Germany:
Munich. England: London. 1963-1982.   1060

Interview with mezzo-soprano Diane Loeb. Canada. 1982.   1061

Interview with tenor Alan Woodrow. Canada. 1982.   1062

Biographical sketch of soprano Emma Albani. Canada. 1847-1950.
                                                                            1063

Brief biography of Pauline Tinsley. England. 1961-1982.   1064

Opera singer Jon Vickers' approach to roles. England. Twentieth
cent.   1065

Survey of critic Herman Klein's work. England: London. 1920-1939.
                                                                            1067

Biography of baritone Gabriel Bacquier. France. 1924-1982.   1068

Interview with tenor John Brecknock. Great Britain. 1938-1982. 1069

Feodor Chaliapin as an actor. Russia. 1873-1917. 1070

Overview of singer Patricia Wise's career. USA. Twentieth cent. 1071

Career of opera singer Siegfried Jerusalem. West Germany. 1976-1982. 1072

Interview with Lorin Maazel, new manager of Wiener Staatsoper. Austria: Vienna. USA. 1982. 1073

Summary of preceding administrations of L'Opéra de Paris. France: Paris. 1973-1982. 1074

Career of composer Emmerich Kalman. Austria: Vienna. 1883-1953. 1075

Analysis of Bartók's opera and ballets. Hungary. -1945. Twentieth cent. 1076

Creation, production and reception of Béla Bartók's operas and ballets. Hungary. 1910-1981. 1077

Description of Le Grand Macabre. Hungary. Twentieth cent. 1081

Genesis of score and libretto for Prince Igor. Russia. 1870-1879. 1082

Problems concerning production of modern operas. East Germany: Karl-Marx-Stadt. 1981. 1083

Conductor Carlo Maria Giulini's cooperation with director. USA: Los Angeles, CA. England: London. 1982. 1084

Interview with director Robert Carsen. Canada. 1982. 1085

Directors' and designers' interpretations of operas. Canada. Twentieth cent. 1086

Gianfranco de Bosio's production of Aida at Arena of Verona. Italy: Verona. 1913-1982. 1087

Impact of theatre directors on opera. USA. 1982. 1088

Operetta singer Fritzi Massary's career. Austria: Vienna. Germany: Berlin. 1904-1930. 1089

Universal Producing Company viewed as small-town show business. USA: Fairfield, IA. 1928-1935. 1094

Reconstruction of a folk festivity. Italy: Siena. 1974. 1097

Itinerant storyteller Ken Feit. USA. 1981-1982. 1098

Education and memoirs of storyteller Ken Feit. USA. 1940-1982. 1099

Memoirs of itinerant storyteller Ken Feit. USA. 1970-1982. 1100

Experiences of storyteller Loren Niemi. USA. 1981-1982. 1101

Career of dancer/clown Bill Irwin. USA: San Francisco, CA. 1968-1982. 1102

Kwagh-Hir technique as means of native expression. Nigeria. 1960-1982. 1103

Itinerant storyteller Loren Niemi's theatre experiences. USA. 1982. 1104

Account of spectacle at Cirque d'Hiver. France: Paris. 1920. 1105

How to be a successful clown, juggler, mime, magician or puppeteer. USA. Twentieth cent. 1106

Origins and development of Russian cabaret. Russia. 1882-1921. 1107

Critical examination of cabaret comedian Karl Valentin. East Germany: Berlin. 1882-1982. 1108

Acting style of cabaret performer Karl Valentin. Germany: Munich. 1908-1948. 1109

Examination of Frigyes Karinthy. Hungary. 1887-1938. 1110

Account of theatrical experience at carnival. Italy: San Giovanni Valdarno. 1979. 1111

Developments of the Teatre de la Carrièra. France. 1976-1982. 1112

Setting up the carnival and text of the performance. Italy: San Giovanni Valdarno. Twentieth cent. 1115

Leo Bassi's clown training and experiences. Twentieth cent. 1116

Annual Swiss-American Wilhelm Tell pageant. USA: New Glarus, WI. 1845-1981. 1122

Participation of Bread and Puppet Theatre in March for Nuclear Disarmament. USA: New York, NY. 1982. 1123

Gaston Baty's poetics, with focus on puppets. France. Twentieth cent. 1124

Interview with puppet player about concept and scenery. East Germany: East Berlin. 1982. 1125

Report on Third Festival of Puppet Theatre. East Germany: Magdeburg. 1982. 1126

Career of Hans-Dieter Stäcker with Zwickau Puppet Theatre. East Germany: Zwickau. 1938-1982. 1127

Traditional puppet movements in shadow theatre. Indonesia. Twentieth cent. 1128

Thunderbird American Indian Dancers' powwow. USA: New York, NY. 1981. 1130

Celebration of Indonesian independence day. Indonesia. 1977-1981. 1131

Voodoo and dramatic presentation. Haiti. 1980. 1132

Sacred rites of Demeter recreated in workshop. Greece. 1980. 1134

Ritual performances of nora chatri in Kedah. Malaysia. Twentieth cent. 1135

Crisis and fragmentaton in Beckett's plays. Twentieth cent. 1136

Analysis of Beckett's Ohio Impromptu and meaning of title. Twentieth cent. 1137

Appraisal of Beckett's later works. 1977-1981. 1138

Beckett's verbal play in A Piece of Monologue. Twentieth cent. 1139

Dialectical nature of laughter in Endgame. Twentieth cent. 1140

Analysis of Beckett's Rockaby. USA. Twentieth cent. 1141

Aesthetic theories of tragedy. Germany. Twentieth cent. 1142

SUBJECT INDEX

SUBJECT INDEX

SUBJECT INDEX

Way, Brian

Three approaches to creative dramatics. USA. England. Twentieth cent. 584

Wayang kulit

Traditional puppet movements in shadow theatre. Indonesia. Twentieth cent. 1128

Celebration of Indonesian independence day. Indonesia. 1977-1981. 1131

Waylan, Francis

Parallels between *King Lear* and 19th century familial relationships. Great Britain. USA. Seventeenth cent. Nineteenth cent. 939

Webber, Andrew Lloyd

English theatre imported to America. USA: New York, NY. England: London. 1981-1982. 543

Eleven critics review Trevor Nunn's production of *Cats*. USA: New York, NY. 1982. 1003

Creation of *Cats*. England: London. USA: New York, NY. 1980-1982. 1013

Webster, John

Historical context for John Webster's major plays. England. 1600-1620. 711

Wedekind, Frank

Character similarities in plays by O'Neill and Wedekind. USA. Germany. Twentieth cent. 1177

Similarities between Frank Wedekind and Eugene O'Neill. USA. West Germany. Twentieth cent. 1184

Weill, Kurt

Lotte Lenya discusses early life and marriage. Germany. 1920-1949. 431

A biography of Weill and an analysis of his works. Germany: Berlin. USA: New York, NY. Twentieth cent. 1011

Weimar classicism

Documents concerning Goethe as theatre manager. Germany: Weimar. 1790-1817. 1150

Weiss, Alexander

Adaptation of novels to stage. Sweden: Stockholm. 1980-1981. 475

Weiss, Peter

Interview with designer Gunilla Palmstierna-Weiss. Sweden: Stockholm, Gothenburg. Germany. Twentieth cent. 216

Brief obituary of Peter Weiss. West Germany. Twentieth cent. 761

Welch, Raquel

Raquel Welch comments on *Woman of the Year*. USA: New York, NY. 1981-1982. 996

Well of the Saints, The

J.M. Synge's use of medieval material. Ireland. Twentieth cent. 812

O'Neill's *The Iceman Cometh* compared to works by J.M. Synge and Joseph Conrad. USA. Ireland. Twentieth cent. 1172

Weller, Michael

Fourth of July as symbol in definition of American consciousness. USA. 1977-1979. 758

Playwrights working in film and television. USA. 1982. 942

Werktheater, Het

Review of Second International Children's and Youth Festival. West Germany: West Berlin. 1981. 346

Werner, Oskar

Actor Oskar Werner's reservations about today's acting. Austria: Vienna. 1922-1982. 676

West Side Waltz, The

Playwright Ernest Thompson uses 'ordinary man' as subject. USA. 1982. 818

Westside Arts Theatre

Seven critics review collective theatre presentation *Pump Boys and Dinettes*. USA: New York, NY. 1982. 997

Weymer, Marguerite. SEE: Mademoiselle George.

What the Butler Saw

Study of Joe Orton's farce *What the Butler Saw*. England. Twentieth cent. 893

Where Do We Come from? What Are We? Where Are We Going?. **SEE:** *Woher Kommen wir? Was sind wir? Wohin gehen wir?.*

Where the Cross Is Made

O'Neill's use of language in *Where the Cross Is Made*. USA. Twentieth cent. 1185

Whitmore, James

Eight critics review Jacques Levy's production of *Almost an Eagle*. USA: New York, NY. 1982. 656

Whittaker, Herbert

Career of designer, director, critic Herbert Whittaker. Canada. 1911-1982. 207

Whodunnit

Eight critics review Michael Kahn's production of *Whodunnit*. USA: New York, NY. 1982. 669

Why Marry?

Evaluation of image of 'New Woman' in *Why Marry?*. USA. 1918. 822

Wieland, Guido

Brief biography of actor Guido Wieland. Austria: Vienna. 1945-1980. 677

Wild Duck, The. **SEE:** *Vildanden.*

Wilde, Oscar

Nikolai Evreinov's theories, plays and productions. Russia. 1879-1953. 558

Wilhelm Tell

Annual Swiss-American *Wilhelm Tell* pageant. USA: New Glarus, WI. 1845-1981. 1122

Williams, Billy Dee

Vignettes of Black stars. USA. Twentieth cent. 136

Williams, E.C.

Two notable panoramas of whaling. USA. 1849-1866. 230

Williams, Jesse Lynch

Evaluation of image of 'New Woman' in *Why Marry?*. USA. 1918. 822

SUBJECT INDEX

SUBJECT INDEX

Women's Theatre Project

Women's Theatre Project and oppression of women by organized religions. USA: Seattle, WA. 1982. 533

Wooster Group

Europeans examine subsidies of American groups. France. Netherlands. Italy. USA. Twentieth cent. 260

Route 1 & 9 examines the Wooster Group's history and philosophy. USA: New York, NY. 1982. 328

Workers' theatre

Shakespeare productions in principal cities. East Germany. 1945-1980. 1194

World Theatre Day

World Theatre Day message by playwright Michael Cook. Canada. 1982. 89

Worm, A. Toxen

The Shuberts' financial arrangements with, and promotion of, Gaby Deslys. USA: New York, NY. 1911-1914. 463

A. Toxen Worm, press agent for the Shuberts. USA: New York, NY. 1910-1921. 484

Woyzeck

Analysis of Georg Büchner's life and work, with stage history of plays. Germany. 1750-1982. 724

WPA Theatre

Seven critics review Howard Ashman's production of *Little Shop of Horrors*. USA: New York, NY. 1982. 993

Württembergische Landesbühne (State Theatre of Württemberg)

Acting in children's theatre. West Germany: Esslingen. 1980-1982. 138

Yale Repertory Theatre

Financial relationship between resident theatres and playwrights. USA. 1982. 753

Dramaturgical study of play by Richard Nelson. USA: New Haven, CT. 1981. 836

Yeargan, Michael

Trends in designs and designers' working conditions. USA: New York, NY. 1970-1980. 222

Relationship between Michael Yeargan and Andrei Serban in designing productions. USA. 1982. 234

Yeats, William Butler

Abbey Theatre peasant drama. Ireland. 1902-1908. 783

Yen, Lu Wong

Women's Theatre Project and oppression of women by organized religions. USA: Seattle, WA. 1982. 533

Yeston, Maury

Evolution of *Nine*. USA: New York, NY. 1963-1982. 1012

Young people's theatre

Documentation of Canada's professional theatre activity. Canada. 1981-1982. 68

Acting in children's theatre. West Germany: Esslingen. 1980-1982. 138

Changing young people's behavior through positive images on stage. East Germany. Twentieth cent. 147

Young people's behavior in the theatre. East Germany: East Berlin. 1982. 148

Designing costumes for high school productions. South Africa, Republic of. 1982. 167

Review of Second International Children's and Youth Festival. West Germany: West Berlin. 1981. 346

Workshops for young playwrights. USA. 1980-1982. 473

Young Playwrights' Festival

Workshops for young playwrights. USA. 1980-1982. 473

Your Arms Too Short to Box with God

Personal/professional history of actress Patti LaBelle. USA. 1982. 991

Four critics review Vinette Carroll's production of *Your Arms Too Short to Box with God*. USA: New York, NY. 1982. 999

Yugoslav Festival Theatre. SEE: Sterijino Pozorje.

Zaloom, Paul

Bread and Puppet Theatre's Resurrection Circus. USA: Glover, VT. 1962-1982. 319

Zarzuela

International contributions to musical comedies. Spain. Italy. France. 1700-1770. 988

Zauberflöte, Die (Magic Flute, The)

Karl Friedrich Schinkel's designs for *The Magic Flute*. Germany: Berlin. 1815-1816. 210

Zecha, Fritz

Review of *The Talisman*. Austria: Vienna. 1980. 902

Zednik, Heinz

Austrian opera singer Heinz Zednik's career. 1964-1982. 1057

Zehntausend Bäume (Ten Thousand Trees)

Interview with playwright Dieter Kühn. West Germany. Twentieth cent. 759

Zeisler, Peter

Gordon Davidson, Alan Schneider and Peter Zeisler comment on artistic issues. USA. 1982. 127

Zerbin, Gaspard

Development of theatrical farces. France. 1530-1640. 1114

Ziegfeld, Florenz

Eddie Cantor's involvement with the Shuberts and Ziegfeld. USA: New York, NY, Philadelphia, PA. 1919-1923. 995

Zillmer, Gertrud-Elisabeth

Director discusses means of emphasizing social values. East Germany: East Berlin. 1982. 545

Zimmermann, Karl-Friedrich

Karl-Friedrich Zimmermann's work with children's theatre. East Germany: Magdeburg. Twentieth cent. 546

Zoete, Beryl de

Commercialized ceremonial dances for tourist audiences. Sri Lanka. Multi-period. Twentieth cent. 609

Zorina, Marta

Costuming Oriental dances. USA: New York, NY. Twentieth cent.
586

Zürich Opera

Theatre consultants impose technical tasks with serious consequences. West Germany. 1982.
252

DOCUMENT AUTHORS

DOCUMENT AUTHORS

Russell, Lawrence. 947
Rydzyk, Hans-Jürgen. 210
Ryga, George. 113, 950
Rzhevsky, Nicholas. 652
Sacheli, Robert. 986, 1023
Salgãdo, Gãmini. 1192
Salzmann-Čelan, Marija. 768
Sander, Anki. 261, 312
Sanders, Charles L. 1005
Sarlós, Robert K. 339, 1187
Satgé, Alain. 1145, 1146
Sauter, Wilmar. 94
Savarese, Nicola. 434
Savran, David. 828
Saz, Natalja. 975
Scabia, Giuliano. 1115
Scales, Robert R. 153, 196, 243
Schaefer, Gabriele. 911
Schaefer, James F., Jr. 824
Schaper, Karen K. 517
Schechner, Richard. 527, 572, 578, 879
Schechter, Joel. 754, 836
Scheepers, Elize. 581
Scherer, Barymore Laurence. 605
Schérer, Jacques. 1167
Schick, Rick. 154
Schickel, Richard. 1268
Schindler, Otto G., ed. 52
Schleiner, Louise. 1225
Schlemmer, Oskar. 211
Schlischefsky, Alexander. 46
Schlösser, Anselm. 1226
Schmid, Estella, transl. 86
Schneider, Guntram, ed. 52
Schneider, Horst. 459
Schoeman, Liesbet. 167
Schofield, B. St. John. 915
Schoyer, Maxine Allen. 1094
Schoyer, William T. 1094
Schreiber, Hans Peter. 1126
Schumacher, Ernst. 1108
Schwanbom, Per. 475
Schwarzer, Erwin. 398
Sears, David. 623
Seehose, Georg. 1227
Segalini, Sergio. 1068
Seligman, Kevin L. 22, 23, 162
Senelik, Laurence. 762
Serafini, Giuliano. 703, 973
Shafer, Yvonne. 697, 781, 880
Shank, Theodore. 232
Shapiro, Michael. 116
Sharp, Christopher. 660, 666, 669, 674, 1000
Sharpham, John. 100
Shea, Ann Marie. 1130
Shearing, Jack. 243
Sherbo, Arthur. 1193
Sherrill, Grace. 827
Shewey, Don. 340, 755
Shively, Donald H. 634
Shyer, Laurence. 233, 234, 881, 1037
Siegel, Joel. 656, 660, 661, 663, 668, 669, 670, 671, 673, 674, 1003, 1004
Siegel, Marcia B. 590
Siegmund-Schultze, Annette. 989
Simon, Richard Keller. 1140
Simpson, Herbert. 287
Sircar, Badal. 910
Sirett, Mark. 1044
Sito Alba, Manuel. 1118
Skasa, Michael. 884
Skerritt, David. 1151
Slabaugh, Richard. 197
Sloan, Lenwood. 268
Smart-Grosvenor, Vertamae. 136
Smedmark, Carl Reinhold. 734
Smith, Alan. 424
Smith, Louise. 341

Smith, Mary Elizabeth. 1260
Smith, Raynette Halverson. 235
Smith, Ronn. 173, 205, 985
Smith, Ronn, ed. 29
Smith, Yvonne. 756
Sobieski, Lynn. 485
Soellner, Rolf. 1228
Soviet Ministry of Culture. 573
Spina, James. 999
Sprinchorn, Evert. 1155
Sprovieri, Giuseppe. 214
Squarzina, Luigi, ed. 302
Stallybrass, Peter. 1229
Stansbury, Joan. 1212
Stasio, Marilyn. 993, 994
Staud, Géza. 1030, 1077
Stauffacher, Paul K. 648
Steane, John. 1029, 1067
Stephens, Judith L. 822
Sterritt, David. 997, 1000
Stetka, Boris. 1087
Stoop, Norma McLain. 589, 594
Stössel, Marleen. 544
Strachan, Fiona, transl. 550
Strauss, Botho. 884
Streitberger, W.R. 967
Stribling, Lauretta. 174
Stuttgarter Ensemble. 344
Sudano, Gary R. 100
Surgers, Anne. 871
Sutcliffe, James Helme. 1274
Swortzell, Lowell. 476
Sydow, Annegret. 46
Szafkó, Péter. 555
Szyszkowitz, Gerald. 955
Tallmer, Jerry. 1268
Tamberlani, Carlo. 1188
Tanzman, Carol M. 473
Tarkiel, Jacqueline. 872, 904
Tarleton, Bennett. 369
Taviani, Ferdinando. 1117
Tawil, Andrea. 236
Taylor, Gary. 1249
Taylor, Neil. 1222
Temin, Christine. 616
Temkine, Raymonde. 418, 845
Ten Cate, Ritsaert. 260
Tendulkar, Vijay. 833
Tener, Robert L. 829
Tennhardt, Hans-Peter. 244
Terry, Walter. 595, 622
Tessari, Roberto. 966
Testaverde, Anna Maria. 1091
Thibeau, Alice. 137
Thomas, Jeffrey. 361
Thomas, Richard K. 249
Thomsen, Christian W. 297
Thorpe, John. 145
Tiger, Lionel. 106
Timár, Esther. 1174
Tindemans, Carlos. 149
Tinterri, Alessandro. 542
Tognoloni, Daniela. 433
Tolnay, Paul. 193
Tome, Konrad. 192
Tosi, Guy. 406
Trauth, Suzanne. 543
Trucco, Terry. 587
Tuck, Susan. 1177, 1184
Turner, Victor. 486, 1129
Turrini, Peter. 77
Ubersfeld, Anne. 937
Ullrich, Peter. 547
Ulriksen, Solveig Schult. 430
USITT Graphic Standards Board. 218
Usmiani, Renate. 709
Valenti, Cristina. 1092
Valle, Outi. 802

Vallee, Lillian, transl. 493
Van Dijk, Maarten. 680
Van Kleef, Deborah. 912
Vaughan, David. 633
Ventrone, Paola. 851
Venturelli, Gastone. 1097
Verdone, Mario. 157, 215, 980
Visser, David. 257, 278
Vivis, Anthony, transl. 82
Vlad, Roman. 980
Vogel, Frederic. 368
Volkmer, Rüdiger. 638
Volli, Ugo. 518
Volpi, Gianna. 303
Volz, Ruprecht. 57
Vorenberg, Bonnie. 853
Waddington, Raymond B. 1230
Wagner, Anton. 114
Wagner, Cosima. 33
Wagner, Richard. 1271
Wakabayashi, Akira. 490
Walker, Alice. 1250
Walker, E.A., transl. 125
Wallach, Susan Levi. 173, 175, 176, 237, 238, 239, 240, 342, 482, 984
Walne, Graham. 183
Walser, Martin. 1144
Walsh, Paul, ed. 68
Wardetzsky, Kristin. 147, 148
Warren, Michael. 1251
Waschinsky, Peter. 111
Watermeier, Daniel J. 929
Watt, Douglas. 656, 657, 658, 659, 660, 661, 662, 663, 664, 665, 666, 667, 668, 669, 670, 671, 672, 673, 674, 1002, 1003, 1004, 1006, 1007
Watt, Stephen. 823
Wayne, Don E. 850
Wearing, J. P. 10
Wechsler, Bert. 598
Wehle, Philippa. 260
Weiner, Bernard. 970
Weinstock, Gloria. 146
Weisfeld, Zelma H. 159
Weitz, Hans J. 844
Wekwerth, Manfred. 526
Wells, Stanley. 772, 1205
Wendrich, Fritz. 497
Wendt, Ernst. 537
Wennergren, Jan. 732, 766
Wennersten, Robert. 431
Werner, Hans-Georg. 641
Wertheim, Albert. 847, 1178
Wever, Klaus. 395
Whaley, Frank Jr. 191
White, Kathy. 308
Wicke, Henry A., Jr. 101
Wilcher, Robert. 1252
Wilk, Gerard H. 800
Wilkerson, Margaret B. 357, 447
Williams-Mitchell, Christobel. 166
Williams, George Walton. 1253
Williams, Simon. 1265
Williams, Tennessee. 757
Wilmeth, Don B. 35
Wilson, Edwin. 87, 657, 658, 660, 661, 664, 669, 670, 671, 672, 673, 674, 993, 994, 1003
Wilson, Garff B. 97
Wilson, Marg, ed. 68
Winkler, Helgo. 244
Winterstein, Eduard von. 686
Wise, Debra. 108
Witham, Barry B. 320, 758
Wolf, William D. 1231
Wolff, Fred M., ed. 194
Wolfram, Gerhard. 548
Woodruff, Marci. 519

DOCUMENT AUTHORS

Work, William.   24, 25
Yamaguchi, Masao.   125
Yarbo-Bejarano, Yvonne.   343
Yates, W. Edgar.   715
Yearling, Elizabeth M.   1232

Yohalem, John.   1088
Young, William.   1179
Yousof, Ghulam-Sarwar.   1135
Zanderová, Aděla.   1233
Zarrilli, Phillip.   1122

Zeigler, Joseph Wesley.   269
Zotzmann, A.   378
Zotzmann, Adolf.   161

DOCUMENT CONTENT GEOGRAPHY

990, 991, 992, 993, 994, 995, 996,
997, 998, 999, 1000, 1001, 1002, 1003,
1004, 1005, 1006, 1007, 1008, 1009,
1010, 1011, 1012, 1013, 1014, 1015,
1016, 1017, 1018, 1019, 1020, 1021,
1022, 1023, 1034, 1035, 1037, 1051,
1052, 1071, 1073, 1084, 1088, 1094,
1098, 1099, 1100, 1101, 1102, 1104,
1106, 1122, 1123, 1130, 1141, 1151,

1170, 1171, 1172, 1173, 1174, 1175,
1176, 1177, 1178, 1179, 1180, 1181,
1182, 1183, 1184, 1185, 1186, 1187,
1192, 1201, 1253, 1262, 1268

USSR. 109, 393, 424, 538, 573, 640, 652,
838, 974

Vatican. 983

Wales. 382

West Germany. 46, 66, 81, 82, 83, 84, 85,
86, 98, 99, 138, 139, 160, 161, 192,

241, 252, 254, 270, 271, 272, 273,
274, 275, 344, 345, 346, 347, 348,
349, 350, 383, 394, 395, 415, 452,
453, 458, 459, 468, 474, 537, 544,
565, 574, 608, 701, 710, 759, 760,
761, 811, 841, 882, 883, 884, 917,
1038, 1039, 1072, 1184, 1275

Yugoslavia. 351, 768

MASTER LIST OF PERIODICALS IN ACRONYM ORDER

Asterisks follow the names of publications that are represented in this bibliography. A plus sign (+) identifies the publication as dedicated to theatre subjects.

ABNPPA	Annotated Bibliography of New Publications in Performing Arts		CJC	Cahiers Jean Cocteau +
			CJG	Cahiers Jean Giraudoux +
AbqJ	Arabesque (Johannesburg, Republic of South Africa)		Cjo	Conjunto: Revista de Teatro Latinamericano +
AbqN	Arabesque (New York, NY)*		CO	Comédie de l'ouest +
ACom	Art Com		Com	Communications +
Act	+		CompD	Comparative Drama +
ADS	Australasian Drama Studies +		Con	Connoisseur
Alive	+		CORD	CORD Dance Research Annual
AltT	Alternatives Théâtrales +		COS	Central Opera Service Bulletin +
AmAr	American Arts		CrAr	Critical Arts
AmTh	Theatre Communications Guild [After 1984: American Theatre* +		CRB	Cahiers de la Compagnie Madeleine Renaud-Jean Louis Barrault +
ArNy	Arte Nyt		Crisis	*
AsCTR	Association For Canadian Theatre Research +		CRT	La Cabra: Revista de Teatro +
ASTRN	ASTR Newsletter +		CS	Canada on Stage* +
ATA	The American Theatre Annual +		CTA	California Theatre Annual +
ATJ	Asian Theatre Journal +		CTL	Cahiers Théâtre Louvain* +
Atr	Acteurs +		CTR	Canadian Theatre Review* +
BALF	Black American Literature Forum*		CU	Cirque dans l'Univers
BaNe	Ballet News*		Cue	(London, England)*
BAQ	Black Art Quarterly		CueM	The Cue (Montclair, NJ)* +
BATD	British Alternative Theatre Directory +		CuPo	Cultural Post
BCl	The Beckett Circle +		D	Dialogue: Canadian Philosophical Review/Revue Canadienne de Philosophie
BGs	Bühnen Genossenschaft +			
BiT	Biblioteca Teatrale +		DAI	Dissertation Abstracts International
BK	Bauten der Kultur*		DB	Deutsche Bühne +
BlC	The Black Collegian*		DBj	Deutsches Bühnenjahrbuch +
BM	Burlington Magazine		DC	Dance in Canada
BMTY	The Best Plays: The Burns Mantle Theatre Yearbook +		DGQ	Dramatists Guild Quarterly +
			DialogW	Dialog: Miesięcznik Poświęcony Dramaturgii Współczesnej: Teatralnej, Filmowej, Radiowej, Telewizyjnej
BOT	Bühne: Das Österreichische Theatermagazines +			
BPAN	British Performing Arts Newsletter			
BPM	Black Perspectives in Music		DiN	Divadelni Noviny +
BPTV	Bühne und Parkett +		Dm	Dancemagazine*
BR	Ballet Review*		Drama	+
Brs	Broadside +		DrammaR	Dramma (Rome, Italy) +
BSOAS	Bulletin of the School of Oriental & African Studies		DrammaT	Il Dramma: Mensile dello Spettacolo (Turin, Italy) +
BTD	British Theatre Directory +		DRJ	Dance Research Journal*
BtR	Bühnentechnische Rundschau* +		DrL	Drama-Logue +
Buhne	Die Bühne* +		DrM	Dramatics Magazine +
CAM	City Arts Monthly*		DnC	Dance Chronicle +
CB	Call Board +		DRs	Dance Research
CDO	Courrier Dramatique de l'Ouest +		DSGM	Dokumenti Slovenskega Gledaliskega Muzeja +
CDr	Canadian Drama* +		DSS	XVIIe Siècle*
CDT	Contributions in Drama & Theatre +		DTr	Drama and Theatre +
CdU	Cahiers dans l'Univers		DTh	Divadlo Theater +
CF	Comédie-Française* +		DTi	Dancing Times
Cfl	Confluent		DTN	Drama and Theatre Newsletter +
ChinL	Chinese Literature		DW	Dance World
ChTR	Children's Theatre Review* +		E	Essence

Ebony	*
EDAM	EDAM Newsletter +
Egk	Engekikai +
EHN	Europaische Hefte/ Notes from Europe*
EIT	Escena: Informativo Teatral +
EN	Equity News +
Enact	+
Encore	* +
Entre	* +
EON	The Eugene O'Neill Newsletter* +
ERT	Empirical Research in Theatre +
Estreno	Estreno: Journal on the Contemporary Spanish Theatre
ET	Essays in Theatre* +
FDi	Film a Divadlo
Fds	Freedomways*
FMa	The Fight Master
FO	Federal One
FR	The French Review: Journal of the American Association of Teachers of French
FrF	French Forum*
FS	French Studies: A Quarterly Review*
Ftr	Figurentheater +
Gambit	* +
Gap	The Gap
GaR	Georgia Review
GdBA	Gazette des Beaux Arts*
GerSR	German Studies Review
GQ	German Quarterly*
GSTB	George Spelvin's Theatre Book* +
GTAN	Gay Theater Alliance Newsletter* +
HArts	Hispanic Arts
HgK	Higeki Kigeki +
HP	High Performance
HSt	Hamlet Studies: An International Journal of Research on *The Tragedie of Hamlet, Prince of Denmarke* +
HTHD	Hungarian Theatre/Hungarian Drama +
HwR	Hollywood Reporter
I	Indonesia*
IÅ	Contemporary Approaches to Ibsen: Ibsenårboken/ Ibsen Yearbook* +
IAS	Interscena/Acts Scaenographica +
IdS	L'Information du Spectacle +
INC	Ibsen News & Comments* +
ITY	International Theatre Yearbook +
JAAS	Journal of Association for Asian Studies
JAML	Journal of Arts Management and Law
JASt	Journal of Asian Studies
JBeckS	Journal of Beckett Studies +
JCT	Jeu: Cahiers de Théâtre +
JdPC	Journal du Palais de Chaillot +
JGT	Journal du Grenier de Toulouse +
JJIT	Journal of the Japanese Institute for Theatre Technology +
JJS	Journal of Japanese Studies
JMH	Journal of Magic History
JNZL	Journal of New Zealand Literature
JRASM	Journal of the Malaysian Branch of the Royal Asiatic Society*
JTV	Journal du Théâtre de la Ville +
JSSB	Journal of the Siam Society
JWCI	Journal of the Warburg & Courtland Institutes*
Kabuki	+
KoJ	Korea Journal
KS	Korean Studies
KSGT	Kleine Schriften der Gesellschaft für Theatergeschichte* +
LATR	Latin American Theatre Review +
LDA	Lighting Design & Application +
LDM	Lighting Dimensions Magazine +
LDr	Letture Drammatiche +
LFQ	Literature/Film Quarterly
LPer	Literature in Performance: A Journal of Literary and Performing Art* +
LTR	London Theatre Record +
M	Marquee* +
MAL	Modern Austrian Literature: Journal of the Arthur Schnitzler Research Association
MD	Modern Drama* +
MET	Medieval English Theatre* +
MfS	Meddelanden från Strindbergs sällskapet* +
MHall	Music Hall +
MHRADS	Modern Humanities Research Association Dissertation Series
MID	Modern International Drama +
MimeJ	Mime Journal +
MLet	Music & Letters
MMDN	Medieval Music-Drama News
MN	Monumenta Nipponica
MoD	Monthly Diary +
MP	Modern Philology: A Journal Devoted to Research in Medieval and Modern Literature*
MRenD	Medieval and Renaissance Drama +
MuK	Maske und Kothurn: Internationale Beiträge zur Theaterwissenschaft* +
NConL	Notes on Contemporary Literature
NCPA	National Center for the Performing Arts*
NCTR	Nineteenth Century Theatre Research* +
NFT	News form the Finnish Theatre* +
NIMBZ	Notate: Informations-und Mitteilungsblatt des Brecht-Zentrums der DDR +
Ns	Nestroyana* +
NSEEDT	Newsnotes on Soviet & East European Drama & Theatre* +
NTMP	The Newsletter of the Theatre Movement Program +

NTTJ	Nederlands Theatre-en Televisie Jaarboek	Scena	+
NWR	NeWest Review +	Scenaria	+
NYO	New York Onstage +	Scenarium	+
NYTCR	New York Theatre Critic's Review* +	SCPU	Scena: Časopis za Pozorišnu Umetnost +
O	Opernwelt +	SD	Simon's Directory
OC	Opera Canada* +	SDi	Slovenské Divadlo +
OCN	O'Casey Newsletter +	SDS	Slovenské Divadlo V Sezone +
Opera	* +	SEEA	Slavic & East European Arts
OpN	Opera News +	SET	Selected Essays of Theatre +
OQ	Opera Quarterly +	SF	Shakespeare on Film
Ob	Obliques	SFC	Samuel French Catalog +
OvA	Overture* +	SFo	Szinháztechnikai Forum +
Ovs	Overtures +	Sg	Shingeki +
PAC	Performing Arts in Canada	ShakS	Shakespeare Studies +
PAR	Performing Arts Resources +	ShawR	Shaw: The Annual of Bernard Shaw Studies
Part	Partenaires		[Formerly Shaw Review +
PArts	Performing Arts	ShN	Shakespeare Newsletter* +
PaT	Pamietnik Teatralny +	ShS	Shakespeare Survey: An Annual Survey of
Pb	Playbill* +		Shakespearean Study and Production* +
Pe	Performance	Si	Sipario: Il Mensile Italiano dello Spettacolo +
PerAJ	Performing Arts Journal* +	Sin	Sightline +
Pf	Platform +	Sis	Sightlines
Pja	Pipirijaina +	SJH	Shakespeare Jahrbuch (Heidelberg, West
Plays	Plays +		Germany)* +
PlPl	Plays and Players +	SJW	Shakespeare Jahrbuch (Weimar, East Germany)* +
PM	Performance Magazine	SMR	SourceMonthly: The Resource for Mimes, Clowns,
PMLA	PMLA*		Jugglers, and Puppeteers
Podium		SNJPA	Sangeet Natak: Journal of the Performing Arts
PQ	Philological Quarterly*	SoTH	Southern Theatre +
PQCS	Philippine Quarterly of Culture and Society	Spa	Shilpakala
Prolog	+	Spl	Der Spielplan +
PrTh	Pratiques théâtrales* +	SQ	Shakespeare Quarterly* +
PS	Passing Show* +	SSSS	Szene Schweiz/Scène Suisse/Scena Svizzera +
PTh	People's Theatre +	Staff	Staffrider
PuJ	Puppetry Journal	STILB	STILB
Pz	Proszenium +	STT	Szenicheskaya Tekhnika i Tekhnologya* +
QT	Quaderni di Teatro* +	STw	Schriften zur Theaterwissenschaft +
Raritan	*	Sz	Szinház: Theatre, the Journal of the Institute of
RdA	La Revue de l'Art		Theatrical Arts +
REEDN	Records of Early English Drama Newsletter* +	Szene	+
RenD	Renaissance Drama* +	TA	Theatre Annual (Akron, OH)* +
REsT	Revista de Estudios de Teatro +	Tabs	* +
RHSTMC	Revue Roumaine d'Histoire de l'Art: Série Théâtre,	Talent	
	Musique, Cinéma	TArch	Teatro Archivo* +
RHT	Revue d'Histoire du Théâtre* +	TAT	Theatre Annual (Tokyo, Japan) +
RN	Rouge et Noir	TD	Theatre in Denmark +
Room	Roomer +	TDR	The Drama Review* +
RORD	Research Opportunities in Renaissance Drama* +	TDS	Theater & Dramatic Studies +
RRMT	Ridotto: Rassegna Mensile di Teatro +	TD&T	Theatre Design & Technology* +
RT	Revista de Teatro +	Teat	Teatteri +
S	Segismundo +	TeatL	Teatr Lalek +
SAADYT	SAADYT Journal +	Teatoro	+
SAITT	SAITT Focus +	TeatrC	Teatro Contemporaneo* +

TeatrE	Teatro en España +	TkR	Tamkang Review: A Quarterly of Comparative Studies between Chinese and Foreign Literatures
TeatrM	Teatr (Moscow, USSR) +		
Teatro	+	TN	Theatre Notebook: A Journal of the History and Technique of the British Theatre* +
Teatrul	+		
TeatrS	Teatr (Sofia, Bulgaria) +	TNS	TNS Actualité +
TF	Teaterforum* +	TNU	Theatre News Unlimited +
TGDR	Theatre in the GDR +	TP	Théâtre en Pologne +
TH	Theater Heute* +	Toneel	Toneel Teatral +
THC	Theatre History in Canada* +	Tre	Theatre +
ThCr	Theatre Crafts* +	Tret	Tréteaux: Bulletin de la Société Internationale pour l'Étude du Théâtre Médiéval Section Française +
TheatreS	Theatre Studies +		
Theatro	+	TST	Teatro Stabile di Torino +
Theatron	+	TT	Theatre Times +
ThIr	Theatre Ireland +	TTT	Tenaz Talks Teatro +
ThM	Theater Magazine* +	TU	Théâtre et Université +
ThNe	Theatre News* +	TW	Theatre World +
ThPa	Theatre Papers +	TWNew	The Tennessee Williams Review [Formerly The Tennessee Williams Newsletter* +
ThPr	Theatre Profiles +		
ThPu	Theatre Public	TY	Theatre Yearbook +
ThR	Theatre Research International* +	TZ	Theater der Zeit* +
ThS	Theatre Survey: The American Journal of Theatre History +	Tzs	Theaterzeitschrift* +
		UCrow	The Upstart Crow +
THSt	Theatre History Studies* +	USITT	USITT Newsletter +
TI	Theatre International +	V	Valiverho +
TID	Themes in Drama +	VV	Village Voice* +
TIn	Theatrical Index* +	WCP	West Coast Plays +
TJ	Theatre Journal* +	WJBS	Western Journal of Black Studies
TJV	Teater Jaarboek van Vlaanderen +	WPerf	Women & Performance
Tk	Theaterwork* +	YCT	Young Cinema & Theatre
Tka	Theatrika +	ZDi	Zahranicni Divadlo

Photocomposition and printing services for this volume
of the International Bibliography of Theatre were
provided by Volt Information Sciences Inc.,
Garden City, New York.

Cover Design by Irving Brown